SON OF FORTUNE

Alfred A. Knopf
NEW YORK

VICTORIA McKERNAN

Text copyright © 2013 by Victoria McKernan
Jacket photograph copyright © 2013 by Eva Kolenko

All rights reserved. Published in the United States by Alfred A. Knopf,
an imprint of Random House Children's Books, a division of
Random House, Inc., New York.

Knopf, Borzoi Books, and the colophon are registered trademarks
of Random House, Inc.

Visit us on the Web! randomhouse.com/teens

Educators and librarians, for a variety of teaching tools,
visit us at RHTeachersLibrarians.com

Library of Congress Cataloging-in-Publication Data
McKernan, Victoria.
Son of fortune / by Victoria McKernan.
p.   cm.
Summary: In mid-1860s San Francisco, sixteen-year-old Aiden gains a hoped-
for chance at a change in fortune when he wins a ship in a poker game, but
soon he is involved in Peru's savage guano trade and the exploitation of its
Chinese workers.
ISBN 978-0-375-86456-8 (trade) — ISBN 978-0-375-96456-5 (lib. bdg.) —
ISBN 978-0-375-89585-2 (ebook)
[1. Conduct of life—Fiction. 2. Seafaring life—Fiction. 3. Commerce—
Fiction. 4. Race relations—Fiction. 5. Chinese—Peru—Fiction. 6. Peru—
History—1829–1919—Fiction. 7. San Francisco (Calif.)—History—19th
century—Fiction.] I. Title.
PZ7.M4786767Son 2013
[Fic]—dc23
2012042506

The text of this book is set in 11-point Iowan Old Style BT.
Printed in the United States of America
November 2013
10 9 8 7 6 5 4 3 2 1
First Edition

To my niece, Therese Thomas
(the high school teacher everyone wishes they could have),
with a heart for social justice

Also by Victoria McKernan

The Devil's Paintbox
Shackleton's Stowaway

Aiden Lynch walked off alone into the night forest. He had no real idea where he was going, but his body needed to move, so he went along with it. He had slipped past exhaustion into a restless exhilaration that demanded motion. The path was faint, but as long as he walked west, he would come soon enough to the sea. The sea offered escape, and he needed escape, for he had just killed a man. The stain was still on him. The blood had soaked through his coat and through his sweater and the shirt beneath that and onto his skin, where it had dried and itched for hours: a rude smear, crisp and foul like a smashed bug. He had washed at the river, rubbing the place with cold handfuls of water until his skin felt raw, but even now, many hours later, it seemed he could still feel it, the poisonous crackle of another man's blood drying slowly on his own flesh.

William Buck was no loss to the world, but Aiden could have easily gone his whole life without killing him. That the death was in fact mostly accidental changed little. Buck was not a virtuous man, nor really even liked by anyone, but the raw truth was, at the time of his death, he was pursuing a thief, a highway robber who had ambushed a medical team and stolen its precious smallpox vaccine. In another day or two, Aiden knew, the name of that thief would reach Seattle, and that name was his own. So Aiden Lynch, sixteen years old and alone in the world, was on the run.

1

The fight wasn't even a whole day ago. His left leg throbbed where Buck had clubbed him, and there were splinters still buried in his palm where he had grabbed the stick. There was a deep pain across his lower ribs, a tender, swollen eye and raw cuts on his face where little shreds of broken skin were beginning to curl. He had a dark, pulpy bruise just below his collarbone where one end of that stick had landed; the other end, accidentally sharper and more fatefully positioned, had pierced the neck of William Buck. The blood had poured out amazingly fast, awful red and dense as mercury, steaming a hole in the fresh snow.

Aiden's legs felt shaky and he stopped, light-headed. He bent over and rested his hands on his knees. The sharp tang of urgency that had carried his muscles along so far was starting to evaporate. He felt frail and drenched with mortality. The sweet scent of pine needles drifted up from the ground like incense. He slumped into the fragrance, resting his head on his arms. In the few months that he had worked as a logger, he had come to love this land and was sad to be leaving it. These northwest woods, with their enormous, ancient trees, were insane and delicious, strange as Mars yet calmly beautiful.

He yearned just to lie down and sleep, but he struggled to his feet again. It was January, and even on a mild night like this, with no wind and the temperature in the forties, he knew that he could freeze to death lying on the bare ground. The moon broke through the clouds and spilled silver on the tips of branches. In a far part of his brain, Aiden recognized it was lovely, but he was numb to beauty right now, numb to everything but the rhythmic solace of his footsteps. Tree roots braided the path before him. He didn't know what came next, and he wasn't sure he had the strength to find out, but there were, as always, only two choices. He could go on or he could die. There had been grander chances to die so far, so it didn't seem justice to do it now.

The sky was beginning to lighten behind him as Aiden stood on the last hill overlooking the Seattle harbor. It would still be a while before the sun actually rose above the trees, but he could see the flat, square shapes of the city streets and the shimmering water of Puget Sound just beyond. He saw fourteen ships anchored. Nine were lumber ships, in various stages of loading. The rest he didn't know. Aiden had never seen the open ocean and knew little about ships, but he did know the ones in Seattle always needed men. There was a gold rush in British Columbia, and it was common for whole crews to desert in Seattle to chase their fortunes. He also knew he had to be careful. Seattle and Portland had long been notorious for shanghaiing—men were fed knockout potions in saloons and dropped through trapdoors only to wake with throbbing heads, far out to sea with the roll of the ocean beneath them, forced into service as deckhands on their way to China. Aiden was determined not to fall prey to anyone. If he did decide on the sea, it would be on his own terms, and those terms, he knew, would be best made in San Francisco. He found his way down to the harbor as the sun rose behind him.

"You have never been to sea." The captain squinted at him suspiciously and twitched like a fly had landed on his ear. "And so I should hire you as sailor for why?"

"I'm not asking for pay," Aiden replied. "Just to work my passage."

"The fare to San Francisco is ten dollars. The pay to a sailor is two dollars a day. It is four, maybe five days to San Francisco. Can you think the numbers?" The captain tapped one finger on the side of his head. He had a thick Swedish accent, so the question sounded almost like a child's rhyme. *Caan you tink da nuumbers?* So many of these lumber boats that ran along the coast were run by Scandinavians that they were sometimes called the Swedish Navy.

"I can sleep on deck."

"Go away," the man said. "You are no use to me."

"I've worked lumber," Aiden said.

The captain shrugged. "The lumber is already loaded."

"I just meant I know hard work," Aiden pressed.

"I have no hard work. I have a steam engine. I have a winch. I have a crew. We do not sail to China."

Aiden knew this boat was the only one ready to leave that day. Besides, even to his inexperienced eyes, it looked like a good ship. The decks were clean, the sails were neatly reefed, the wooden railings were recently varnished and the lumber was well stacked and secured. He had some money, almost two hundred dollars. It was a modest fortune but hard won, and he didn't want to spend it unless he had to. Fortune, for most of his life, had been a box of pennies on the shelf above the stove, saved against hard times and emptied far too often. He knew San Francisco was expensive, and he had no idea what sort of work he could find there. He had no formal education and little experience. He could plow a field, skin a wolf, cut down trees and fight. He had read most of

Shakespeare, all of Dickens and the *Atlas of the World,* but he knew that didn't count for much.

"I'll give you five dollars' fare for passage, and sleep on the deck," Aiden offered.

"Your face was in a fight," the captain said, flicking a disapproving hand at Aiden's bruises. "It looks like trouble."

"Well, it never looked all that good to start with."

The captain twitched in what might have been a laugh. "Did you win?"

"I'm here, aren't I?"

"What is this?" He tipped his prickly chin at the bundle that Aiden carried. "A gun?"

The bundle was long and narrow, wrapped in oiled cloth and tied securely with rough twine.

"Bow and arrows," Aiden answered.

"You are not the Indian."

"No," Aiden said simply. He wasn't sure what he looked like these days, but he was pretty sure he didn't look Indian.

"Where do you come from?"

"Logging camp up north."

"Before that?" the captain pressed suspiciously.

"Kansas mostly, then west. I came out with a wagon train." The facts were true, though they left out a lot. His parents had been godforsaken bog Irish who had escaped famine in the old country as indentured servants, their passage to Virginia paid for with nine years of work: the regular seven, plus two for the children they brought along—his two older brothers. After the indenture was completed, the family had worked in coal mines and rock quarries, saved every penny and bought land of their own. But that land turned out to be a barren plot of desperate Kansas, where drought and blizzard and fire made the plagues of Egypt seem like sniffles and hangnails. That land had ultimately killed most of them. A pile of woeful history, he thought, that mattered to no one.

"What is your name?"

"Aiden . . . Madison, sir," he said, thinking only now that he ought not use his real name. He did not imagine himself a very grand outlaw and doubted a manhunt in Seattle would chase him very far, but his real name—Aiden Lynch—might be tainted for a while in local parts, and a lumber ship on regular runs might hear it. His sister's name had been Maddy, so Madison would be easy to remember.

"How old are you?"

"Nineteen," Aiden lied, adding on three years. He was tall and still lanky, but months of plentiful food and hard work in the logging camp had given him some muscle. His face, angular and roughened by a life outdoors, had never really looked boyish, but a close inspection would betray little need yet for shaving.

The captain frowned but didn't challenge him.

"Are you a good shot with this bow and arrow?"

"Yes," Aiden said evenly.

"What do you know about polar bears?" the captain asked abruptly.

"Um . . . they live in the Arctic," Aiden replied, quickly trying to switch his brain around. "They can weigh six hundred pounds and are solitary animals. They eat seals, which they hunt from ice floes—"

"Are you being smart?" the captain snapped.

"No, sir." Aiden flushed with confusion. Hadn't the man just asked him? Wasn't he just answering? "I had a book," he explained. "It told about all the regions of the world and their native peoples and animals and so on." The *Atlas of the World* had been nightly reading for most of his life, and the only thing that had kept him and his little sister, Maddy, going through the desperate last winter. He could call up most pages entirely by memory.

"So I could ask what do you know about headhunters or yaks and you would tell me that too?"

"Not yaks, sir," Aiden said. He suspected the man was now teasing him but decided to play it back straight. "They were mentioned only briefly, as Mongolia is still a largely unknown region," he added. "Though I could probably build a yurt if I had to."

"Ha!" The captain jerked his head back once, overly quick like an amateur sword swallower. He seemed too young to be captain of a ship, Aiden thought. No more than thirty, though he did have a beleaguered air of experience about him. He was shorter than Aiden, and stockier. He looked like he might once have been athletic, but now had the slight softness that came from spending long periods of time on a small ship with a steam engine, a winch and a crew.

"Ha! All right, then, Mr. Atlas of the World. So you know all about polar bears! Are you afraid of polar bears?"

"I've never seen one, sir."

"Well, think! Think!" It came out *Tink! Tink!* and Aiden, his nerves already on edge, had to work hard not to laugh. "Use your imagine! It's a bear!" He lunged at Aiden in bear pose, with curled finger-claws and a toothy snarl. Two of the other sailors working on deck briefly looked up but didn't seem to think their captain's behavior all that peculiar. Aiden took some hint from that. Crazy people were in charge of lots of things in the world, he had learned, so you just had to go along with them.

"Well, if I saw one in the wild, I suppose there wouldn't be much I could do," he said. "I suppose it would kill me regardless, if it wanted to, so being afraid wouldn't matter much either way." He gave a quick glance around the deck, suddenly wary that there might actually be polar bears on the loose. "But if I saw one anywhere else, it would probably be in a cage." He shrugged. "So I'd be all right."

"Yes!" The captain jerked his head again in his odd way of maybe laughing. He actually had a kind face, Aiden noticed, once you got used to the twitches.

"These are in the cage." He grew still and looked at Aiden with a sudden piercing concentration. "See. Here. I have bears. For a rich man's zoo in San Francisco. Special order from Alaska. We go all the way for the special trip. It is the long trip and now mother bear is sick. We give the fish but she will not eat. My men try to kill the seals but they are not hunters. One time when they do shoot the seal, God knows by what luck, it swims away before we catch it. So here you come now with the Indian bow." He gave one tiny twitch, then went on. "This morning when we leave the harbor, we will pass by a little island full of seals. So you will put string on your arrow like the harpoon, yes? And so you can shoot the seal and pull it in." He mimed this vigorously, tugging an invisible rope hand over hand. "And then you feed the bears."

"Uh, sure," Aiden said. He doubted the string-and-arrow plan would work, but he certainly wasn't going to talk himself out of an opportunity.

"Keep the bears alive and you have free passage. Ten dollars you pay if they die. Yes?"

"Five dollars if they die," Aiden countered. "Though I promise I will devote myself."

The captain shrugged. "*Ja*, all right. But no coffee! Only food, and you eat last."

"Fine," Aiden agreed. He liked coffee, but he could go without. He held out his hand, but the captain just turned away and shouted to the deckhands in Swedish. Three of them began hauling in lines and preparing to cast off. The fourth, a small, bowlegged man, muttered something that sounded, even in the unknown language, to be more grumbling than a ship captain usually heard. But the captain didn't react. The bowlegged man was at least fifty and could have been much older—his weathered skin and rough gray beard made it hard to tell. His watery eyes were the palest blue Aiden had ever seen.

"I am Captain Neils. That is Sven the Ancient. Go with him now. He will show you the bears!"

"Yes, sir."

Aiden followed Sven the Ancient down a narrow ladder and through an even more narrow passageway. The ship smelled like tar and rope, stale smoke, dubious meat and the fusty damp of men living in close quarters. The old man ducked at a beam, then led him through the center of the ship. The ceiling was so low Aiden could barely stand upright. There was a wooden table, with benches on three sides and two chairs on the other. Not two feet away was a tiny galley, where a little stove was just going cold, with a pan half full of breakfast biscuits still sitting on top. Aiden's stomach lurched with hunger. His last meal had been over twenty-four hours ago, some scraps of stolen bread and cheese, eaten in a cave while hiding out a blizzard and waiting on death.

The old man led Aiden through a final dark passageway, then slid back the bolts on a door. He handed the lantern to Aiden and turned away, still without saying a word. Aiden crept cautiously into a small hold. The light shone on the bars of an iron cage and cast stripes on a yellowish heap inside. At first it looked simply like a pile of old sacks or moldy straw. Then two little polar bear cubs rolled out of the pile and stumbled awkwardly toward him. They chirped and whimpered. Their little legs didn't seem to know quite what to do with their dumpling bodies.

"Hello there," he said as he pressed his palm against the bars. Both cubs began to lick eagerly at his hand. Their tongues were soft as lettuce. Then the moldy pile snorted, snuffed, lifted a massive block of head and charged. Great black paws slammed against the bars, claws carving the air. The mother bear roared, and Aiden felt her hot breath on his face. He scrambled back as far as he could, which didn't feel anywhere near far enough. The cage rattled and clanked, but held together. It was barely big enough for the bear to turn around in.

"There now, bear," Aiden said stupidly. His heart pounded so hard his fingertips throbbed. Yes, he thought, cage or not, polar bears were frightening. Then the mother bear fell back weakly into the dirty straw. Her breathing was heavy, and the enormous ribs pulsed beneath the thin yellowed fur. The two cubs, oblivious to her distress, burrowed into her side, trying to suckle. The mother bear lifted her head a few weary inches, then gave a great sigh and lay still. The cubs gave up and stumbled back toward Aiden with pitiful cries of hunger.

Aiden added up the days that must have been required for her capture and transport from Alaska, and came up with a month or more. And it was January, so she must have been taken from hibernation in her birthing den, so she would have gone two or three months now without food, maybe longer. What a wretched journey she must have had, he thought. One day her world was all snug den and nuzzly babies. Then crashing men with shovels and nets and chains. Now this place of dank darkness and iron bars.

The cubs were certainly fat enough and could last the four or five days to San Francisco, but the mother might not. He knew the tortured breath and glazed eye of starvation; man or animal, it was pretty much the same. And the cubs would probably need to nurse for at least a few months more once they got to their new home, so if the mother died, they would likely be doomed as well. He felt the ship start to rumble as the steam engine roared to power. He had to decide now. His last attempt to do good had resulted in pain, death and banishment. But this time it was only bears.

Aiden liked hunting. He did not like the factual stab of death or the moment when life seeped from an animal's eyes, but he did not feel sad either, for death was meat and he had lived too long with hunger. But he liked tracking an animal. He liked testing his own skill, human and mechanical, against the animal's, responsive and instinctual. He had a weapon, but animals owned the world, so it seemed pretty fair. There was always a moment when he had the bow drawn and the prey in his sights that he felt connected to the animal. It was a sensation of both total excitement and total calm.

But hunting seals wasn't real hunting. They just lay on the rocks like plums. All he really had to do was not spook them. The big ship with its noisy steam engine would clearly spook them, so Aiden suggested Captain Neils anchor a few hundred yards out from the rocks and let them row in close with the dinghy. The sea was calm and the wind mild. The late-morning sun was a watery shimmer through the light fog. Aiden knew a little about how Indians along the coast hunted seals, but that was a group effort with many men in several canoes, armed with harpoons, nets and clubs. He had one rowboat, three other men, his bow and arrows, a gaff, a blunt hatchet, an odd scrap of cargo netting and a shotgun so old it might have hunted woolly mammoths.

"Can we just drift in from here?" Aiden whispered as they neared the rocky island in the rowboat. He was pretty sure all the sailors spoke English, though two of them had said no more than "Hello" or "Sit there." The third was a bit friendlier. He had offered Aiden the leftover biscuits and, defying his captain, a cup of coffee, still slightly warm. He had introduced himself as Fish, and at first Aiden thought he was misunderstanding some odd Swedish name.

"No—Fish," the man had said, wiggling one hand in a swimming motion. "Like a sardine." There was no further explanation. He might have been related to Captain Neils, Aiden thought, perhaps a brother, for they shared the same stocky build, blue eyes and thick blond hair, but Fish had none of the captain's odd twitches or strange manners and seemed in general more easygoing. He was younger, maybe twenty, and had no accent, only a slight lilting rhythm to his speech.

The island was the size of a small-town churchyard, with about thirty seals basking lazily in the weak sun, and another dozen swimming around the broad, rocky fringe. A sharp odor sliced over the boat. One of the sailors murmured some words of Swedish disgust.

"Go on," he growled. "Shoot one and let's go."

Aiden stood, braced his leg against the wooden seat and lifted the bow. He had not tied any string to his arrow, since any string, except for sewing thread, would be too heavy, and sewing thread would be useless. He was hoping for a good shot and an instant kill. He didn't know if a seal would float or sink, so he picked one that was dozing near the center of the island, hoping the rocks would prevent it from rolling far. But a kill shot from a bobbing boat was going to be luck as much as aim. He tried to feel the rhythm of the swells, but it was like playing the accordion: nothing remotely like anything he knew. Besides that, he was feeling a bit seasick: coldly sweaty, hollow behind the eyes and ghastly full in the stomach. As he drew the bow, he felt pain stab through his injured ribs. He loosened the pull, closed his eyes, took a deep breath and focused beyond the pain. *Find your center.* Aiden opened his eyes, drew again, sighted his prey and shot. The seal reared its head, gave out a bellow, twitched its flippers and tumbled down the rock, coming to a stop just a few feet from the water's edge. The little island erupted with noisy chaos as all the other seals lumbered toward the sea.

"Go! Go!" Fish cried out excitedly. The rowers gave a few hard pulls, then steered carefully through the skirt of rocks. It looked for a minute as if the seal were in hand, but just as they neared, it suddenly lurched up, flippered wildly and splashed into the water. A faint trail of bubbles frothed up through the calm surface.

"Back!" Fish directed the rowers. "Watch the rocks."

Aiden kept his eyes on the seal. "There!" he shouted. It floated motionless just below the surface.

"Grab it quick and hold on," Fish said. "I'll get the gaff."

Aiden leaned over and grabbed one of the rear flippers just as the body began to sink. It felt so strange he almost let go. It was furry but slick, dense but bony, impossibly heavy but somehow delicate. He strained to hang on until Fish came alongside with the gaff and hooked the body. Together they held the carcass until the men rowed them out of the surf zone.

"How do we get it in the boat?" Aiden panted. His arms were trembling from the effort to hold it. From the sea the seals had looked no bigger than dogs, but this one, though medium-sized, still weighed at least two hundred pounds.

15

Even if they could manage to haul the dense jelly body into the boat without tipping it over, the extra weight might sink them.

"We don't," Fish said. "The captain will bring the ship to us, then haul it up with the winch. We only have to row out a little more, away from the rocks to deeper water. Get the rope there—we'll tow the seal."

Of course. Someday, Aiden thought, he might not always be stupid. He tied one end of the rope securely around the seal's tail, took a turn around one of the flippers just for good measure, then fastened the other end to an iron ring in the stern. He suspected the sailors would be judging his knots, and he wasn't going to risk embarrassing himself by them coming loose. Once the seal was secured, Fish deftly unhooked the gaff. The body drifted back, trailing a wide slick of blood. The boat jerked as the cumbersome weight tugged on the rope.

"Okay." Fish waved at the other sailors to continue rowing, until they were twenty yards from the island, over clear, deep blue water. Then Fish pulled out a whistle and gave a few short blasts, which were answered by the ship's bell. The fog was starting to burn off, so they would be able to see the ship approaching in just a few minutes. The sailors shipped the oars and took out their pipes. Aiden leaned back against the stern and watched the seals swim and splash, still barking objections to the disruption. Now that the excitement of the hunt was over, lame as it actually was, he felt extraordinarily tired. He had traveled many miles and slept only five or six hours in the past three days. But soon enough they would be back on the boat and he would have nothing to do for days but ride along. Soon mother bear would eat and her babies could nurse and all would be well. Aiden trailed his right hand idly over the side. The cold water felt good on his scraped palm. For the first time in days, he felt safe. There were no plans to make, no action to take. He was half dozing when he felt a slight push of water wash over his hand. Then something hard brushed across his knuckles. Thinking it a bit of driftwood, he pushed it away. Odd feeling for driftwood, though, he thought vaguely. It was smoother than any log, and rough, like sandpaper. He felt it again, a harder knock this time. Suddenly the seals all erupted in loud, urgent cries. Aiden opened his eyes and saw them leaping frantically out of the water onto the rocks. Then he saw a dark shadow pass beneath the little boat. He thought at first that they had drifted over an old sodden log. Then the log turned and showed a white belly and a great black eyeball. A glossy fin split the tranquil surface.

There is a big gap in the brain between seeing a shark and realizing it is indeed actually a shark. Time went slow and strange. Five seconds or an hour passed, then a huge gray head thrust out of the water. White dagger teeth flashed. The shark grabbed the dead seal, shook it violently and tossed it into the air. A spurt of blood arced across the sky. Red drops hit the water, loud as stones. Then the shark disappeared. The dead seal bobbed behind the dinghy, still tied, but with a ragged bite mark slashed across the middle of its body. Strings of flesh and intestine drifted out like party streamers. A thread of air bubbled out from some punctured inner cavity. A thick swirl of blood stained the water.

No one spoke, no one moved. For many long seconds, the only sound was the gentle lapping of water against the fragile hull of their very tiny boat. Then the shark roared up again, mouth open like a bear trap. The shark was nearly as long as the dinghy, and almost half as wide. It clamped down on the seal's body and thrashed it side to side, so hard a wall of water washed into the little boat. Time shifted again, speeding up now. Aiden felt all his senses overlapping. Somehow he understood what was about to happen. The rope had not snapped, and the shark's glistening gray head, unnaturally fine and terribly real, was alongside, the seal carcass in its mouth. The two-hundred-pound seal looked as small and limp as a dead dove in the mouth of a dog.

The shark yanked the boat hard. A wave of cold water rushed in. The rope held. The knots held. The bolt held. The shark let go again but swam back and forth in tight, jerky passes, puzzled by the unexpected difficulty of obtaining this simple morsel that had been dangled in front of him.

"The hatchet!" Aiden shouted. "Give me the hatchet! We have to cut it loose!"

Aiden saw Fish struggling to his knees and reaching for the shotgun. Aiden doubted that the wet gun would fire or that it would do much to such a huge beast even if it did. He crawled forward, climbed over the seat and grabbed the little hatchet.

Then one of the sailors screamed, and Aiden saw the rush of water as the shark charged again. He heard the futile clink of the gun. He saw a constellation of teeth. The shark clamped once again on the dead seal and yanked it away. But still the rope didn't break. One side of the boat was dragged completely underwater, pitching the other side up. Aiden managed to grab the high-side gunwale and hold on. Fish did not. Aiden watched him topple soundlessly over the side. The little boat righted itself, but as it did, the rope recoiled, pulling the seal into the swamped dinghy. Now the dead seal was bobbing right there between their legs, entrails swirling around Aiden's ankles. Aiden grabbed hold of the rope, flung it over the oarlock and whacked it with one stroke of the little hatchet.

"Push it out!" Aiden yelled, groping at the carcass. His hand sank into the pulpy flesh. Then the shark rushed in again, mouth peeled back, showing a thousand savage teeth. As if tired of their nonsense, it clamped hard on both the seal and the boat. Aiden felt the boards splinter beneath him. Without thinking, he kicked at the monstrous head and felt the crunch of a tooth breaking beneath his boot sole. Then he raised the hatchet and slammed it onto the shark's head. The shark merely twisted away and vanished into the depths with half the seal in its mouth, the hatchet still stuck in its skull. A trail of blood swirled up like ink from an artist's brush dipped in water after painting sunsets. Aiden wiped the stinging salt water from his eyes. The sea was eerily calm.

"Where's Fish?" Aiden shouted.

The side of the dinghy had been ripped open and water was rushing in fast. Aiden's palm tingled from the impact of the hatchet. His brain felt dull as moss. For some reason, he couldn't hear anything but a roaring sound. Then one of the Swedes pointed a trembling hand. Aiden saw Fish flailing at the surface about twenty feet away. It wasn't far to swim, but it was clear that Fish could not swim. Then sound returned. Aiden heard a strangled cry and saw Fish's head sink, his heavy clothing dragging him down. The sun broke through the fog and dappled the water. The clang of the ship's bell rang out again and the men turned hopefully. They could see the ship steaming toward them, but it still looked miles away. It hadn't been five minutes, Aiden realized, since Fish had first whistled for pickup. The man was now floating motionless, just beneath the surface. How long before he sank completely? How long until the shark finished its meal and returned for more?

Aiden pulled off his jacket, wrenched off his boots and dove into the water. Although he had already been soaked through, the cold of total immersion was shocking. He gasped for breath. It felt like a giant icicle had been driven up through his chest and into the center of his brain. Aiden reached the drowning man in half a minute, but his limbs were already so numb he could barely grab hold of him. He managed to turn Fish over and get his face above the water, but Fish did not gasp at the sudden air. His head just flopped to the side. Aiden tried to tow him by the jacket, but his fingers would not hold. The freezing water made his hand little more than a club, unable to grasp. Well, he thought with an odd tranquillity, I've learned another stupid thing not to do in life. Desperately, he managed to thrust his arm down the back of Fish's jacket, hooking it with his elbow. Aiden kicked and pulled with his free arm, but it was like towing a log. His heart was made of leather. He stopped trying to swim and focused on simply keeping both their heads above water. He had almost drowned once before, but he felt none of that panic now, only a sense of awe at the power of cold that now owned him. It was strangely peaceful. Then, just before he surrendered completely to the peace, he felt something hard bump against his back.

4

Aiden woke gasping for breath, hot and crushed. In his brain fog, he was certain there was a polar bear lying on top of him, but when he shoved against the suffocating weight, he found that it slipped off easily, spilling only a pile of blankets. He leaned up on his elbows and cautiously tested reality. Dim gray light came in through a small, round window, casting shadows on strange cupboards and foreign boots. He was in a narrow bed in a tiny cabin. On a boat. He sat up all the way. Sense and memory flashed like lightning through his brain, tumbling the dramas of the past few days together. He raked his fingers through his greasy hair. Slow facts began to assemble in his brain.

A polar bear was starving and he shot a seal and a shark ate half their boat. The ocean was cold and Fish was terribly heavy while drowning. The hard jab against his back had not been the huge shark returning but the jagged gunwale of the sinking rowboat. He remembered hands grabbing hold of him, then a rope digging under his arms and pulling him up through the air. He remembered feeling amazed to be back on the ship, separated from the evil ocean. He remembered Fish's blond hair swinging back and forth as the other men rolled him across a barrel, and the magnificent gasp as his lungs came back to air. Then he remembered the warmth of the polished deck against his cheek, and nothing else.

Aiden tried standing and found it possible. He felt his

way through the narrow passageway toward faint daylight. All five of the Swedes were on deck, with Captain Neils at the helm. A watery gray light made everything flat and slightly unreal. The men looked at him, and Aiden couldn't tell what anyone was thinking. He had worked with Swedes in the lumber camp and knew them as a mostly taciturn bunch, so this didn't surprise him.

"Is it evening time?" he asked.

"Morning," Captain Neils replied. "Morning of tomorrow. You slept a long time."

"Sorry," Aiden said.

"It's fine." The captain smiled. "Have some coffee." He said something to Sven the Ancient, and the old man went below and returned with a coffeepot, mug and plate full of food. Aiden devoured the breakfast: fried apples and onions, some kind of pickled fish, fatty bacon and biscuits with jam.

"You should have seen the mama bear eat!" Captain Neils said.

"Eat what?" Aiden asked, puzzled.

"Too many knots!" Captain Neils yelped his strange burst of laughter. "Too many knots!"

"The shark bit through the seal's body just as you cut the rope," Fish explained. "The cut end of the rope snagged on the broken boards, still tied to a good chunk of meat." He held his hands out to show the size. "Maybe thirty pounds."

Aiden felt himself suddenly gagging at the image of the torn seal flesh, guts swirling around his feet, weird prehistoric flipper scrabbling at his knee.

"So she ate it?" He tried to picture the little cubs instead.

"Oh *ja!*" Captain Neils nodded happily. "She has milk now for the little ones!"

"That's great."

"But I am sorry to say your bow and arrows are gone," Captain Neils went on. "Everything in the boat was lost. Except for one oar and all the men."

"Oh," Aiden said dumbly. "Yes. I don't suppose they would have floated." The news hit him like a punch. He had had the bow since he was ten years old. It was the last bit of anything left from his old life. He looked out over the low swells and worked to make his voice sound normal. "Is this the real ocean now? Are we out of Puget Sound?"

"*Ja,*" Captain Neils said. He waved a gnarled hand toward the western horizon. "China is just over there." He laughed and nudged the wheel.

Sven the Ancient began clattering loudly in the little galley, washing up the breakfast dishes, while the other men went about their ordinary tasks. In the sanctuary of day, on a sturdy ship with a fair wind filling the sails and genial dolphins escorting them along, they had little work to do, yet there is never time for real idleness at sea. The sailors passed the morning splicing ropes and patching up the dinghy. The sight of the torn wood made Aiden shudder. He could clearly see tooth marks in the wood, as if an expert carpenter had cleanly struck his sharpest chisel there. The men talked in Swedish as they fitted new planks across the gap. When they saw Aiden and Fish, they began to laugh and talk with more animation.

"When a bad time is over and we tell the story afterward, everything changes," Fish explained. "Now you are the warrior king who has split open the head of the sea monster with one stroke of a magical axe," he translated. "Our little boat was tossed twenty feet into the air, but a great school of fish leaped up and whirled around it like a waterspout and brought us gently back down By evening, they will have goddesses coming down from Valhalla to pluck us from the waves and feed you goblets of mead."

"Well, I wouldn't turn any goddesses away," Aiden said.

The sailors made some comments that, even in Swedish, sounded ribald.

"They all understand English just fine," Fish said. "Except Sven the Ancient. But they aren't good at speaking it. They all grew up on Swedish ships. They don't spend much time on land, and when they do, it is among other Swedes."

"How come you speak it so well?"

"I lived on land with my mother and little sisters until I was twelve."

"In San Francisco?"

"Yes. My mother was a cook in a dining house. She wanted to keep me from the sea, but as you see, that didn't work. My family all have salt water for our blood."

"Are all these men your kin?"

"The captain is my brother. Though he is ten years older and more like a father. His name is Magnus. Our own father died when I was five. A storm put his ship on the rocks. Sven the Ancient is my uncle." Fish pointed at the two men fixing the dinghy. "Jonas, there with the hammer, is his son; Gustav is another cousin. His father also died with mine." Fish looked up at the sails, which were taut with the wind. "You have never been on a ship?"

"I've never even seen a ship before, except in books. My family has dirt, I suppose, for our blood."

Fish laughed. "Well, come then, I will show you a ship."

They spent the morning looking at ropes and winches, pumps and sounding lines, sails and the steam engine—still only half of the hundred things that made a ship work. In one way everything was very foreign, but in another way it was also somehow familiar. It was all solid and functional and quietly ingenious. Fish took Aiden below and spread out charts with wavy lines and striped shades of blue and cryptic numbers sprinkled all over like tiny seeds.

"These lines mean deeper water," Fish explained. He tapped a few spots along the coast. "This indicates shoals, and these are visible rocks." He traced his finger across the thick paper with casual command. To Aiden, it was all strange and exotic. He had always loved maps and could have looked at the chart for hours, but Fish rolled it up with an abrupt dismissal.

"But we've sailed here so long we almost never need the charts," he said. "Back and forth, back and forth, with the lumber. I am twenty-one—it's nearly half my life! But someday I'll sail blue water."

"What is blue water?" Aiden asked.

Fish waved his hand toward the horizon. "Out there— open ocean—where you see no land for weeks or months. Where there is nothing familiar—nothing to depend on but what you have learned and what you feel and knowing the stars. Just the soundness of your ship and your crew and your own decisions. Hawaii, Tahiti, China, Europe, maybe Australia!" He put the chart back in its niche, then opened the top of the chart desk and took out a wooden box. "For blue water—real sailing—you need this." Inside, cushioned well in a nest of red velvet, was a complicated brass instrument with gears and wheels, tiny mirrors, a lens like a miniature telescope and numbers etched along the arc of the bottom.

"It's a sextant?" Aiden guessed.

"Yes!" Fish lifted the instrument out of the box like it was the crown jewels. "With celestial navigation, you can go anywhere! With the sextant, the whole world belongs to you!" He traced one finger longingly over the smooth brass. He sighed and looked away, out the tiny porthole, where the shoreline was always visible. "Come, it's almost noon—I'll show you how to shoot the sun."

Since they didn't really need an accurate reading, Fish let Aiden take the sight. It was a tricky business, balancing on the moving boat while staring through the eyepiece, trying to keep the horizon level and the sun in view just exactly as it turned noon. Fish grabbed a handful of Aiden's sweater to steady him, but shooting the sun was only the beginning. After that there were pages of calculations to do. Aiden had never been really good with math and was soon lost in azimuths and angles. He realized that if his fate were ever in fact to take him to sea, it would certainly not be as a navigator.

"Well, according to your reading, we should be seeing Japan any minute now!" Fish said. "That's the thing with navigation—one small error changes the course of the whole voyage."

So navigation was just like real life, Aiden thought. Errors went back forever, each one building into the next—a deadly daisy chain of fate. The wind was steady and the sails well set, so Fish let Aiden try his hand at the helm. He was nervous and zigzagged at first, turning the wheel too hard one way, then the other.

"Don't think," Fish said. "Just feel." He spread his legs slightly and bounced, sweeping his hands up with surprising grace, like a dancer. "The ocean is a live thing. The ship is a live thing. They are like lovers who love but sometimes want to kill each other. You must keep them both on the loving side."

"You're kind of poetical for a Swede, aren't you?"

"A sailor spends a lot of time inside his own head," Fish said.

They sailed along in companionable silence until the clouds came in and the wind turned gusty enough to require Fish's more experienced hand at the helm. Aiden went below to check on the polar bears. The mother bear seemed in much better health. Her eyes were bright and her breathing was steady. Aiden sat quietly for a while just watching them, until the mother bear's wariness ebbed and the cubs' curiosity overflowed. Then he eased the cage door open just enough to sneak the two babies out. Soon they were romping and tumbling all over. Aiden wrestled them, rolled them about and tossed them into the straw. They chirped gleefully, galloped gracelessly back and flung themselves upon him with furry vigor. The mother bear watched nervously at first, woofing and huffing, but eventually she seemed to understand that he was not going to hurt them and settled down. Once the cubs were tired out, he raked the dirty straw from the cage, shook in a fresh bale, then squeaked open the door and pushed them back in. The mother bear scooped them into her arms, sniffed them suspiciously and started licking them free of every dreadful human scent. Aiden leaned back against a bale of straw and watched the little cubs suckle contentedly. Despite his previous twenty-four-hour sleep, he was still deeply tired and dozed off himself. It was a fitful sleep, full of violence, and he woke with tiny scratches all over his arms from thrashing in the straw.

The bears were sound asleep, snoring in oblivious bliss. The ship creaked gently. He could smell the rich aroma of frying potatoes and hear the easy cadence of Swedish conversation from the deck above. In the main salon, the men were just sitting down for a meal. They had left a place for him. Evening came early in January in this northern latitude, and though it was only about four-thirty, the sun was already low, slanting sharp gold beams through the small portholes. It was all so totally foreign, yet so easy and comfortable.

After supper, Captain Neils went to his tiny cabin to update the ship's log, while the other men, like all sailors eager to take advantage of sleep when it was possible, took to their bunks. As long as the weather stayed fair, they would keep only one man at the helm throughout the night, each taking a two-hour watch. Aiden went up on deck and sat on a pile of lumber, watching his first sunset at sea. The clouds slid through ripples of gold and crimson, with fringes of purple. A hundred shades of blue melted gradually down through the sky. The ocean was the color of black plums ripened to bursting.

He heard a noise and looked up to see Fish approaching. He carried a bottle and two glasses and sat down beside Aiden. He pulled the cork from the bottle and poured two small drinks. A dense aroma—spicy and slightly medicinal—floated up. The liquor was smooth and scouring at the same time and tasted very foreign. Aiden gasped and managed not to choke. He leaned back on the pile of wood. The fresh smell of lumber made him feel strangely sad. That part of his life was over now. It was a rough, harsh life, but there was a lot of good about it too. Logging was challenging and dangerous, but at the end of every day he always felt satisfied. And there were few decisions to make, nothing to wonder about. Eat this, sleep here, chop down this tree.

"Here—a present for you." Fish pressed something smooth and sharp into Aiden's hand. It was a glossy white triangle, nothing like a stone, though closest to a stone, the size of a playing card, smooth on one edge, jagged on the other two.

"Shark tooth. It was stuck in the sole of your boot."

The tooth was surprisingly heavy and had an odd prehistoric elegance. Aiden found a bit of leather boot sole caught between two of the tiny saw points. He pried it free and rolled it between his fingers. It was like mitten fuzz, only rubbery and dense. His hands began to tremble. Fish said nothing but poured them both another drink. The clear, pungent liquor was thicker than water but less so than blood. Still, there was the harsh iron smell to it that reminded him of blood. Or maybe everything now made him think of blood. Would he ever again be free of blood? "What is it?"

"It's called aquavit—water of life."

"Then, to life," Aiden said. They drank, then were silent for a few minutes, watching the sun sink into the water like a single burning coal.

"Why did you go in the water for me?" Fish asked quietly.

Aiden shrugged. "I know how to swim. It seemed like you didn't."

"I don't," Fish confessed. "Sailors almost never do, unless they sail the tropics. But the shark could still have been near."

"I figured it was busy eating already. Figured I had a little time. I wouldn't have gone in otherwise. So you know."

"No. That's good to know."

"No offense."

"No."

"I didn't think about the water being so cold," Aiden said.

"It was awfully cold."

"Just—it wasn't a good-deed kind of thing. I only went in because I was pretty sure I would come out again."

Fish reached for the bottle and poured another ounce out in each glass.

"I figured the odds were pretty good for me living," Aiden went on. "If you lived too, so much the better. But if it came down to just one of us, me or you, well, it wouldn't be me all drowned or in the belly of that shark right now."

"That's reasonable."

"It wasn't a question of who ought to live or not, or why or why not," Aiden went on. The strange Swedish liquor, plus the piled-up shock of the past few days, was making him strangely talkative in a way he somehow couldn't stop. "Only what could I probably do at the time with the way things were."

Fish looked at him with a puzzled expression. "Well, whatever reasoning you like, I am glad to be topside of the sea and outside that shark." He raised his glass and clinked Aiden's, and they both tossed back the water of life. They watched the last red arc of the sun vanish into the sapphire sea. Fish looked at the shark tooth that Aiden was absently rubbing. "Sven the Ancient can drill a hole in that if you like," he said. "So you can wear it around your neck. Maybe even scrimshaw on it."

"Thanks, but I think I've had teeth close to my skin enough for now," Aiden said. He pulled out the little leather pouch he wore around his neck. "I have a place for it." He did not look at the other tokens already there—the memories they held were still too sharp. The tooth was almost too big to fit.

"Is that an Indian thing?" Fish asked.

"Yes," Aiden said, not offering more explanation. If his luck was strong, Tupic might be through the mountains by now, on his way back to his tribe with the smallpox vaccine. Aiden pulled the strings closed, and the weight of his new life tugged gently against the back of his neck.

5

The sweetness of that first day at sea was gone by morning, with a storm that terrified Aiden, though it seemed only to slightly annoy the experienced crew. Sven the Ancient just cursed a little more as he fried the eggs and boiled the coffee, his bony legs braced casually against the galley cupboards. Aiden huddled in the bunk belowdecks. He was halfway between trying not to die and hoping with all his might that he would, and soon. The ship pitched and groaned. The sky churned and the sea heaved. He lay twitching and curled in a ball. Seasickness was a unique and disconcerting ailment, especially bad because it seemed ridiculous and weak. This was not the smashing bullet of war. This was not the sword's deadly stab through the haphazard organs that turned out to matter so terribly much. It was not the gouge and tear of wild animals or the smash of an enemy's club. It was not influenza that killed half a town in one sweep. It was not smallpox, lockjaw, ague, rabies, cholera, typhoid, pneumonia or any of the vicious maladies of awful everyday life. Seasickness was relentless and dull as bad wallpaper. It was just stupid. But horribly, inescapably, nauseatingly stupid. Aiden felt like someone had turned his body inside out, scooped up his guts with a spoon, boiled his bones into jelly, sprinkled it all with poison and hung him out on the fence for coyote bait. Fish dragged him up on deck a few times to gulp at the fresh air, but the sight of the heaving gray waves just made Aiden worse. At least he learned to throw up over the downwind side of the ship. Finally, by evening, the seas eased and he found he could sit up on deck without fear of vomit boiling up and pushing his eyeballs out of his head.

"The barometer has steadied out," Fish said. "So the roughest may be over with."

Aiden splayed his jelly bones out on the deck and stared pathetically at the gathering stars. He had never thought in a million years that he would miss the plains of Kansas, but right now their absolute immobility was very enticing.

The next couple of days were milder, though the sky remained gray and drizzly and the sea sloppy. Aiden could not manage platefuls of fried potatoes and pickled fish, but neither was he begging for death. He mostly sat for hours on the piled timber, just watching the ocean. He did spend a few hours each day with the polar bears, playing with the cubs and coaxing the mother to eat. She was accepting fish now, as the gorge on seal meat had apparently wakened an appetite, but she still sniffed each morsel with suspicion and made her displeasure clear, swatting at the fish with a dismissive huff and peeling her lips back before taking it in her teeth.

The last day of the trip, as they sailed into San Francisco Bay, was beautiful and calm. The sky was a clear, deep, cloudless blue.

"Lucky you to see it so," Captain Neils said. "I sail here twice a month since I am ten years old and have seen blue sky maybe a dozen times. Do you know, for a hundred years men sailed by this bay and never knew it was here? And always ships are looking for good harbor. But for a hundred years they passed it by. Paradise just there—but always in the fog."

Aiden had heard about San Francisco, but nothing could have prepared him for the first real sight of it. It looked like a storybook kingdom. Fine wooden houses marched up the hills in every direction, trimmed with what looked like wooden lace, and all with glass windows! Not just one or two windows, but three or four on each floor—and each one with six or eight panes of glass! He hadn't seen a house with so many glass windows since he was seven years old on the plantation in Virginia. His sod house on the prairie had oiled paper or scraped hides covering the windows. The bunkhouses in the logging camp simply had wooden shutters and canvas flaps.

They dropped the sails as they entered the bay and chugged along with the steam engine. There were hundreds of boats here, oceangoing ships and coastal ferries, fishing boats of every size and kind. There were dozens of lumber ships like their own, hauling timber for the vast appetite of this booming city. As they neared the wharf, Aiden saw hundreds of people milling about, most turned out in what seemed like Sunday best. The women wore coats with fur-trimmed collars; the men were in fine suits and hats. Rows of wagons, glossy carriages and buggies were lined up on the road, some with coachmen in livery.

"Do people always come out to the dock like this?" Aiden asked.

"Oh yes," Captain Neils said. "But many more today, for they've come to see the bears." There was more than a hint of pride in his voice.

"Our bears?"

"What others?"

"How do they know?"

"Have you never heard of a telegraph?"

"Yes, of course."

The telegraph had changed the world, connecting both sides of the country, so that messages that used to take months to travel by ship and horse now flew through the air in minutes.

"Ship news is important in San Francisco," Fish explained as his brother steered them through the channel markers. "There are stations along the coast that watch for the ships and wire the news ahead. Every cargo means something to buy and sell, and the merchants want to know what's on the way. I suspect Mr. Worthington's bears have been talk for some weeks now, as there's precious little novelty this time of year," he said as he readied the mooring lines.

Captain Neils turned to Aiden. "Can you get the cubs out of the cage?"

"I thought we were going to winch the whole cage up through the hatch."

"Look at all the people!" Captain Neils tipped his bristly chin toward the crowd. "It's plenty of money Mr. Worthington has paid. I suspect he'd appreciate a bit of a show. Maybe you could walk them out on the leash, show them off. There's a bucket of fish," he said casually, as if the bucket had just appeared out of thin air. "You can make them dance, eh?"

"Shall I tie bows around their necks too?" Aiden asked.

"Do you have some?" The captain's face twitched and cracked briefly in what passed for a smile.

"You should have seen when the kangaroos arrived!" Fish whispered. The crew began tossing mooring lines to the dock, and Aiden went below to arrange the show. In the four days he had cared for her, the mother bear had become somewhat used to him and no longer charged the bars when he approached. A full belly also helped her disposition, so it was relatively easy to coax the docile cubs out. Aiden slipped a bit of rope around each fuzzy neck, slid the door open just a foot and snuck them quickly out of the cage. There were of course no ribbons or bows to be found. He thought about borrowing a couple of the captain's bright red kneesocks— that would serve him right!

Bear cubs were not built for ship ladders. They were fat and wiggly, like sacks of wet grain that had come alive. Aiden was sweating by the time he got them up on deck. He led them to the opening at the top of the gangplank, and there was a swell of oohs and aahs from the excited crowd.

Aiden picked a fish out of the bucket and held it up. The cubs twitched their noses eagerly. The boy cub stood up and pawed the air, but his sister promptly swatted him away and took the treat. The crowd laughed. Many of them were rich, Aiden thought, dressed in fine shoes and clothing. His mother had been an expert seamstress, and he knew she would have needed twenty hours to produce the ruffles and trims on some of these dresses. And people certainly wouldn't be wearing their finest clothes to the docks in daytime, so these would be their second-best or even ordinary clothes—yet each outfit probably cost a month's pay for a lumberjack. For a farmer, they might as well be woven of moonbeams. But even the poor people didn't look so bad off. They all had coats and they all wore shoes. What kind of place was this, he thought with amazement, where the poor could turn out to look at bears in the middle of the day? Wouldn't they be beaten for missing work? Wouldn't their children go hungry for the lost pay?

The girl cub flounced impatiently and clawed gently at Aiden's leg. Her brother just sat on his haunches and surveyed the crowd with the calm aloofness of a raja who accepted adulation as his natural right. Aiden hated having so many people looking at him. He took a deep breath, ducked his head and led his charges down the gangplank.

Children pushed to the front of the crowd and squealed, but even the top-hatted men didn't conceal their excitement. When Aiden got the cubs down to the dock, the crowd erupted in applause. Both cubs cowered at the noise. They yelped and darted about, tangling their leashes as they tried to hide behind his legs. Aiden squatted down and scooped an arm around each one and held them close, trying to mimic the reassuring noises he had heard their mother make. They calmed down and began to lick his face. A few women squealed in delight, and Aiden wished he could slip through the cracks in the dock.

Then the crowd parted and a young man appeared. He looked fair enough to be fifteen, yet he walked with the command of a judge. People fluttered out of the way as he passed, then fell in a wake behind him, like blossoms in a current of air. Even the cubs noticed him. Aiden had no idea what clothes were in fashion, but somehow he knew these were perfect. His coat flowed around him, and the trousers appeared to change shape to accommodate his stride. The leather boots were closely cut and supple as butter.

The man-boy was beautiful, Aiden thought—not like a girl was beautiful, but just because there wasn't a better word for what he was. It wasn't a feminine beauty, but like an ancient Greek or Roman statue's. His features were strong and even, his eyes wide and alert, his hair a thick, lustrous dark blond, perfectly cut and never touched in nervousness. Just behind him, like a royal court, were four little girls—sisters, Aiden guessed, for their similar beauty—plus assorted servants, coachmen and porters and two wagon drivers steering a flatbed cart pulled by a team of draft horses. The young man stopped well out of clawing range and clasped his hands behind his back.

"What lovely bears!" he said. "My father will be very pleased. He regrets he could not be here to welcome them personally, but I thank you, sir, for their excellent care!" He nodded slightly in what was neither a bow nor a dismissal but a graceful acknowledgment of a special effort by an obvious inferior. Aiden couldn't think of what to say, so he simply held out the leashes. The young man stepped back.

"Oh no, the keeper will take them," he said, gesturing with one hand. A tall, long-faced man in plain canvas trousers shuffled out of the retinue and glowered at his new charges. Before he got near, however, one of the little sisters, maybe five years old, scampered up excitedly. Aiden pulled the cubs back and stepped between them and the girl, but the young man, moving with a quick, catlike grace, scooped the child up.

"They bite, Daisy," he said. "They will bite off all your fingers and you won't be able to hold a cookie or pet the cat or pick your nose ever again!" The little girl stared at him in wide-eyed terror for about three seconds, then burst out in giggles and butted her head into his shoulder. He petted her neck affectionately and set her down as an embarrassed nanny dashed up to retrieve her.

The keeper took the leashes from Aiden. The girl cub darted eagerly to sniff his boots, but the startled man kicked her back so she tumbled head over heels with a squeal. Aiden was shocked at the rough response, but before he could do anything, a sudden chorus of frightened gasps and shouts erupted from the crowd. Fish and the crew were hoisting the mother bear over the rail. The cage was halfway down, but the mother bear, closed in the dark hold for a month, terrified already to be swinging in midair, had just seen her missing cubs. She was frantic. She thrashed back and forth, slamming her body against the bars and swinging the cage wildly. She reared up, hitting the top of the cage, sending it spinning. On the dock, the nervous cubs began to cry and strain against their leashes to reach her.

The winch rumbled with awful slowness. There were guide ropes hanging from the corners of the cage, but the longshoremen, who would have had no problem steering an ordinary crate into place, were not about to get anywhere near an angry polar bear. Aiden ran over and grabbed one rope. By hanging with his entire weight, he eased the swinging for a moment, but then the bear lunged again, the cage tilted and Aiden was dragged off his feet. Cutting down trees had made him strong, but strength wasn't much use when he had only his dangling body weight to work with. He hung there awkwardly for what seemed like an hour but was probably only ten seconds. Then Jonas and Gustav reached the dock and grabbed the other ropes. Together they managed to slow the crazy spin. One longshoreman finally took the last rope, and the four men guided the cage safely to the ground.

The crowd cheered. Aiden shook his strained arms and rolled his shoulders with relief. The excited cubs dragged the zookeeper over, their leashes now completely tangled. The man offered little help as Aiden got the cubs back into the cage. The reunited family cuddled together, the mother still trembling and panting with panic.

"She doesn't look very good," the keeper grumbled.

"She'll do all right if you tend her," Aiden said, still catching his breath.

"Awful skinny." The man spat on the ground.

"She just needs feeding and a place to be."

"Mr. Worthington paid for a good bear."

Aiden felt a surge of anger boiling up. He grabbed the man's hand, as if in a handshake, but dug his thumb into the wrist and twisted it sharply. "This is a good bear!" he said, dropping his voice so no one else would hear. "She's come a long way through bad times! She will live fine if you keep her well."

"Let go of me!" the man yelped, and tried to pull away.

"So you keep her well or I will come kill you in your sleep." The man cowered, and Aiden was glad to see real fear in his eyes. "I swear I will," Aiden added. "Knife stabbed through your eyeball straight into your brain. Or just a stick." He twisted the man's wrist harder and leaned into his face. "Most sticks go into brains easy enough."

"You mistook my meaning."

"Good. Because I wasn't liking the meaning that I was mistaking." Aiden released his torturous grip and smiled. The crowd had seen nothing but a handshake. "She needs to eat two or three fresh seals a week, I think. And some fish. Maybe you can get her used to other meat too."

"We have plenty of meat at Mr. Worthington's zoo," the keeper said defensively.

Aiden choked back the bile in his throat. "That's fine, then." He had a quick temper and had learned violence, but he never got to like the taste of it. And he actually had no idea how easy it was to stab a stick into a brain through an eyeball. It seemed like it should be easy—everything between eye and skull was just mush.

He helped Jonas and Gustav get the cage onto the cart and watched with relief as the whole show finally began to roll away. The beautiful man, the flock of little sisters, the nannies and the coachmen all climbed into their carriages and drove off. The crowd drifted apart.

"*Ja*, good, no more bears!" Jonas hitched up his pants. He and Gustav turned and hurried back up the gangplank to the ship. Aiden knew they were eager to start off-loading the lumber so they could get home to see their families. There were no extra minutes in a city like San Francisco. They would have only two nights ashore before sailing north once again for another load. "An idle ship is like a hole in the ocean, and into this hole you throw money," Captain Neils had said.

Aiden went back on board to collect his things. They made a very small bundle. It was strange not to have his bow and arrows. Of course there would be no use for them now; they would in fact be an encumbrance in the big city. The big city—the reality of it was just now hitting him, and his stomach felt queasy with nerves. He had no idea what he would do here. In his sixteen years, he had worked in fields, quarried stone, mined coal and cut down trees. He had read seventeen books, not counting the *Atlas of the World*, Shakespeare or the Bible, but he doubted there were jobs as book readers. He pulled the drawstrings tight on the little canvas bag. It was especially hard to know what he would do when he had no idea who he even was anymore. At least he knew where he would stay.

"Here is the address of our mother's boardinghouse." Fish handed him a scrap of paper as he came back up on deck. "There are six boardinghouses on that street—it's called Swedish Town—but anyone will know where to send you once you're there. The place next door sometimes has a parrot in a cage hanging outside. And a black dog. But ask anyone and they'll know. Tell my mother we should be done off-loading by five, so we will be there soon after. There will be a big dinner." He grinned in anticipation. "After dinner, we will go out. Music halls, dancing girls—just wait!"

"Listen to me, Fish," Captain Neils interrupted. "You can drink in our own places."

"Yeah," Fish scoffed. "With the same twenty old Swedish seamen I've known all my life, in the same three saloons where the barmaids are all the grannies of my friends!"

"The Barbary Coast is dangerous," Neils said, not as a captain this time, but as Magnus, the big brother. "There is a body every night."

"Well, there are a hundred saloons and two thousand men—I don't mind those odds."

"We have only two nights ashore—you should see Ingrid."

"Ingrid should see herself," Fish muttered under his breath.

"What do you say?"

"I said, I can't wait to see Ingrid!" Fish rolled his eyes at Aiden, then contorted his face in a schoolboy gesture for a homely girl.

Magnus swore at him in Swedish, a language that Aiden thought sounded too pretty to be much good for swearing.

"Rest up!" Fish winked at Aiden and leaped to the stack of lumber.

"I do not joke!" Magnus shouted after him. "Don't listen to him," he said to Aiden. "You are too young and it is all danger out there!"

"I'll be careful," Aiden said. "Can I help off-load?"

"You would just be in the way." Magnus blinked a few times as if to clear spiderwebs from his face. "You are a good boy. If I had a job for you on this ship, I would keep you. But you see I have the big family already. But if you like to work on a ship, I will ask around."

"Thank you," Aiden said. "But I think I'll see what the land might hold for me right now." The wash of doubt he had felt moments ago was vanishing out here on this bright sunny day with this whole glorious city before him. Everything felt suddenly possible. San Francisco was the city of fortune. Maybe it was time for some fortune to come his way.

6

Aiden walked through the bustling dockyard, dodging carts and winding through mazes of piled-up crates. The rare sunshine made the day so warm that many men worked in shirtsleeves. With block and tackle, it took only two or three men to swing the most massive cargo. One of the crates he saw was only slightly smaller than the covered wagons that carried entire families and all their possessions across the country on the Oregon Trail. What could it possibly contain? Two elephants? Six pianos?

Aiden saw a man doing nothing, which meant he was probably in charge of something, and walked up to him.

"Excuse me," Aiden said. "Who would I see about working here?"

"Your grandfather," the man said, barely even glancing at him.

"My grandfather's long dead," Aiden said.

"Pity, that."

Aiden sensed there was an acre of complicated understanding that he was missing here.

"I can rig and swing cargo. I've been working as a logger."

"Well, good for you." The man tapped his pipe and took out a little pouch of tobacco. "Far too many trees cluttering up the country."

"I'm looking for a job," Aiden said, trying to be clear. "I could do this sort of work."

"So could a little girl if a boss man said she could," the man spat.

"Ah, I see," Aiden said, suddenly understanding. It was good work, so it was closed work. It was who-do-you-know kind of work. "Well, if I come across any little girls looking for work, I'll surely send them your way." He smiled and touched his cap, then went on his way before the man could decide if that was an insult or not.

Aiden followed the street up from the wharf until he came out onto a broader street. There were grand buildings as far as he could see. Half the people walking by looked like they were dressed for dinner with the president. In the street were wagons and carts and carriages of every size and shape. There were peddlers selling brooms, toys, ribbons, old clothing and blocks of soap. Shopwindows displayed everything in the world: fancy shoes, silver platters, French lace, silk cloth, wheels of cheese, jars of shiny candy. Everything was abundant and everything was for sale. Aiden had never seen so much of everything.

He walked on, mesmerized, for a good fifteen minutes before he remembered that Fish had told him to turn left at the fifth street he came to. Aiden turned and went back to where he had started, and counted. Some of the streets had signposts and some did not. Fish didn't know the name of the street, just said there was a grand house on the corner. Like most people who were familiar with a certain area, Fish took little notice of actual markers or signs; he was used to going home through backstreet shortcuts. The instructions were further complicated for Aiden since he wasn't really sure what was a proper street and what was an alley. As for a grand house on the corner, everything looked grand to him.

He had been so entranced, wandering from one street to another, that he was now lost in a maze. He tried to pick out landmarks, but the buildings all looked so foreign, with their many windows and lacy trim, that he could not rely on any one to guide him. He decided to just go back to the dock, but he soon realized he wasn't even sure which direction the main road was. Besides that, fog was rolling in fast and thick. This was nothing like the morning mist on the prairies, or even the damp gray of the northwest forests. This was like a bowl of porridge. He could not see ten feet ahead, let alone tell north from south.

The streets were suddenly narrower and lined with saloons instead of shops. Garish signs advertised dancing girls and penny whiskey. Crude, plunking piano music echoed from half-open doors, and in front of every door was a man in a bright waistcoat and bowler hat, calling to him as he passed, the voices scratchy and creepily the same. Some of the places had lamps outside, but these were few and far between. Shadowy men passed. A few women flitted in and out of sight, darting across from door to door like bright birds, their skirts clutched up out of the dirt. He almost collided with one. Her cheeks were freshly rouged, her curls still tight from the curling iron. A heavy scent of dismal flowers hung around her.

"Excuse me, miss," Aiden said.

"I work at the Gold Nugget," she said brusquely. "Not the street! And then not till five!" She looked him harshly up and down. "And I cost more than the likes of you can afford anyway!" She disappeared into the fog with a swish of her skirts.

Aiden had never been in a place like this, but he sensed

the joyless mood of this grim hour, when all were steeling for the night ahead. It was the bit of time between hoping for happiness and settling for lack of hurt. He took out the paper with the address of the boardinghouse and asked a lamplighter, but the man did not appear to speak English. He tried one of the saloon doormen, who simply shrugged.

"It's where the Swedish sailors live," Aiden tried.

"Why would I care where the Swedes live?" the man said. "I can send you to Italian Town—there's some fine black-haired beauties there. Or set you up with a guide for China-town, eh? Two bits for a cellar girl—fifty cents for a beauty. He'll bring you back alive, I guarantee!" Aiden walked on and asked at another saloon.

"Don't know the street," the doorman offered. "But there's lots of boardinghouses down by Fremont Street." He gave some more vague directions, and Aiden set out again into the darkening mist. He turned the first corner as directed and was relieved to see the tavern sign the man had mentioned, but shortly past it Aiden's senses pricked. Was it just nerves or real danger? And what sort of danger was there? He was pretty sure he had stumbled into the Barbary Coast, the place that Fish was eager to visit and that his brother had warned against. Aiden was feeling wary, but it seemed a bit early for murder.

But not for robbery.

"Apple just a penny, sir?" A small boy suddenly appeared in front of him, holding out a glossy red fruit. Aiden stepped back, startled. Before he could even begin to wonder what a boy was doing out selling apples in the twilight and fog on a nearly empty side street, he heard the rough scamper of boot soles behind him, then he felt the whack of a club across the back of his knees. As he crashed to the ground, he felt a blow between his shoulder blades and a rough yank on the strap of his canvas bag.

Instinctively, Aiden twisted away and sprang to his feet. He saw, or sensed, the man swing something at his head. He ducked, but the truncheon blow still connected with enough of his skull to jar him. As Aiden staggered for balance, he saw five or six shapes pouring out of the shadows. He knew how to fight. He had once had three brothers. He had learned Indian fighting from his friend Tupic. He had fought for money every Saturday in the logging camp and usually walked away with his pockets full. But this was like no fight he had ever been in. Hands grabbed at him everywhere. He punched and kicked and was startled to hear a yelp of pain that sounded like it came from a boy. Aiden grabbed a twiggy arm. He was fighting off a mob of boys! Wiry bodies wrapped themselves around his legs and pulled them out from under him. Little spider bodies fell over him, pinning him to the ground. His bag was torn away and his coat yanked down off his shoulders. He felt his boots being pulled off. Another yank tore his jacket free. He punched and smacked, but every time he hit something, it was so small and fragile he pulled back. The boys didn't seem to mind causing him pain, however. Little fingers clutched big handfuls of his hair and bounced his head off the ground. Boys or not, the five or six of them were enough to keep him down.

Out of the corner of his eye, he saw his first attacker, the grown man, rushing at him. The little boys jumped back out of the way just as a hard boot kicked viciously at his ribs. Aiden gasped for breath. He saw one small boy's face flinch and turn away. It was the same boy who had offered the apple—a pale, flinty face, with wide blue eyes and sharp, dirty bones.

"Brace," the boy whispered urgently. "Don' fight—they'll do you worse!"

Aiden had heard that advice before. "Sometimes you're just plain down," Powhee, the fight manager in the camp, had advised. "All you can do then is not get broken more than necessary." But Aiden wasn't ready to curl up and endure. He was angry. When the next kick landed, he slammed the heel of one hand into the side of the man's knee, then grabbed the ankle and twisted. The man tumbled to the ground. Aiden jumped on top of him and landed a few quick punches before the man threw him off.

Then a gunshot cracked. Aiden felt the dirt kick up on his face. Another shot rang out, sounding close enough to be a cannon. The mob of boys scampered away into the shadows. The man cursed and backed away, then shuffled off after them. Aiden sat up slowly. Standing not more than ten feet away was some sort of gnome in a gaudy military jacket, with a pistol in one hand and a leash in the other. Attached to the leash was a great hairy brown animal, probably a dog but tall as an antelope, with four-inch teeth and a snarling lust for limbs. Aiden froze. He was familiar with the ways of death, and by dog was not his first pick.

"Quiet, The Moon!" a scratchy voice commanded.

The huge dog immediately folded itself up into a silent, attentive sit.

"Do you live?" It was a woman's voice, high-pitched and cracked with age, though still resonant.

"Yes." Aiden drew a deep breath. "So far."

"Well, know I charge the cost for the bullets," the woman snapped. "And double for those what live! Though not likely you have any money left. Did they get it all?"

"I don't know." Aiden got to his feet, bruised but unbroken. He felt his pants pockets and found the fabric torn and flapping. He thought he had been smart. He knew about thieves. He had hidden part of his money in each boot, part in the lining of his coat, a little in each pocket, some in his bag. Apparently, it wasn't such a clever strategy after all. The swarm of boy thieves had simply scavenged every possible hiding place, tearing everything apart and stealing his boots and coat entirely. His canvas bag with the few spare clothes was gone. He grabbed at his neck and was relieved to find Tupic's pouch. There were a few coins in it, but it was the other treasures, and the pouch itself, that would have been worse to lose.

"How much do the bullets cost?" he said dumbly. His head throbbed. Damp from the street was oozing up through his socks. The gnome woman let out a scratchy laugh.

"Are you just come off the boat, then?"

"Yes."

"Ah, well, I thought as much. There's some bad hang down the docks like that, see? Follow a fresh new man as you are. A sailor just paid off, or an Eastern man, or a foreign man, though clear to me you're none of those. What are you—miner?" She suddenly sprang close and thrust her face up to his, squinting so hard her small eyes almost disappeared into the wrinkled face. Her bony hand darted out and wrapped around the side of his neck, then felt its way over the knob of his shoulder and down along his arm, as if examining a horse. Aiden stood still, too surprised to pull away. She grabbed his right hand and spiraled her fingertips over the palm.

"Ah! I say lumberjack!"

"Yes," Aiden said, startled. "How did you know?"

"You haven't a miner's neck—but there is shape of you from work. And the calluses. And the cloth." She rubbed the fabric of his shirt between her fingers. "I know the cloth. So, that's sense, then. They would've seen as much the same. That's why they didn't just rob you straight off, eh, down the docks, but followed all along and got up the whole pack to swarm so as they did. They saw you wouldn't be a daisy man."

"Do you know them?"

"Not by person. Only the sort what do this. Boys make a little gang all their own, or some might just be standing around this day and idle when the robber man needed hands."

She spoke in a strange accent, like an Italian or Russian who had learned English from an Irish and then just plain gone loopy.

"But even if they was known and found and hanged, there'd be more tomorrow. Always more boys."

"Thank you for helping me." He held out his hand to shake hers, but she made no move to take it. The giant dog lifted his now-placid head and sniffed it. "My name is Aiden—um—Madison, ma'am."

"I'm Blind Sally."

"Blind Sally?"

"Aye."

Aiden recalled the sound of her bullet thwunking into the dirt by his ear.

"Are you really blind?"

"Did I not just say so?"

"But you—you shot at us!"

"I wasn't about to go in swinging my fists, now was I?"

"They let you have a gun?"

"They who? Who's they who ought to let or not? And who needs a gun more than a poor old blind woman, eh?" she snapped. "*They* do nothing little else ever much good to help one what needs help, now, eh? Of course I have a gun!" She tucked the pistol into a pocket of the tattered uniform coat. Frayed ropes of gold braid swished across the lapels as she moved. "Come. We may find your boots before the full dark. Your coat maybe too. Was it shabby as the rest of you?"

"I don't know."

"Well, likely gone if it was any good. Was it any good?"

Aiden prickled. He didn't need to add insult to his already considerable injury.

"It had bloodstains on it," he said. "Will that help or hurt?"

She shrugged. "Can't tell blood from gravy, I've found. But coats are easy to sell along. Not so boots. The fit is easier for a coat. And some decency part of it too. The worst thief won't steal a live man's boots. Not usually. Or cut his fingers off. Not usually. And more so if they're happy with the glint. Did you have coin or greenbacks?" she asked.

"Some of both," he said. "And some gold certificates."

"Happy, then. Maybe they will leave you a packet of sweets besides! Come on, The Moon." The huge dog ambled to its feet, stretched lazily, then fell into place beside her, his shaggy side lightly touching her hip. Aiden had given up trying to understand anything at this point. He simply followed the old blind woman in her ancient soldier's jacket, with her cannon-sized pistol and her ambling dog called The Moon. She and the dog led him down to the end of the small street and around the corner into an even smaller lane. Aiden shivered. The January evening was now cold, and his torn pockets flapped as he walked. His wool socks were soon soaked through and sagged heavily. Stupid, stupid, stupid, he thought as he scanned the edges of the narrow street.

Blind Sally and The Moon navigated the streets without hesitation. She did not speak as they walked, but sometimes she clicked her tongue against her teeth or muttered to the dog. Around the second corner, in the middle of the road, in the faint pool of light from a single gaslight, were his boots, standing upright and together as if by the side of his bed. People walked by with no notice, like it was a normal thing to have empty boots in the middle of the way. Aiden wriggled the soggy socks into the boots and tied the laces. He felt marginally less ridiculous.

"Thank you, Miss—Blind Sally," he said. "I'll give you something for your trouble when I have something, if you tell me where to bring it."

"Bring it here. I'm always here."

"I don't exactly know where here is," Aiden confessed. To his surprise, and horror, he suddenly felt his voice starting to shake and hot tears pooling in his eyes. He hadn't cried in over a year, not since his mother died. There had been plenty of sorrow in the time between, but he'd felt only rage or cold, dead-hearted nothing. Why schoolboy tears just now? He hadn't cried over murder or banishment; he hadn't cried over leaving his only friend behind, or the fate of an entire Indian tribe who might die of smallpox, or the cold-river death of his beloved sister. Why tears now? Why only for wet socks, mild lostness and a bit of a knocking? The physical pain wasn't that bad. The lost money hurt, but it had never seemed real anyway. Was he turning stupid? He coughed to squelch his sobs and thanked the heavens that the old woman was blind.

"Could you point me toward Swedish Town?" he asked.

"You're crying salty tears." The softer tone of her voice told Aiden that he had not disguised himself quite well enough. "How old are you?"

"Sixteen." He rubbed his eyes with his shirtsleeve.

"Ah. Well." She stroked the gigantic dog's head and fingered the braid on her decrepit uniform. "Cheer up—this won't be the worst of things for you, then, will it? Plenty more bad times ahead. Come on, I'll set you on the way."

7

Aiden arrived at Mrs. Neils's boardinghouse just a few minutes after Fish and Magnus, who had not yet even begun to worry.

"We figured you stopped off for a drink or three along the way," Fish said. "It's what I would have done. Have done, actually, many times—including today!" His cheeks were rosy.

"No," Aiden said. "I was just, ah, seeing a bit of the city." He had brushed most of the dirt off his pants, and they didn't seem to notice he was coatless.

"Then clearly you need to catch up!" Fish picked up the bottle of aquavit and waved Aiden to a seat on the bench nearby. Aiden gladly took the drink from his friend's unsteady hand. He tossed it down and Fish refilled his glass. The small room was bright with oil lamps and crowded with men. It smelled of tobacco, tar, damp wool and beer. A small fire crackled cheerfully in the hearth. The door opened, and a woman poked her head in the room and shouted something in Swedish that, even in the foreign language, sounded clearly like a command.

"That's my mother—supper's ready." The men quickly began to assemble at the three long tables, tucking their shirts in and removing their caps first.

"We haven't told her quite everything about the last trip," Fish whispered to Aiden. "The shark events and such. It's bound to get round to her sooner or later, but we thought she might have a night or so with just her usual worries. Which, far as I know, don't yet include me being eaten alive."

"Fine by me," Aiden said. The food was plain but plentiful. Boiled meat and pickled vegetables with a sort of dumpling. After supper, the men smoked pipes and talked a lot of ship talk, while Sven the Ancient played music on a strange instrument. It looked a bit like a fiddle and was played with a bow, but the neck was much wider and there was a row of levers that pressed the strings. It sounded something like a hurdy-gurdy.

"It's called the *nyckelharpa*," Fish explained. "It is too old and fragile to take on the boat, so Sven must come home to his lover!" The other sailors laughed. Aiden hadn't heard the old man speak twenty words on the ship, but his music told a thousand stories now. The night wore on in a warm, dull, lovely way, with the sweet music playing gentle background to nothing much happening at all. He could see why Fish was crazy to escape it, but after this particular day Aiden was quite glad for the utter boredom.

Whether it was simple tiredness catching up to him or his brother's heavy hand with the liquor bottle, Fish also sat drowsy and contented by the stove with the others and did not mention his earlier plans for a night out on the Barbary Coast. By ten o'clock, almost everyone had gone to bed or down to the local Swedish tavern. Magnus slung Fish's arm across his shoulders and helped steer his little brother to their room, while Mrs. Neils took a lamp and led Aiden to the bunk room, already noisy with snoring sailors. After just four days at sea, he had grown used to the feeling of the bed moving and the sound of the wind. It was strange to have everything so still. Though he was very tired, and aching from the fight, he could not fall asleep. It felt like his entire life was stampeding through his head like a herd of buffalo. He had no family, no home, no possessions and now no money. Aiden tossed and sweated in the narrow bunk as weary sailors snored all around him. The world was full of gorgeous things and awful things—things that made no sense and things like the temples of Greece. How would he find his way through it all?

He knew he had finally fallen asleep only because he was awakened suddenly. It was barely dawn, but the entire boardinghouse was noisy with activity. Men were hurriedly stuffing clothes in their bags and downing plates of fried potatoes and onions as fast as Mrs. Neils could cook them.

"The weather is coming in," Fish explained groggily as he finished off a large mug of coffee. "If we don't get out of the harbor, we might be stuck in for a couple of days." He grabbed his cap and kissed his mother on the cheek. She dropped her wooden spoon and yanked him into a real hug instead. No one, Aiden knew, ever went to sea without thinking it might be the last goodbye.

"I'll see you in two weeks or so." Fish tipped his cap at Aiden. "And we will have a grand night then! Good luck."

Then, just like that, the place was empty.

8

"**N**o work, sorry."

"Got nothing. Go on."

"Who sent you?"

After an entire week spent looking for a steady job, Aiden was starting to get worried. He had figured that in a city this big, there would be plenty of work, but every place he went there were lines of men and always the same answer. *Not today. Go away. Nothing here.* In the East, the machines of war had shut down. There were foundry workers laid off from the cannon works, tinsmiths no longer needed for pails and canteens, engineers with no barricades to build. Men were fleeing west: soldiers and bankers, blacksmiths and drovers, shopkeepers and organ-grinders, paperhangers and butchers. There were embalmers, with their satchels full of potions. The profession had barely even existed before the war, but there was not enough ice in the world to carry all the bodies home, so men had learned to plump the dead with arsenic instead. Embalming was now becoming cautiously fashionable in the cities. One undertaker on Montgomery Street proudly displayed a real body in his front window.

The world had changed and no one really understood how, but they all needed to make a living. The East was scorched and tired and so they came west. California had always been the promised land, but the promise was stretched thin here as well. The gold rush was long over. The transcontinental railroad was more than halfway finished, and lots of skilled men were being laid off. There were still places for architects and engineers, for bankers, of course, and for the interior decorators they needed for their sumptuous mansions. But the plain labor that most men had counted on—the digging and hammering and hauling, the factory work that could build a simple but secure life for a family—was getting more difficult to find.

"It's the damn Chinese!" a man muttered to Aiden after they had both been turned away from yet another laborer's job. "Chinese take all the Irish work here, you know! There's not a hole been dug by a white man in ten years! Women's work too! My wife used to get fifty cents a dozen for buttonholes in the shirt factory. Chinese do it for seven. Seven cents! No one can sew more than twenty buttonholes an hour—and that's only if the thread is good! My children used to shuck oysters—Chinese took over that too! One dollar a day for a good white child—Chinese do it for fifty cents!" He slammed the beer glass down on the bar. "And the children had decent hours!"

"What's good hours for shucking?" Aiden asked.

"Ten to noon for the lunchtime, then three to eight for the suppers, right? For the older ones, that is. The little ones, five or six, can't shuck more than three or four hours a day—their little hands, you know? But they still could get ten cents for shoveling away the shells. And always Sundays off. So that's all right, I say—let the Chinese work Sundays, but don't take work from my children!"

Aiden said nothing. Seven hours was an easy day for a child, and three hours off between shifts was extraordinary. Shucking oysters would probably be hard on their hands, but they had clean air, which was far more than mill children and coal children had.

As for himself, not working was very strange. For all his life before this, not working had meant starving. But now he had only himself to worry about. And not working in San Francisco was vastly different from not working in Kansas or the coal mine. A beggar eating out of garbage bins in this city would still fare better than he and Maddy had their last month on the burned-out homestead, when they ate nothing but clay and grasshoppers. Just a mile outside the city were farms and lush orchards where the gleanings—the bruised and discarded produce left behind after the harvest—could feed a hundred families.

But Aiden quickly learned that he did not have to forage in bins or fields. There were saloons throughout the city that offered free lunches. Food was spread out on a long table called a buffet. There was bread and butter, ham, roasted onions, plates of gorgeous oily sardines and pots of creamy oyster stew. There were whole apples! It was the craziest thing Aiden had ever seen, and every day he still could not believe it was true, but he soon saw the strategy behind it. Most men paid three times the cost of the food to buy liquor to go with the free meals. The usual price was twenty-five cents for a glass of wine or spirits, but some places charged as little as ten cents for a glass of beer. He could make his few remaining dollars go a long way.

He was fortunate to have a place to stay at Mrs. Neils's boardinghouse. Forever, no cost, Mrs. Neils had tearfully promised once she heard, as Fish knew she would, about how Aiden had rescued her youngest son.

On his third day of searching, he got a half day's work

unloading a coal barge. Then one of the wagon drivers from that job, impressed by how hard Aiden had worked, hired him for a big furniture-moving job the next day. It was heavy work, but it was interesting to see all the things that rich people owned. It took four strong men to carry one cabinet, and one entire cart just for the carpets. There was one man who did nothing but wrap the paintings. He shouted at the movers if they came anywhere near his wrapping table. Aiden didn't see what the fuss was, since the pictures were all dull, dark portraits of grim old-fashioned people—or dogs. Why would anyone want a picture of a dog? Everyone knew what dogs looked like. If he could have pictures on a wall, if he ever had a wall of his own, they would be of beautiful things, flowers or the ocean or the pyramids of Egypt or any exotic land, really. He liked dogs well enough, but he could go out-side and see one whenever he wanted—why have a painting of one? He wiped the sweat from his forehead and kept on lifting things. The moving job was good, but Aiden knew there were already enough relatives to handle the usual daily work.

As soon as he got paid from the furniture job, he gave Mrs. Neils money for rent and board, despite her protesta-tions.

"I'm taking up a paying bed," he said. "If you want me for free, I'll have to sleep on the kitchen floor, and that won't do since I'm used to luxury now."

The thin mattress in the sailors' bunk room and the sup-pers of pickled fish and boiled potatoes were hardly luxuri-ous, but he was grateful to have the security of a home, no matter how simple. Mrs. Neils had mended his pants and given him the very good jacket of a very old distant cousin who, she had assured him, had died peacefully in his sleep. It was a bit too small all around, but was a soft wool and had nice deep pockets. Even after he paid the rent, he still had enough money to buy two pairs of new socks, two shirts and a pair of sturdy blue pants called denims, which almost all the laborers wore here. The fabric was thick and stiff, but the shopkeeper said it would soften up with wear.

Though he was unnerved in one way to not have a job, in another way it was nice. Aiden enjoyed walking the streets of the city, looking at people and buildings and shopwindows. At first everything was so foreign it felt like he had landed on the moon. But by the end of the week, he was beginning to make sense of the rhythms and patterns of city life. The best and most amazing part of it all was having so much to read. Magazines and newspapers came infrequently to Kansas. News a month old was considered fresh. But now, with the telegraph running all the way across the country, news from Washington or New York could be in the San Francisco papers the next day. Soon, it was reported, there would be a permanent underwater cable across the whole Atlantic Ocean, linking America to Europe.

Books were even more scarce and expensive on the prairie. His family had often gone an extra year patching over patches to buy a book. A trader with a copy of *A Tale of Two Cities* once rode off with six live chickens, half their flock. But Aiden still remembered those wonderful sixteen days of winter when, for one hour each night, the whole family was transported to another world and lost in the story—except for interruptions of stomach gurgles and farts, since they were eating nothing but corn mush and beans.

Aiden had also put aside a few coins for Blind Sally.

Though his daily exploration of the city had brought him back to the Barbary Coast, he hadn't found the old woman in the daytime, and he wasn't about to go back alone at night. But two weeks later, when Fish returned from the logging run eager for a night of adventure, Aiden was willing. Fish washed, changed clothes and bolted down his supper, and they were out the door before Magnus could begin his usual warnings.

"You would think he's sixty-one instead of thirty-one," Fish ranted as they walked. "Sometimes I'm ready to push him overboard! Push them all overboard! The same men, the same stories, the same route, the same everything day after day after day. My sextant might as well be a toy."

"Couldn't you just get a place on another ship? Aren't they always wanting sailors?"

"Sailors, sure. But I don't want to be a sailor. I want to be a navigator, though I'd be happy to start as boatswain and work my way up. But I've only sailed the coast, no blue water. They want experience."

"Well, experience is nothing more than living through your mistakes."

"So I need to make more mistakes?" Fish said with a laugh.

"Exactly." Aiden slapped him on the back. "I can probably help you with that!"

The streets of the Barbary Coast felt different now that Aiden was a two-week veteran of the city, walking with a friend and here on purpose, not just lost. The bouncers in their bright waistcoats seemed far less sinister, more like bored men at a tiresome job. Gaslights flickered at this later hour, and there were lots more people walking about. There was still a desperate taint in the air, an overwhelming stink of piss and the weight of danger everywhere, but it didn't feel like murder was standing square in front of you either. Still, Aiden knew, it was true about there being a body a night. One of the newspapers had a column called "Despicable Crimes of the Barbary Coast" that filled several inches a day.

"It's great, isn't it!" Fish almost outpaced Aiden with his exuberant stride. "Didn't I tell you?"

"Great" wasn't exactly the word Aiden would have used, but there was a certain tawdry excitement to it all. Most of the places were narrow and dark. Some of the bars offered little more than a few rough planks set on top of boxes, and served vile liquor out of a jug to the shabbiest men. But many places had brightly painted signs advertising shows and dancing girls. A few even had women standing outside to lure men in, women dressed in satin corsets and ostrich feathers and little else. Aiden was relieved when they turned a corner and Fish stopped in front of a large, brightly lit building.

"Here's the place." Fish tugged him into a garishly painted doorway. "The top place! The Elysium!"

A bouncer in a blue velvet coat with shiny gold buttons stepped up to open the door. It seemed a little pretentious to Aiden, until he noticed the two hundred pounds of pure muscle inside the silly coat. The man had fists the size of ducks. He probably didn't need to use them much, since his evil-eye glance was enough to make most men cower just at the sight of him. Aiden followed Fish inside, then stopped, awestruck.

Fish grinned. "Look at all this—it's like a place in France!"

The room was grand as a cathedral, only where an altar might be there was an acre-long bar with a marble top and gleaming brass footrail. Instead of organ pipes there were tiers of liquor bottles, all reflected in gilt-framed mirrors that hung behind them. There were marble statues, though not of saints or angels. The walls on either side of the bar were painted with pastoral scenes in which beautiful girls tended fluffy lambs on gentle hillsides covered in buttercups. The artist had clearly never spent any time with any real sheep on any real hillsides, Aiden thought, for he had dressed the girls in floaty white gowns as flimsy as cobwebs, not at all practical for tending livestock.

"Come on, let's have a drink." Fish expertly muscled his way through the crowd to the bar. Aiden had never seen so many people in one place. There were probably two hundred men. At one end of the room, there was a band with a piano, two fiddles and an accordion, a little stage and a small space in front of it for dancing.

Fish nodded at the bartender. "Two whiskey sodas." The bartender poured the liquor into the glasses, then added water from a bottle with tiny bubbles fizzing up from the bottom. Aiden had never seen anything like it, but Fish treated it as ordinary, so he was embarrassed to ask. He watched the stream of bubbles boil up in his glass.

"Skoal!" Fish raised his glass in a toast. Aiden took a big swallow. The bubbles buzzed at the back of his throat and foamed through his head, making him cough and choke. Just as bubbles fizzed out his nose and dripped all over his shirt, two beautiful girls slid up next to them, sparkly as diamonds, silky as cats.

"Need a hankie, sweetheart?" One of them plucked a bit of frilled lace from the very low neckline of her very tight dress and dangled it before him. He smelled a wave of sour perfume. Aiden struggled to squelch the coughs but felt his face turning red.

"He's more of a straight whiskey fellow," Fish explained, clapping Aiden hard on the back.

"Stick with us, boys, and you can have it any way you like," the other girl said, fluffing her blond curls over her shoulders. "My little sister and I have a special tonight for handsome young gentlemen such as yourselves."

"I'm sure you do," Fish said, looking them up and down.

"Then why don't you buy us a drink?" The dark-haired "little sister" trailed a finger down Fish's arm and batted her eyes.

"Thanks anyway," Fish said, reluctantly pulling his gaze up to her face.

"We don't look good to you?" she persisted with an exaggerated pout.

"I've been at sea over a month," Fish laughed. "Your grandmother would look good to me. But I'm afraid my pockets aren't full enough to take care of ladies as fine as yourselves."

"Oh, I'm sure we can find something in those pockets to make everybody happy," the blond girl cooed, and rubbed her hand lasciviously down Fish's leg. He sidestepped her advances and gently peeled her practiced hand away.

"How about you, honey?" The other girl pressed herself on Aiden. "Special price for juniors." Her experienced eye had quickly discerned his youth.

Aiden took a deep breath. He wasn't used to seeing that much bare flesh on a woman, let alone having it pressed against him, however briefly. It felt very hot in here all of a sudden.

"He's a preacher," Fish said, by way of rescue. Aiden glared at him. Fish just shrugged and grinned.

"Is that so?" the blond girl purred. "Well, you know, a preacher ought to have a good working knowledge of sin."

"The Bible says sin is an ugly thing," Aiden said. "So I don't see how you girls can be of any help to me."

The girls were silent, trying to decide if that was insult or compliment, then gave up and flounced away in search of better prospects.

"Damn, that was a good line," Fish laughed. "How'd you think of that?"

"You can always say something is from the Bible," Aiden said. "Anything you want to say for or against, you can find something in the Bible to back it up."

"They're called pretty waiter girls," Fish explained as he watched the bright dresses swish away into the crowd. "And talking is the only thing they do for free. Even then, they'll ask for a tip if they think you're looking too long. Don't ever say you'll buy them a drink. They'll order some expensive French champagne, and you have to pay. Or they'll slip something in your drink, and next thing you know, you're out cold and robbed in the alley. Some of these places have a special room just for robbery, with a chute to slide the bodies out the back. Anyway, they're two dollars to go upstairs here. The girls next door are half that, and just as pretty and clean."

Aiden knew about prostitutes and the business did not shock him, but he didn't want to "go upstairs" with these or any others. It was not a question of beauty or cleanliness, of morality or even expense; it was just impossible to put aside thinking about them as real people and who they might otherwise be. He had become close friends with a woman named Bandy who led a group of women on a circuit through the far northern lumber camps. Her own fate had been cruelly decided by smallpox, which had left her scarred and robbed of any chance at normal life. Society may have reviled her, but she was also his dearest friend and one of the kindest people he had ever met.

He reached for his drink and took another, more cautious sip, but he still couldn't get the hang of drinking bubbles. He pushed the rest of the hornet fizz to Fish.

"Soda water is all the fashion, you know," Fish said.

"Well, I've never been so good with fashions."

Fish met some other sailors he knew, and they caught up on ship talk. Aiden mostly just looked around and listened to snatches of conversation and watched for glimpses of the pretty waiter girls as they flitted in and out of the crowd like bright tropical birds in a drab forest of men. At the other end of the room, men crowded around gambling tables in a thick blue cloud of cigar smoke, shooting dice or spinning the roulette wheel. There were at least a dozen card games under way, and Fish was eager to join one called faro, but Aiden didn't know the game.

"It isn't hard," Fish said. "Do you play poker?"

"Not well," Aiden confessed. Fish joined a game and Aiden stayed at the bar. Just one year ago, on the bare plains of Kansas, the possibility of ever being in a fancy saloon in San Francisco with music and dancing girls was about the same as being crowned king of England. But now here he was, and it was oddly disappointing. He wasn't sure why. He slowly sipped his drink. He was careful with alcohol now. In the logging camp, he had started relying on it a bit too much, especially after a fight. It was plentiful and soothing and softened the harsh world for a while. But he had also seen it make men stupid and mean and ruined. He wanted his wits sharp, especially in a place like this.

"Oh my God, you're the shark killer! I was sure it was you!" The tall, handsome, fair-haired young man was suddenly walking toward Aiden. Other men slipped out of the way to make room for him, not in deference but automatically, the way people turn to the sun on a winter day. "Boys, come on—I told you it was him!" Christopher Worthington called back to his friends. Four other young men slipped up through the crowd and pressed close around. They were all dressed in shabby coats and worn old work pants, but the crisp collars of their tailor-made shirts and their fine boots immediately marked them as impostors. They were all seventeen or eighteen years old, Aiden suspected, except for one who looked around fourteen, and they were all, except for that young one, very tipsy.

"This is the fellow I told you about," Christopher went on. "Fought off a man-eating shark with his bare hands! Cracked its head open with a hatchet, then dove in the water to save his shipmate!" He focused, as much as he could, on Aiden. "We've only heard it roundabout, so you must tell us the whole story! They say you kicked out a tooth and you wear it now in a pouch around your neck. Can we see it?" Christopher smacked a hand on the bar. "Sir!" he shouted at the bartender. "Another round, and one for our friend here!"

"I don't know where you heard all that—" Aiden said, embarrassed at the attention.

"Oh, it's all the talk in the sailor bars," Christopher interrupted.

"Since when do you go to sailor bars?" One of his friends laughed.

"Oh no, not me! This is the deepest into rough I ever wish to visit!" He waved a dismissive hand around the gilded room as if it were a cowshed. "My father sent his clerk back around to the dock that evening to tip the crew. One always tips for special services," Christopher explained. "It got overlooked that morning, with all the snarling and fangs and such. But our clerk learned this fellow here"—he grabbed Aiden's arm with drunken familiarity—"saved our bears! He shot a seal with a genuine Indian bow. That he got from real Indians—in—in—well—Indian lands! Right?"

Aiden glanced back toward the faro tables, hoping Fish would come to his rescue. "I did shoot a seal," he said simply.

"You see! Just as I said! And then the shark attacked them!" Christopher clapped his hands together, accidentally slamming them against the bar. "Ow!" he yelped. He examined the wounded knuckle carefully. "Go on—tell us the whole story!"

"That's about it," Aiden said.

"There must be details!" Christopher's eyes were blurry and he swayed unsteadily. "Our lives are dull. Give us a story!"

His friends laughed, but it was an embarrassed sort of laughter. The youngest one tugged on Christopher's coat sleeve. "Christopher, it's getting late."

Christopher shrugged him off. "At least show us the tooth," he said to Aiden.

Aiden had never thought about the lives of rich people

being dull. They had books and food and were usually warm. But if this tale had come through Captain Neils or any of the crew, which of course it must have, he didn't want to be rude. Mr. Worthington was obviously a good client, and it wouldn't do to antagonize his son. Aiden drew open the leather pouch, took out the tooth and held it out to them on his palm.

"It's enormous!" Christopher said, his bright demeanor restored.

"You can hold it," Aiden offered.

The young men passed the tooth around with murmurs of admiration, noting the size and weight of it, the sharp jagged edges. They peppered Aiden with questions. How big was the shark, really? Did he think he would die? Could it take off a leg in one bite? Aiden was eager to escape but decided the easiest way at this point was just to give them what they wanted.

"The waves were high as mountains," he said. "The unpitying beast bit so continually at our oars that the blades became jagged and crunched, and left small splinters in the sea!" He paused for dramatic effect and hushed his voice. "I could see the bluish pearl-white of the inside of its jaw, not six inches from my head." His audience murmured with appreciation.

"I remember the sound of its body slicing through the water." Aiden concocted what he supposed would be the proper sound. In reality, he had heard nothing but the low roar of his own panicked blood pounding inside his head. The group leaned in close like eager children. "It was of prodigious size and strength," he went on. "It had no mercy, no power but its own."

Christopher Worthington gave him a suspicious look.

"Then slam!" Aiden finished with an exaggerated flourish that startled a few. "I hit it with the axe. The blood poured out red as—as a—a red rose." It wasn't the best simile, but what else was red but roses and blood? He hurried to finish. "Then the monster vanished, and the great shroud of the sea rolled on as it rolled five thousand years ago."

"Wow." The youngest boy's eyes were wide, and Aiden could tell they were all satisfied with the story. They grew very quiet, sipping their drinks and reflecting on the brevity of life, the savagery of nature and the tenacity of the warrior hero. Or maybe not. An instant later, when a couple of the pretty waiter girls paraded by with feathers and promises of a fandango dance, the young men followed eagerly, ready for a new diversion. Except for Christopher. He watched his friends go off and gather around the stage, then turned and looked at Aiden with a slight, knowing smile.

"I've read *Moby-Dick,* you know. Have you memorized the whole damn thing?"

"No," Aiden laughed, surprised Christopher had recognized it. "Just those bits. 'Bluish pearl-white jaw' is the kind of thing that sticks in the mind. I've read it seven times." He took a well-earned sip of his drink. "I wasn't mocking you, sir."

"I'm not a 'sir,'" Christopher said with a laugh. "I'm hardly older than you, I think. And even if you were, mocking with Melville isn't such a bad thing, I suppose. But seven times? I did like the book—though, honestly, did it really need to be so long?"

"It was a long voyage," Aiden said. "And a big whale."

"True." Christopher tossed back the rest of his drink. The bartender immediately brought him another. "And one for my friend here."

"No thanks." Aiden held his hand over his glass. The bartender glowered, nudged his hand out of the way and poured another one anyway. He was quick to add two ticks to the tally card.

"How are the bears, then?" Aiden asked. "Are they all right? Are they eating?"

"Oh, they're fine, I suppose. But what a stupid showboat that was! Father owes me big, I do say."

"What do you mean?"

"Greeting the bears! And with the ducklings in tow!"

"Ducklings?"

"The sisters. Dear sweet things. I do love them. But you saw it, didn't you? All those nannies, and still at least one always escapes. Father was meant to go himself, of course, holding court and all that—what do I care about bears—but he came down with a bad cold."

The younger boy pushed his way back through the crowd. "Come on, Christopher! It's nearly ten, and you know Lawrence and I have to be back by ten!"

"Little Tom Tom, if you can't sneak into your own house after curfew, you don't deserve to go out," Christopher said sharply. "Getting through your pantry window is like dropping a marble down a well."

"But we have exams tomorrow!"

"I know the capital of Egypt!" Christopher said. "And the square root of pi or whatever. Go on without me if you want. I can certainly find my own way home."

"Not from here!" The boy looked genuinely worried and glanced nervously back to his brother and friends, who were waiting near the door. "You'll be murdered!"

"Go on." Christopher shooed the boy off.

"I'm serious, Christopher," Tom Tom said. "We will leave you."

"Fine."

Tom Tom turned away.

"I should go," Christopher said, looking at his friends. "We do have exams this week, and some of them aren't as rich as me."

"Why does that matter for exams?"

"It means that someday they'll have to work at real jobs, and if they're not smart, they'll be doomed to being minor bank managers or to sitting on the city council for the sewer department or on the commission to teach poor boys to read or something."

"I'm poor," Aiden said evenly. "And I like to read."

"Well, there you have it!" Christopher gave him his brightest smile. "We can stay out all night and fail everything and not be worthless after all!"

Aiden saw Christopher's friends apparently arguing over what to do. Lawrence craned to see over the crowd and waved at Christopher; another just shoved Tom Tom out the door, his rigid shoulders betraying a resigned frustration with Christopher Worthington's antics.

"Ah, well. I suppose I should join them." Christopher reached into the shabby coat and took out a fine leather wallet. The bartender brought over the bill. The total was a week's wages in the lumber camp, but Christopher pulled out the notes as if they were play money. He got unsteadily to his feet and stumbled into a man standing nearby.

"Hey! Watch it!"

"Sorry," Christopher muttered.

"Who do you think you are?"

Aiden stood up between them, experienced by now in defusing a fight. "No harm meant, sir. Have this with our compliments." He slid his untouched drink to the man and steered Christopher aside. "Come on, I'll walk out with you," he said, grabbing Christopher's arm and holding him up.

"Fine. If you like. But *Moby-Dick* was still too long."

"Not if you live in Kansas."

The cold night air felt good. The streets were quiet, with most of the men settled and drunk inside by now. Aiden guided the wobbly Christopher down the two stairs into the street and looked around for his friends.

"They won't really have left you, will they?" he asked.

"I suppose they did. We came in Lawrence's carriage. His parents are out at some fete. If they come home and see the carriage gone, he'll be—I don't know—scolded."

"Where do you live?"

"Just point me toward Pacific Street. There will be cabs there."

Aiden paused. He certainly couldn't let Christopher stagger off through the streets of the Barbary Coast alone, but he didn't want to disappear without telling Fish, who was still inside playing faro.

"Wait here a minute," he said, propping the young man against the side of the building. "I'll be right back, and then I'll walk with you."

It wasn't even a minute later when Aiden returned, but Christopher was almost out of sight, swaying drunkenly up the muddy street. The blue-coated bouncer leaned nonchalantly against a porch railing, watching him with the cool disinterest of a vulture eyeing a lame bunny, his muscled arms folded across his bulky chest. Aiden felt a rush of anger.

"What the hell are you doing letting him wander off like that?"

The man shrugged. "I'm not a nursemaid."

"He can barely walk!"

"Bother me anymore and you won't either."

For a moment, Aiden considered the pure pleasure of punching the bouncer in his fat nose, but he could see a more urgent fight brewing down the street. Men were already coming out of the shadows after Christopher. This little drunken bunny was hopping straight into the stew pot. The man that reached him first started groping at his coat. Christopher barely reacted, perhaps thinking it was his own friends come back to play a trick on him, but when he saw the stranger, he ducked and pivoted away more deftly than Aiden would have expected. But the real danger was just arriving: two more thieves, one armed with a club. Aiden had not clearly seen the faces of his own attackers, but something about this man's posture and the way he carried that stick was all too familiar. Even the initial pickpocket was frightened and took off running. They didn't even bother trying to sneak up on Christopher—they simply grabbed him.

"Hey!" Aiden yelled. "Let him go!" The man with the club turned to meet Aiden's charge, weapon raised. Aiden ducked, spun around and tackled the man at the knees, taking him down. The man lost hold of the club. Aiden drove the heel of his hand hard under his chin and followed with a hard punch to the gut. This wasn't boxing. Damage was the point. It was a messy brawl, but short. Christopher managed to pick up the club and wave it around. He did not manage to actually hit either of their attackers, but his wild swings distracted them enough to help Aiden a little. Even with two against mostly one, Aiden landed more blows than he received, and when he felt the slippery warmth of blood on his knuckles, he was pretty sure it was not his own. Men came out from the nearby saloons to watch, and finally a couple of the bouncers stalked over waving their own clubs, and the two attackers gave up and dashed off into the darkness. As quickly as it had started, it was over.

Christopher Worthington sat in the middle of the road looking confused. He pulled his coat back up into place and wiped dirt off his mouth.

"Did we just have a fight?" he asked.

"Something like that," Aiden said. The energy rush was starting to make his muscles tremble, but he felt unbroken—he felt good, actually.

"Did we win?"

"Can you stand?"

"Was I standing before?"

Aiden laughed, offered a hand and pulled him up. Christopher brushed the dirt off his coat and pants, standing fairly well now, the attack having sobered him up quite a bit.

"Did they get your purse?" Aiden asked.

"Of course not," Christopher said indignantly, pulling out a handkerchief. "It was in my boot. I'm not entirely unacquainted with the practices of the Barbary Coast, you know." The crowd that had gathered quickly evaporated, back to the warm interiors and ready drinks.

"You did much better this time." A familiar voice came out of the darkness. Aiden squinted and saw the old woman and her gigantic dog standing nearby.

"Thank you, Blind Sally," Aiden said, still panting. The old woman tapped her stick in the dirt and The Moon sat down.

"It's nice to see you again," Aiden said. "I have come looking for you—since that day."

"Not at the right time, you haven't."

"No, I suppose not."

"Better late than never." She held out her palm with a regal gesture. Aiden dug into his pocket for some coins.

"Who is that?" Christopher strained to focus.

"This is Miss Blind Sally," Aiden said. "Miss Blind Sally, Christopher Worthington."

"Is that some kind of real animal?" Christopher stared at The Moon. "Or a very shaggy piano?"

"Don't try to make sense of it," Aiden whispered. He placed the coins into the old woman's palm. The skin was soft and papery. In a flash she closed the witchy fingers and stuffed the payment into her pocket. Aiden jingled a couple of other coins so she could hear.

"Blind Sally, would you happen to know where we could find a cab to take my friend home?"

F ish was disappointed that he had missed the drama, but he had done well at cards, so they both came home winners. Magnus said nothing to them the next morning about their late night out, though he twitched more than usual and barely let his brother finish breakfast before dragging him off to the boat.

"We have two days in port," he said as he stomped into his boots. "Last man on deck will be scraping barnacles!" He was out the door and halfway up the street by the time Fish got his coat off the hook.

"Maybe I *will* be an ordinary sailor if it gets me on a real ship!" Fish grumbled. "Hell, I'll be a galley slave! I've got to find something else."

Mrs. Neils gave him a gentle slap and said something in Swedish—clearly a scolding for his ungratefulness to his brother.

Aiden spent the morning as he usually did, walking the city, making the rounds of the laboring jobs, looking for work and coming up empty. As he headed to the cheapest of the saloons for a free lunch, he ran into Bobby O'Brian, one of the men he knew from the moving job, hurrying out.

"Hey, laddie," Bobby said. He gave a quick, furtive glance up and down the street. "A word?" A little boy dashed out of the saloon behind him, jumped down the step, stopped and stood with his palm open. "Here you go." Bobby pressed a penny into the child's hand. "Breathe a word to any other and I'll turn you inside out!" The child ran off. "Come on with me," Bobby whispered to Aiden. "There's a nag just gone down on Second Street by the greengrocer's—knackerman will need hands. Hurry."

He set off at nearly a run, and Aiden followed.

"The boy's mum works in the kitchen there," Bobby said. "He knows to come with news of work. He's a fast one, but anyone can well enough see a dead horse in the street."

The horse was not yet dead, but Aiden knew it was not going to stand ever again, despite the angry whipping of its owner. It was old, and like too many cart horses had been overworked for so long that it had finally simply given out, collapsing, still in its harness, in the middle of the road. Bony ribs still moved as the animal drew shallow breaths. The cart was blocking the street, with two other wagons and a carriage already backed up. The greengrocer was shouting at the horse's owner. A small crowd had gathered.

"The knackermen always hire off the street," Bobby explained. "It's a quick job with two strong men." There were a couple of other men heading purposefully down the street, even as they spoke. "We'll stake our claim," Bobby said. "You stand by the arse end. I'll take the head."

As they went to their posts, another man stepped out of the crowd and glared at Aiden.

"Back off, boy," he growled. Two other men arrived and stopped to size up the situation. Bobby gave Aiden a worried glance. They weren't really going to brawl over a dead horse, were they?

"Sir." Aiden turned quickly to the owner. "Shall I unharness it for you?" The man stopped whipping the horse.

He was sweating from the exertion. "It'll be quicker for when the knackerman arrives," Aiden went on. "Then we can move your wagon over there—clear a bit of the street."

The man spat, looked with disgust at the fallen horse and threw the whip in the wagon. "Go on, then. Goddamn worthless animal!"

Aiden made quick work of unbuckling the harness, then Bobby helped him drag the shaft out from under the beast and back the cart up. The horse lifted its head and looked at Aiden. Its eyes were sad but still luminous. Foam flecked the sides of its mouth. Dust had settled on its hide in stripes between the protruding ribs. It kicked feebly and drew its forelegs up as if to try once more to stand, but the effort was little more than a spasm. Aiden shuddered. A child in the crowd shrieked and began to cry.

"Goddammit, man—put the beast out of its misery!" the grocer yelled.

"How long before the knackerman gets here?" Aiden asked.

"Could be soon, could be an hour," Bobby said.

"If you can bring us a gun, I'll take care of it," Aiden said to the grocer.

"I don't keep a gun in the onion bin!" the man snapped. "It's his damn horse! He should shoot it!" There were some more arguments, more cries from the crowd, more jostling for position as more men arrived wanting the work. Finally someone did show up with a pistol and handed it to Aiden. Aiden said nothing, but waited a few minutes until all the bystanders had seen the gun and understood what was about to happen. It was a job someone had to do, so Aiden did it. He knew where to shoot. You had to get the angle just right.

The knackerman arrived about ten minutes later. He was a tall, blocky man with small, piercing eyes and a head bald as the moon, oiled and polished so it glistened. The cart was brightly painted and pulled by a fine, strong horse with a plume on its head, like the ones funeral horses wore. The knackerman said nothing at first. He walked over to the dead horse and pressed on its eyeballs, checking to see that it was really dead. He looked up at the owner. The man nodded at Aiden and Bobby.

"Them," he said tersely.

"Fifty cents each," the knackerman said.

Aiden and Bobby both nodded without even thinking. What was there to think about? Twenty men could be plucked from the crowd at half that price. It was surprisingly quick work. The cart was just a flat platform on two large wheels. There was a roller fastened at the front between the braces. They tipped the platform down, wrapped a chain around the horse's rear legs, then just cranked the levers until the body began to slide up. Aiden could feel the weight slowly dragging up over the boards. He heard the creaking of wood and iron as the weight transferred to the axle. Inch by inch it came, and this was oddly worse than actually shooting the horse. Once the body was hauled up, they tilted the cart back up level, braced it into place and hitched the knackerman's horse back in. The drama over, the crowd drifted away. The knackerman paid them.

"Who shot the horse?" he asked.

"I did, sir," Aiden said.

The man gave a quick nod of approval. "Farm boy, were you?"

"Some."

82

"You're idle in the midday," he said. "So you must need a job. I'm short a man in the yard."

"I don't know the business, sir," Aiden replied. He didn't know, but he could guess, for the stink of it clung to the knackerman. It would be foul and revolting work.

"Not much to it," the knackerman said. "We skin off the hide. Hair goes to the mattress factory, butcher off the meat for dog food, boil up the rest for tallow and glue. Burn the bones for fertilizer. Five dollars a week to start. But if you last a month and do well, I'll offer seven."

Flies were already massing around the dead horse, lining up like piglets at the edge of the eyeball to suck the juice.

"Could I come by in the morning and take a look?" Aiden said, desperate to get away.

"Suit yourself. Plenty of men looking for work." He climbed up on the cart, slapped the reins and drove off. The dragging tail of the dead horse scrolled curlicues in the dirt.

Bobby suggested they go get some lunch with their wage, but Aiden wasn't feeling hungry anymore. He turned up his collar, shoved his hands deep into his pockets and set off down the street. The day had been gray as usual, but now the afternoon felt especially cold and bleak. He wasn't sure exactly what he had expected to happen in two weeks in this big new city, but somehow it should have been more than this— begging and bribing to get a shovel job or boiling dead horses into glue. He couldn't complain, really—he was better off than he'd been most of his life, and better off than more than half the people he had ever met in his life. But better off than dying of starvation or smallpox or cold just didn't seem like much of an achievement now that he wasn't actually in danger of any of those things. He felt angry and wanted to smash something.

He was tired of always being at the bottom of the pile. There was fortune everywhere in this city, and he had just as much right to try for it as anyone. Who decided all this anyway? Was it just luck? Were some just born sons of fortune?

He walked back to the boardinghouse in a dark mood. Though he had not felt terribly thumped the night before, Aiden was tired and aching and cold to the bone. But when he got home, he found excitement in the air, as there was a package waiting for him.

"It's from Mr. Worthington," Mrs. Neils said excitedly, pointing to the return address. "Such beautiful handwriting he has! A man brought it to the ship this morning, and Magnus sent him along here."

She watched eagerly as Aiden pulled open the string and carefully unfolded the brown paper wrapper. Inside was a book: *A Journey to the Centre of the Earth* by Jules Verne. It had just been published in 1864 and looked expensive, bound in good leather, with the pages edged in gold. Aiden had never seen a book so new. The binding creaked and the pages smelled rich. Tucked inside the cover was a folded note, written in elegant script on thick, creamy stationery with a fancy crest embossed at the top.

Please accept this as a small token of my appreciation for your welcome companionship and assistance last night. I think you will find it an interesting read. My father is hosting a party this Saturday night for the grand introduction of our polar bears, for whose company we are forever in your debt. We would be honored if you would attend. Enclosed is an invitation. I understand that you lost many of your possessions in the dramatic events of the voyage with our

bears and do beg you to accept the services of our tailor, who
has been instructed to manufacture new apparel for you.
Respectfully, Christopher Worthington

Just then the door swung open and Fish, Magnus, Sven the Ancient, Jonas, Gustav, two other cousins, four sailors from the boardinghouse and the barkeep from the Viking pub crowded into the room.

"Well?" Fish said excitedly. "What is it? We've been wondering all day. Give us a look!"

Aiden handed him the book.

"A book? That's all?" They looked disappointed.

"What did you think it would be?" Aiden said, annoyed at their response. "A block of gold?"

Fish snatched the letter out of Aiden's hand.

"'Please accept this as a small token of my appreciation for your welcome companionship and assistance last night,'" he read aloud. "There is also an invitation to a party! At Mr. Worthington's own home, and a tailor to make him a new suit for it!"

The other Swedes murmured their approval.

"'Elsworth Winsor IV, world-renowned tailor of royalty,'" Fish read. "That's a high-class street, and not a Chinaman—maybe English!"

"I'm not getting any fancy suit or going to any fancy party," Aiden said.

"Of course you'll go!" Fish slapped the book back into Aiden's hands. "What do you mean, not go? You must go, if only to tell us all about it after! Have the tailor make extra-big pockets, and you can fill them with sweets and cakes and bring them home to us poor shabby lot!"

"What does he mean, 'your assistance last night'?" Mrs. Neils stared suspiciously at her youngest son. "What happened last night?"

"Nothing at all," Fish said innocently. "We met the young Mr. Worthington and his friends and Aiden gave them a good story, that's all." Fish folded the letter away. "That's all."

The sailors, who had speculated all day over the mysterious package and were now gravely disappointed to find it only a book, soon shuffled out and took themselves quickly to the Viking.

"We should get you to the tailor right away," Fish said eagerly. "Even a 'world-renowned tailor of royalty' will need time to make a gentleman's suit."

"What would I do at a party?" Aiden said. "What could I possibly talk about with any of those people? Christopher probably just wants me to tell them all the stupid shark story, which I don't want to do—only if I don't, I'll have nothing to say at all."

"Don't say anything, then," Fish said. "Just stand around in your fine new suit and let them think you're someone."

"But I'm not someone."

"It doesn't matter! Look, Aiden, everyone in San Francisco is someone they're really not. Even those who actually are someone weren't always someone and know they could be no one again like that!" He snapped his fingers. "No one is no one here, and everyone can be anyone! Come on, what's the worst that can happen?" Fish went on. "You have a fancy night, then go back to ditch work. Or you have no fancy night and go back to ditch work." Fish grabbed his arm and dragged him toward the door. "Either way, you can always sell the suit!"

10

Aiden stared at himself in the mirror as the tailor whipped a measuring tape around his body and shouted out numbers to an assistant. The tailor seemed displeased, as if there weren't quite enough inches somehow, or they were all in the wrong places. Though he kept his drawers on, Aiden still felt naked. He had never seen all of himself at once in a mirror. He didn't know a mirror could even be this big. It was an acre of polished glass, big as a front door. The body he saw there was familiar, but utterly foreign all the same. He recognized the roughened hands and muscled arms, but not the sharp ridge of collarbone, or the complicated ropes that made his neck. He had never seen his own bare chest before and thought at first he was looking at one of his older brothers. He was taller than he remembered either of them being, but he had been only fourteen when they died. He had seen his face, of course, but only in small pieces of a hand mirror or as a blurred reflection in a pond or shopwindow.

The tailor poked a finger in his ribs to make him turn.

"Arms up!" he snapped. Aiden lifted his arm up.

"No—out! Like this!" The tailor slapped his elbow to straighten it. Aiden hadn't expected haberdashery to be quite so rough. But he endured the prodding, and three days later he left the shop looking every bit the gentleman.

Aiden tried to act calm as he walked into the Worthingtons' home, but it was like walking into Aladdin's cave. It seemed like every surface was painted with gold, every object dipped in gold, then all of it painted with even more gold, as if decorated by mad elves and dragonflies. The floor was a kaleidoscopic swirl of green and pink marble that reflected the starlight flickers from the crystal chandelier hanging above. Against one wall was a massive mahogany table with legs carved to look like a lion's paws and a polished slab of marble for the top. Upon the table were two silver vases stuffed with bouquets of flowers as tall as children. Beside the vases were china saucers full of glistening candies, and huge silver bowls overflowing with sugared grapes. Aiden was dizzy from looking at it all, and this was just the foyer. It was nearly as big as his entire sod house in Kansas, where his whole family, as many as eight, had lived. Four gold cherubs flanked the arches that led to the even more opulent rooms beyond.

"May I take your hat, sir?" A tall man in an elegant black suit and blindingly white shirt gave a slight bow and held out a hand.

"Mr. Worthington?" Aiden said, quickly extending his own hand.

"No, sir." The man waited quietly. Only then did Aiden notice there were actually three more of him. Servants.

"Oh—yes." Aiden snatched off his stiff, heavy hat and handed it to the man. "Thank you." He had a moment of panic, for how was he supposed to get it back again? It wasn't even his, but borrowed from an undertaker cousin of a friend of Fish's. Aiden had no idea what a hat cost to replace, but it probably wasn't cheap. He quickly glanced around and saw another man casually reach into his pocket and take out a card, which he slipped into his hat before surrendering it. But Aiden had no card.

Then the old butler smoothly dipped his thin hand into his pocket and drew out a slip of paper. He tore it in half and dropped one half into Aiden's hat and slipped the other into his palm.

"Thank you, sir." The butler nodded, gave him a kind smile and disappeared silently into the cloakroom.

As Aiden walked through the entryway, another servant stepped forward with a tray. On it were delicate little glasses with a golden-colored drink. He took one, but noticed with dismay that there was a stream of bubbles fizzing up. What was it about bubbly drinks here? He cautiously wet his lips. He wasn't about to risk choking on an actual sip.

The room was crowded with women dressed bright as tulips and men looking all so identical in their suits and whiskers that Aiden didn't know how he would ever tell any of them apart.

"There you are!" Christopher Worthington strode through the crowd, silk and whiskers swishing out of his way. "I'm so glad you came. What a rotten dull party it was until now. Oh God, you don't have to drink that swill." He snatched the glass of champagne out of Aiden's hand. "They make it down the road, you know! Father says he wants to support our local businesses, but really, he's just cheap when it comes to these parties. Mr. Butter"—an attentive servant stepped immediately to his side—"would you please bring my guest a glass of whatever this is I'm drinking?" He held up a glass of ruby-colored wine. "From Father's study."

"Of course, sir." The man bowed and pivoted neatly on his impeccable shoe.

"And here." Christopher handed over his own glass. "Top

mine up, would you, please, we're about to venture into the wilds and need fortification."

"The wilds?" Aiden asked suspiciously.

"The zoo." He waved toward a bank of windows at the rear of the house, through which Aiden caught a glimpse of an ornate gate. "I'll show you before Father starts his official tour. He'll go on for hours. All about reproducing the optimal habitat of each and every creature, and how many natives it took to capture the things."

"I should like to see it. Thank you for the invitation," Aiden said stiffly. "And the book. It was an excellent book."

"You read it already? The whole thing?"

"Yes," Aiden said, then paused. Was that maybe an insult—that he had read the whole thing so quickly? Would Christopher think it wasn't a worthy present since it was too short? "I have many idle hours these days," he added. "And it was a very exciting story."

The servant returned with two glasses full of red wine. Aiden, suspicious now about all new beverages, took a cautious sip, but found it smooth and quite delicious.

"Come on," Christopher said.

Afraid of spilling the red wine on his crisp new white shirt, Aiden took a big gulp to lower the level. He looked up to see a whiskered face frowning disapprovingly at him. There were probably a thousand rules here he did not understand, Aiden thought. There was probably a whole bible full of rules and he had probably done half of them wrong already. He stared the disapproving man directly in the eye, tipped up the delicate glass and drank down the whole thing in three great gulps. Then he smiled at the man, set the empty glass on a spindly little table and turned neatly on his heel. There was a certain sweet freedom in having nothing to lose.

Christopher led him deftly through the crowd, through a set of tall carved doors with glass windows and into a room that seemed to be made entirely of windows. There was a tropical jungle growing inside, complete with parrots in enormous wire cages. Aiden could have lingered here for at least a month, but Christopher hurried him outside through another pair of tall doors, across a sort of plaza made of stone, down a manicured path and up to the huge wrought-iron gate.

"Here it is." Christopher swung open the gate. "The Worthington Zoo. Come on, your bears are down the path."

"Have you always been interested in animals?" Aiden asked, trying not to sound as amazed as he felt, or gawk at everything like some bumpkin.

"I'm not the least bit interested in animals," Christopher laughed. "It's just something for the old man to do, you see? We already have the grandest house in San Francisco and all the ice cream we could ever possibly eat. But he is a dear old man, and if it makes him happy to give us an ocelot or aardvark, well, how could I refuse? There's the aardvark." Christopher pointed to a curled-up lump of fur in the corner of a cage.

"He likes the hunt too, you see? Not shooting—the old pussy won't kill a mouse! No, for Father, hunting animals is about writing letters and arranging ships and hiring trappers," Christopher explained. "He spent a year getting the polar bears, arranging for the Eskimos to catch them and the ship to bring them down. And then, of course, there was having the architects design the cage—you wouldn't believe how hard it is just to get enough ironworkers for a fence these days! He shipped them up from Mexico City. Look at the pond—it took a dozen coolies a week to dig that, and you know how fast they work!"

"What are coolies?" Aiden asked.

"Chinamen," Christopher replied. "They're very good diggers." They stopped in front of an extravagant enclosure with ornate iron bars and a pool. The mother bear was curled up sleeping between some rocks, the cubs nestled against her. Aiden was glad to see they all looked well.

"And having a zoo is brilliant for the girls," Christopher went on.

"You mean your sisters?"

"No! Real girls—the kind you court. Of course they'd be coming around anyway, but it is much nicer to have a zoo, for otherwise one would have to sit around in the parlor and always be thinking up conversation."

"Do you have a girl?" Aiden asked.

"A sweetheart?"

"Yes, I suppose, a girl you especially like."

"I like them all. They're all fine."

"What do you mean, all?"

"Well, all the girls in our set," Christopher said. "There aren't that many of them. Thirty-five, I think, maybe forty if you count the ones over twenty. And, well, another fifty if you go down to the picnic girls."

"Picnic girls?"

"The daughters of merchants or minor officials—the next tier down. The ones we would invite to a picnic or a casual dance but not a ball. You know, an open house, like this, but not a served dinner."

"But what's wrong with them?"

"Nothing's wrong, they just aren't, you know, in our set," Christopher explained. "Look, society here is really very movable. I mean, look at yourself—you're nobody, and here you are, welcome in my home. Most people came here with nothing, after all, my father among them. But the gold rush was seventeen years ago."

"Is that how your father made his fortune—in gold?"

"No, iron," Christopher said. "Nails mostly. The city grew so fast, and burned down so often, there was always a need for nails. He started scavenging nails from burned houses, then manufacturing them. He made nails, then factories, then machinery. You've heard of the Comstock Lode? In Nevada, 1859?"

"Of course." It was the biggest silver deposit ever discovered in the United States.

"It was different from the gold rush—a different sort of mining. You needed machinery, and most of all you needed financing. Father provided both. And here we are." Christopher waved toward the elaborate estate. "But the point is, there is a real society now, not just some lucky gold diggers. There are about a hundred top families, give or take a few who are in scandal or bankruptcy or are just too dull. We have to maintain standards. So picnic girls are just for fun."

"What if you fell in love with one?"

"Why would I?"

"Maybe she's beautiful and—nice. I don't know, maybe it just happens?"

"It isn't shameful to marry down a bit. But why? I mean, there are forty good ones available, so chances are that at least one will be all right for a wife. I'm in the top, oh, five, I suppose, of a dozen very rich young men—top three, if you count looks—so no one is likely to refuse me. I can take my pick." He looked down at the last ounce of wine in his glass and swirled it around. "And even if all forty of them turn out to be bores, it's easy enough to ship some in from abroad. Chile is bursting with rich daughters, some of them royalty from Spain. I suspect with our fortune, I could easily get one from Europe if I wanted to. And she would speak a foreign language, so I wouldn't even have to listen to her!"

"You're an ass!" Aiden said before he could stop himself. Christopher's blithe candor was both appalling and wickedly funny.

"Oh yes!" Christopher laughed. "But I'm the emperor of asses! Now come see the monkeys."

Later, as they came back into the conservatory from the zoo, the servant Christopher had called Mr. Butter approached them.

"Mr. Madison," he said with a little bow to Aiden. "Mr. Worthington has requested to meet with you in his office."

"Right now?" Christopher asked.

"If Mr. Madison would be so kind."

"Oh. Well. He probably wants to hear some more about his bears," Christopher said, quickly recovering his nonchalance. "Do go along—he hates to be kept waiting."

Christopher had made his father sound like an old man pottering around his zoo all day, so when Aiden entered the office, he was completely unprepared for the actual person awaiting him. For one thing, his physical presence was startling. The rich men Aiden had seen about San Francisco, and indeed at this party, were all stout, soft men, most with elaborate whiskers and broad mannerisms—men who, even if they weren't actually tall or big, seemed to take up twice the space of ordinary men. But Mr. Worthington was a very small man—at least three inches shorter than Aiden—lean as the newsboys on Market Street and clean-shaven. He had a coiled alertness about him, like a falcon.

"I'm very pleased to meet you, Mr. Worthington," Aiden said nervously. He had never been in a room so grand and sumptuous except on the day of the moving job. These carpets were even bigger and thicker, this furniture even heavier. It would take four strong Irishmen to lift that desk. The glass windows were taller than most houses. The yards of velvet in the draperies would make a hundred ball gowns.

"Welcome, Mr. Madison. And did you like the zoo? The polar bears are quite the attraction."

"I am glad to see them well."

"I would like to thank you personally for their care. Please sit." He waved a small hand at the chairs facing his enormous desk. They were extravagantly carved of exotic wood and, Aiden quickly discovered, extremely uncomfortable to sit in. The seat was flat and shallow, forcing him to perch more than sit. The knobby carvings pressed against his back.

"I understand you were recently in the lumber business. In what capacity?" Mr. Worthington opened a rosewood box filled with cigars.

"Capacity?" Aiden said. "Well—chopping, sir."

Mr. Worthington looked momentarily puzzled, and Aiden wondered what Christopher had told him.

"I cut down trees."

"Oh, I see." The old man sliced him up and down with a sharp, assessing gaze. "Cigar?" He offered the box to Aiden.

"No thank you." Was it rude to refuse? He knew cigars were important, but he had tried smoking and hated it. This life was so hard to figure out. But Mr. Worthington didn't seem to care.

"And now you have come to San Francisco seeking your fortune."

Aiden wasn't sure how to answer that, but he didn't really have to.

"Of course you have, lad, of course you have! Everyone does!" Mr. Worthington sat down behind his desk, his own chair creaking with plush leather. "Would you like some coffee? Some brandy or wine?"

"No thank you. I've enjoyed well and plenty of everything, sir."

"Very good. I won't have my guests wanting." Mr. Worthington leaned back in his chair and took out a cigar cutter and a silver box of matches. "So," he said as he went about the complicated business of snipping and twirling and puffing the cigar. "Logging—a business I am also engaged in. In fact, I was recently offered a contract for advance guarantee of five hundred thousand board feet of lumber at eight dollars a thousand," he said casually. "That is ten percent below current market rates. Shall I take it? Would you advise me so?"

Aiden hesitated. He had the feeling he was being tested, but he had no idea exactly how.

"No, sir. I wouldn't."

"Why not?" Mr. Worthington looked surprised.

"There were some big snows this winter. That means,

come spring, the rivers will be extra-high, able to float out a lot more logs. There are camps up in the far valleys, where I worked, with three years of logs ready to float out, just waiting for high water."

"And you think that high water will come this spring?"

"Yes, sir. Also, with the snow, we dragged a lot of logs out of the woods to the riverbanks."

Mr. Worthington's slender fingers tightened across his velvet waistcoat. "Can the mills handle all these extra trees?"

"Yes," Aiden said. "I know mill workers who've come to be loggers because there wasn't enough work sawing boards."

"The trees that will move on these high rivers—are they good?"

"The best, sir," Aiden said enthusiastically. "Because logs are so hard to move in the high forests, we only cut the very best ones. They've been logging on the coast for a hundred years, so what they cut there now is second growth. Trees from the interior are older, so the wood is dense and very fine. Not wood for common framing, but beautiful wood for furniture and paneling."

"So what should I offer? What price would you advise?"

Aiden thought of Napoleon Gilivrey, king of the high valley logging, in his fastidious little house, squeezing out his profit in overlooked pennies.

"If you could offer to buy the whole lot, and make your deal now, you might expect to pay seven dollars or less, depending on how you bargain."

"I bargain well." Mr. Worthington smiled. He leaned forward, uncapped a crystal inkwell, plucked an ivory-handled pen from a marble holder, opened a ledger to a blank page and quickly began scribbling. He finished his calculations with a slashing underline and turned the book around for Aiden to see.

"Do you have a thousand dollars to give away, Mr. Madison?"

"No, of course not."

"Well, that's what you just did!" Mr. Worthington tapped the ledger page. "Your information given just now will gain me an extra thousand dollars of profit and you not a penny. That isn't very good business for you."

"Mr. Worthington, I didn't think we were conducting business. You simply asked me—"

"Everything is business, young sir," Worthington interrupted. "Knowledge is a commodity as much as wheat or coal or iron. I've just earned a small fortune off your knowledge. Where is your profit?"

Aiden was used to the quick reversal in a fight, but this verbal switch took him by surprise.

"My profit, sir, is—is to know I have been helpful to those who, even if for a short time of acquaintance, I consider my friends."

"Very honorable," Worthington said. "And how well will you live off that honor, young Mr. Madison?"

The man was toying with him, probably insulting him in a dozen different ways, which made Aiden even more embarrassed because he wasn't really sure how.

"Well—honorably, sir," he said. The stupid collar and tie were choking him; the world-renowned-tailor-of-royalty jacket was crushingly heavy. He didn't belong here. Maybe he was suited only to the knacker's yard, boiling dead horses into glue. His back was cramped from sitting in the rigid chair.

"Thank you for inviting me to your party, Mr. Worthington." Aiden stood. "I will go now." He turned and walked toward the office door.

"Wait, Mr. Madison. Please."

Aiden paused, his hand already on the brass knob.

"I did not wish to offend you," Mr. Worthington said. "I apologize. Please indulge an old man with a few more minutes of your time. Perhaps a little fresh air." He crossed the room and unlatched a pair of glass doors to a little balcony that overlooked the garden. He gestured toward a pair of armchairs. "Please," he said. "I have been harsh in my chastisement just now, and I am sorry. I have been in business so long I am like a fish that forgets how those above the sea draw breath. Will you forgive me?"

"Yes, sir." Aiden blushed even hotter. "Of course."

"Then sit with me for a minute more and we will discuss other business."

"I doubt I have any more useful—or profitable—knowledge to offer, sir."

"I don't," Mr. Worthington said in a kinder tone.

Aiden took a deep breath, came back into the room and sat down. This chair was soft, and the cold air felt good on his burning face.

"I test everyone—please do not take it personally. It was not an insult. It is part business and part sport—and wholly cruel, some would say—but as it turns out, it tells me much about a man's character. Now, in regard to the thousand dollars, I will offer that to you as salary."

"Salary? For what job, sir?"

Mr. Worthington went to a nearby table and poured from a crystal decanter into two enormous round glasses. Aiden did know enough about rich men to recognize cognac as the mark of something important.

"I know that you rescued my son from harm last week," he said as he handed Aiden a glass. "Very little goes on in this city that I do not hear of. I am grateful to you. Christopher is a smart boy, but often an idiot. He is the prince of San Francisco, but he is of the age and the mind to . . . rebel. He is welcome in every gentlemen's club but prefers to explore the seedier establishments. I would like him to stay alive long enough to have a chance to straighten himself out and make something of himself in this world. I had a man in my employ charged to be observant and available to assist my son as might be needed. Clearly, he failed. So, to that end, I wish you now to look after his well-being."

"You want me to be a guard for him?"

"I want you to be a friend to him. And perhaps teach him something of the real world. Christopher and his friends were raised without challenge or want. And"—Worthington held up his hand—"I can anticipate all protestations of friendship without recompense, which I do respect. But I am paying for your time, not your devotion. If you work elsewhere, you will not be available in my household."

"I don't think he'll have it, sir. All due respect—"

"Of course he won't have it! Coddled or not, he isn't a damn nancy boy. You will not be employed as his bodyguard, but as a tutor to my youngest son. He is a sickly boy and cannot go to school. That will bring you into residence here in my house and thereby make you available as a natural friend to Christopher."

"I'm not a teacher, sir," Aiden said. "I have no formal schooling myself."

"He's eleven years old, and unfortunately, it appears his mind is also afflicted," Worthington said, growing impatient. "You can certainly read ahead."

"How do you know—" Aiden was so surprised that his voice caught in his throat and he had to swallow before he could speak. "How do you know you can trust me, sir? How do you know I'm not a robber or something?"

"If you robbed me, you wouldn't get very far." Mr. Worthington smiled but could have been brandishing a dagger. "I am practiced at assessing men quickly. So I do not fear for my candlesticks. I have done business with Captain Neils for many years, and he spoke well of you." He put his cognac down and sprang from the cushy chair with a single smooth motion, like a cat. "Perhaps I can sweeten the deal. Christopher said you like to read. Come here."

He strode across the office and slid open a pair of twelve-foot-high mahogany doors, revealing the adjoining library. It was like walking into heaven. Every wall was covered with shelves from floor to twenty-foot ceiling, and every inch of every shelf was packed with books. In the center of the room were two tall, slanted reading desks, and upon each was a huge folio of maps.

"Will this coax you?"

Aiden was already thinking he would pretty much sell his soul to the devil for a single day in this library when a door at the other end of the room slid open and an angel appeared instead. She had silky gold curls that shimmered around a face that was smoother and more perfectly carved than any of the marble statues in the garden.

"Oh, hello, Father. Whatever are you doing here? I hope I'm not interrupting," she said coyly. "But a question arose"—she gestured toward the atlas on one of the desks, but her eyes were fastened on Aiden—"about Patagonia."

"Yes, that happens so often at parties," Mr. Worthington said with a sigh.

"You must be Christopher's new friend!" she said, gliding toward them with a soft rustle of skirts and a trail of butterflies. Trumpets and harps sounded. The earth paused in its revolutions and tilted on its axis, tossing penguins from ice floes in the distant Antarctic.

"Mr. Madison, may I present my daughter, Miss Elizabeth. Elizabeth, Aiden Madison."

She extended her hand. "I'm so pleased to meet you. I've heard so much about you." Aiden hadn't heard anything about her. Christopher had referred only to a flock of little sisters, and though she was clearly a sister, there was nothing little about Elizabeth. She was small in stature like her father, and more delicately boned, but she had her brother's strong features, the same bright confidence and easy manner. Her eyes and her dress were the color of the ocean, and this time Aiden longed to sink.

"I'm very pleased to meet you," he managed to say. He gingerly touched the very tips of her offered fingers, afraid they might break off like sugar flowers on a fancy cake.

"I understand you have many stories to tell," Elizabeth said. "Will you be staying long?"

"Yes," Aiden said. "I believe I might be."

11

A

iden never knew life could be so soft—the feel of new shirts against his skin, the buttery leather of his new boots, this goose-down comforter like a cloud. His room had carpets, and his bed was big as a horse stall. Even after a month here, he woke up startled every morning, disoriented and incredulous at his fortune.

The kitchen had two iceboxes—the estate had its own icehouse, with ice brought down from the Sierra Nevada. Milk was delivered every day. There was a greenhouse that grew lettuce even now in February, and whole chickens were common as potatoes. He and Christopher could come home at midnight on any day and forage up a feast. There was hot water whenever he wanted to bathe, no stove to light or bucket to boil. It simply came from boilers somewhere deep in the house. Each morning silent servants appeared with pots of coffee and freshly baked bread.

The whole family rarely ate supper together, but they were always gathered for breakfast, stretched out around the huge dining room table, Mr. Worthington at one end, his wife at the other. Edith Worthington was not yet forty, a good twenty years younger than her husband, though his first and only wife and the mother to all seven of the children. She was a little taller than her husband, a sturdy woman to whom the years had not been terribly kind, but who had clearly contributed some of the best features to the beautiful children. The fair skin, pale hair and gray eyes that once must have made the younger woman as lovely as the painted shepherdesses on the walls of the Elysium now, in the morning light, made her wan. Even after a month in the house, Aiden hardly knew her. She had accepted his new position in her household with a distant politeness and little more interest than if he were a new animal in the zoo.

"Oh, how lovely to meet you. A tutor for Peter? What a good idea."

She was a loving though distracted mother, more than willing to trust the details of daily care to a staff of nannies and nursemaids. After raising Christopher and Elizabeth largely on her own for four years back east and shepherding them safely across half the world to rejoin her husband, she had given birth to Peter and had assumed her family was complete. She had begun to enjoy the life of leisure that their new fortunes allowed. There was a party, the theater or a concert every night of the week. There were long luncheons and teas with the other wives, and drives in the countryside. Then suddenly little girls started showing up: Charlotte, now eight; seven-year-old twins Annalise and Annabelle; and finally Daisy, the oddest of the odd quartet. She was a solemn, dark-haired child who, although barely five, spoke in long and often complicated sentences. "I do not want the dog to sit there," she would declare as she pushed the poor spaniel out of the afternoon sunbeam. "She dirties the sun."

These little girls, Aiden had discovered, were connected to the rest of the family only at their choosing, living most of the time in their own world, like a little tribe of changelings. They often spoke in a private language, full of odd allusions, sometimes with no more than a gesture or a glance.

The boy Peter, though eleven, was nearly as small as Daisy, with a mild palsy that kept him mostly in his wheelchair. Mr. Worthington had shipped in doctors from all over the world, but none offered a cure, or even a diagnosis. No one knew if his mind was normal, but most thought not. He would not look directly at people and seemed not to understand anything that was said to him. He was transfixed by objects, especially a collection of smooth river stones. He would stare endlessly at sun patterns on the floor of the conservatory. There was a private live-in nurse to tend to Peter's bodily care, so Aiden's duties were devoted to the boy's mind. Peter could barely speak, and though the ducklings had an uncanny ability to understand his attempts, their translations were limited by their own childish sensibilities. "He wants to sit in the garden," Charlotte explained. "He says he would very much like some treacle taffy," said Annalise. "He would like us to dance for him now, not go to bed."

"*Candy* is his word for anything good," Daisy explained. "This is the candy cat." She pulled the enormous orange cat up and dropped him onto Peter's lap. "The word for *bad* is *tsin*—for *medicine*. That one"—she pointed at the striped cat—"is the cat he doesn't like. That is the medicine cat. Tsin!"

Aiden spent the mornings with Peter, often accompanied by Daisy, who was considered too young to join the older ducklings' lessons. Charlotte, Annabelle and Annalise were tutored for two exact hours by a cheerless woman who valued penmanship above all other virtues and wielded alphabet cards at them like a crusader's sword. She wore stiff black dresses, always clasped at the throat with a brooch the size of a vulture's egg. Two days a week, the science teacher came after lunch, and the dancing and arts teacher the other three.

The science teacher, Professor Tobler, was a genial old German at least seventy years old who took the girls for walks in the garden, collecting things to look at under the microscope, or tried to get them to copy the parts of a plant from the illustrations in a pebbled-leather folio. They generally preferred to draw volcanoes and lions.

Aiden's friendship with Christopher grew easily; it was mostly enjoyable and definitely never dull. Their lives could not have been more different. In his seventeen privileged years, Christopher had never slept on the ground, killed any animal larger than a fly or gone hungry unless he was feeling too lazy to walk down to the kitchen for some bread and jam. Aiden could never quite forget that he was paid to be Christopher's companion and protector, but they might have been friends anyway, although Aiden would have indulged his exasperation more frequently.

Christopher was either summer or storm. He drank too much. He gambled outrageously. He was kind to the servants and sometimes vicious to his friends. He smuggled sweets to the ducklings and bribed their nannies to let them out for adventures with him, then ignored them completely for days. He loved to roam the city and would talk to anyone about anything with genuine interest, but he also started senseless arguments, which often turned into fights that always left Aiden with more bruises. He was easily bored and often restless, physically vigorous but loath to suffer any discomfort. There were some excellent riding horses on the estate, and he loved to go for long gallops west across the open country to the sea, riding hard for hours. But once home, he fussed like a child if his slippers were not warmed and a hot bath was not ready immediately.

He flirted with every pretty girl he saw, society girl, picnic girl and waiter girl alike, and felt no guilt about breaking their hearts.

"They know how I am." He shrugged. "I can't control their hopes."

Even after attending several parties and meeting most of Christopher's friends, Aiden could never speak to a girl much beyond "Hello" and "Lovely weather."

"How do you think of things to say to a girl?" Aiden asked Christopher after one unsuccessful party where he had thought one particularly pretty red-haired girl would be interested in the details of loading a knacker's cart.

"You've read three shelves of poetry books by now," Christopher said with a laugh. "Plus all of Shakespeare. If you can't come up with sweet talk, you should probably just throw yourself off a cliff."

"It's different outside of books. You don't just go up to a girl and smack her with Shakespeare."

"True. There's rule number one, then—no smacking with Shakespeare. So, rule number two—pay her compliments. Say that her skin is like porcelain and her arms graceful as a young plum tree waving in the summer breeze and her hair spun gold as gossamer!"

"What is porcelain?"

"Fancy china."

"Like china plates?"

"Yes, but thinner and finer—like my mother's best teacups. You can see light through the bottom of a porcelain teacup."

"So girls want to look like teacups?"

Christopher shoved him.

"And what if her hair is black?"

Christopher gave an exaggerated sigh. "Well, then, say it looks like a woodland pond shimmering under a full moon! Just use lots of poetry words and pay her compliments. But start off easy—hold off on the porcelain and plum branches at first. Start with her beautiful eyes. Eyes are perfect. Unless she's totally crazy cross-eyed or something, you can't go wrong with the eyes. Hands are good too: 'What lovely hands you have'—no, *elegant* is better. That can go easily into 'Do you play the piano?' And there—you have something to talk about."

"I don't know anything about piano," Aiden said.

"Well, she will, so just nod and listen. Of course, don't go to piano if she has stubby little fingers."

"Of course not," Aiden said. "I'd say what useful hands for a washboard, and has she ever thought about taking in laundry."

"You asked for my advice," Christopher said in a wounded tone. "You asked about girls, and I know about girls. If I wanted to know about . . . farming, I would—well, I'd never want to know about farming, really."

"All right, compliments and piano."

"Though you do have to be careful," Christopher went on. "A really beautiful girl is distrustful of compliments, and the ugly ones know you're faking. But for the average pretty-enough girls, just focus on their good bits. You don't have to get specific, just say something is flattering: 'That color is so flattering on you.' 'That hairstyle flatters you.' You're not lying, because it doesn't mean anything, really. A bow on the forelock will flatter any nag."

"You're awful," Aiden said, though he couldn't help laughing. "I wish you could be ugly for just one day."

"It wouldn't matter," Christopher said. "I'd still be rich. And American. And a man."

Aiden said nothing. It was simple truth.

For all his protestations about dry old dusty books, Christopher actually did well in school. He had an eager mind and pursued anything that interested him, but he had to work hard at the duller subjects required for graduation: Latin, chemistry and ancient history. Aiden had never gone to a real school, so in every subject that required actual book learning, his knowledge was spotty. He was exceptional with geography and foreign cultures, thanks to reading, at least a thousand times, the *Atlas of the World*. He had a decent command of history, but Christopher knew more about the Civil War, even though Aiden had lived on its doorstep and lost a brother to the fighting.

"There's one professor at the academy who followed every battle and reenacts them in class with little lead soldiers and tiny paper flags," Christopher explained. "He'll go on for hours with this charge here and that flanking there. It's to teach us military tactics, though I don't know why. It's not like any of us are ever going into war!"

"What if you had to?" Aiden asked.

"Had to what? Go to war?"

"Yes."

"Why?"

"Maybe there was something worth fighting for?"

"Well, anything worth fighting for, we would just buy," Christopher said, genuinely puzzled. "Or pay the politicians to give it to us! Why ever go shooting people? Unless, I suppose, you've invested in guns and powder or cannon factories—then a war does make sense. But even if, for some reason, some stupid reason, we absolutely had to have a war—well, we would simply pay some armies and generals who know what they're doing, right? I mean, I don't have to personally know about flanking anybody!"

Aiden was still never exactly sure how much Christopher was teasing him. The little circle of wealthy families certainly did seem rich enough to buy pretty much anything they wanted, including armies and the governments that made them work. The real question, Aiden realized, was exactly how did they get that money in the first place? And—as he grew more used to the luxury it offered—how could he get some himself?

Christopher spent every afternoon working in the office with his father, so Aiden had a few hours alone in the library. Here the world was opening up to him in ways he could not have imagined. It was like he had an axe and was chopping his way through all of civilization. He burrowed through the stacks, from the Magna Carta to the American Constitution.

Then, at three or four each afternoon, Elizabeth would come home and here would be a whole other world altogether. Even after a month, Aiden had no idea what to make of her. Sometimes she flirted and teased him like a pretty waiter girl would; sometimes she wanted to discuss Darwin for hours. Sometimes she felt like a sister, sometimes like his heart's desire. How was a man ever supposed to know? When he was around her, Aiden felt nervous and peaceful, happy and confused, all at the same time. There really needed to be an *Atlas of Girls*, he thought. For all her dainty posturing, Elizabeth was a physical girl who came home each day restless and eager for exercise. Her choices were limited, of course. There would be no wild gallops to the ocean with her, certainly no rambles through the city, but within the protection of the estate, they were allowed to walk together or play tennis on the lawn. They often walked through the zoo, talking of nothing at all, just happy to be away from the prying eyes and ears of the servants.

Aiden's days fell into a comfortable routine. He worked with Peter, played with the ducklings and tidied up after Christopher, defusing or winning his battles as needed. He escaped for easier nights with Fish whenever his friend was in town between trips. He read books until his brain hurt. He watched this new world and tried to understand it. And so the months passed in the house of riches.

For most of Aiden's life, the turn of the calendar page from February to March had always been a day of grim cheer. It was a mental leap toward spring, but in reality, the snow was still waist-deep and the winds promised only more harsh days. Real spring, the end of winter's attempts to kill you, did not usually come until April.

But in San Francisco, March was a real shift. It helped that the winter was mild to begin with, but even with that, there were such quick changes day to day that spring felt generous and real. There was lettuce growing outside by April, and fresh peas at the end of May. He watched jealously as the kitchen girls sat out in the sun shelling them, their quick fingers splitting the pods open and spilling the sweet contents into copper bowls. The first few dinged like hail, but after that, with a cushion already at the bottom of the bowl, the peas made a soft tattoo. When he saw a girl pop one into her mouth, he nearly died of desire. He was both amazed by the bounty of the spring and oddly angry. Scarcely one year ago, he was a stick man of a hundred pounds, with nothing to eat but clay and grasshoppers.

CHAPTER 12

It was June 25, the night of Christopher's graduation. One of his friends was hosting a grand house party, but Christopher was in a strangely dour mood and not eager to go.

"It's everyone I've seen all my life," he said. "And celebrating only what we were supposed to do all our lives, and what we are now supposed to go on to do with the rest of our lives, which is all laid out and all the same. University, then business, then more business, then die."

"There may be a bit more to it than that," Aiden laughed.

"Not for me," Christopher said. "My future is fixed." He spun a gold collar stud around on his dressing table. "And infinitely dull."

"Dull? But you can do anything you want."

"What should I want?" Christopher flung back. "Maybe I'd like to be a farmer. I've never dug a hole—is it satisfying?"

"No," Aiden said. "Not at all."

"But then you get to plant seeds and watch them grow."

Aiden stifled a laugh. "That's plowing. Holes are what you dig for fence posts. Holes are just work."

"Well, exactly my point—if I don't even know a plow from a hole, how can I know what else I might like to do?"

"Believe me, you wouldn't like plowing."

"Still, I'm tired of my future being all laid out," Christopher said. "And I don't want to go to this party."

"You've got to at least make an appearance," Aiden said, well versed in protocol by now. "It would be rude not to."

"What good is it being rich if you can't be rude sometimes? Anyway, it's early. The party will go on forever. Let's go play a few hands at the Elysium." Christopher pulled out his pocket watch. "It's barely eight o'clock. We can arrive at the party by ten and no one will even blink. We can make it eleven with a good story. Come on—we've plenty of time!"

Of all his "guard duties," the most difficult for Aiden at first was playing poker. He could not avoid the game, for there was no excuse for him to go out with Christopher for an evening and just sit idle for hours while his friend played. He had learned to play in the lumber camp, but only enough to know how much he didn't know. So he found a book about poker in the library and began to deal practice hands with Peter and the ducklings. Aiden wasn't sure if the boy could discern the suits, or even red from black. He had tried twenty different ways of communicating with the boy by now: a giant chart of letters; colored blocks, red for *yes*, blue for *no*. He had tried wrapping a pencil in rounds of cloth to make it easier to hold, even tying it to Peter's hand and guiding him to make letters, but Peter would only scribble madly or smash the pencil so hard it broke. Aiden brought in a box of damp sand that he thought Peter might trace in, but when he pressed the boy's finger into the sand, Peter howled and jerked back as if a wasp had stung him. Peter had a bell on his chair, but Aiden could not get him to ring for *yes* or *no*.

"He doesn't need *yes* or *no*," Daisy finally explained one day.

"What do you mean?"

"Whatever is usually fine."

"Do you mean he doesn't care? Or he doesn't notice?"

Daisy looked down and pulled at her dress. "He notices more."

"I don't know what that means," Aiden said. "You don't care if you have applesauce or bread?" Aiden asked the boy directly. "If I read to you or someone plays the piano?"

Peter only looked up at the draperies, as he often did—mesmerized, it seemed, by the scrolled pattern.

"*Yes* and *no* don't matter the same way to him," Charlotte explained, though it explained nothing.

"In his head," Daisy said, "he can make anything be whatever he wants."

"So he can make bread taste like applesauce in his head if he wants to?" Aiden pressed, frustrated. Peter turned his head back and forth, and Aiden was sure he was laughing.

"No," Charlotte said. "It's that bread has a thousand ways to taste and applesauce has a thousand ways to taste and he hasn't finished all the ways with either of them yet." The other ducklings smiled in agreement, happy that their biggest sister had managed to explain.

"I expect it will change," Charlotte added. "As he gets older."

"After he tastes all the thousand ways?"

"Yes!" The four little girls nodded together in perfect solemnity.

"But he does communicate with the four of you," Aiden persisted.

"Oh yes." Daisy nodded, as if it were a silly question.

"How?"

"We are inside his head."

"Can I go inside his head?"

The ducklings conferred in their secret way of looks, then solemnly shook their heads.

"Maybe sometime," Charlotte offered kindly. "Now you have too many colors." She brushed her hands alongside her face as if flicking away spiderwebs.

"Colors?"

"Mad colors," the others said in accidental unison.

"I have no idea what that means." Aiden sighed. He dealt a new hand of cards out on the table. "But look at his cards and ask him what he wants to bet."

Over the months, the nursery room poker games did sharpen Aiden's skills. The little girls played with both the impulsive glee and the simple logic of children. Annalise and Annabelle didn't care what cards they were dealt, they just liked to raise each other. Charlotte was good with numbers and tried to figure out her odds. Daisy had the simplest strategy, only betting when she had a good hand, never bluffing. She understood the concept of bluffing—but she thought it the same as lying, and lying offended her. This was not for any moral reason, but because she thought it just messed up the games and made them boring.

These games, however odd, did give Aiden good practice, and soon he began to hold his own in the real games and finally to win more than he lost. His strategy was a combination of Charlotte's and Daisy's, though improved by his own discipline. He made only small bets and quickly folded when he had bad cards, but went bold when he knew he had a strong hand. Even if other players recognized this strategy, it didn't hurt him, since they were more likely to fold when Aiden bet heavily. They knew he didn't bluff. It drove Christopher crazy. Christopher's strategy was exactly the opposite. His play was as mercurial as everything else about him.

This night at the Elysium, Aiden was doing especially well, and after an hour he had a great pile of chips in front of him. They were playing with nine men; bets tended to be fifty cents to a dollar, and few pots topped twenty dollars. Christopher, still in his funk and distracted, had lost almost everything. It was an ordinary night with an ordinary group, but the energy of the table changed when a new man sat down. He was a brown-haired man of average height, clean-shaven, though not in the past few days. He was not soft as a gentleman nor roughened as a laborer, though his hands, Aiden noticed, bore signs of hard use: callused palms, tiny scars, swollen knuckles. But he had no accent to place his speech, no posture or gait that would mark him in any way. He was in fact of such unremarkable appearance that you could spend a week with him and still not pick him out of a dozen other brown-haired men of average height and build. Unless you looked into his eyes. There was a haunting about him.

"Welcome, sir," the dealer said. "Your entry?" The man opened a purse and tipped out a pile of coins. The dealer gave a quick nod to a floor man, who quickly came over to judge the worth. There were so many coins and notes in use it took an expert to know what they were worth. The floor man placed stacks of chips on the table. The man barely looked at them before giving a sharp nod of acceptance. The dealer snapped the cards down, and the game continued.

The man gave his name simply as Newgate. Aiden, as he

always did, watched the man closely, but got few clues. He hardly seemed to breathe. It was as if he were trying to take up as little space in the world as possible.

The game went around for an hour with shifting stacks of profit, but gradually the better players built piles and the lesser ones dropped out. Aiden continued to win, though Newgate also accumulated a steady pile. Christopher was playing badly. He called in all his credit, which was plenty, and continued to lose. Newgate sloughed off both wins and losses with no emotion. Another player dropped out, so there were only five of them left now. Aiden felt vague misgivings—Newgate was manipulating the game in some way, but he could not tell how. Aiden had learned to spot all the common cheats and scams, but there was nothing clearly wrong here, just a sense that the man was steering the game a certain way. There was no obvious sleight of hand, no flagrantly stupid bets, but no real sense to it either. Aiden could usually tell when men were working in partnership, but the only one profiting from the game was himself—and that made no sense at all. Why would a complete stranger turn a game his way? Twice, when it was down to just Aiden and Newgate, Newgate had folded, even after having raised several times. It wasn't all that suspicious, since Aiden's technique was pretty obvious. He had had very good hands both times, but because Newgate folded, neither of them had to show their cards. Aiden began to worry, for if he felt it, the other players must have sensed it too and might think he was cheating.

"We need to take our leave soon," Aiden said. "We've already stayed far too long and are late for an engagement."

"Not that late," Christopher said brightly. "We can't leave while you're on a streak and I've still got, oh, nearly two dollars left! Cover me this one round, and if I lose, I'll step out. I promise. Truthfully and swearing."

The betting went two rounds to the draw and three after. One of the other players won with three fours. Christopher had a pair of twos, Aiden a pair of tens, Newgate a pair of nines; the fifth man had bluffed with nothing, having tried to draw to a straight. There were no clocks in the Elysium, but one of the players pulled out a pocket watch and announced with dismay that it was a quarter to ten.

"Come on," Aiden said to Christopher. "We're past late."

"We can't both leave losers!" Christopher waved at the table. "One more hand. Raise the stakes—let's go out grand!"

"Yes, one more hand," Newgate said softly. He had to stop and clear his throat. It was the first time he had spoken in the game. "I have no more cash, but I will wager my ship."

"Your ship?" the dealer said.

"She's wholly mine, free of debt." He pulled tattered papers from his coat pocket and laid them on the table gently, like an unsure offering to a doubtful god. "She is sound, with all sails and rigging. She is the *Raven*. We are arrived in the harbor this very afternoon."

"You would do better selling her anywhere else, sir," the dealer said. "The pot won't go near your value." He waved toward the piles of chips in front of each man. The total of everything on the table might make five hundred dollars. "A hulk is worth more for scrap."

"She is no hulk."

"Then you could sell her outright."

"I leave the city this night and have no wish for negotiations," Newgate said, his voice sharper.

"So what will you do, then, if you win?" one of the players asked, thinking it a joke. "You will have money and still a ship. What will you do if you win this hand?"

"Burn her."

The table fell silent. It was clearly no joke.

"Is she cursed, then?" the man asked.

"A ship is a thing. There is nothing to curse in a thing, only in a man."

The dealer caught the eye of the floor manager, who swooped in to examine the papers. Meanwhile, all the other men at the table shifted and murmured. No one knew quite what to make of this.

"Are you known to anyone here?" the floor manager asked.

"To the harbormaster," Newgate said softly. "And Addington's chandlers."

"Gentlemen," the floor manager said. "If you all wish to play, I will recess the game for fifteen minutes. If the hand commences, to be fair, this will be a high-stakes game. There will be a fifty-dollar ante. As you are all known here, you may speak to the house manager if you desire a house credit. Please stretch your legs and accept a complimentary drink."

"We're in," Christopher announced. "Well, Aiden here is."

"No." Aiden held up his hands. "Thank you—I get seasick," he said lightly.

"He's in!" Christopher said, dragging Aiden away from the table before he had a chance to object any more. "You have to play, Aiden. Don't you see? This is a chance to make

our fortunes! You win the ship, I'll finance the business—
we'll be partners!"

"What business?"

"The shipping business, of course! We will ship things—
pineapples! From Hawaii!"

"You're crazy. And you already have a fortune."

"I have my father's money," Christopher said. "But for
that I am eternally bound to him and his business. This is
my chance to break free! And your chance to make your own
fortune."

"I have a fortune right now on that table!" Aiden said.
"Two hundred dollars is more money than has passed through
the hands of my whole family in all of our lives combined." It
was exaggeration, but not by much.

"All the more reason to risk it!" Christopher declared.
"For where did it get them?"

Aiden stiffened.

"I'm sorry," Christopher apologized. "That was a cruel
thing to say. But true."

"Can you be more awful?"

"Oh God, yes, unfortunately. But I'm trying to help you
here. This is our time for daring!"

"Dare with your own money, then," Aiden said.

"You know I can't draw any more tonight. My father has
seen to that. And I've no luck at all anyway. Win this ship and
with it your way to real fortune, or lose the money you never
had two hours ago. I will even repay you if you lose."

"Your father won't allow that."

"Exactly why we need to escape his infernal thumb on
our lives!" Christopher said desperately.

"The papers appear genuine," the floor manager announced as he returned. "The house has agreed to hold all monies and deeds in trust for verification. Whoever wishes to play may be seated."

"You like this life, don't you?" Christopher said quietly. "I know you do. You pretend not to care, but you do. You will never have this life working as a tutor or a clerk for my father."

The truth of that stung.

"Come on." Christopher pushed him back toward the table. "Fortune favors the brave!"

The five men sat down. Aiden counted out fifty dollars' worth of chips and pushed them to the center of the table. It was two months' pay for a logger. But he wasn't a logger anymore, nor a dirt farmer nor a refugee. He was a son of fortune.

The seal was cut from a new package of cards. The cards were dealt. Aiden fanned his out to see a very good starting hand: two jacks, a two, a three and a seven. The pot grew quickly. The table felt like it was vibrating. The chips, of wood, bone and ivory, made a slippery pile in the center. At the draw, Aiden drew three cards. One man drew two. Two other players each drew three. Newgate drew only one. Aiden looked at his new cards—he felt heat creep up the sides of his neck. Another jack—now an exceptional hand. Except there was a chance one player had a full house, or that Newgate, drawing only one card, now had a full house, a straight or a flush.

The first bet was twenty dollars. Aiden raised twenty. Newgate also raised. What was the man's real intention? If he really wanted to lose the ship, all he had to do was fold.

Was it really a ruse just to get a high-stakes game going? Was the story of haunting and burning the ship just to tantalize them into losing all their money? It didn't matter at this point. Aiden was in the game. Whoever won the hand owned the ship. When it was Aiden's turn, he needed sixty dollars to call. Then he raised a hundred.

One man turned his cards down. "I'm out."

There were only four of them left now. The other players hesitated. One looked hard at Aiden, searching for any clue. Aiden held steady. The man called. The next man called. It was up to Newgate now. He had no chips—he was playing on house credit.

"I raise," he said, his voice raspy, "five hundred dollars."

A buzz erupted throughout the room. Aiden didn't flinch but his mind was spinning. If he lost, he was out nearly half his year's salary as Peter's tutor. Christopher might or might not actually cover a loss this big. What was Newgate's game? Aiden was pretty sure at least one of the other players would fold. Aiden looked up at the floor manager and nodded.

"House credit for five hundred," the manager said.

Another of the players threw down his cards in anger and pushed back from the table. That left just the three of them. The whole room was silent, everyone now watching the game. The other player called the bet. Newgate laid out his cards. A three, a four, a five, a six . . . The crowd murmured in excitement as the sequence appeared, then gasped to see the last card: an ace of spades.

It was Aiden's turn next. He put down his three jacks. The final player's hand shook slightly. He held two pair. Kings and tens. A very good hand. But not good enough. Noise came rushing back through the room. The piano started up a gay tune, and flocks of pretty waiter girls began to swarm around the table. Christopher whooped and flung his arms around Aiden. Aiden blinked and stood up.

"A bottle of champagne for the table!" Christopher waved at the waiter, then turned to Newgate. "We assure you, sir, we will take most excellent care of your ship. Will your captain stay on?"

"I was the captain," the man replied. "Now I am done." His face looked transformed, peaceful, almost radiant, though his whole body was trembling. "I will have no more of it."

"All right, then," Christopher said, blithely undaunted. "So we have a ship—now we just need a captain, crew and some place to sail it!"

"She has a place to sail," Newgate said quietly. "She has a license for guano."

"What's guano?" Christopher and Aiden asked together.

"Precious stuff," the man said. "More precious than gold."

CHAPTER 13

"**I**t's bird crap!" Christopher moaned. It was bright afternoon, and they hunched woozily over the library table with a dozen weekly shipping and mercantile reports spread out before them.

"It's fertilizer!" Aiden said.

"That comes out the back end of a seagull!"

"Well, yes, but farmers need fertilizer."

"That doesn't mean we have to haul it around in our own dear ship! It's so . . . farm-ish."

"Where does your food come from if not a farm?" Aiden laughed, then winced. After the triumph at the Elysium, they had gone on to the house party, where they had drunk far too much more, and they now suffered extremely.

"Pineapples!" Christopher said. "Last year Mrs. Larson paid twenty dollars apiece for nine pineapples for her cotillion party. She was the talk of society for months."

"The fastest ship in the world still takes three weeks from Hawaii," Aiden reminded him. "The whole cargo could rot on the way and lose us every penny. Guano is already rotten! And look at the prices!" He thrust a commodities report at Christopher. "See what they're paying in Baltimore? Or Liverpool!"

"We are not sailing to Baltimore or Liverpool. I'm not going to sea for months and months, beating round the Horn, eating hardtack with worms in it and losing my teeth from scurvy. No. I need my teeth. We stay on our side of the world."

"Exactly," Aiden said. "Look—half the food in San Francisco now comes from the Salinas Valley, and the city is getting bigger every day. They've been farming there for decades now, and the best soil is dead in three or four years unless you fertilize it. They need guano. Cow poop and burned bones are not going to do it."

"Why not?"

"Well, cattle take up space, for one thing, and pastureland isn't close to growing land. And cow dung is heavy. You can't just train them to go marching through the crop rows and drop it fresh on command. You have to go out to their pastures and shovel it up and haul it to the barn and pile it up with straw for a season and then haul it out to the fields in a cart and shovel it off again. If this guano is as good as they say, one man could probably fertilize in one day what it would take ten men a whole year to accomplish!"

"But why is bird shit from Peru better than any other bird shit?" Christopher pressed, still hating the idea.

"I don't know. But if farmers are paying fifty dollars a ton for it in Baltimore, there must be something to it. And think," Aiden said, getting up, a little too fast for his aching head, and crossing to the map of the United States that hung on the wall. "If it does well in the Salinas Valley, well, we could sell guano to half the country!"

"You might have a bit of the businessman in your tender heart after all," Christopher said appreciatively. "But you haven't even considered the real possibilities here, have you?"

"Well, we need to figure out the freight costs—"

"I don't mean that." Christopher went over and stood beside him, staring at the map like Napoleon designing the conquest of Europe. "What have you learned about business thus far? How does it work?"

"You buy something at a low price that people need or want and you sell it for more."

"That's not business, that's shopkeeping. Look"— Christopher traced his finger along the little black line of tracks—"in two or three years, the railroad will connect the whole country. It's got to be cheaper to sail the stuff up here and ship it by rail than to sail it all the way around the Horn to Baltimore. Newgate said something about a license. If there are licenses involved, there are monopolies to be had. That's business!"

14

"Y̵ou want to sail to Peru for a shipload of bird crap?" Fish said with a laugh. "Are you out of your mind?"

"It isn't just any old bird crap—it's the most valuable crap in the world!" Aiden tried to spark his friend's enthusiasm.

"What could possibly make this bird crap worth more than other bird crap?" Fish said disparagingly.

"There's a current, the Humboldt Current, that brings all these fish—rich oily fish like sardines—up close to the coast," Aiden explained. They had managed to find out something about the guano islands from the ducklings' science teacher, old Professor Tobler. "So millions of seabirds live there. They gorge on these fish, and their droppings are extra-rich. They basically poop out money! There are three islands—the Chinchas—where it never rains. The wind dries the guano out, and it just piles up and lasts forever. It's hundreds of feet deep—and look at the prices!" Aiden thrust the commodities report beneath his friend's nose. "You will have a share of the profits."

"I've never captained a ship," Fish said.

"I've never won one in a card game either."

"And I've never sailed blue water."

"This isn't like crossing an ocean," Aiden pointed out. "We'll be along the coast the whole time—or close anyway. And you know how to navigate. Every captain has to have a first time, doesn't he?"

"Yes, but usually it's after years of experience as a first mate. I sailed one year as a deckhand on a schooner when I was sixteen. It wouldn't be fair to you."

"It wouldn't be fair to send us out into the unknown with anyone else," Aiden said. "Isn't this the chance you've been waiting for? No more boring timber runs up and down the coast with the same old relatives in the same old boat!"

"It's crazy."

Of course it was crazy. The smart thing to do would be to sell the ship and the guano license to someone who knew the business already and give the money to Mr. Worthington to invest in something sensible. The smart thing was to be a shopkeeper. But last night at the table, the idea of fortune had suddenly become real to him, and Aiden was intoxicated. He had come to know something about the world, and it was a much better place with money.

"If you pick an experienced crew, you won't have to do anything but boss them around," Aiden said.

"It doesn't exactly work that way."

"You're related to half the Swedish Navy, and friends with the other half, aren't you? Surely there are some experienced men who would want a little adventure and the chance for a share in the wealth?"

"Have you seen this ship—the *Raven*?"

"Not yet—we just won her last night. Christopher has a lawyer checking it as we speak. I thought we could go look at it now."

"And where will you get the money to outfit her?"

"How much do we need?"

Fish laughed. "You have no idea what you're doing, do you?"

"No," Aiden said brightly. "Not in the least."

Recruiting Fish was the easy part. Explaining the plan to Mr. Worthington was much more difficult. He sat in silence as they told him. If he thought the venture wicked or wise, canny or foolhardy, neither Aiden nor Christopher could tell. He dismissed them without admonition, chastisement, advice or encouragement. For the next two days, he was silent and absent, not even going to his office downtown. There were more than the usual messengers to the house, and Mrs. Worthington was fretful, as if there were sickness about.

Finally he summoned Christopher and Aiden to his office, where his lawyer was waiting with a stack of papers.

"It would be wiser to sell the ship," he said. "But I expect you will not do that."

"No, sir," Christopher said solemnly. "I believe our venture, though bold, is well reasoned. And your own life, sir, demonstrates the advantage of boldness."

"My boldness," Mr. Worthington said grimly, "never put me at risk of being lost at sea."

"The ship is sound, sir," Aiden said. "And our captain is very good. You needn't worry. Very few ships sink, really."

"Of course," Mr. Worthington said sharply. He pushed the papers toward his son. "If you are determined to go, you will go. But I am divested entirely of the enterprise. Understand that. The investment is yours alone. You will draw against your inheritance. My lawyer has prepared the papers."

"Yes, sir." Christopher picked up the pen. His hand shook slightly. Aiden could not tell if it was from excitement or fear.

15

W hen you are on a ship at sea, the sea is all the world and time is just the sky. The *Raven* was a self-contained world, like a little village, only with all men and no dogs. There was a cat, however, and chickens, four small pigs that would be fattened on scraps along the way, two goats and three obnoxious geese. Strange as it was, there was also something familiar about it to Aiden. The isolation, the self-containment, was not so different from the months he had spent crossing the country in the wagon train.

The voyage was mostly good and sometimes not, terrifying a dozen times to Aiden but only twice to the more experienced crew. Only once did they all fear death, in a storm that built fast as Genesis. The sky was blue, then green as pus. The sea went flat and oily, and the cat grew twice her size and sparked when touched. It was not fifteen minutes from calm day to full storm. The weather sliced in fast and sharp as ice over ice, smelling of iron. Waves crashed over the deck. A spar twisted and broke like a twig the ducklings might use to build one of their fairy houses. But Fish steered them well, the men knew what to do and somehow at the end of it, which was a long, awful time coming, they were all alive and the ship was whole and there were stories for days—no more nor less than a thousand storm tales from history, but truly their own.

Even on routine days, nothing was ever really ordinary at sea. A thousand dolphins would suddenly burst out of the waves around them, leaping and playing along with the ship like children in some spontaneous game of chase. There were popping schools of flying fish almost every day, and whales almost as long and broad as their ship. To see a dozen or more whales was not uncommon but still felt like a miracle.

"They have their babies in Mexico during the winter," Fish explained. "Then they swim north all the way to Alaska to feed during the summer."

They ate fresh fish most days, and in the six weeks it took to reach their destination, hardly any weevils invaded the biscuits. Most of the cabbages, carrots and onions lasted. Every desperate sea story Aiden had read seemed false and overwrought. So sprits were high the morning of August 20 as they neared the Chinchas. The sea was churning and tumbling with life. Schools of silver-blue mackerel boiled through the water. Chasing after them were a hundred sea lions, supple and glossy as pulled taffy. They dodged and spun through the swarms of mackerel, pausing just long enough to lift glistening heads with mouths full of sparkling fish, as if showing off before gulping them down. Their barking cries were so loud the men on the ship had to shout to be heard.

"I've never seen fish thick as this," Fish shouted. "It's like a carpet you could walk across!" This boil of fish sounded like a waterfall.

The sky was also impossibly thick with life. Millions of seabirds soared and skittered across the dense blue sky. Not millions like the way people casually say "millions," but millions like real millions. In the distance, they could see the snowy peaks of the Andes.

Aiden, Christopher and Fish stood on the quarterdeck like kids on Christmas morning. The long voyage was over, and here they were, ready to scoop up their fortune in guano and sail triumphantly home again. But the mood changed as they neared the islands. At first they saw no land at all, just a strange low yellow cloud on the horizon. It was something like fog, but it did not melt off over the water or wisp away up into the sky. It simply hung there, immobile and fuzzy, like an ancient dog in its ancient place. They took turns looking through the spyglass, but still no one really knew what it was. The morning passed and the miles closed and the dense yellow cloud grew larger.

As they got closer, the actual islands began to appear out of the yellow haze. It was like no place anyone had ever seen or even imagined. There was not a scrap of vegetation, not a tree or bush to be seen—only guano. The color ranged from rusty ocher to almost white. Years of mining had carved out one whole side of the mountain. Aiden shuddered. What was this place?

"Jesus—there are a hundred ships anchored there!" Christopher said, scanning the anchorage. "How long does it take to load a hundred ships?"

"There can't be that many," Fish said. "Here, give me the glass." Christopher handed him the telescope, and Fish scanned the forest of masts. "Not more than seventy, I think," he offered lamely. "Maybe eighty."

"Two ships loading every day would still put us waiting here a month for our turn!" Christopher held his handkerchief up to his nose. "And no one said it would smell so ghastly!"

"It's shit," Fish said. "How did you think it would smell?"

In reality, it smelled nothing like ordinary waste, animal or human. It was more acrid and penetrating, with a taint of ammonia. It stung their eyes and left an odd soapy feeling in their mouths.

It took the rest of the afternoon to maneuver the ship into place and get it securely anchored. The water was deep, so plenty of chain was required to anchor safely, and with so many ships, swing room also had to be carefully calculated. The sun was setting by the time everything was all secured. The smell of the guano was less pungent without the steaming power of the sun and was soon overshadowed by the smell of cooking from nearby ships.

Fish gave most of the sailors leave, keeping only two volunteers for the evening watch. There were two "saloon ships" in the near vicinity, older vessels, no longer seaworthy but not quite ready to be sunk, that were permanently anchored to sell necessities and serve as saloons for the sailors who were stranded here with no other outlet. The sailors dropped the launch as if the ship were on fire and rowed away so fast Fish swore their wake bobbled the *Raven*. Throughout the harbor, yellow lamps flickered aboard other ships, and a fiddle tune floated over the still water. The yellow haze of dust settled, and the island, in the gibbous moon, looked almost beautiful, like a half-eaten wedding cake. Aiden, Christopher and Fish ate a cold supper on deck, with a bottle of champagne.

"Here we are, then." Christopher leaned back in the canvas chair and raised his glass. "Three Kings of the Chinchas! Sons of fortune!"

They toasted, and tried hard for merriment, but it never felt like a real celebration. There was a deep gloom that hung about this place. Bits of music and talk floated over from the other ships, but the island was silent and dark. Christopher drank enough to fall asleep easily, and Fish never had trouble, but Aiden could not quiet his mind. There was almost no wind and the little cabin was hot and stuffy, so he finally gave up and went up on deck and watched the stars until he fell asleep in the chair.

Everyone was awake by sunrise, and after a quick breakfast he and Christopher set off in the launch to register with the office onshore. As owners of the ship, they should have sat like gentlemen and let the four sailors row them in, but they were both tired of idleness, so each took an oar for most of the way, sometimes racing each other to see who could pull hardest. It was at least a half mile to the island, and they were both sweating but energized by the time they arrived.

The landing dock for small boats was sheltered by a rocky breakwater. It protruded barely twenty feet from the shore, offering space for only three or four boats to tie up.

"I don't suppose crowding is often a problem," Christopher said. "It hardly seems a place for sightseeing." The acrid smell was strong and the island radiated heat even at this early hour.

About two hundred yards away, partly obscured by the rocks, was the loading wharf, which had been built out from a high cliff edge. Right now there were two ships tied up, one on each side, loading the guano. Bags of it were slid down canvas chutes, one on each side, directly to the ships, where men tossed them into the holds belowdecks. The sailors wore kerchiefs over their mouths and often ran to the bow of the ship, bending over the rails, gulping fresh air.

"What are they doing?" Aiden asked one of his own crew.

He knew that after just a few hours aboard the saloon ship last night with the other sailors, the men probably knew ten times as much about the business as he and Christopher did.

"Trimming the load," the sailor replied as he expertly rowed them through the surf. "Making it balanced in the hull," he explained, remembering that Aiden had no experience with this. "It's foul work, but there's no one else can do it. The coolies aren't allowed."

"Why not?" Aiden asked.

"They're not allowed to even talk to a white man. Never allowed near a ship for fear they'll try and escape."

"Escape what?"

The sailor shrugged. "This place."

Before he could ask any more questions, they pulled alongside the little dock. When Aiden climbed ashore, his legs were so unused to solid ground that he almost fell. He turned and gave a hand to Christopher, who was equally wobbly but, being more practiced with drunkenness, better able at negotiating it. They started up the path that led to the manager's compound. After about a quarter mile, the path came into an open area, where they could see, for the first time, the actual mine. What they had seen from aboard the ship, even with the telescope, was not a tenth of the true operation. It was like they had suddenly landed on another planet. Christopher and Aiden both just stopped and stared. It was one thing to know that there was a pile of bird droppings here three hundred feet high; it was quite another to actually see it, a pile as high as a castle or cathedral, built over thousands of years, plop by plop, a spoonful at a time. With the weight of centuries and the uniquely dry atmosphere, it was now compacted hard as cement. And everywhere they looked, hundreds of men were working furiously to chip it away. Perhaps a quarter of the mountain had already been gouged out, in tiers that stepped back from the shore.

The workers were all Chinese—skinny little men, men of only bones. They looked so frail it seemed impossible they could even stand, let alone swing a pick or shovel, but all over the vast site, they smashed away at the guano mountain. As quickly as the chunks fell, other men scooped them up and carried them away. Some had wheelbarrows, but most used baskets that they carried on their backs, held on with a strap across their foreheads or braided ropes that dug into their shoulders. They scurried back and forth in a quick-step shuffle, bent forward to keep from falling over under the load. There were at least two hundred men laboring, and no one ever paused. Dotted throughout the site, ensuring that no one ever would, were a dozen tall Negro overseers armed with clubs and bullwhips.

"I suppose I thought there would be machines," Christopher said quietly. "Not just . . . this." It was the first time Aiden had ever seen him rattled.

"Yes," Aiden said blankly, unable to tear his eyes away from the awful scene. "But how would they get machines out here? Or the coal to run them. And the dust would be hard on machines. . . ." He trailed off. Talk of machines was just to fill up the air. What level of hell was this? A track ran from the center of the dig site straight to the cliff edge above the loading wharf, but the carts that ran on this track were pulled by men, not mules. A cart that size, Aiden knew from coal mining, could carry one ton. But mules needed more food and water than men did, and they probably could not work long in this blistering heat. So it was men—hundreds of men.

"What do we do?" Aiden whispered, his voice choked more by horror than by the toxic dust.

"What do you mean?" Christopher grabbed his arm, his fingers digging into the flesh, and turned him away from the scene. "Business," he said. "We do business."

As he followed Christopher toward the office, Aiden thought about the strange, haunted captain so eager to wager away his ship, so ready to burn her if he could not. What kind of business was this going to be?

The office compound was a collection of shabby little buildings that would have been considered poor anywhere else in the world, but here, where every plank of wood had to be hauled in from the distant mainland, were probably considered quite grand. There was one main building with three separate doors opening onto a narrow veranda, barely wide enough for two men to walk side by side. There was a separate little kitchen building, essentially just a thatch roof for shade with some woven mats for walls, and two sturdier sheds to store supplies, with locking doors and no windows. There were two large water barrels, also with locks, set under the shade of a lean-to.

A large, dark Negro sat in a cane chair at one end of the veranda, where he had a view of both the compound and the digging below. His clothes were worn, but his short hair was meticulously cut, smooth and even as the perfect hedges outside the Worthingtons' front door. Propped against the wall behind him was a wooden club the size of a baseball bat, though thinner, meant to be swung with one hand. It had leather lacing wrapped around the handle, stained darker in the middle from a sweaty grip. Coiled neatly beside the Negro's chair was a braided bullwhip. He said nothing as they stepped onto the narrow porch, just looked them quickly up and down, then nodded toward the middle door.

Mr. Koster, the manager of the island, sat at his desk. He was a small man with heavy bones, not fat exactly, but soft and unworked. He, like the Negro, was clean-shaven and had his hair cut so short it was impossible to tell the color. His skin was ghostly pale and puffed the way it got to be for men too fond of brown liquor and tinned meats. Aiden had assumed he would be Peruvian, but now he couldn't guess what his heritage was.

"Good morning, Mr. Koster. We are so pleased to meet you." Christopher took his hat off and made a formal bow. "I am Christopher Worthington; this is my partner, Aiden Madison, of the *Raven*. We arrived yesterday from San Francisco."

Koster's desk looked like a schoolteacher's castoff, and there was a crack down the front from top to bottom, as if an angry student had kicked it in a temper. The top of the desk was almost entirely covered in little decorative knickknacks: carved wooden birds, embroidered pincushions, small blobby glass animals, china angels crowded together on painted tin trays. There was barely enough space for a ledger in the center. The office was covered in calendar pictures. Covered wall to wall, ceiling to floor. Some, dated as far back as 1857, were just faded bluish shapes with curled, crispy edges by now, the Alps indistinguishable from Tahiti.

"The *Raven*?" Koster looked puzzled. "I know that ship." His accent was impossible to place, but there were suggestions of German.

"She has sailed here before," Christopher said. "Under Captain Newgate. We are the new owners. We have the guano license as well." He produced the paper, with its official signatures and stamps. "We are looking forward to conducting our business here. We haven't had much chance to look around, but it seems like a splendid operation!"

Aiden was startled to detect Mr. Worthington in Christopher's voice, cadence and even posture. How easily he had slipped into business mode, like a lady whipping out her painted fan. Koster leaned back in his chair, an ornate construction of carved mahogany—a bishop's chair, though spidery with cracks and pocked with tiny wormholes. He examined the papers.

"They appear to be in order," he said. Christopher and Aiden waited awkwardly, neither sure what to say next. Koster controlled the fate of every ship in the anchorage, determining who would load and depart in a few weeks and who might languish for months. The Worthington name had clout in the United States, but the biggest shippers in the guano trade were from England or Germany and had been dealing here for a decade. Koster would have to be courted carefully.

"This will do." Koster tapped the papers together and handed them back.

"We would be honored if you would dine aboard our ship," Christopher offered. "Our cooking is undoubtedly less fine than you are accustomed to, but we do have a fattened live goose and some excellent wines that have been carefully kept."

"Very nice." Koster creaked forward in his chair, sliced his nail beneath the ledger page and turned it with a heavy sigh. "I could come Tuesday, a week from now, though it must be early—say, six? I have another engagement at nine." He closed the book and looked at Christopher with a smug little smile. "Will your wine keep that long? I would hate to see fine wine spoil on my account."

"Yes." Christopher fumbled for the first time Aiden had ever seen. "As it suits you, sir," he recovered. "We will await your company."

Aiden could tell Christopher was annoyed by the man and was working as hard as he could to hide it. "Is there anything else?" Koster asked.

"No. Good day, sir."

"Is it possible to explore a bit?" Aiden asked impetuously.

"Explore?"

"To walk around on the island."

"Whatever for?"

"I have some interest in the natural elements," he said, grasping for the best excuse. "Birds and such."

Koster looked at Aiden as if he had asked to be dropped into a pit of spiders.

"Fine, if you stay away from the digging," Koster said. "It's dangerous. Nature is filthy, but I know there are those who must have a look at it, so fine if you must. You know there is no water anywhere?"

"I do, sir."

"And where the guano is fresh, you can fall through. We will not rescue you."

"I will be careful and expect no rescue."

"There is something of a path beyond the compound

141

here." Koster waved vaguely. "Those so inclined do occasionally walk there to observe nature. There is a surveying team working up there that may have advice about birds and whatnot."

"Thank you, Mr. Koster," Aiden said.

"What are you on about?" Christopher said the moment they left the office. "Since when do you go observing nature?"

"I want to see more of the place."

"God—why?"

"We have to know what we've become part of."

"No, we don't," Christopher said. He stood at the top of the stairs with his back to the digging, his arms folded resolutely. "I know you. I know what you're thinking. We've seen something harsh—"

"Harsh?"

"—and you have a dangerously tender heart," Christopher went on. "But what is going to change? Whatever you discover?"

"I don't know, but—"

"Then I'll tell you. Nothing!" Christopher spat, trying in vain to get the acrid guano dust out of his mouth. "We're here now. We've invested every penny and sailed four thousand miles. It looks a bit rough—"

"A bit?"

"—but we have a contract for guano. We have loans to pay off and a crew to pay. You are a businessman now, not a laborer, not an indentured servant, not a farm boy or a rock digger or—whatever rotten life you once had!"

"These men are slaves."

"They are not."

"What do you need overseers with whips for if not for slaves?"

"There is no slavery in Peru. They abolished it before we did! I'm not going to argue out here all day in the sun." Christopher sighed, pulling out his handkerchief to wipe the dusty sweat from the corners of his eyes. "This is reality. We cannot change it. And this is our fortune. We must take it! Have your walk. I'll send the launch back for you at noon."

"No," Aiden said. His head was spinning. "We can't ask the men to row out in the noon sun."

"For God's sake, Aiden, we own the ship! We can tell the men to do anything we want!"

"There must be other boats coming and going. I'll try and catch a ride with someone—otherwise, four o'clock."

"Fine. As you wish." Christopher hurried down the path. Aiden turned around and started walking up the guano mountain. He had no idea what he really expected to learn. And regardless, Christopher was right—what could they do about it? Haul up the anchor and sail home empty?

The path wound along the back side of the island, so after only about a hundred yards, Aiden could no longer see into the open pit. Once he was away from the digging, where the guano was undisturbed, it really did not smell bad at all. It was like a sourish kind of ordinary dirt. The taint of ammonia was definitely still there, but it did not burn. The fresh breeze blowing in from the ocean also helped. The path was little more than a slight trail of packed footsteps. The guano on either side of it, fresh and not yet trodden on, was surprisingly light and spongy, though also sticky, a bit like fresh soap. It was honeycombed all over with little holes, and sometimes, even on the path, his foot plunged through up to his knee. Lizards popped in and out of the holes, skittered across the surface and stopped to twist a curious eye at him. There were also immense flocks of a type of blue-gray bird, like a pigeon. It had a bright red beak and jaunty little yellow feathers on each side of its head. The birds sat so thick in places that Aiden couldn't see the ground beneath them. Then he noticed that they had actually made burrows in the guano. Little heads popped in and out like nosy cottage wives peeping out on a village. They did not seem to be bothered by his presence, or even to notice him, but sometimes a group of them would rise all at once and wheel about in a swoosh of wings so strong it was like a wind against his face.

Millions of seabirds filled the sky like a blizzard. Some he had learned on the voyage—cormorants and terns and boobies, pelicans, frigate birds with their great black wings thin and sharp on the sky—but others were completely new. Their cries were wild and ghostly. He had never seen so many live things crowded into any one place. The rocks down below along the shoreline looked like they were made of brown velvet from all the sea lions lying there, and there were easily just as many splashing in the surf. Aiden wondered if they shared the rocks in shifts, for there could not possibly be room for all at once.

He walked for about twenty minutes, covering no great distance, partly because there wasn't much distance to cover on such a small island, but mostly because the soft guano made for slow walking. Concentrating as he was on his steps, and with his hat pulled low to protect from the sun (and anything dropping from above), Aiden came upon the surveyors almost without warning.

The trio looked as out of place as hummingbirds on a glacier. One man stood bent over a theodolite, while the other two played cards on a colorful woven blanket beneath a small canopy. The cardplayers were in their mid-twenties, Aiden guessed. One sat on a small canvas camp stool and held his cards in a tight fan. He had a gentleman's smooth hands and thick chestnut hair curling over his shoulders. It was clearly too hot to have such a loose blanket of hair, Aiden thought, which marked it as a vanity. The other man reclined on his side, propped up on one elbow. He was very fair, with short reddish-blond hair. His shirtsleeves were extra-long to cover his pale hands, and a broad-brimmed straw hat lay at the ready beside him. The two men looked up, startled, as Aiden approached.

Then the man at the instrument turned, and Aiden was surprised to see that it was not a man. She wore trousers and a waistcoat like a man, and rough boots dusted white with the dust of the place, but she was clearly a woman. Her face was framed with a straw hat but still browner than any proper woman would allow.

"I'm sorry to disturb you," Aiden said. "I was just exploring. I wanted to see the birds and nature." Aiden snatched off his hat, the thing to do upon meeting a lady, and felt the sun immediately burn his scalp. "I'm sorry. I interrupted you."

"Not at all." Her glance darted quickly to the men on the blanket, like a child caught playing in a forbidden parlor. "We just aren't used to visitors up here."

"I'm Aiden Madison, of the *Raven* from San Francisco."

"I am Alice Brock," she said. "This is Mr. Nicholas Brock." The chestnut-haired man got up and ducked out from under the little canopy. He shook Aiden's hand.

"And this is my assistant, Gilbert Windemare," Nicholas said. The fair-haired man gave a little wave from the blanket. "We're surveying the island." Nicholas had to speak loudly to be heard over the birds and barking seals.

"We're pleased to meet you." Alice took off her hat, and a brown braid dropped out and swung over her shoulder. She wiped her sweaty forehead on her sleeve. Aiden noticed that her nails were chipped and her hands were rougher than her husband's.

"Nicholas lets me play about with his surveying instruments," Alice quickly explained, as if reading his mind. "There is so little else to do here that I grow bored."

Alice was not beautiful, and nothing would ever make her so, though Aiden had learned a little about what powders and styling and luxurious clothing could do for a plain woman. The mousy hair could be burned into curls, the hands covered with gloves and the thin lips colored crimson, but her face was a bit too long, her features a bit too strong and her shape too straight to ever be a beauty, no matter the assistance. But she did have startling green eyes, a lovely voice and a graceful way of moving. A woman could be attractive, he had learned, without being a beauty. She was around twenty-five, he guessed, though it was hard to tell. She had clearly spent more time outdoors without a parasol than most women, but unlike poor women, who could look fifty at twenty, she had the good health to stave off the worst effects. Her cheeks were naturally pink, her face unlined.

"Will you rest awhile in our shade?" She waved a weathered hand toward the tent.

"Thank you, but I won't impose."

"We would be glad of the company and eager to hear about San Francisco," Nicholas said. "It is one of the places we are thinking about visiting after this. Please."

Gilbert sat up cross-legged to make room, and Nicholas opened up the other two little camp stools. By their accents, Aiden knew they were English, and despite the ordinary clothing and peculiar occupation, he sensed an air of aristocracy.

"And how are you finding our little dung heap so far?" Gilbert asked, tucking the cards away in a box.

"I've never seen anything like it," Aiden replied. "Or even imagined."

"Why would you?" Gilbert said. "It's the last place on earth anyone would ever imagine. In fact, it was really rather cruel of God to think it up in the first place."

"The birds seem to like it," Aiden said diplomatically.

"Oh yes. You're on a nature walk," Gilbert said.. Aiden wasn't sure if he was teasing. There was a sketchbook with some excellent pictures of a cormorant and a sea lion open on the blanket beside him, so the man had to like something of nature.

"I wanted to see something more of the island," Aiden said. "And stretch my legs. We only just arrived and I'm tired of being aboard ship. Does this path go all the way across the island?"

"Not really," Alice said. "People from the ships come up this far sometimes, to enjoy the view and the birds, but there is no real reason to go on much further. We have made a path with our own walking, but there is nothing different to see beyond here. Will you have some water?" she offered, taking a bottle out of a canvas knapsack.

"Thank you, but I'm quite all right." He was in fact very thirsty, but it was his own fault and he wasn't about to take their water.

"We always bring too much and would rather not have to carry it back," Alice said as she poured some in a tin cup. Aiden smelled oranges. "We won't be working much longer—it gets far too hot by afternoon."

"Thank you." Aiden took a grateful sip. "It's delicious!"

"Just a bit of orange oil twisted from the peels," Alice said. "Ship's water is always so stale."

"What ship are you with?" Aiden asked.

"The *Lady May*," Nicholas said. "Of the Brockleton Line. We arrived a week ago."

"Are you surveying for them?" Aiden asked.

The three exchanged glances.

"There are many parties with an interest in the future of guano," Nicholas said simply.

"With millions of dollars at stake, I'd say so," Gilbert added, less diplomatically.

Even after his months with the Worthingtons, Aiden didn't really know what a million dollars was. In Kansas, his family's one good crop had brought in three hundred eighty-nine dollars, and they had felt rich. Mr. Worthington had recently bought a chandelier from Europe, the size of a shed, for two thousand four hundred ninety-one dollars, including shipping. One year ago, Aiden would have sold the whole farm for one dollar's worth of cornmeal and a bit of stringy meat.

He changed the subject. "How exactly do you measure guano? Is it like surveying land?"

"Basically," Nicholas said. "The North Island has already been stripped bare, and there are plenty of shipping records to get a good estimate of the total tonnage mined there over the years. So once we figure out the area of this island and the average depth of the guano, we can calculate the volume. It's pretty simple math."

Aiden had never found math all that simple, but he did know how to estimate the amount of wheat a field could produce, or how many tons of coal could be chipped from a seam.

"The topography of all these islands is similar," Alice added. "And I don't imagine the birds have been favoring one island over another in deciding where to leave their gifts."

Nicholas went on explaining the basics of surveying, which involved a lot of angles and triangulation. Alice said nothing during the lecture, but Aiden noticed that there was a notebook sticking out of her pocket, not Nicholas's, and a pencil poked through her plain hair, not his glossy mane.

"Oh, enough," Gilbert finally said, putting an end to Nicholas's windy explanation. "We're helping rich men understand the depth of their riches. That is really all of it."

"Shut up, Gilly," Nicholas chastised. He looked back at Aiden and gave a little shrug. "He's right, but crass. Tell us about San Francisco."

"Yes. Have you felt an earthquake?" Alice asked excitedly.

"There have been four since I arrived there in January," Aiden said. "But little ones. The plates on the table shook, but the ones in the cupboards didn't fall out. There were nineteen last year."

"Nineteen earthquakes?" Alice's green eyes shone, and he thought she might clap with delight, like one of the ducklings upon finding an exceptional beetle.

"People take it as ordinary," Aiden said. "Like blizzards if you live in the north."

"Nicholas," she said, clutching her husband's hand. "That is surely where we must go next!"

Nicholas laughed. "Besides the geological thrills, what is the city itself like? The talk in London is that it's become very cosmopolitan and worth a visit. They call it the Paris of the West!"

Aiden wasn't sure what "cosmopolitan" meant, but he had certainly heard of Paris.

"It is a grand city. I like it very much."

"Then stay and tell us all about it," Gilbert said. "We're always desperate for smart new people to talk with. Come, join us for lunch."

Aiden hardly thought of himself as smart, but he was equally happy for the new company.

"Please do," Alice said. "It's just some bread and cheese. It's too hot to do any work in the afternoon, but we always spend the whole day here," she explained. "Even with the heat, it's much nicer up here with the ocean breeze than on the ship. Do you have a launch waiting for you?"

"I hoped to catch a ride back with one of the supply boats. Otherwise, they will come for me at four."

"Perfect," Alice said as she opened a basket and unfolded the cloth inside. "Our launch returns for us at three and can take you back to your ship as well."

The morning that had started with a scene from Dante's *Inferno* now turned into an afternoon of blithe picnicking. They sat in the shade and ate soft bread, crumbly white cheese, a sort of pickled vegetable relish and some dried figs. The conversation was bright and easy. He told them all about the city that he now considered home, describing the elaborate houses and society of the fashionable neighborhoods, the crowded lanes of downtown boardinghouses, the opulent hotels and the busy docks. He told them about Blind Sally and the Barbary Coast. Nicholas and Gilbert were very keen on operas, theater and music halls; Aiden felt he was letting them down by not having gone to a performance every night of the week.

They told him about Rome and London and Venice. They had even been to Egypt. Aiden was fascinated by these exotic people. They had such a different way of thinking and talking, and such different things to talk about: science and philosophy and art and all the new ideas of Europe and England. Sometimes they bickered, sounding more like annoyed siblings than scientists.

When it finally came time to fold up the stools and take down the canopy, it was a shock to step back into the reality of the place. The sun had baked the top layer of guano into a crispy stink. Two sailors from the *Lady May* came up the path to help carry the equipment down. The day was frantically hot by now, and the blizzard of birds was starting to feel oppressive—like a swarm of locusts. When they passed Koster's office compound, there was no one in sight and all the louvered shutters were closed against the dust. Yet in the mine below, the work was still going on as vigorously as it had been that morning. The ant men working their ant labors. Watery shimmers of heat rippled above the guano, and the sun reflected brightly, causing Aiden's eyes to burn.

"No good to think about it," Nicholas said, pausing beside him. "It will just depress you."

"Why are they all Chinese?" Aiden asked.

"Because China's a bigger dung heap than here," Gilbert said. "The poor buggers are glad for any chance to escape."

"Gilly!" Alice chastised him.

Gilbert shrugged. "It's true. Sad but true."

"It's complicated," Nicholas said. "Peru ended slavery ten, twelve years ago. But the Negroes, after they were freed, mostly stayed. They had nowhere else to go. So they had first pick of the jobs."

"Of the horrible jobs," Alice added pointedly.

"Yes, well," Nicholas went on. "The Negroes preferred the plantations. But someone has to work the guano. Guano finances the entire nation of Peru—it would collapse without it. They tried shipping in convicts, but there's only so much you can make a convict do. Even the Irish won't do this work! But China is teeming with people, half of them starving, all of them desperate. It's harsh, to be sure, but they sign up for it. Civilized men just aren't suited to this kind of work."

"From what I've read, China does actually have some civilization," Aiden said.

"Oh, of course," Nicholas said. "But you know what I mean."

Aiden did know, and it angered him, this casual racism. Gilbert started back down the path, clearly tired of hearing this discussion. Aiden thought it best to drop the subject for now.

The *Lady May*'s launch was a sleek, light boat, freshly painted red with gold trim. It was twice the size of the *Raven*'s, but much faster, though rowed by only six men. The launch stopped first at the *Lady May* to let off the surveyors and their equipment; the men then rowed Aiden over to his own ship. It was nearly four and the *Raven* was quiet. The sailors had rigged canopies all over the deck, beneath which they now dozed, except for the one man on watch. Fish was sitting in a canvas chair on the quarterdeck, reading a British magazine called *Punch*. There was a stack on the chair beside him, the top one dated only five months ago, and Aiden felt a sharp thrill of anticipation to have something new to read.

"Watch out," Fish said as Aiden climbed aboard. "The deck is slick with the guano dust. We washed it down this morning, but it settles again almost immediately."

The railings were also slippery. Aiden wiped his hands on his trousers. "Is every day like this, do you think?"

"With the dust, you mean? That's what I hear. There is clear seawater in the forward cask to wash with," Fish said. "The trick is to pull it up first thing in the morning, after the night has settled the ship's filth and before the dust starts to fall again."

"You've learned a lot in one day," Aiden said.

"It's like a small town here. A thousand sailors sitting around with little to do but talk. Christopher asked to see you as soon as you got back. He's in the cabin. He is not cheerful."

"Are you?"

"Cheerful?" Fish shrugged. "No. Of course not. Who could be?"

"I'm sorry."

"For what?"

"This place. I had no idea."

"I guess that's part of sailing off into the unknown, isn't it?"

The cabin was stiflingly hot, but only the porthole was open, not the overhead hatch. Christopher sat at his desk, his face shiny with sweat and his shirt soaked through. He was writing notes and needed a towel on the blotter beneath his right hand to keep the sweat from soiling the paper.

"We're invited by Captain Nickerly of the *Lady May* for supper tonight," he said without preamble. "It's a very important engagement."

"The *Lady May*?"

"She's the premier ship in the Brockleton Line."

"Yes, I've seen her. How did we come to be invited so soon?"

"I sent our card over this morning, announcing our arrival. I sent our card to everyone of importance here."

"I didn't know we had a card," Aiden said.

"I've been working here for hours on our business," Christopher snapped, clearly annoyed. "While you were out—bird-watching! I've had seven invitations in reply already and had to write back to each and every one."

"In your own blood?"

"Very funny." Christopher jabbed the pen in the inkwell, dabbed his sweaty wrist on the towel and painstakingly wrote a few more words. At home, of course, there were secretaries for writing, and the careful penmanship required of him now was laborious.

"I'm sorry." Aiden sat down on the edge of his bed, as there was only the one chair. "I can help you if you tell me what to say. My script is passable. I've copied some letters for your father."

"It's the last one," Christopher said indignantly. He blotted the paper and blew on it. "There is a mail boat that comes around every morning and afternoon, carrying letters between ships." He folded the letter, addressed the outside with the name of the captain and ship, then tucked all the notes into an oiled-canvas bag.

"How did you know who was important?" Aiden asked.

"Well, no one here actually is," Christopher said. "Important captains are hauling silks and ivory, not guano. But some of the losers are still more important than others, so I encouraged the harbormaster to tell me all."

Aiden knew *encouraged* really meant *bribed*.

"So we need to be dressed by five," Christopher went on. "Things start early around here."

Aiden wanted to do nothing more tonight than sit quietly and let his brain unravel, but he understood the obligation.

"And we need to decide what to do about Fish," Christopher said, still snappish.

"Do what about him?"

"Customarily, it is the captains who visit and dine with other captains. Most owners aren't aboard, after all. But in this case, we have been invited because, well, I am who I am. If this were an ordinary little ship with just Fish for captain, he wouldn't be invited to dine on the *Lady May* at all. He isn't very—captain-like."

"He's done a rather good job of it, though," Aiden said.

"You know what I mean."

"You mean he's a picnic girl."

"Exactly!" Christopher said, with no trace of irony. "So will you go sort it out with him? I do like Fish and we're lucky to have him, but it would just be awkward!" Apparently, there was no escaping the strictures of society even out here. Aiden knew that Fish wouldn't want to go anyway, but he still felt sad to have it all laid out so plainly.

"I'll take care of Fish. It's the least I can do."

No, he certainly did not want to put on a starched collar and tie and wool suit and sit for two hours making small talk with stuffy Brits in a stuffy salon belowdecks and probably have to play a few hands of whist afterward. No, Fish said, he couldn't in fact think of a worse way to spend an evening, except maybe being buried headfirst in a pile of guano with needles stuck in the soles of his feet. He was sorry, but they would just have to make up some excuse for his absence.

Aiden was relieved. He knew Fish would be miserable dining on the *Lady May*—he expected he himself was going to be miserable—but he also knew his friend was in a lonely position here. All his life, Fish had been a sailor in the company of sailors, but now, as a captain, he had to be apart from the crew, even though he had been friends with half of them before this voyage. Fish did not enforce the rigid separation between officers and crew practiced on most ships—he would still play a few hands of cards or games of chess—but still, there was no escaping the fact that he was no longer one of them.

Dressing in a suit had become ordinary for Aiden in San Francisco, but after six weeks of shipboard freedom, it seemed constricting and absurd. He feared he had not exaggerated any aspect of tonight's party when describing it to Fish, and he wished he could get out of it as easily. But business was business. The right connections could mean the difference between waiting here two weeks or two months.

The wind had dropped and the guano dust was just a low yellow haze over the island as Aiden and Christopher were rowed over to the *Lady May*.

When they climbed up to the deck, Aiden and Christopher found the captain and his wife waiting to greet them at the companionway. Aiden almost laughed, for the man looked like a caricature of a sea captain from a musical comedy. A perfectly round belly strained the buttons on his waistcoat. He had an extravagant mustache that looked like two white mice sitting on his lip, hunched nose to nose, tails flung out and curled beneath his rosy cheeks. Thick white hair fringed out from his hat. He was probably in his mid-fifties, but his face was remarkably unweathered, especially for a sea captain's.

A tidy little steward with deer-brown eyes and a hooked nose stood beside the captain to announce each visitor and make formal introductions. He was barely five feet tall, but his rigid posture, piercing gaze and elegant bearing made him appear formidable.

"Captain and Mrs. Nickerly, may I present Messrs. Christopher Worthington and Aiden Madison, owners of the ship *Raven*, newly arrived from San Francisco. Mr. Worthington, Mr. Madison, Captain Nickerly and Mrs. Nickerly." His voice was strong and his enunciation precise.

"So pleased to meet you, very pleased indeed," Captain Nickerly said. He was radiantly cheerful. This cheer, Aiden suspected from the smell of him, had been fortified with a good deal of liquor in anticipation of the evening's festivities. His wife, at least ten years his junior, appeared to be depressingly sober. She was a sturdy woman who had probably once been pretty and might still be if she unfroze her face for a smile. She wore a plain dress of dark green serge, practical for shipboard life, but adorned with a fine cutwork collar and embroidered cuffs. Aiden knew this sort of handiwork, for his mother had painstakingly sewed such things long ago as an indentured servant in Virginia. Fine work like this was expensive and so declared a family's wealth but was not valuable in any way that would tempt thieves. Thieves were after silver candlesticks, not linen cuffs.

Aiden shook hands and made small talk. He no longer felt out of place at parties, but he doubted he would ever have Christopher's smooth social talent. He was glad when Nicholas and Gilbert appeared. They were freshly washed, with hair still slightly damp. They both wore coats in the latest cuts, exquisite brocade waistcoats, daringly striped trousers and ties that even Aiden could tell were slightly more fashionable than the one Christopher wore. He saw Christopher notice this as well, and bristle a bit, but Nicholas's natural charm quickly eased the awkwardness and soon they were chatting like old friends. Though they were in their twenties, Nicholas and Gilbert were still much closer to Christopher's world than to the world of these moldy old captains.

A servant came by with a silver tray of silver cups. The low sun reflected off the tray and burned on Aiden's chest in a hot beam the size of a coin. Aiden took a cup. The light beam sliced across his chest, cut through the mast and daggered across the deck, then vanished as the servant moved on. Always suspicious of rich people's drinks now, Aiden took a cautious sip, but he found it delicious, with no stinging bubbles. It was sweet and fruity and even slightly cool. He took a big gulp. He saw Alice on the other side of the ship, standing next to a group of chatting wives but not included in their talk, looking almost as awkward as he felt. With relief, he went to join her.

"You look very different—very nice."

"Was I so completely frightful this morning?"

"No—no, of course not," Aiden stammered. "I didn't mean that at all!" His face went hot.

"Oh stop, I'm teasing you." Alice laughed and touched his arm. In fact, she looked, happily, much the same person, only with a dress on. It was a different kind of dress. It had no corset or hoops; the skirt was merely cinched with a wide ribbon high on the waist. It was made of a light, gauzy linen, with loose, flowing sleeves. It might almost have been a nightdress, or something the shepherdesses in the mural in the Elysium might wear, though of course nothing was transparent, wet with dew or falling undone on Alice. Crocheted gloves covered her sun-browned hands. Her hair was twisted up and stabbed into place with an ivory comb, and she had stained her lips and cheeks a little, but otherwise she had put in no great effort with powders and perfume, unlike the other women.

"You're quite the surprise guest, you know," she said. "The captain and missus were atwitter all afternoon. You didn't say you owned the *Raven*."

"Only half of it," Aiden said. "Christopher and I are partners."

Mrs. Nickerly, hovering nearby, turned at this mention, eager to ferret out more information.

"But it's just the two of you?" Mrs. Nickerly said. "In charge?"

"We have a captain," Aiden replied. "He regrets he could not come tonight."

Mrs. Nickerly looked him up and down with a sharp eye. "You're hardly more than boys."

"Christopher is eighteen. I will be soon." He had just turned seventeen in June, so "soon" was a bit of a stretch. "And we have had some experience in the world."

The woman frowned and looked over at Christopher, who was comfortably chatting with the other men by the starboard rail.

"Men often go to sea at a young age," Alice offered.

"They may go to sea, but they don't usually own ships!" Mrs. Nickerly snapped suspiciously. Aiden had no idea what to say. Fortunately, he was rescued as the steward announced more guests at the companionway and Mrs. Nickerly left to greet them.

"I didn't know it was such a sin to be young," Aiden said.

"To the old, it is always a sin to be young," Alice said. "She's been aboard for twenty years. Six times around the Horn on this ship. Her world has become small. You must be kind."

"I will."

"And you are rather shocking with your youth."

"As shocking as you are with your theodolite?"

"Ah, well. She doesn't like me much either."

160

Aiden suddenly bent down and whispered to Alice, "We won the ship in a card game."

Her green eyes sparkled, and she pressed her fingers to her mouth in amusement. "No!" she giggled. "My goodness, don't let Nicholas and Gilbert learn of that! A card game?"

"I'm not actually supposed to tell anyone," Aiden admitted. He wasn't sure why he had told her, just that he felt conspiratorial and liked her very much.

"I am very good with secrets," she said with a smile. "And be careful with that," she added as he took another drink of the punch. "It's loaded with pisco brandy, but you hardly taste it with all the fruit juice."

"Thank you for the warning." Aiden set his cup down. He had eaten very little of their light lunch, and the drink was already making his head spin. Then the party swelled up all around them. Aiden worked hard to remember every name and to fashion the proper conversation. Asking questions, he had discovered, was the key. People were always happy if you just kept asking them questions about themselves. The questions directed at him, Aiden casually deflected. He owned land in Kansas, he explained, had worked in the timber business in Washington Territory, then had recently expanded into shipping in San Francisco. It sounded rather grand without all the details. Perhaps it was just the novelty of talking to new people, but Aiden began to find the conversation less difficult and, with some of them, even interesting.

After a while, he found he was actually starting to enjoy himself. Here he was, aboard a fine ship, wearing a fine suit, surrounded by fine people—in fact, he was one of those fine people! He was a shipowner, a businessman, no longer bound or indentured or simply poor. No longer a dirt farmer to be thrashed about by the whims of a hostile planet, he was, like these others, a man who could carve his own destiny and set his own course. He felt bold and deserving. A little over a year ago, he was eating dirt. Now servant hands swept plates away and slipped new courses in front of him. The main course was roasted pork loin. "Brought out live this afternoon," Captain Nickerly reassured them. "So don't worry about the native filth." Aiden cringed. Not long ago they would have considered *him* "native filth."

For a few strange hours, the whole world existed in this little room with the smell of the powdered rich and the beady pork. It was hot and Aiden felt like he was breathing soup. He drank only one glass of wine, yet when they were finally released from the table, the world was tipped eight ways from center. He was glad to climb up into the fresh night air. Captain Nickerly, who was now sweating and swaying, invited them to stay for cigars and a game of cards, but Christopher managed to make excuses.

"I think all the excitement of arrival has been a bit much," he explained. "Your excellent hospitality has made us forget our fatigue for a while, but I believe it will soon catch up to us and we will be poor company."

As they waited their turn for their launch, Alice came up to Aiden and took his hand in farewell. "It was lovely to meet you," she said. "I hope we will have more occasions to visit during our stay here."

"I would like that very much," Aiden said. He had not touched a woman in six weeks, and the softness of her hand half melted his brain. "I was in fact, um, quite interested in your geology and surveying and such things. Might I come along with your party again? I would find it very interesting. I could help carry things."

"You would be welcome," Alice said with a slight hesitation, her cool glance taking his measure.

"I am always eager to learn new things," Aiden said, immediately thinking it sounded stupid.

"Very well." Alice smiled. "We leave at first light. I will have our launch stop for you."

The *Raven* was quiet as Aiden and Christopher climbed aboard, except for the hushed talk of a few sailors still on deck and the soft lapping of water against the hull. Lanterns cast warm pools of light on the polished deck.

"That went well, I think," Aiden said. "It seemed we were very well received."

"A dancing poodle would be well received by that crowd!" Christopher's mood, always mercurial, was suddenly gloomy. "What dullards and bores! We cannot stay here two months waiting to load. I'll absolutely die." He leaned against the railing and looked out over the village of ships. "God, I wish there was something else I could do."

"What do you mean? To move us up the queue?"

"No—well, yes, of course to move up the queue, but I mean in life. Something to do in life besides business!" He yanked at his tie and clawed at the button on his stiff collar. "I want to do something more than scheme for deals and toady up to influential bores. I want to do something that matters! I want to be a painter or a poet!"

"You do not!" Aiden couldn't help laughing. He knew his friend was drunk, but he also knew the raw honesty that drink sometimes let out. "I'm sorry. But I doubt there are many rich painters, and certainly no poets."

"No, I suppose not," Christopher sighed. "But I could always find a rich patron."

"Like who?"

Christopher looked out over the calm black water to the dark heap of their treasure island. "Well, like a guano merchant, I suppose," he said.

It was funny, but also sad, and Aiden felt a pang of compassion for his friend. Aiden had no real direction in his own life and certainly not a thousandth of Christopher's fortune, but he was freer in many ways.

"All right," he said. "When we come home rich, I will be your patron and I will commission you to paint my portrait."

"You'd do much better commissioning the ducklings," Christopher said. The teasing did not ease his gloom. He got up and slapped his hands against the side of his trousers, brushing off the ever-settling guano dust. "Those surveyors, are they anyone?"

"I don't know."

"You've got to get better at finding out, dear boy. Connections to the Brockleton Line would be very useful. Their ships never spend more than two or three weeks here. The gossip is that the *Lady May* would be out even sooner, except that Nickerly buys their ghastly pisco by the barrelful, so they like to milk him for a while."

"Well, I am going to the island with them tomorrow for their surveying," Aiden said. "I'm sure you would be welcome to join us."

"The next time I set foot on that dung heap will be the day we sign our departure papers," Christopher said. He scrunched up the tie and tucked it into his pocket. "Are you staying up?"

"A little while, I think."

"I'm spent. Don't clatter about when you come in." Christopher went off to their cabin.

Aiden spent the whole next day with Alice, Nicholas and Gilbert, then the day after that and the next and the next. The actual surveying work took up only a few hours in the morning, but it was much nicer to spend the afternoons lounging about beneath the canopy than aboard any ship in the anchorage. Except for the few minutes coming and going each day as they passed by Koster's office, they could neither see nor hear the mining site. Once on the crest, they were upwind of the dust, so it was easy to pretend the awful place didn't really even exist.

By noon, as the sun grew hotter, they retreated to their little camp for lunch and an afternoon of leisurely amusement. It was surprisingly easy to forget they were picnicking atop a mountain of bird shit. They read poetry aloud or played cards, backgammon, chess or word games while the birds skittered across the sky and the occasional whale spouted in the distance. One morning they were rowed around the entire island while Gilbert drew dozens of sketches, capturing details of cliff faces and rocky inlets for the survey. Aiden still wasn't sure if they were "anyone," as Christopher had so bluntly put it. The surname of Brock certainly hinted at a relationship to the Brockleton Line, but Aiden couldn't ask them outright. The long afternoons began to melt away in their easy friendship. As smart and worldly and exotic as they were, they never made him feel ignorant.

Aiden tried to get Christopher to join them, but Christopher was repulsed by the very idea of walking over the mound of guano, let alone lying around on it for a whole day. He spent his days instead on the North Island, where there was something of a club set up in the abandoned buildings. Most of the captains and officers spent the days there.

"There are awnings and gaming tables—nothing fancy, but it's a place to go," Christopher said. "There's even a restaurant of sorts for lunch, where the Peruvian fishermen grill their catch and sell some vile stuff they call wine. It's an awful ugly place, of course—but we must make do. The men play cards, and the wives do their needlework or stroll back and forth with their gossip and umbrellas. Cabin boys brush a path clean for them. It's all rather well organized."

Society in the anchorage was vigorous. There were dinners or parties every night of the week on various ships. After just a few days, Christopher began hosting his own gatherings aboard the *Raven*. He quickly found the few young and interesting people among the hundreds of stranded souls. Nicholas, Alice and Gilbert were at the very top of any ship's guest list, but they actually enjoyed parties on the *Raven*, where everything was lively and fun. Someone always knew a comic recitation, a poem or a song. Christopher found musicians and arranged recitals and dances.

Fish, quite unexpectedly, was an excellent dancer. He certainly hadn't been raised, as Christopher had, with dancing masters and ballroom practice, but growing up on ships had made him nimble. He also had a natural musical sense. And a natural ease with women. His blond hair and Nordic blue eyes captivated them. Alice delighted in teaching him all the dances, and he was a quick student. He easily mastered the waltz. It was still regarded in provincial circles as a scandalous dance, but Fish made it look like pure, innocent fun as he clutched Alice close and spun her around the small deck.

Aiden watched them one night and felt—what? It wasn't jealousy. It couldn't be—Alice was several years older, and married. She was more like a big sister or a teacher to him. So why should it bother him that Fish clutched her so close, his hand covering half her back, fingers spread as if measuring his acreage? He could not be angry with Fish for monopolizing her. But still, he was—something. It wasn't fair for Fish to just step in, swoosh her about, make her laugh and brighten her cheeks so. Aiden knew that the rules of dancing—and friendship—would allow him to cut in, but he would no sooner try to dance than to fly. He did not have to cut in after all, for the next minute all the dancers stopped as a bell began to sound from the island. It was a harsh, flat tone, somber and relentless. The musicians stopped playing. All eyes looked immediately toward the island, then most dropped their gazes downward, the way people did to avoid an ugly scene: horses with broken legs or shamed housemaids. Aiden looked at Christopher, who just shrugged. Alice, Nicholas and Gilbert also seemed puzzled. They were apparently the only ones who didn't know what was going on.

"What does the bell mean, sir?" Christopher asked one of the visitors. "Has there been an accident?"

"No accident." The man was the son of an experienced captain, on his second voyage here. "It's the punishment bell. Probably a coolie tried to sneak off. A provisioning boat came out from Pisco today. They always guard the boats, of course, and search them before they leave, but these devils can be tricky. The bell reminds all the rest of them what will be done to escapees."

"And what will be done, sir?" Aiden asked.

"The proper thing," the young man said vaguely. "Only that. Only what's due. Shall we have a reel? Something merry to finish up the night?"

Christopher waved to the musicians and they began to play again. What could they really do, Aiden wondered, to punish men who already endured such hardships as daily life in this place? He remembered the overseers with their black whips. A whipping was bad but not unusual. Every captain in this fleet had probably had sailors flogged. His own father had raised welts on his sons with his belt. What had made these people look away and shudder? The fiddler played a lively reel, but the dancing seemed forced and artificial. Soon after, the party broke up.

"I will see you tomorrow at dawn, then?" Aiden said to Alice. He had not missed a day with them since their first meeting.

"We'll be collecting guano samples from the mine tomorrow," she said. "It will be quite different."

"Oh." He had been picturing another breezy afternoon of gay talk and companionship up on the ridge. "Well, I do like to see different things."

"I fear it will be very dusty and unpleasant."

"I've had dusty and unpleasant times before."

"Gilbert will not even come."

Aiden shrugged. "He is an artist."

Alice laughed. "Yes, he is that. Very well. You will need a scarf or kerchief to cover your face."

"All right. Tomorrow, then." Impulsively, he bent over and kissed her on the cheek.

The launches all departed, the merrymakers vanishing into the night. Night sounds drifted over the ship: the lapping of calm water on the anchored hulls, the murmured conversation of sailors, the soft percussion of the cat leaping onto the deck. In the background were all the steady little rattles and tinks of the ship's rigging, and behind that the steady bass drum of surf on the rocks. It was a little while before Aiden picked out the one different sound of this night. From the dark island, he could hear the faint sound of distant screams.

17

The screams had stopped by morning. The man made no sound at all now, or if he did, it was lost in the waves. It wasn't until the *Lady May*'s launch rowed past the rocky curve of the breakwater that Aiden and the others saw him. Alice gave a little gasp and pressed her hand to her mouth. Nicholas said "What is—" then stopped. It took a few long seconds to realize what they were looking at. A man was chained to a rock. Only his arms were chained; his feet dangled free. There were no marks on the man. There was no visible blood. But there wouldn't be, of course; the waves had crashed over him all night. He probably had kicked for a while, trying to get a heel to rest on some slippery niche, trying to ease the pull on his wrists and to push himself a few inches higher from the choking surf. But now he just dangled. He appeared to have sunk halfway into the rock, like a man lying in soft sand. But it was his flesh that was the soft part.

Aiden just stared in silence. How did they drill the holes to secure those chains? he wondered. The rock face was nearly vertical, and the biggest waves crashed completely over it. How did anyone stand there long enough to drill into the rock? Where would you tie up your boat? And how did you fix chains into a rock anyway? You couldn't use cement. It wouldn't dry, being wet all the time. Even small splashes would wreck the mixture. But someone had figured it out. Someone had figured out a way to drill the holes and sink the bolts and fix the chains. Then they had figured out a way to secure a boat long enough to haul a man up, wrestle his arms into place and clamp the shackles around his frail wrists. Perhaps it was just a matter of having the right tide. At any rate, they had done it. It had been done.

Black vultures perched on nearby bluffs, their tiny claws grabbing for balance, waiting. How did they know to come? Wouldn't the waves keep washing away the smell? Maybe the vultures had learned the punishment rock like crows on the prairie had learned the butchering frame. They began to gather at any activity there, even before blood was let.

The rowers lost their rhythm. One oar rattled in the oarlock, missed the stroke and hit another oar. The clap of blade against blade was loud as a gunshot. The coxswain shouted. The sailors regained their rhythm, and the launch rowed quickly past. It bumped softly against the dock. One of the rowers vomited over the side. Aiden got out, held out a hand for Alice and helped her up. Her face was very pale and her eyes were shiny with tears.

"Are you all right?" he asked quietly.

"No. Of course not. Who could be all right?"

Aiden said nothing. He actually was all right, for he was outside himself in a floating glass ball and nothing was real and he wasn't really there and felt nothing at all but the warm hum of the yellow sun and the strange firmness of solid ground.

Nicholas climbed up, and Alice whirled around to face him. "Did you know?"

"No." He looked away. "I—I heard something about it last night. But I didn't expect—"

"What did you expect?"

"I don't know—"

"A softer rock?"

"Stop!" Nicholas took her arm and steered her away from the launch. "Please," he whispered. Aiden couldn't tell if it was from tenderness or embarrassment that the sailors might overhear. "You must go back to the ship. You can't work here today. You know you shouldn't be here at all—not in the mine. And especially not now."

Alice pulled her arm away.

"There is nothing to do but scrape up bits of guano and put them into envelopes," Nicholas pleaded. "Your disguise will not fool anyone. I can collect the samples myself. Or you can send Gilbert. Go back and tell him I said he must come or—or I'll fire him." The threat did not sound convincing. "You must go back, my dear. The coolies will be upset. You would be provocation."

"We should all go back, then."

"No," Nicholas said firmly. "One mustn't appear weak in these circumstances. Go back. I can manage on my own. I will ask Koster for a guard."

Alice tucked some escaping bits of hair up under her hat. Despite the baggy men's clothing and the wide-brimmed hat, Aiden knew she would be recognized as a woman the moment she stepped into the mining site. On an ordinary day, that might be all right, no more than a bit of curiosity. The sailors in the launch twitched their hands on the oars, eager to be away.

"I will stay," Aiden offered. Staying on the island was about the last thing in the world he wanted to do right now, but the thought of Alice staying was worse. "If it's just collecting bits of guano into envelopes, I may be capable enough. It seems a waste of your expertise anyway."

Aiden watched two small sharks cruising in the shallows. One of the vultures landed on the rock. But everything inside his glass ball was very calm.

"Thank you," Alice said, her voice trembling. Nicholas helped his wife back into the launch, and the sailors began to row away as fast as they could.

"Good chap." Nicholas patted Aiden on the back. "Koster hasn't liked her being on the island at all since day one, and certainly would not want her mucking about the dig site even on the best of days." He sighed and looked around nervously. "This won't be the best of days. But I don't suppose the coolies would do anything drastic. I mean, this sort of thing must happen often enough. I'm sure the guards can handle things."

"There are plenty of guards," Aiden said.

Nicholas picked up the bag of equipment. "Right. Well, let's soldier on."

"What exactly am I meant to do?"

"Oh—sorry, yes." Nicholas stopped, opened the canvas bag and showed Aiden a stack of small paper envelopes, each one already labeled. "We'll take a little sample every three vertical feet, starting from the bare rock, hopefully all the way up to the top. You keep the envelopes in order and hand them to me. I'll also need to do some measuring, so you'll hold the stick. Shouldn't take more than a couple of hours. We'll be back in time for lunch."

They started walking up their usual path toward Koster's

compound, but then Nicholas led Aiden off onto a smaller path where rough stairs were cut into the bare rock. The guano had been stripped away here, but the scrolls and spatters of fresh bird droppings were already starting to replace it, making for slippery walking. The steps led up to the loading area at the top of the wharf. Aiden had previously seen this area only through the telescope from the ship, and it was always shrouded in a cloud of dust. Now he could see there was a sort of corral, made from canvas and sticks, to hold the deposited guano before it was shoveled into the waiting ships. Loaded carts came in on the track from the quarry area, pulled by men straining in the harnesses. Four shorter sections of track were spiked out at the end, allowing the carts to veer off and dump their loads. Around each of these piles, a few old men sat, picking at the guano.

They looked like no men Aiden had ever seen, unless men could be salamanders. They sat propped upright against bags of guano, their tiny bodies folded up knees to ears, shoulders hunched and heads barely erect, bony feet splayed for balance. With skeleton fingers, they scratched at the piles. Aiden walked closer and saw that they were picking little stones out of the guano. To lighten the load for the ships, he realized. If the stones were only two percent of the weight, it would still matter to a ship carrying twenty tons across long, vicious seas. It was all really math, wasn't it? Tons and miles and profit.

"Gear up, lad," Nicholas said, tying his kerchief around his nose and mouth. "Let's be done with this as quick as we can." Aiden tied his bandanna over his nose and mouth, and they set off walking along the rails to the base of the guano mountain. Now the sound of waves was replaced by the chink of picks, the rumble of the carts and the occasional shout of the overseers and the crack of their whips.

What Aiden and Christopher had seen from the path that first day, shocking as it was, had really showed nothing. Now he could see the actual men as they swung their picks and shovels. He could see the stretched sinews of their arms and the rivulets of sweat that ran down their backs, making little curlicues around the poking bones. He could see the yellow dust caking in the hollows of their ankles and the napes of their necks, clinging in ribbons between their ribs, like scalloped lines on a frosted cake. They were so thin and frail it seemed impossible that any one of them could even lift a pick, yet they lifted and swung in a constant motion. Aiden only vaguely remembered the Negro slaves on the plantation in Virginia, but he was sure they had been twice as big as these men, and with flesh and muscle. The cruelest masters still fed them enough, for they were valuable property and needed for work. These men most resembled the coal miners he had worked among, small, wiry men with skeleton cheeks and bony chests. But even in the coal mines, the sickest old men were more robust.

Some of the coolies glanced at them as they passed, but none ever stopped digging. The guano here was different from the spongy surface on the top of the ridge. This was dry, and compacted hard as rock. As the guano was chipped out, men with sledgehammers smashed the bigger chunks into smaller pieces; other men shoveled the pulverized guano into the wheelbarrows, which were hauled to the rail carts. The carts were then dragged to the corral, the piles were dumped, the old men picked out stones, the precious dust was shoveled into sacks, the sacks slid down the chutes, the ships sailed away, crops grew, distant people ate bread. Aiden shuddered. Where was he in this chain?

Nicholas dropped his bag, took out his trowel and scraped out a bit of guano. Aiden opened the first envelope to receive it. Even with the noise and clatter of the mining, he could hear it rustle down through the stiff paper and feel the crumbles settle in the bottom upon his fingertips. He had been here less than ten minutes, and his lungs ached. His eyes burned, and his mouth felt both soapy and dry, like he had eaten a spoonful of lye. But the coolies would work all day feeling this way. One man staggered past him, carrying a basket. Aiden could see the forehead strap digging into his skin. His toes left wide, clear prints in the dust, though his heels made barely a mark. A few of the men wore sandals, but most were barefoot, and the dusty ground was dimpled all over from their toes. Not one of them made a sound, or even looked at them, but Aiden could feel an angry tension in the air.

A worker filling a wheelbarrow on the terrace above accidentally spilled a shovelful of guano that barely missed them as they walked past. Nicholas cursed and shook the dust off his hat. Ten minutes later, as they were collecting on a higher level, one of the men lost his grip on a sledgehammer, and the heavy tool landed within inches of their boots. A guard ran over and lashed the man a vicious blow. The man dropped to his knees and bowed his forehead to the ground in apology, but when he stood up again, he glared at Aiden with murderous fury in his eyes. Chinese, Negro, or Irish, Aiden knew that men might endure plenty of abuse but always had a breaking point.

"Nicholas," he said. "I think you were right about the coolies being upset. It might be better to put this off for a few days."

"What? Nonsense—we're halfway up the mountain." Suddenly he realized what Aiden meant. "Are you saying the coolies—" He glanced around and dropped his voice to a whisper. "Do you think that was deliberate?"

"I think our people chained one of theirs to a rock."

"Regardless," Nicholas said, trying to sound confident, "one must never let the natives bully! My family were all foreign service—I know this!" He shook the dust off his kerchief and tied it back over his mouth and nose. "You can't let them take an inch. Come along, let's finish and be done with it."

As they worked their way to the top of the quarry, Aiden saw more glares and glowering looks. Even the Negro guards seemed tense and angry. Every time they took a sample, Aiden kept a cautious eye all around. The tension felt even higher as he and Nicholas made their way back down. Aiden heard muttered curses and hissing as they passed. The little accidents became more common. Showers of guano crumbled down on them from above. Several times, men with full wheelbarrows nearly knocked against them. So when one of the diggers suddenly sprang toward them, Aiden instinctively swung at him. The coolie ducked and nimbly dodged away, then bowed his head and held up his hands in supplication.

"Sorry! So sorry. No bad!" He bowed rapidly. "No bad me! No hurt! Only you take!" He held out something in his hand. "Free you take—take! Free take!" He was grinning and bobbing in the most obsequious manner, and would not even raise his eyes to look at them.

"Go away!" Nicholas made a shooing motion. "Get back or I'll call the guard."

"You take!" the little man insisted. He risked a glance at Aiden. "For you science! Very old. History! I give!"

Cautiously, Aiden held out his hand. The man dropped a small object, about the size and shape of a shark tooth, into his palm. It was a shard of pottery, grayish brown with some dark lines painted on the curved side.

"More!" The man's eyes darted around nervously. "I have more. You come see!"

"We don't want any trinkets," Nicholas said. "Don't encourage him, Aiden. Come on."

"Thank you," Aiden said to the man.

"More—history—Inca—yes? You know Inca? Very old!" The man pointed again at the shard, then patted his hand on his bare chest, leaving a palm print in the dust. "I am Jian Zhang. You come—more!" He pointed at one of the Negroes on the terrace below. "See!" He drew his finger down the side of his cheek. Aiden looked and saw that the guard had a ropey scar across his cheek. "He show! Yes?"

"Yes," Aiden said, wanting only to be far away from this crazy coolie and gone from this place. He closed his hand around the little bit of pottery. "Thank you."

Jian Zhang picked up his shovel and bowed. Then, for an instant, he looked Aiden directly in the eyes. "Now you watch!" he whispered. He tipped his chin and pointed a finger up. "Bad men—bad!" Then he turned and darted away, back to his digging. Aiden tucked the bit of pottery into his pocket. It was just one more strange thing in a long, strange day.

Two tiers down, Aiden heard, or felt, something wrong.

It had been years since he had worked in the rock quarry as a child, but instinctively he recognized the rivulet of dust and pebbles that indicated a rock slide. He looked up just in time to see a huge chunk of guano break off above and tumble down toward them. *Watch—bad men.*

"Look out!" He shoved Nicholas, but the landslide of guano was already rushing down on them. Aiden grabbed Nicholas's arm, pulled him across his own body and rolled them both out of the way just as a chunk of guano big as a steamer trunk crashed down inches away. They were buried in choking debris. The terrace cracked beneath them, and they were pushed along in an avalanche of guano. For a few long seconds, Aiden could not even tell which way was up. This was not the way to die, he thought. Of all the ways there were, this was especially not it. The ammonia stench was a cloud of gas that steamed through his lungs.

But finally everything slowed and he got his feet under him. He pushed himself up and dragged Nicholas to his feet. Aiden groped at his eyes and tried to brush away the burning dust, but that just made it worse. He could hear shouting and Nicholas coughing and spitting. Then many hands began grabbing at him—small, rough, scaly hands. Aiden swung wildly, thinking the coolies were attacking them now. He couldn't see or breathe. Then a whip cracked, and he saw the black legs of Negro guards. The dust began to settle, and Aiden saw Nicholas also blinking and spitting and coughing, coated in yellow dust from head to foot like a sugared cookie.

"Are you all right?" Aiden gasped.

Nicholas nodded and began to brush himself off. There was much shouting and whip cracking all around them. It might well have been an accident, Aiden tried to convince himself. They probably wouldn't really have been buried alive. But his heart was pounding and his skin prickled with panic. He forced himself to stay calm. He found the collection bag, dusty but undamaged, and got out their canteens. He handed one to Nicholas, pushing it blindly into his hands. Aiden swished his mouth out, poured some water over his eyes and even splashed a palmful up his nose. The guano boulder had shattered upon impact, but there was still a large chunk the size of a cannonball that had made a crater several inches deep just where they had been standing minutes ago.

"Oh my," Nicholas said, still brushing himself off. "Good eye there. Thank you. Wherever did you learn to flip someone about like that? Did you wrestle in school?"

"Old Indian trick," Aiden said, spitting and wiping his tongue.

"What? Oh yes—ha, good there. Well done, ah, however it was, ah, done." He coughed violently. "Well, I suppose we have enough samples," Nicholas said in a louder but shaky voice. "Get the bag there, will you, and let's be on our way." He brushed the guano dust off his trousers. "Calmly," he added in a whisper. "Remember—never show the natives fear."

The *Lady May*'s launch was waiting for them, sculling in place fifty yards off, well outside the breakwater.

"Why aren't they at the dock like they should be?" Nicholas said crossly. "What the bloody hell are they doing bobbing around out there?"

There was a splash nearby, and Aiden saw the dark flick of a sharp tail. The water all around the dock was riffled by sharks. There were five or six, maybe seven, all small, the biggest no more than four feet long. They swam around lazily, like contented dinner guests casually browsing the dessert tray to see if there might be a few of the best sweets left.

"Sorry, sir," one of the sailors said as the launch glided up. "It was a bit dodgy here for a while." He stood and offered his hand to Nicholas. His face was gray and his fine livery blotched with vomit stains. "Watch your step, sir."

With a few hard pulls, the sailors rowed them swiftly away. Aiden squeezed his eyes shut, but he did not have to look to know the awful truth. The punishment rock was now empty.

The *Raven* was quiet as Aiden climbed back on deck. The sun felt closer and hotter than ever, as if it could beam a hole through the whole ship. Aiden imagined her sinking quickly into the cold water with only a slight hiss. It seemed a peaceful resolution right now. It was not yet noon, but Aiden felt a year had passed since he woke at first light that morning, eager for exploration.

"Good morning, sir." Sven the Baby stepped up to the companionway as Aiden boarded. There was no one else on deck.

"Where is everyone?" Aiden asked.

"The captain is visiting the *Bristol Star*. Mr. Worthington has gone to the North Island as usual." Sven the Baby, Sven the Ancient's great-nephew, was the most junior of the crew and so was often one of those left behind to man the ship while the others enjoyed an outing. "Um—if you'd like to join him, I can row you over. There's only the little boat, so it will take a while longer—"

"What? No," Aiden interrupted. "I don't want to go anywhere." He suddenly felt as if the ship were rocking beneath his feet, though he knew they were calmly at anchor. He grabbed the rail to steady himself. The wind was roaring in his ears.

"Are you all right, sir?" Sven said in a faraway voice. "You're very pale."

"I don't want to go anywhere," Aiden repeated. His own voice sounded far away. And being called "sir" suddenly seemed awfully strange. "I will be in my cabin."

"Very well, sir. Shall I bring you some lunch?"

"Please just let me be," Aiden snapped. The air felt dense and prickly, like just before a storm. He brushed past Sven and managed to stumble down the companionway. The cabin was impossibly hot. Aiden pushed open the hatch, and a carpet of dense air rolled in. He didn't care if the yellow dust came in with it. He felt sick and angry, and more so because what right did he have to feel sick and angry? He had only seen this awfulness, he wasn't living it. He wasn't a coolie, he was a master. He owned escape.

But how could he have been so oblivious? For nearly two weeks, he had been picnicking every day on the edge of hell, with his back to the abyss. He had sat at fancy tables, eating fancy food with wealthy people. The memory of the rich pork and sweet punch now made him nauseated, and he barely got to the bucket in the passageway before he vomited. He went back into the cabin and fell down on the bed just before the woozy sweat of darkness laid him out. He lay still for minutes or hours, until the world stopped spinning and his bones firmed up enough to stand. He sat up and saw a jug of water and a plate of hardtack on the little table. The bucket had also been rinsed and placed strategically by his bed. Sven the Baby was a quietly thoughtful man. But instead of making him feel better, these easy comforts just incensed Aiden more. He got up and opened the desk drawer, got the key to the liquor storeroom, found a bottle of whiskey and drank himself unconscious.

"Wake up—we're having a party," Christopher said. "What are you doing down here? It's like a hothouse! And you've let the dust in!"

Aiden blinked open his crusty eyes to blinding sun stabbing in through the porthole. He sat up, sweaty and confused. The slant of the sun told him many hours had passed. "A party? What time is it?"

"Party time!" Christopher said brightly. "One of the German ships has an oompah band." He sat down at the tiny desk that also served as his dressing table. "I've got every danceable woman in the anchorage promised to come, though that's only three, and two are ugly." He had already rinsed the dust out of his hair and now carefully combed it back. "But I haven't got a reply from Alice yet. Do you know if they have plans tonight?"

Aiden's mouth was so dry he could barely talk, and his skin crackled when he moved. He poured some water from the jug into a glass and gulped it down. "What are you talking about? We can't have a party."

"Why not? We have a band, we have drink, we have nothing else to do. In any math that equals a party."

Aiden rubbed his eyes and immediately regretted it, for the dust made them burn like a hornet sting. Christopher pulled the hatch closed. "What are you doing down here anyway? Look at you—you're filthy! You need to wash before the party."

Aiden saw that Christopher was in what they called his

"bright mood," but he did not want to deal with it now. He pressed the heels of his hands against his eyeballs, hard enough to cause a comforting pain. "We can't have a party."

"Why not?"

"Do you know what happened today?" he said.

"Of course." Christopher pulled off his damp shirt. "Unpleasant business."

"Unpleasant?" Aiden's voice caught in his throat. Unpleasant was an overcooked roast or a rough seam inside a new shoe. He felt his anger rising like a storm. "Last night, while we were waltzing, they chained a man to a rock!"

"I know. He tried to escape."

"They chained him to a rock, where he hung all night being smashed by waves, and then through the morning until his wrists finally stretched enough for all the little bones to break apart and the skin to tear—or maybe, I don't know, maybe the skin didn't tear—" Aiden rubbed his own wrists as if examining the construction to be sure. "Maybe the little bones just finally got crushed enough to slip through the shackles, I don't know—"

"Shut up," Christopher interrupted.

"Then his body fell into the sea and was eaten by sharks and little fish."

"Shut up! I know what happened."

"Hopefully he was already dead before that."

"We didn't chain him there," Christopher said, annoyed. "It wasn't us."

"Of course it was us!" Aiden slammed the little table so hard the water jug crashed. "Why would any of them be here—if not for us?"

"It was a barbaric thing," Christopher said. "Everyone

agrees, and some of the senior captains are going to talk to Koster. But the fact is, the coolie did try to escape."

"Oh—yes. So now we all just polka to an oompah band?"

"Oh stop!" Christopher jumped up, equally angry. "Do you think me such a monster? Or incapable in my heart—because I haven't had your damn infernal prairie suffering—dead starving family—awful suffering? You think that I don't care for a man—even a Chinaman—being dashed to bits on the rocks? Am I a toy man with a toy heart? I won't have this argument now! We are here for business!" He flung open the cabin door and strode out. "You need a bath."

"We are not having a party!" Aiden, enraged, ran after him. Christopher started to climb up the ladder, but Aiden grabbed his leg.

"Let go of me!" Christopher kicked free and scrambled up the ladder. Aiden tore up behind him and tackled him, so they both fell. They rolled and wrestled across the deck.

"Stop it!" Christopher cried. "Are you crazy?"

Aiden did feel crazy, but he stopped himself. He knew too well how to fight, and how easily he could hurt his friend if he did. He took a deep breath and slowly got to his feet. Every sailor was on deck, staring.

"Get up." He held out a hand to Christopher. Christopher took it, staggered to his feet, then punched Aiden in the face. Aiden fell back and stumbled over a hatch.

"Ow!" Christopher crouched and rubbed his hand. Aiden felt a warm drip of blood fall on his chest. He wiped his nose. A landslide of fury rocked through him and he lunged at Christopher. But before he could get to him, strong hands grabbed his arm and spun him back.

"Stop it, the both of you!" Fish said angrily. "I'll have no fighting on my ship, even from the masters." He held Aiden's arms behind him. "All hands aft!" Fish shouted at the sailors. The sailors ducked their heads and retreated to the back of the ship, some thankful to escape the confrontation, some eager to see more of a fight.

"We cannot stay here." Aiden dropped his voice. "We cannot be part of this!"

"I would throw you overboard right now except I know you probably want that exactly!" Christopher shouted. "And if we didn't have a contract that would be awful to sort out if you were dead."

"I will sign any papers to make it easy for you," Aiden said bitterly.

"Stop it, the both of you, now!" Fish turned Aiden loose but stood between the two of them.

"You stupid hypocrite!" Christopher's blue eyes turned dark with anger. "You are crumbling now because one man died whose face you saw today. But don't you realize that everything we have—every nice and comfortable thing that you have lapped up like a little milk dog in my father's house for the past six months—has come from some horrid labor! Every orange and plum, every carpet and book. What do your nice boots really cost? Or the sugar in your coffee? Do you lie in your comfortable bed on your soft sheets night after night fretting for the slaves picking cotton and the little children who work in the mills?"

"Take your sugar and your sheets. I don't need any of it!" Aiden shouted. "We cannot be part of this! We cannot make our fortune from slavery!"

"The coolies have signed for this!"

"No one would sign for this!" Aiden lunged again, but Fish pulled him back.

"Stop it, the both of you!"

"I would not have signed for this!" Aiden said bitterly.

"You said yourself how the guano is needed!" Christopher said. "People are starving all over the world! They can't eat grass."

"My parents ate grass! So don't you dare tell me about starving! But to save all my family, I would not have signed for this!"

"Enough!" Fish said. "We are here. And nothing here will change. We can leave tomorrow, with an empty hold, and nothing here will change. You can write to the president or the pope or any god you like, and nothing here will change. You can have a bloody fistfight or a goddamn duel if you like—but not aboard my ship!"

A heavy silence dropped over the ship. They could hear the faint sounds of an accordion drifting across the water. The lowering sun painted the island a lovely copper color. In the cloud of yellow dust, Aiden knew that the tiny ant figures were still working with their picks and wheelbarrows to meet their daily quota. Five tons per man. The accordion music grew louder as the launch with the band came nearer. Besides the accordionist, there were two men playing brass horns with little enthusiasm. Men on other ships applauded as they passed. Any entertainment, no matter how lame, was welcome in this place.

"You aren't the only ones upset." Fish lowered his voice. "Our men have heard about the rock. It is cruel to everyone."

"Of course." Aiden's face burned with embarrassment. "I apologize."

"Permission to board!" A shout rang out from the German launch. The horn players lowered their instruments, but the accordion player kept playing all the while. He had a vacant, glazed expression and did not seem to care or even notice where they were. Aiden had pictured a jolly little man in lederhosen like the illustration from the *Atlas of the World*, but this fellow was a lean giant, with huge, knobby elbows that poked out like albatross wings, and giraffe legs that spread the width of the launch. His head was a cornerstone, his jaw an anvil, but his eyes were tiny black stones. Though his face was expressionless, his fingers flew over the instrument like small, happy birds, spinning a bright tune.

"Oh God, it's worse than I feared," Christopher said quietly. He smoothed his hair, brushed off his jacket and poised himself like a general awaiting the charge, for there were already two launches approaching with party guests.

"Are you finished?" Fish glared from one to the other.

"Yes," Christopher said. "Excuse me, I must speak to the cook and the steward." He nodded to Fish and walked off without another word.

"The steward?" Fish could not help laughing. The steward was actually Sven the Baby, who had the duties of steward only because he was the most junior of the crew.

"Go clean yourself up," Fish said to Aiden. "What have you been doing—rolling in the guano?"

"Yes," Aiden said. "Actually I have. I can't stay for a party. I will go fishing. I'll take the small rowboat by myself."

"You can't take a boat alone," Fish said with a sigh. "It is a ship rule for everyone. You know that."

"I won't go far."

"It's dangerous. The wind comes up, the sea becomes choppy, a sea lion jumping for a fish knocks your boat over. I will ask for a volunteer."

"No." A smear of blood was crusting on his lip, and Aiden wiped it roughly away. "The men should have their leave. They might enjoy the music. I promise I will stay in the anchorage. I won't go beyond where the farthest ships are anchored."

Fish rubbed his hand across his forehead. "You will still not escape this infernal music."

"I know."

"Promise you will return before dark comes."

"I will," Aiden said.

"And promise you are not going mad from this place—" Fish said quietly. "As I've learned too often happens."

"I promise," Aiden said. "But if a man were mad—well, he wouldn't be likely to tell you so, would he?"

"I suppose not."

"Perhaps a man not going mad here would be more horrible."

Fish nodded. "Go on, then."

A gunshot cracked in the distance. A flare went up and streaked across the sky. Cheers erupted from every ship. The *Diana*, a ship out of Liverpool, was leaving the anchorage, starting her homeward journey. She was heavy in the water, her great hull loaded full with guano. Aiden and Fish watched as she unfurled her topsails and picked up speed.

"What a terrible machine we are," Fish said softly. "With our ships and desires."

18

Aiden honored his promise to come back before dark, but he still hung off in the little rowboat once he knew Fish had seen him. He waited until the last of the visitors were rowed away before he climbed aboard. The smell of the party lingered. Perfumes, powders, hair oil, tobacco and the unique smell of sweaty linen, like burned toast and sour milk. The crew was gathered on the aft deck, enjoying an after-party ration of pisco. Christopher was sitting in a canvas chair in the bow, his feet propped up on the capstan, his eyes closed. His tie was undone and his shirt collar open. A lantern cast flickering shadows across his face. Aiden sat down in a chair beside him. Christopher opened his eyes and looked at him, then picked up the lantern and held it closer to Aiden's face.

"My God!" he said with unseemly delight. "Have I given you a black eye?"

"It wasn't a fair punch," Aiden said.

"Of course it wasn't fair! I'm not stupid—I've seen you fight. I wouldn't last ten seconds with fair. Does it hurt?"

"No."

"Well, it ought to. My knuckles are still aching."

Aiden's face did in fact hurt quite more than he thought it should, but he would never admit that.

"How was the party?"

"Horribly dull." Christopher leaned back in his chair. "Exactly as I expected. The people were dull, and the pretty girl was dullest of all. And whoever invented that god-awful oompah music ought to be shot."

"If you knew it would be horrible, why did you have it?"

Christopher sighed and spoke with exaggerated slowness, as if explaining things to a dull child. "Because Captain Heifer-weasel is well placed here. He plays chess every day with Koster and lets him win. Because the accordion player is his wife's idiot nephew. He loves to play his accordion. He plays dawn to dusk, and they love to have one evening on the ship free from his playing. It is simple as that. Heifer-weasel is a man with influence. And now we have done him a favor."

"Ah," Aiden said. "So, basically, you're flanking?"

"Yes, I suppose." Christopher laughed.

A fish splashed in the water nearby. Soft murmurs of conversation drifted back from the sailors. Twinkling lanterns from all the ships draped a blanket of tiny stars over the water. It could almost be a normal evening in a normal world.

"I am sorry I hit you," Christopher said quietly.

"I know."

"Why did your parents eat grass?"

It was a very unexpected question. "It was the famine," Aiden said. "In Ireland, when all the potatoes went bad. Have you not heard of that?"

"No."

"How do you go to your fancy school and not know that?"

"It's the past."

"Rome is the past and you know about Rome."

"They have ruins," Christopher said.

"Well, I am a ruin," Aiden said. He looked over toward the island. It was so still and silent now. "It is true, what I said—that I would not have signed on for this place. Not in the worst starving, not to save my own family. But I confess, I would have killed any friend, or any man's child, for a bag of this magic dust. I would have swung the lash myself, as hard as any overseer, to make them dig it out. I would have chained any one of them to the rock. I would have chained you. I would have chained Elizabeth or any one of the ducklings."

"You wouldn't."

"I don't know that."

"You oughtn't go off brooding alone in rowboats," Christopher said. "Contemplation always muddles up the mind."

They sat silently for a few minutes, then Christopher spoke again, his voice tired, resigned.

"We couldn't have expected this."

"We should have asked—"

"Asked what? Asked who? Asked the mad captain— 'Please, sir, what haunts your soul? Is it a thousand coolies worked to death on an island of bird shit and chained to a rock if they try to escape?' It was a poker game! It was a chance."

"And now it's just business."

"Damn right," Christopher said. "For painters and poets don't really feed anyone, do they? You want to feed the world? Well, this is how it works!"

The *Lady May*'s launch did not stop by the next morning to collect Aiden. Alice sent a note on the afternoon mail boat, thanking Aiden for his help with the sample collecting and explaining that they would spend the next few days testing and cataloging everything. But then nothing. Christopher invited them to a games party aboard the *Raven,* but they declined. More days passed, all alike. The weather never changed. New ships arrived and old ones departed, while those still at anchor waiting to load counted off the days that never changed. Aboard the *Raven,* there was little to do. Every morning and evening the sailors hauled up buckets of water and rinsed and brushed the decks stem to stern, but they were still always slippery from the dust. Laundry was hung out only overnight but was still often coated and slimy. Hatches were closed during the day, making the cabins generally unlivable. Fish kept the sailors busy in the mornings with repairs and general maintenance, but they were mostly idle the rest of the day. Everyone in the anchorage was mostly idle. Nearly two thousand men and at least a hundred women simply passed the days in small hours, seeking any entertainment or diversion they could.

One couldn't swim or even take a dip in the anchorage because of all the garbage from the ships, and the sharks that prowled about feasting on it. Some of the sailors rigged little sailing boats and held races around the islands. Some rowed out and passed the days fishing. But most of the idle hours were spent on the saloon ships. Fights were common and sobriety was rare. Guano ships, after all, did not attract the best of men.

Christopher went to the North Island every day, easing his boredom in the card games and always seeking the vital connections that might speed their escape from this place. Fish often went with him, but Aiden found the place too depressing. It was littered with detritus from the mining days, valueless bits of machinery, rusting gears and the splintering scraps of wood that were too flimsy even to be hauled over to the Middle Island for coolie shacks. The North Island was now nothing but bare rock, with only a glaze of new guano. Ten thousand years of accumulation of guano—three hundred feet, five million tons, countless millions of dollars' worth—had been hauled away in just ten years. Aiden tried taking walks there but always felt depressed after; there was a bleak and ghostly desolation in the air. None of the locals who sailed out from Pisco to do business in the anchorage would even spend a night in a boat offshore.

"Too many spirits," one of the cooking women explained to Aiden in halting English. "Very bad place."

Bad place or not, there was nowhere else for most of the ship-bound to go to escape the boredom, confinement and dust, so they came here to frolic amid the ruins.

It was five days after the day of the rock before he saw Alice again, on board another ship for another dinner party. She was distant and formal with him. As the punch was passed on deck before dinner, she stood fixed by Nicholas's side. Throughout the evening, she was the very picture of a quiet, proper wife. She was even dressed differently than she had been at the *Lady May*'s dinner, in the more traditional boned corset and full skirt with petticoats, and looked very prim. Aiden was seated too far from her to have any conversation at the table. Instead he nodded his way numbly through an endless discussion of labor unrest in England and the lack of quality house servants in India these days. But after dinner, when brandy was being served on the deck and Nicholas was smoking cigars with the other gentlemen, Aiden managed to have a few minutes alone with her.

"Have I done something wrong?" he asked. "Have I offended you someway?"

"No, no, of course not! Don't think that."

"You won't talk to me and will barely look at me. What should I think?"

"That life is complicated and often goes askew," she said quietly. "I'm sorry."

"I miss your company," he said simply. "And here," he added less formally, "I have something for you." He took the little shard of pottery from his vest pocket and handed it to her. Alice's eyes brightened immediately.

"One of the coolies gave it to me," Aiden explained. "I forgot about it for a few days, then, well, I didn't see you until now."

"Did he say where he got it?"

"He found it in the guano. He says he has more. Probably wants to sell them."

Alice examined it closer. "It could be from the Incas," she said. "I don't know much about pottery, but I would love to see more. Will you go back and see what else he has? Oh, please, Aiden?" Her eyes were suddenly full of tears.

"Of course—but have I upset you?"

"No, not at all." Alice wiped her eyes quickly on her handkerchief and glanced around the deck as if expecting to be scolded. "You are the least upsetting thing in the world. It is just this place. I am trapped here. I have nothing to do and nowhere to go. I am kept from all that is interesting. Captain Nickerly never approved of me climbing all over the guano in the first place, and after the . . . troubles, I am forbidden to return." Her voice was strained. "It is selfish of me to complain that I have lost my small freedoms when a man has lost his life." She squeezed the little shard in her hand and pressed it to her chest like it was a magic charm. "But this is the sort of thing a lady scientist is allowed to do—look at bits of pottery. I have some books on the Inca civilization. It will give me a pursuit and keep me from stabbing every single person on our ship through the heart with a dagger at night as they sleep."

"Well, I am generally in favor of not stabbing," Aiden said. "So I will gladly go." Returning to the guano mine would never be done gladly, but he felt honored—was that the right word?—to be given this task for her. His feelings for Alice were a complete jumble, scattered somewhere in the broad plain between sisterly affection and romantic desire, complicated further by his admiration for her intelligence and his simple happiness to be near any woman after these months of only men.

"I'll go tomorrow. Will Nicholas and Gilbert want to come?"

"No!" she said, a little too quickly. "I mean, you are better alone." She glanced around nervously. "This place is a horrid little village," she whispered. "Full of gossip."

Aiden had no idea what she was talking about. But before

he could ask anything more, Nicholas walked over to join them.

"Our launch is second in the queue, dear," Nicholas said, slipping possessively back to her side and resuming his hold on her arm. "Are you ready?"

20

Aiden had not been back on the island since the day of the execution, and he felt a sick twist in his stomach as they rowed toward the dock. But the punishment rock was empty, the chains clinking faintly as they were knocked by the occasional high wave. Everything was back to normal. He walked up the path past Koster's office and down into the mine site. He glanced at every coolie he could as he passed, but he didn't recognize the one who had given him the pottery shard. Aiden didn't expect he would. He had only briefly seen the man's face, and then he had immediately been nearly crushed by an avalanche of guano. Besides that, the coolies were all of similar build, with identical hair and clothing—and covered in dust. People in San Francisco joked about the Chinamen all looking the same, but Aiden had to admit that their features were still so foreign to him that he probably couldn't have picked the man out even with close inspection.

But whatever the Chinaman's real game—the sale of genuine artifacts or some kind of scheme—Aiden knew all dealings would have to be done through the scar-faced guard anyway. The coolies had little to offer for sale or trade, but what they did have was always brokered through the guards. Some made small wood carvings or decorative bone buttons that were popular as souvenirs. There was one valuable business, but it was never done in daylight. The bodies of coolies who had been buried for a while in the guano were passed off to museums or collectors in Europe as ancient Peruvian mummies. Sailors rowed out in the dark of the moon and returned with tightly wrapped bundles that, if successfully smuggled home, might earn them double their pay.

Aiden walked around the mine site pretending to be taking more samples of the guano, waiting for the scar-faced guard to approach him. He had no idea how he would receive the rest of the pottery bits. Neither the coolie nor the guard would have known he was coming. But there were always ways to arrange commerce.

It wasn't long before the guard appeared almost silently at Aiden's side. Aiden had seen plenty of rough-looking men in the lumber camp, but this man had the most frightening appearance. His eyes shone red in a face so black that, with the glisten of sweat, it looked like ink. The scar on his cheek was raised and ropey, knitted down the whole side of his face, from eyebrow to chin. His bare chest was coated with the yellow dust but striped with trickles of sweat. Aiden took the pottery shard out of his pocket and held it on his palm. The guard nodded slightly.

"Go to the houses at noon," he said in Spanish, glancing toward the coolies' village. "Do not let others see you go there."

Aiden knew enough words in Spanish to understand. But then the guard spoke in English, the words clearly learned just for Aiden's benefit. "See man near Buddha shrine."

"*Gracias,*" Aiden said. He had assumed that the guard would expect some kind of payment for his part in the arrangements, so he had brought a few twists of tobacco, a universal currency. The guard tucked it into his pocket and walked quickly away.

Aiden climbed up to the first terrace and crossed to the far side of the quarry. No one seemed to pay him much attention. He skidded down a rough path and walked toward the village. The shacks were clustered haphazardly, as the rocky terrain allowed. There was one main path, barely a yard wide, with dozens of narrower paths snaking off it into the warren. The ramshackle buildings tumbled and leaned into one another, so it looked as if one strong push would topple them all. The walls had such large gaps between the boards that Aiden could see through two or three rooms sometimes. It would have been crowded for a hundred men, but Aiden knew there were twice that many living here. Each shack held only a pathetic collection of rough wooden bunks with rolled-up reed mats and a few wooden crates. Aiden followed the main path until he came to what seemed like the center of the place, an open area, no more than twenty feet on each side—the village square. There were pieces of driftwood, a few canvas stools and some ancient, rusted pieces of a wheelbarrow arranged as seating. At one corner, a smooth, flat stone had been carried up from the shore and set upon a bed of smaller stones. In the middle of this altar was a Buddha statue about six inches high, carved from wood.

Aiden had seen shrines in Chinatown in San Francisco, but they were always cheerful and brightly painted, garlanded with flowers and surrounded by little dishes for offerings of rice, candies, fruits and incense. But this poor Buddha shared the barren world of his worshipers. There were, of course, no candies or fruits, but some pieces of old newspaper had been folded into flowers and placed carefully at his feet. Some kind of grass or reed had been cleverly twisted into a necklace for the idol, with tiny shells woven in like jewels. Tin can lids had been hammered into bowls. One held the stub of a candle, another a few grains of rice, a third a shriveled twist of orange peel. There were also three cans filled with water. Beyond recognizing the Buddha, Aiden knew nothing about the religion, but like all the other religions he was aware of, it didn't seem to be doing much good for its people.

In the corner opposite the shrine was a pile of rags on a reed mat, perhaps dirty clothes or bedding waiting to be carried down to the shore for washing. The rest of the square was empty—there was clearly no man waiting here for him. Had he misunderstood? Was the guard toying with him? The wind swayed through the flimsy shacks, making them creak eerily. There were no signs of life except for tiny lizards darting in and out of cracks and the omnipresent seabirds scraping the sky.

Where might a bag of pottery shards be left for him? Would such a thing have enough value to the other men that it would be well hidden? Of course, anything that might be sold for a few pennies to a sailor would have value here. Aiden searched all around the shrine but saw nothing. There were no weeds or brush to hide anything in, and the ground looked well trampled—no hole had been dug or rocks obviously rearranged. He walked carefully around the perimeter of the square, looking under every crate or bit of scrap. He came to the pile of rags and hesitated. It was dirty and stinking, but it was really the only place to hide something. Gingerly he plucked at the corner of one cloth and lifted it up, then jumped back in horror. A skull stared up at him from the pile of rags.

Was this a hideous joke? Then the skull gasped. Aiden realized, with even more horror, that the thing was not yet a skull. There was still skin over the bone, but it was pulled so taut over the cheekbones and forehead that it looked glossy and mottled, like mother-of-pearl. The man was still alive. His mouth was open, and shriveled lips curled back from toothless gums. There was a twitch in the sunken eye sockets, and two tiny jet buttons appeared, staring wetly at Aiden. The man breathed a faint, bubbly exhalation that smelled vaguely sweet and yeasty, like when you opened a cask of cider. A thin, witchy hand reached out from under the rags and tapped at the wizened lips, clearly begging for water. Aiden felt both a rush of compassion and a stab of revulsion.

His hands shook as he took out his canteen and pulled out the cork. He did not want to touch the man, partly afraid to damage him, partly revolted. But mostly he didn't know how to do it. Even if he sat the man up, his mouth was too tight and his jaw too stiff with rigor to drink from a cup. He couldn't just pour some in his mouth—the man would choke. Finally Aiden took off his bandanna, shook out the guano dust and soaked a corner with water. He dabbed the wet rag on the man's lips. The jawbone jerked forward and the man began to suck eagerly on the wet cloth. Aiden wet the bandanna a few more times, suckling the dying man like a newborn calf until he grew too weak from the exertion to suck anymore. The skeleton man's head sank deeper into the rag pile. The bony fingers spasmed at the air in a gesture of thanks, then groped weakly at the cloth that covered his body. He pulled back a corner, and Aiden saw a small bundle nestled against the man's sunken belly. The man's arm fell on top of the bundle, but he lacked the strength to pick it up. Aiden picked up the bundle and felt the crunch of broken pottery inside.

"Thank you," Aiden said to the man. What should he do now? Say a prayer? He didn't know if the Chinese believed in prayer. He didn't know if he believed in prayer himself. And the man didn't speak English anyway. Did the Chinese believe in heaven?

"Rest in peace," he finally said. Everyone believed in peace. He turned to leave, but the man made another sound, the desperate, frightened cry of a small animal. His eyes opened wide and the tiny claw-hands groped at the rags. He thrashed his head side to side and blinked rapidly. Then he raised one useless hand and waved it at the sky. The birds. Of course. Aiden shuddered. He lifted the ragged cloth back up over the man's face, tucking it around him and carefully covering his eyes.

Aiden stood motionless. He wanted to run away but couldn't. Movement equaled time. If he didn't move at all, time would not pass. If time did not pass, nothing more would happen. He clutched the bundle of broken things against his heart. The relentless birds filled the sky. The almost-dead man did not move. Nothing moved but the birds and the wind and the useless ticks of time.

21

Aiden rinsed himself at the shore, head to toe, wading in fully clothed and rinsing until the shallows were cloudy. Since he was on an errand for her, Alice had arranged for one of the *Lady May*'s launches to carry him to and from the island, so the trip across the anchorage was quick. The rhythmic swish of the oars was soothing as he was rowed back to civilization. His clothes were nearly dry and his mind numb as they approached the *Lady May*. He saw Alice waving at him, and he felt his mood switch as suddenly as a lamp lit in a dark room. She stood at the rail in a pale green day dress with a blue sash, her hair loosely twisted up beneath her straw hat. The dress was of light fabric, and the breeze blew her sash out like a kite tail and puffed her sleeve when she waved. Aiden felt a rush of happiness and relief. Everything that was not the rag pile man was beautiful, but she was the most beautiful of all. How long had it been since he had seen anything pretty? There were no flowers in this place, no grass, no greenery at all. There were no children, no dogs, no bunnies nibbling clover in the morning garden. Even the birds were harsh in this place, sharp and angular with their stabbing beaks, and always screeching. No chickadees or sparrows or mourning doves. There was nothing soft for a thousand miles. But right now Alice looked like an angel.

"You are a vision of loveliness," Aiden said impulsively as he climbed on board.

"How silly you are!" She blushed with surprise and dropped her head demurely. There were sailors nearby. "Please come and have some refreshment, and we will examine your artifacts," she said. Her tone was formal, but there was a brightness about her that he hadn't seen since the first day he met her with her theodolite. She led him to the aft deck, where there was a comfortable lounge area set up beneath awnings. Aiden sank gratefully into the shade. The ship's steward (a real one) wheeled over a trolley with a pitcher of water, a silver tea set, a bottle of sherry and all the proper silver tankards, bone china cups and cut crystal glasses required. There was a plate with oranges, dried fruits and cookies, which the English, to Aiden's amusement, called biscuits. Aiden felt like he had stepped through a magical door between worlds. Maybe that was the trick to this new life he was inventing—keeping everything in its own world with the doors neatly closed. If he closed the door to the island world, the ant men and the dying rag pile man did not exist.

"Everyone has gone to the North Island today," Alice said in a hushed but excited tone as soon as the steward left them alone. "Even the captain and missus, and she almost never goes. They're having a cricket tournament! It's the social event of the season. Everyone is gone, and I feel like I've been let out of prison!"

"I'm glad to see you happy again," Aiden said. "And you do look very pretty."

"I'm not and never was," she replied, not in the coy way a girl fishing for more compliments might, but in her usual factual way.

"Not like fancy girls are pretty, or girls in magazine pictures, but you are pretty as any regular woman ought to be."

Now she laughed. "And how pretty is that, exactly?"

Aiden cringed. That hadn't come out as he had meant it to. Christopher would never say something that clumsy to a girl. "Well, a man might not drive his ship onto the rocks upon first seeing you," he said, groping for repair. "But once knowing you, he would certainly long for you after leaving port."

"You are a terrible young Shakespeare." Alice's green eyes sparkled with amusement. "Or Homer, I suppose. But enough of the taxonomy of beauty—show me the treasures!"

He took the bundle out of his bag and set it down on the table and untied the knots. There were thirty or forty pieces of pottery, from coin-sized shards to pieces almost as big as saucers.

"Oh my!" Alice began examining them like a jeweler with a plate of gems. All the pieces were painted with lines and geometrical designs, a few had relief details and one had what looked like part of a man's face molded into it. Though Aiden knew nothing about artifacts or pottery, there was something about these broken bits that gave him a jolt of excitement. He could tell that several of them came from one vessel. Perhaps they could be put back together.

"They're nothing like the modern pots we've seen," Alice said excitedly. "They really might be genuine! See the wear on the surface? And something about the clay itself is different."

"You think they could be from Incas, then?" Aiden asked. "Do you think they came out here to collect the guano?"

Alice held one of the larger pieces up to the light. "They

had millions of people at the peak of their civilization, and it was an agricultural society. They must have needed fertilizer."

Aiden felt a small chill of horror slip back in through the bright afternoon. Who did the Incas send to collect this magic dust? As if reading his mind, Alice looked past him to the brutal yellow island.

"I doubt they would have had permanent operations," she said. "Bringing enough water out would be a problem, for one thing. I think it would have been more like temporary work parties. The Incas had a system where people were required to give some of their labor to the empire every year. Like a tax. That's how they built their cities and temples and pyramids."

She placed the piece reverently in Aiden's hand. "You could be touching something that an Inca touched hundreds of years ago. A sacred pot or ceremonial urn."

"Or his lunch pail?"

"Yes," she laughed. "I suppose so." She nudged some pieces away from the others into a separate pile. "These bits are definitely modern," she said. "Probably just a common broken bowl that your fellow put in to make it seem like he had more."

Aiden could see these pieces were different from the others. The edges were sharp, as if they had recently been broken. And just looking at the pile, he could see three or four pieces that would fit together into a shallow bowl, the same common style one saw everywhere, probably made in local workshops. He turned one piece over and saw letters scratched into it. It looked like the letters *a* and *n*. He picked up another shard and saw there were letters there as well. Not stamped or etched into the wet clay before firing, such as would be made by the potter to sign his work, but scraped into the finished bowl itself with the point of a knife or nail. Perhaps the bowl had belonged to a sailor who had scratched his name into the bottom. He fitted two obvious pieces together and saw what appeared to be parts of words—*ped, Fathe*—perhaps a bit of verse or rhyme. He swept all these bits up and put them in his bag. It would be fun to try to puzzle them out.

He and Alice spent the afternoon looking through the older pieces, sorting them by color or similar design, even piecing a few bits together. They drank sherry and flipped through the books, trying to match some of the designs and decipher the Spanish. It was a surprise when they heard the sound of laughter and shouts coming from the water. The afternoon had passed, and boats were starting to return from the North Island, loaded with the boisterous company from the cricket match. Alice's face darkened, as if an actual cloud had suddenly shadowed them. The carefree lightness vanished from her eyes.

"Thank you so much for bringing me these, Aiden," she said as she wrapped them back up in the dirty cloth. "I will take them to the university in Lima. If they are important, I will see that you are credited."

"I did nothing for credit," Aiden said. "The coolie collected them. Perhaps he has more," he added impetuously. He wanted to see happiness on her face again. "There might even be a tomb, a ceremonial place like in the book— something important. I'll go back tomorrow."

"We are leaving," Alice said. "The day after tomorrow."

"Leaving? But I understood the *Lady May* was not due to load for another week."

"Just our party," she said. "Nicholas and Gil—Nicholas and I and Gilbert. We have—he has—no more work here. We will take a steamship from Pisco to Callao, then spend some time in Lima." She tied the corners of the bundle.

"Must you really go so soon?"

"You would not be eager to leave this place as soon as possible?"

"Yes, of course," Aiden said. "I'm just being selfish to wish for your company." He reached across and touched her hand, which lay protectively on top of the bundle. Alice jerked her hand back as if his were hot. Aiden blushed and quickly sat back. "The three of you," he stressed, "are the only interesting people in this place." He dreaded the thought of languishing here another month or more without them. "And what if there is some important archaeological discovery to be made here—with more pots, and even bones?"

"I'm not an archaeologist."

"You still would know more than anyone here."

"I have no say in where we go or what we do," she said. "Nicholas is the one in charge."

"Perhaps Nicholas and Gilbert would also be interested in examining the site. Gilbert could draw it."

"Nicholas will not go back to the island under any circumstances. He said the coolies tried to kill you."

"It might have been an accident," Aiden said.

"Even so, he will not return. And Gilbert—" She stopped as the steward approached.

"We are nearly finished," she said to him. "Please go tell the coxswain that Mr. Madison is ready to leave."

"You're really the geologist, aren't you?" Aiden said.

Alice looked away. "It is Nicholas's name on the diploma," she replied flatly. "You have brightened many dreary afternoons and now brought me this treasure. I will remember you fondly." They watched the boats splintering off in different directions toward their home ships.

The steward returned. "Pardon, ma'am. The launch is ready."

Alice stood, and Aiden sprang to his feet as well. "Thank you." She waved her hand toward the tea table. "You may clear."

Aiden made a polite, formal bow. "Thank you for a lovely afternoon, Mrs. Brock," he said. "I enjoyed our scientific pursuits."

"My pleasure, Mr. Madison," Alice said. "Goodbye."

22

Aiden got back to the *Raven* just as Christopher and Fish and the crew were returning from the North Island. Everyone was tired and tipsy but in a good mood, even the sailors, for they had spent the day at their own party, with a generous supply of pisco and a whole roasted pig.

"Cricket—what an absurd game that is!" Christopher said as he sank with exaggerated weariness into a canvas deck chair. "You have no idea!"

"It's like baseball, isn't it?" Aiden replied.

"Well, yes, in the way that stale bread is like meat since they both are chewed and swallowed." Christopher wrenched his boots off and put his feet up on a hatch. "A game of cricket goes on twice as long and makes half as much sense. It's boring as hell. It may *be* hell—at least the official sport of hell. If anything will ever cause me to repent my evil ways, it will be the thought of an eternity at a cricket match."

"It wasn't exactly horse racing," Fish agreed.

"It wasn't even snail racing!" Christopher sighed. "They just try to knock some little sticks off of other sticks and then run back and forth. Plus they spent a whole day yesterday flattening out the pitch—that's what they call the playing field—because the pitcher—who is called a bowler—God knows why—has to bounce the ball off the ground. But of course it isn't ground at all, but guano, a fact no one seemed to take into consideration when they were planning the whole thing. So hardly anyone wanted to touch the ball. Mostly, we just drank punch all day."

Clearly, it had not been children's punch. Aiden was worried that Christopher was falling into the drinking habit of this place—which for most, with so little to do, was basically a daylong pursuit.

"So how was your day?" Christopher asked brightly. "You were after some old broken dishes?"

"Yes." The day rushed through Aiden's mind: the scar-faced overseer with his red eyes and striped sweat, the forlorn Buddha, the dying rag pile man, lovely plain Alice waving from the rail, the sweet taste of sherry, the playroom joy of the pottery shards, the stab of Alice's loneliness, his own confused longings, the sadness of impending loss.

"It was fine," he said. "Did you know they're leaving? Alice and Nicholas and Gilbert?"

"Yes. I'm surprised they lasted this long. Not exactly the place for such fine gentlemen. But they did serve us well! I told you friends on a Brockleton ship would be helpful." He glanced around and lowered his voice. "We're getting out next week anyway—maybe sooner!"

"It's certain?" Fich looked suspicious.

"Not ink in the ledger yet, but I'm quite sure." Christopher beamed his most triumphant smile. "This could put our whole trip just under four months! If we can do every trip in four months instead of six, that is one more cargo every year!"

"Cargo?" Aiden stared at him in shock. "You mean guano?"

"Of course guano! We can't carry anything else in a guano ship—you know that. The smell never goes away."

"We are not coming back to this place!" Aiden said.

"Of course not! God no!" Christopher flicked his hands dismissively toward the island. "This was just for the adventure. But we've had it now—adventure and experience and all that—so after this we'll just send the ship with Fish. You and I stay in the comfort of home and manage our empire!"

Fish frowned. This was the first he had heard of this scenario. Aiden could see that Christopher was not only drunk but also in one of his euphoric moods, so there was little chance of any reasonable conversation.

"Excuse me. I must see to the ship." Fish was starting to look more like his serious older brother, Aiden thought. The weight of a captain's responsibility and the dreariness of life here were heavy upon him.

Christopher yawned and smacked dust out of his hair. "I will wash and sleep," he announced to himself. "There are no parties tonight—well, no important ones anyway. God, what a ridiculous sport," he muttered as he got up and weaved unsteadily toward the wash barrel.

Aiden sat on deck and watched the last traces of sunlight vanish from the far snowy peaks. The first stars appeared, and then the Andes began to fade away into darkness. How in the world had he ever come to be in this place?

He considered writing a letter to Elizabeth. But whatever would he say? He thought about her sometimes, pictured sitting with her in the garden, but truth be told, it was the cool green garden that enticed him right now as much as her memory. Was that bad of him? He liked Elizabeth very much, and she had certainly smacked him hard when they first met, but he did not ache for her now. Had she been standing by the rail that afternoon instead of plain Alice, on a wreath of roses like Mary on a holy card, Aiden wasn't sure he would have been any more excited. Alice was older and plainer and treated him with nothing more than sisterly affection. And she was married. He enjoyed being with her. He was always excited to see her. But he never wanted to touch her hair or kiss her. He always wanted to kiss Elizabeth, but now that he was away from her, he did not find himself longing for her. He missed her, of course, but the feelings he had had when he first met her seemed to have evaporated over the months of familiarity. Life never made sense, and even less when you added in women.

But at least the pieces of a broken bowl could be sorted out, he thought. He picked up his bag and tipped out a little pile of broken pieces on the hatch cover. The cat roused herself from the coiled rope where she liked to sleep, stretched lazily, strode over and began to sniff at the pieces. Aiden petted her silky coat and she purred.

"What's all that?" Fish asked as he walked by.

"Just some bits of a broken bowl," Aiden said. "A coolie gave me lots of broken bits—mostly old, but these pieces were mixed in. They're modern. There are words scratched in." He offered a piece to Fish, who examined it closely.

"I imagine all sorts of rubbish from the ships winds up with the coolies," Fish said. "Probably a sailor scratched his name in his dinner plate."

"Probably," Aiden agreed. "How is our ship? All well?"

"The hull is grassy from these idle days. And the men are eager to be off."

"Did you tell them about leaving soon?"

"Not until I know that it's more than Christopher's fancy. Though I do hope it's true." Fish rubbed the back of his neck and looked up at the stars. "I won't do another trip," he said. "I must tell you up front. . . ."

"I never expected you would. What will you do? Go back to lumber?"

"Up and down the coast on my brother's ship—ah!"

"You've got blue-water experience now," Aiden said. "You could be a captain for anyone. Or at least a first mate. We would certainly give you a high recommendation. Which might actually mean something coming from Christopher anyway."

"How do you stand him sometimes?" Fish said. "If you weren't partners, if you didn't have to be in his company, would you still be his friend?"

"I'm not sure Christopher has friends," Aiden said. "He has more like collections of people. Like a little girl has dolls—only we can move our arms and legs on our own. But yes, I do honestly like him. When he isn't being infuriating or stupid or horrible or drunk."

"When is that?"

"Sometimes."

"Do you trust him?"

"In a way."

"You either trust someone or you don't," Fish said.

"I trust him to be how he is."

"Like you trust the shark will bite when there is blood in the water?"

"Something like that, yes."

Fish laughed and went off to complete his inspection. The cat leaped onto the hatch, sniffed around the curious bits of pottery, then settled herself in Aiden's lap. Aiden nudged a dangling paw out of his way and began to piece the puzzle together. Without all the other ancient shards to distract him, it was pretty easy, and within minutes he had most of it assembled. But now the words were really puzzling.

Help. Kidnapped. Father pay riches. Jian Zhang.

What in the world was this? Jian Zhang—was that the name of the coolie who had given him the shards? But how did a coolie know how to write in English? That coolie only spoke a few words. The kidnapped son of a rich family? Here on the guano islands of Peru? That was absurd. Kidnappers anywhere in the world wanted ransom money. Aiden suspected there were many levels of people profiting from the procurement of coolies for this place—from the agents in China to those who arranged their transportation here. If the son of a rich man had somehow been snared up by accident or trickery in China, he should have been able to pay his way out long before he wound up here.

It had to be a joke. And if it wasn't a joke, well, what was Aiden supposed to do? He looked around for Fish, but he was up in the bow. Just then the cat tensed and her yellow eyes went giant with fear. Her fur bristled the way it did before a storm and she gave a weird yowl. The broken pottery pieces began to tremble. Aiden felt the deck vibrate. Then the world fell out from beneath him. The ship lurched sideways and the deck pitched up. Aiden's chair toppled and the pottery pieces skittered all over the deck. The cat dug her claws deep into the flesh of his leg. Aiden looked out toward the sea, thinking a ship had come loose and crashed into them, but he saw nothing. The sea was gone. Fish came running, almost sliding across the steeply pitched deck.

"What's wrong?"

"I don't know!" Fish said.

Suddenly there was a terrible quiet—as if all regular sound had been sucked out of the world. Then the ocean roared and the *Raven* was thrown up into the sky. Aiden fell backward, slid across the deck and crashed into the rail. Coiled ropes unwound and snaked through the air. Aiden tried to get his feet under him, but the deck was heaving so much it was like trying to stand in a racing wagon. He saw only shadows of men in the twilight as they came running, tumbling and grasping at the shrouds. All the stars on the horizon lurched up, like bread crumbs tossed off a picnic blanket.

Time froze. In the bright starlight, he saw the Andes bearing down upon their ship. This was odd, for the mountains were on the opposite side of the ship and didn't usually move. Then he realized it was not a mountain bearing down on them, but a wave. A monster wave, taller than the mountains, rising with impossible force out of the darkness.

The *Raven* was spun hard, pivoting around her anchor like the last child in a game of crack the whip. Rigging lines flapped, and a spar snapped up above. Aiden was thrown up in the air like a stuffed toy. Then he was in the water. The ocean surged and foamed and tumbled around him. A hunk of wood smacked his shoulder, then grazed his ear. He tried to grab it, desperate for anything to help keep him afloat, but it was gone the next instant. Debris swooshed and crashed all around. Salt water burned up his nose and down his throat. He felt a thump across his chest, as if he had been slammed into a tree trunk, then realized it was another ship's anchor chain. He tried to grab hold of it, but it was slick with algae. He did not bother to shout, for who could hear him, and he had no breath to spare anyway. Was the *Raven* sunk? Was every ship sunk? Something smacked hard against Aiden's knee—a shark? But sharks were probably too smart to be here now. Something smooth and wide slid under his arm. A sea turtle, Aiden thought, come to carry him safely to shore! He grabbed hold, pulling his body up over the shell, and grasped frantically for a handhold on a flipper. It wasn't a turtle, of course, but a broad piece of wood—a hatch cover torn from some ship. It was only about three feet square, but enough to help him float. He clung so hard his fingers went numb. After a while—minutes or hours, he could not tell—the violence eased a little. He looked around for a light, but every ship seemed to have vanished. He was still being pelted with debris and whirled around in little eddies that left him dizzy. His limbs grew cold and heavy, but finally he could lift his head enough to get a deep breath.

He felt the acrid sting of guano at the back of his throat—the smell could never have been so fabulous. He must be near the island! This ugliest, most wretched place in the world was now very desirable. A slimy drift of seaweed draped around Aiden's neck. He shuddered and combed it away. Then he could see it, just ahead, the pale guano mountain illuminated by the starlight. But Aiden's relief did not last long. Solid land didn't count for much if he couldn't get to it. The island was ringed by jagged rocks that in the mildest conditions could splinter a rowboat, let alone a man. It was like a bowl of candy guarded by a pack of rabid wolves. He had no idea where he was, and so no idea where he might get ashore. He might find one of the few tiny beaches where the sea lions rested, but would they attack him if he crept up among them? He had seen their yellow teeth and the scars they left on each other. He rested, such as it was, for a few minutes and tried to figure out what to do. He could try to swim back toward the anchored ships—if he had any idea what direction that was. And were there even any ships left? Could the giant wave have sunk them all? Could it have sunk every living thing in the world, like Noah's flood, and he was the only one left?

He heard the surf dangerously close. But he could also hear a change in the sound of the waves that signaled an opening through the rocks. There was no time to consider or doubt. He had to take the chance and swim for land. Aiden could barely feel his arms and legs, but somehow he made them move. It was here or nowhere, he thought as he began to swim toward the invisible beach. He crashed hard against a submerged rock and a sharp pain daggered through his leg, but there was no time to think about it. He could hear the crash of waves upon rocks on either side of him, meaning there might be some channel between them. He swam as hard as he could and soon his hand hit sandy bottom. A wave pushed him forward onto a pebbly beach. Air was everywhere and the land was real. Death loses again, Aiden thought as he collapsed onto the beach.

23

This is a nightmare, Aiden thought as he limped along the narrow beach looking for a path. Any minute I will wake up in my chair on the deck of the *Raven* with Fish laughing at me because I drooled in my sleep. But right now he was terribly awake in a terribly real time and place. He had no idea where he was, but open beaches were so rare on this island that any one of them would have a path leading inland. He just had to find that path, and somewhere up it he would find a way across to Koster's compound. The starlight cast only faint shadows, but he did begin to grope his way up what seemed to be a path. Still, the way was rough, and Aiden often stumbled, which sent lightning bolts through his injured leg. He stopped and vomited a salty bile, then limped on. The path was narrow and slippery, and quite steep at first, but finally it leveled out, and after a little while he saw flickers of light up ahead and realized he was at the edge of the coolie village.

The shacks were dark, but there was a dim orange glow coming from farther in, and he could hear voices. Aiden walked toward the glow, winding his way through the warren until he came to the little square in the center of the village. There were at least fifty men squatting or sitting around a tiny fire. More men stood behind them, pressed against the weathered buildings, squeezed shoulder to shoulder. With their thin bare chests and loose white trousers, they looked like moths. They all fell silent as Aiden walked into the circle of light. Then soft whispers and murmurs began. Every eye was on him.

"Hello," Aiden said dumbly. "I am from a ship. There was a giant wave. . . ."

He couldn't read their faces. Surprise? Pity? Hostility? The fire popped and everyone jumped. Aiden saw a smooth piece of wood bubble in the flames. It was a piece of a ship's spar, the varnish blistering. The fire, he realized, was built from broken bits of ships that had just washed up. Of course—wood in this place was otherwise too rare to waste on a campfire. Maybe the coolies were burning bits of the *Raven* right now, he thought, rejoicing over the wreckage of their oppressors.

"I—I am sorry to bother you," Aiden said. "There was a wave—"

Harsh laughter roared around the square. There was a shout from the back that, even in the unfathomable language, was clearly a taunt. A clod of guano hit his chest. Aiden couldn't see their faces, but he could sense the mood. The wave had not helped their own wretched circumstances, but it had hurt their enemy and so was an occasion to celebrate. Aiden's skin prickled with fear. He remembered the day when he and Nicholas had been harassed with "accidents" and nearly buried in guano. There had been guards around then. Aiden was alone here now. They had every reason to hate him, and they could kill him if they wanted to. A rock hit Aiden on the leg. He flinched. They could torture him if they wanted to—and why wouldn't they want to?—then kill him and dump him into the sea. His body, if it was ever found, would show no more damage than it already wore. He could not fight and there was nowhere to run.

Another rock whizzed by his face, and he ducked. There was more laughter, louder rumblings, more stones. He squared his shoulders and stood ready to fight, which was stupid since he was half lame and totally exhausted—and would still be stupid if he were fit since there were at least a hundred men in the square, and how did one fight against stones anyway?

Then one of the men stood up. He looked like all the others, but something in his posture set him apart. He had a certain grace of movement, a natural authority. He spoke to the group in a firm but conciliatory manner, like a good schoolmaster to unruly students. More angry shouts followed, but he appeared to deflect them with laughter and murmurs of calm. To Aiden, the foreign language sounded like complicated birds—the man could just as well be auctioning off his bones as negotiating his salvation. A thin crescent moon spliced itself into the starry sky. Then the man walked over and stood beside Aiden.

Aiden, to his embarrassment, was beginning to shake uncontrollably. His defender did not say anything, did not even look at him, but simply gripped his arm with a dry, roughened hand. More stones hit him, but they were small, taunting pebbles. There wouldn't be any big stones here, he remembered with sudden relief. Only the beach stones that might have been carried up for building, or small stones from seabird gizzards that may have dropped over the eons. But did seabirds even have gizzards?

He felt his legs wobble. The coolie pulled Aiden's arm around his shoulders and continued to talk to the crowd in Chinese. Though the anger remained palpable, there gradually seemed to be some resolution. His tone, even in the foreign language, sounded both commanding and consoling. There were a few more angry shouts, but also a wave of bitter laughter. Men began to get up and disappear into the dark. The fire was burning down, and they had to be back at the picks and shovels before dawn.

"Come now," the coolie whispered in Aiden's ear. "Say nothing." He dragged Aiden out of the square and back through the maze of narrow lanes. The coolie didn't say anything more until they were well outside the village. Then he eased Aiden down to sit on the ground.

"I am sorry," he said. "I am dishonored for that. Please accept my deep apology."

"No—" Aiden said, shocked to hear the man speaking perfect English. "I mean, thank you—you have done nothing to apologize for."

"Those men are barbarians." He spat. "Unworthy peasants!" He sat down beside Aiden, dropping his arms and forehead onto his knees and breathing heavily.

"Did they want to kill me?"

"Of course."

"What did you say to them?"

The man turned his face, and Aiden saw his eyes glint in the faint starlight. "That killing a white devil is not worth the stain of his blood on this great pile of bird shit," he said.

"Oh. Well—thank you."

"In Chinese, it has more poetry."

"I should probably go now," Aiden said.

"Do not fear these men." He flicked his hands as if shaking off something disgusting. "They are unworthy insects. In China, they would be lucky to empty the night pots from my family's house. Now we must talk quickly. The guards will come soon. They must not see that we talk."

"How is it you speak English?"

"I am the educated man. I come from the noble family. My name is Jian Zhang. I am kidnapped." He spoke quickly, overenunciating the words like someone out of practice who had been rehearsing in his head. "I am sorry—my heart goes very fast now."

Help. Kidnapped. Father pay riches.

"You gave me the pottery pieces," Aiden said.

"Yes."

"How did you know I would find the message?"

"I did not know," Jian said. "It was a chance. I take every chance. I scratch a message inside the water barrels that come to us. I sneak out at night to look for bottles on the shore and I put a message into the bottle. The first piece of bowl I give you in the quarry, I carry that piece tied in my clothing every day for more than one month waiting for a chance. I think I will drop it in the path of a sailor. Sailors come for trade for mummy—maybe one will be curious. Then I see the science men and think this is the best chance. So I beg that you will help me now," Jian went on. "And also I offer the great reward."

Aiden could barely make sense of anything. And he didn't really like a man who thought of other men as unworthy of emptying his piss pot. But Jian Zhang had certainly helped him just now, quite possibly saved his life.

"Who kidnapped you?" he said.

Jian looked around nervously, but the immediate night was still silent and dark. Every lamp in the coolie village had been extinguished. "I sailed from China to bring my sister to San Francisco to be married," he said. "But the man—the husband—was false. This man, Silamu Xie, had me put on a ship and brought here." His voice was pinched as he groped for the English words. "The family of Silamu Xie has bad feelings with my family for one hundred years in China. This marriage was to fix this—to bring our houses and our fortunes together. I am my father's only son. If I am dead, our fortune goes to my sister and so to Silamu Xie."

"So why aren't you dead?" Aiden asked.

"Ah, yes." Jian nodded. "You ask the wise question. If Silamu Xie had me killed, the revenge would be great. This way, he can explain that I was kidnapped without his hand. And I think it is more pleasure for Silamu Xie to have me here as a slave."

"I'm sorry," Aiden said cautiously. "But any man might tell this story to escape the life he has signed on for."

"No man signs for this place," Jian said angrily. "All are brought wrongly. They are promised a job in California for the gold or work on the railroad. Some are simply taken—fishermen or poor farmers. They are locked up in a prison and beaten until they agree to sign the papers. Some are sold by the family to pay off a debt. But you hear that I speak English very well—although not so right now. Also, look at me. You see the other men here. When men come here from China, they have been on a ship for six months. In that ship, they lie the whole time on bare boards. They are crowded like firewood. They cannot move or sit up. They lie in their own waste, in the dark, at the bottom of the ship, always wet and with disease and rats. Many die. The ones who live and come here alive are skinny as the bones of a dead man. And their skin is all covered with sores. But on our journey from China, we slept on cushions with silk sheets. We ate fresh eggs and pork." He ran his hand down the side of his thin belly. "I was a fat man then. My sister teased that I would not find a beautiful wife. After I was kidnapped, I spent only one month in chains. So, compared to the other men, I was fat like a seal when I landed here."

Aiden could see that while compared to any normal person Jian would be considered wasted, in this place he did indeed seem almost robust. His skin did not have the brittle yellow color, his joints were not swollen, his gums were still pink and all his white teeth were still there.

"Also, in China, who will have teachers from England except a rich family?" Jian went on, pressing his case. "I know Shakespeare." He closed his eyes and took a quick breath. " 'To be, or not to be: that is the question,' " he spoke rapidly in a soft monotone. " 'Whether 'tis nobler to suffer—to suffer—arrows—ah—' " Aiden saw that the strain of this desperate confession was wearing.

"Stop," Aiden said. "I believe you." *Hamlet* on the guano mountain after a tidal wave was more than his brain could handle. The story was absurd. The kidnapped son of a wealthy merchant—it was something straight out of Dickens. Aiden lay back and looked up at the stars. There were so many the sky looked like a lace tablecloth. His body felt like stone.

"Did you tell Mr. Koster all this?"

"No coolie may speak to Koster, or even go near him."

"I can talk to him on your behalf—"

"No!" Jian said sharply. "He will not believe. He will

227

make things bad for me. Say nothing to anyone else. Promise this!"

"All right, I promise. But then what do you want me to do?"

"Take me on your ship," Jian whispered. "I must free my sister from this man and restore honor to my family. Take me to San Francisco."

"I could sooner take you to the moon."

"Whatever it costs, my father will pay five times."

"Five times or ten times, I still need Mr. Koster's permission."

"I will hide."

"There is no place to hide."

"The *Lady May* is a big ship. There will be a place."

Aiden leaned up on his elbows. "I'm not aboard the *Lady May*," he said, puzzled. "I'm on the *Raven*."

Jian frowned. "I know the science men come from the *Lady May*. My guard told me."

"The geologists?" Aiden said, gradually understanding. Jian Zhang, always looking for his chance, had observed him with Alice, Nicholas and Gilbert.

"I'm not a scientist. I'm just a friend of theirs," Aiden explained. "I was helping them. I'm on a different ship. The *Raven*. A very small ship. There is no place to hide."

"I will hide in the guano."

"It's impossible. They would know you were missing. They count you before any ship sails."

"Once you are sailing, no one can stop you. They have no cannons."

"You could be whipped just for asking me this!" Aiden

said, looking around nervously. "And then shackled the rest of your days here."

"Then I will jump off the cliff knowing that my death is good. If I do nothing, I will die badly."

At least once a week, a coolie leaped to his death. There would probably be one a day except that the guards were punished for not stopping them.

"I will take a letter for you to San Francisco," Aiden whispered. "I can speak to someone there on your behalf."

"Do you have a sister?"

"I did," Aiden said. "Two. They're gone—dead."

"When I was a boy, ten years old, my father tied a rope around me and dropped me from a bridge into the river. It was the way to make me swim. But I had only fear. Then little Lijia picked flowers. She ran up along the riverside and threw the flowers in the water to float to me. She called to me that the flowers were her tears of love and I must catch them. I reached my arms to catch the flowers and so my arms learned to swim. Do you see? She is the flower of my life."

A bobbing light appeared in the dark distance.

"The guard is coming," Jian whispered nervously, jumping to his feet. "I cannot be found outside our village."

"I will explain to the guard."

"No! Say only that you came ashore from the wave. You climbed up and found this path. You did not come into our village. Please."

"All right."

"You must help me," Jian said. He tensed up like a rabbit about to dart away.

"I will deliver a letter for you. That is all I can do."

The guard shouted from the darkness and the lantern rose higher. Jian ducked and vanished. Aiden quickly brushed his hand across the dusty ground, obliterating his footprints.

"Hello?" the guard called. "Is someone there?"

The light swung across Aiden's face, then a dark shape appeared behind it, only the Negro's eyes visible.

"I am a sailor," Aiden said. The tremble in his voice was not forced. "I was washed overboard in the wave. I hurt my leg. Will you help me, please?"

A large, rough hand grabbed his arm and hauled him to his feet.

24

The sky was just turning blue when Aiden woke. It was not the light that woke him, however, but the dusty steps of two hundred men as they walked past on their way to the mine. He sat up too fast and his head spun. He had been covered with a cotton blanket but was still chilled through, for there was a cool mist that fell on the island at night. He had been sleeping on a reed mat outside a hut. The hut was made of planed lumber, nicer and more sturdy than the twig houses in the coolie village. Aiden vaguely remembered the guard bringing him here last night. None of the coolies looked at him as they passed. Any boldness they may have felt last night had vanished with the bondage of morning. They walked silently and their silence was enormous. Aiden started to get up, but winced at the pain in his knee. It was so swollen it stretched the leg of his trousers. He was also covered in cuts and scrapes from the rocks, with guano dust caked in the drying blood, leaving slimy daubs. His lips were coated with dust. He wiped them as clean as he could on a corner of the blanket. He tore open the knee of his trousers and managed to get to his feet. As the last of the coolie crew shuffled past and their dust settled along the morning path, a Negro guard came toward him and handed him a cup of water.

"*Vámonos.*" The guard pointed at the path. "That way."

* * *

"You're alive!" Christopher cried as Aiden was rowed along-side the *Raven*. "You are, aren't you?"

"I'm no ghost," Aiden said.

It was a glad reunion aboard the *Raven*, with shameless hugs and some all-out tears. With all the chaos, it was almost noon by the time Aiden could get a ride from the island to the *Raven*, so they'd had plenty of time to mourn him.

"Is everyone all right here?" Aiden asked.

"We are now," Fish said. His eyes were red with fatigue.

"I was tumbled from my bed and smashed about the cabin like dice," Christopher said triumphantly. He pointed to a tiny wound on his cheekbone that had been sewn closed with two neat stitches. "So thank God you're alive—for I've been getting no pity at all with everyone thinking you were dead!" He swiped his sleeve across his eyes. "Why aren't you dead anyway?"

Aiden told them very briefly what had happened, leaving out much. He wasn't sure why. But telling them about Jian Zhang would make it too real, and he wasn't sure he wanted it to be real yet. Or maybe it was just because reality had changed so drastically. In spite of the lumps and aches all over his body, the wave now seemed like something that had happened to another person on another planet in another time. The feel of wooden deck under his feet was strange.

"Here, sit." Fish helped Aiden to a crate. "Your leg looks bad."

"I can stand on it," Aiden said. But he couldn't bend it, and sat awkwardly. "The *Raven* is all right—no damage?"

"The rudder is twisted," Fish said. "But nothing we can't fix. And the cat is missing."

"She was on my lap," Aiden said, feeling oddly guilty. Sven the Baby appeared with mugs of sweet tea and the bottle of brandy. Christopher poured a generous measure into the mugs, and Aiden didn't object.

"What about other ships and men?" he asked.

Fish raked his fingers through his sweaty hair. "No one is sure of anything yet. There are two known dead, and eight missing, but that was early this morning and there may be more or less by now. The *Lady May* has become the place for lists and keeping track," he said. "We have a captains' meeting there at four."

"They are all right—on the *Lady May?*"

"Yes, everyone there," Fish said. "What about the island? We can see from here that the loading wharf is damaged—do you know how bad?"

"The pylons looked secure, but most of the cross braces are smashed," Aiden said. "Both the chutes are damaged. One was completely knocked off into the sea. The coolies were at work to salvage it this morning."

Aiden looked out over the anchorage, where every ship buzzed with activity. "I thought—I thought for sure every ship would be sunk." His voice cracked. "Have you ever seen anything like that before? A wave like that?"

"No." Fish rubbed the back of his neck and rolled his shoulders. He had said nothing about his own bashing, but his face was bruised and his hands were leaking blood through bandages. "I've only heard stories. It's thought to come after an undersea earthquake somewhere. I think we got off lucky. This anchorage is so deep. Maybe that absorbed the force."

"Maybe God just loves us," Christopher said, raising the bottle of brandy in a toast. "And wants us to drink lots more before we die."

The afternoon was a time for repair—of both men and ships. Most of the injuries to men were split heads and broken limbs. There were only a handful of surgeons in the fleet, but every ship had someone who could sew up wounds, and many had bonesetters as well. But more essential than doctors were carpenters. A ship could sail with damaged men but not with a damaged hull. The wave had broken masts, torn sails away, blown out portholes and twisted off hatch covers. Everything loose on decks had been swept away. Fish had been diligent about keeping things stowed well despite the calm anchorage, so the *Raven* had lost nothing but a few chairs and lanterns and some laundry.

Throughout the day, messages were relayed from ship to ship with semaphore flags. The good news—a missing sailor returned—was healded with cheers. The bad news—a body found—was greeted with silence. By afternoon, fifteen more men were confirmed dead, three of the missing had been accounted for and three were still lost. It was rumored that as many as thirty ships had serious damage, but only one seemed in real danger of sinking.

Aiden sat uselessly on deck, watching everything from a distance. A chair had been brought up from below, and a crate propped up his leg. Sven the Baby, who had assumed the role of ship's medic, had stitched the gash on Aiden's head, spread a foul-smelling ointment on his other wounds, cut away his torn trouser leg and made a poultice of capsicum and mustard for knee. It burned mightily but did help the swelling go down. They had laudanum for pain in the medicine chest, but Aiden was wary of it and stayed with the more manageable dose of brandy instead. Christopher, who had no compunctions about the opiate and actually had been quite painfully battered, took a dose and slept away the afternoon.

It was annoying to have nothing to do when there was so much to be done. But Aiden couldn't very well hang over the side to help repair the rudder or crawl around belowdecks helping restore order. He tried to read. Alice had given him *On the Origin of Species,* but it was far too dense a read for right now. And evolution seemed suddenly irrelevant anyway. Everyone could die at any minute from all sorts of catastrophes, so what was the point? Tornados, blizzards, drought, famine, awful disease and war, of course—how was it that anyone lasted at all? And why? The people who lived were mostly cruel and awful to each other anyway. If either Darwin or God had the answer in his book, Aiden had not found it yet.

But it was the fate of one man that most concerned him now. What to do about Jian Zhang? His story was crazy, but there was enough feel of truth to it that Aiden couldn't just let it go. Besides, the man had helped him, maybe even saved his life. What was due him now? More to the point, what was possible now? There was absolutely no way to sneak him off the island. Perhaps he could convince Koster to let him take Jian—to buy him, really, for he would have to offer some price. They could take Jian back to San Francisco with them; he could find his sister and go back to his princely life in China. While every other Chinaman here—the peasants and barbarians that Jian considered unworthy to empty his chamber pot—slaved out the rest of his brief life in hell. Aiden was conflicted. Was he thinking more harshly because Jian was a son of fortune?

But what could he do? Certainly he couldn't try to smuggle Jian aboard the ship. Aiden thought again of the man on the rock. The penalty was too real. He felt vomit creeping up his throat again and forced it back down. The sea was uneasy, with low, choppy waves that seemed to come from every direction. Fish appeared and sat on the hatch cover beside him.

"I'm going to the *Lady May* now for the captains' meeting," he said. "Shall I take a message to Mrs. Brock for you?"

"Mrs. Brock? Oh, Alice—yes." Aiden was filled with a sudden longing and also an urge to cry. "Tell her that I am well and hope to visit with her soon." He took a deep breath and looked away.

"Are you all right?" Fish frowned.

Aiden sat up and tried to look all right. "I'm tired, is all. I didn't sleep well."

"I wouldn't think so." Fish combed his fingers through his tangled hair. Aiden noticed that the blond locks that so enchanted the native girls were now thinning and streaked with gray. "You've had a rough go," Fish said. "But there is more on your mind besides all the near-death parts."

"Do you read my mind now?" Aiden said.

Fish shrugged. "No one's mind is so different," he said. "We all want the same things: safe home, love and dinner."

"Only that? A pretty wife and fat babies?"

"As long as she's nice and the babies don't howl all the time."

"Isn't that what we adventured out to escape? When you

come home from a timber run, I don't recall home and hearth being the main attraction."

"This is true." Fish laughed.

Aiden looked out over the harbor. "I was wondering about the coolies," he said. "Do you know, is it possible for a coolie to buy out his indenture? Or to have someone buy it for him?"

"You mean pay a sum of money and the man be allowed to leave?"

"Yes. What if, for example, one of them found a gold nugget while digging the guano—just say."

"It would be taken away from him," Fish said. "And he would be put back to the digging, poor as ever."

That was awfully true.

"Well, what if a coolie had relatives, let's say, who came and offered Koster the price of the contract to buy his freedom?"

"Has someone approached you about this?" Fish said suspiciously.

"I was just wondering," Aiden said.

"Whatever you're thinking—don't."

"They aren't slaves. Supposedly."

"What happened on the island? Did a coolie speak to you?"

"All I asked was if you know whether one can buy out their indenture. If you don't know, just say so," Aiden said, more snappish than he intended. He wasn't exactly sure why he didn't want to tell Fish more. "I thought you might know. That's all."

"Fine. Then the answer is, I don't know."

"Fine. That's it, then."

"No, it isn't." Fish glanced around to be sure no one was nearby to hear them, then leaned in close. "You know I abhor this business," he said quietly. "And I will never sail this trade again. But these aren't just rich men with a stake here—these are governments. This is the wealth of nations. Peru would go bankrupt without the guano. The economy of Europe could collapse." Fish wiped the sweat from his face with both hands in a scoop, like a monk in supplication. "I know something of you by now," he said.

"Of course you do," Aiden said. "We've been on a small ship for three months. We know every man by the smell of his farts by now."

"I know what happened in Seattle," Fish said seriously. "The Swedish Navy is a small world. News travels fast between the logging camps and ports."

"I don't know what you're talking about."

"I'm talking about smallpox vaccine stolen for some Indians. About a man killed in the theft and his killer on the run. And about you arriving in Seattle the day after it all happened, desperate to leave and wounded from a fight."

"Seattle is always full of busted men desperate to leave," Aiden said.

"You were well known from Napoleon Gilivrey's fight circuit."

Aiden looked out over the messy ocean and wished to be any other creature but a man.

"Don't worry," Fish went on quietly. "None of us have said a thing and no one will. You are our shipmate—and friend."

"It wasn't murder," Aiden said. "It was just a man getting dead in a fight."

"I wouldn't have sailed with a murderer. But right now I think I might be better off with a murderer than a man who has shown a dangerous heart."

"Dangerous?"

"A tender heart is dangerous."

"My heart is not tender—it's angry."

"I might agree with what you did for the Indians," Fish went on. "But listen to me carefully now. I am not a missionary. I am a practical man. And this much I do know: any ship trying to help a coolie escape will be found out. You know what they do to the coolie—but there is punishment for the ship as well. They will take back the guano and revoke the license. A guano ship can never carry another cargo; the smell is sunk forever in the timbers. You've smelled it—you know it never goes away. So you have no cargo, no profit— plus the debt you took on—no license and a useless ship. And besides that, I would be blacklisted as a captain. Who will pay off the crew? Not Mr. Worthington. This endeavor is yours and Christopher's alone. He made that very clear, in writing, with two lawyers and lots of signatures."

"What if it were your brother trapped here?"

"Every man on this ship is a brother to me, and I will not risk their futures. They have their children and the children of the dead to care for. They have the old and the cripples. We came on this voyage prepared to die in a storm or ship-wreck like any sailor. But we are not ready to risk everything for a wrongheaded action, no matter how honorable it might seem."

"Captain, sir?" Gustav stood at the gangway. "The launch is ready."

Fish nodded. "Yes. One minute." He turned back to

Aiden. "We are caught up in an ugly business. Promise me you will not be foolish."

"You don't trust me?"

"I do trust you. That is the problem. I trust you to be how you are."

"Very well. I promise you," Aiden said, "I will not save any coolies." It was a cruel way to say it, and Aiden knew it and felt bad. But the blow had been struck. Fish stiffened, stood up and turned away.

"Forgive me," Aiden said. "I've had too much time to think this afternoon, sitting around idle."

Aiden watched the boat row away. Nothing was solved, but how could it ever be? It seemed everything he touched turned foul.

25

All the next day the sound of hammers and saws drowned out the birds and sea lions as everyone worked to repair their industry. Broken masts were salvaged from the shores of the islands, and lumber was scooped from the sea, where random bits floated in the filthy waves. Besides the obvious physical damage to the ships, the wave had left behind a thousand small catastrophes. Chickens and livestock had all been washed off the decks. Water barrels were smashed. In this eternally rainless anchorage, hatches had been left open to keep away the damp, so the wave had flooded the holds and soaked tons of food.

Even with all the damaged ships, repairing the wharf was the main priority. The guano was already piling up in the corral, and one new ship had already arrived just that morning, with more certainly on the way. Every carpenter and sailor who could be spared was put to work on the wharf. Sailors who were used to mending sails made quick work of repairing the canvas chutes. Even some of the coolies were lent to the effort, mostly to fetch and carry and haul.

Since the *Raven*'s damage had been only to the rudder and only a few men were needed to work on that, Fish sent six men ashore in the morning to help work on the wharf, and Aiden rode along with them. He had promised Jian that he would say nothing to Koster, but he thought he might still talk to the man without telling him the particulars. What was a coolie actually worth? There had to be a price. There was always a price. The *Raven*'s launch dropped him off at the dock. It had been thoroughly smashed by the wave but was already rebuilt enough to walk on, if one took very big steps over the missing planks. The stairs to Koster's compound had also been shattered, and a carpenter was at work on them.

"Mr. Koster's not here," he told Aiden as he drove a huge nail down with three powerful blows. "He's moved aboard one of the ships until things are settled." His accent was Irish, his complexion pale, but the back of his neck was dark and charred to turtle skin.

"His house was damaged?" Aiden asked. "All the way up there?"

"No," the man laughed. "He's just fearful to be stuck up there on his cliff with no escape." The carpenter waved toward the broken steps. "Coolies are meek little men for the most part, but when they come up a madness, they can't be stopped. There've been mutinies on the ships, you know, on the way from China. I've heard it firsthand. You can put a sword through their hearts, an axe in their skulls, and still they'll keep coming when they're in the madness. Even with those big blackie drivers, I suspect a mad enough pack of coolies could pull them down, whip or no whip. This is the truth." He held a board against the others, measuring the length with just a practiced eye. "Though why the buggers don't rampage and come murdering every day, I don't know," he said as he began to saw. "They know soon enough how it is here. They know they'll none ever leave. None but those who jump." He fitted the board into place. "Those ones we do respect."

"What do you mean, respect?"

The carpenter looked Aiden up and down, then ducked his head and turned back to his work. "Sorry, sir, speaking out of turn."

How was he suddenly a "sir"? Aiden wondered. He wore a cotton shirt and canvas trousers—not a common sailor's garb, but nothing fine either. His hands were brown and roughened—not beaten as a sailor's hands, but not a gentleman's either. What had marked him as a "sir" to this man?

"Please speak freely," Aiden said.

The carpenter glanced around to see if anyone else was within hearing. "It's just—a man oughtn't to take it," he said. "No other race of man would work and live this way. They tried here with the natives, the blackies, even the Irish. Think on that, eh! Even the Irish! It would be one thing if there was some hope to come away at the end. Even your slaves in America had some kind of hope. Or at least women. But this place . . ." The carpenter looked away and shook his head. "A man who's any kind of a man ought to die instead. 'Tisn't a godly way to think, sir." He shrugged and picked up his hammer. "But it's the way most feel."

"But some do leave in the end," Aiden said. "Some do finish the time and come away."

"If you say so, sir." The carpenter pounded down another nail. "I'm sure Mr. Koster will come ashore sometime this morning," he went on, clearly wanting to get off the topic.

"Yes. Thank you." Aiden limped along the rocky shoreline toward the wharf. Would I slave or would I jump? When he and Maddy had been starving on the prairie at the end of winter, with no hope in sight, he had thought about ending their lives. It was the difficulty of actually doing it that

243

had stopped him, more than courage or hope. There was no cliff nearby to jump from, nor enough water in the creek to drown in; no bullets for the gun, and he was too weak to trust a knife. Women on the prairie sometimes drank lye, but that was a slow and horrible death. And they had no lye anyway. There were no trees tall or sturdy enough to hang from. He shuddered and pushed away the memory.

At the wharf, repairs were under way at a furious pace. Sailors dangled from boatswain's chairs on either side, prying off broken boards and hammering on new ones. On top of the wharf, a few coolies were helping to get the canvas chute back into the braces. Aiden looked around for Jian but didn't see him.

"You're with the *Raven,* aren't you?" the harbormaster said brusquely as he appeared suddenly beside Aiden. "She's a small ship?"

"Yes." Aiden offered his hand. "I'm Aiden Madison. I'm one of the owners—"

"Yes, yes." The man gave his hand a quick shake, then took out a small notebook and pencil from his pocket.

"What's her draft, fully loaded?"

"I don't know."

"Sound?"

"Excuse me?"

"Is she sound?" he said impatiently. "Was she damaged in the wave? Is she able to load?"

"Load the guano?"

"No, the gold dust," he said sarcastically. "The wharf will be repaired enough to load a small ship tomorrow. I can't risk a bigger ship yet. I don't know what the bottom is like. The wave could have dredged up sand and muck. My men are sounding the depth now, but I can't risk a ship being grounded. You're high up the list anyway—certainly have some well-placed friends. Can you be ready?"

"Yes," Aiden said eagerly. "I will ask our captain, but I'm quite sure we would be ready. I will go now and send back word immediately. Thank you!"

The stressed harbormaster turned away, scribbling in his little book as he strode off. When Aiden got back to the *Raven*, the sailors were all lying about the deck, napping in hammocks or on beds of coiled rope, crowded close in the scant squares of shade from the canopies. Two new kittens were sleeping peacefully atop two of them. They were a gift from Alice, who had departed that morning. Fish was on the quarterdeck.

"How is our ship?" Aiden asked excitedly. "Could we be ready tomorrow, do you think? Strong enough for a voyage home?"

Fish's eyes grew wide. "Tomorrow? What do you mean?"

Aiden grinned. "The harbormaster asked if we could be ready to load tomorrow."

"Are you serious?"

"The wharf can only handle a small ship. Could we be ready?"

"Yes—oh, shoot me, yes! The rudder is fixed. There are some small things left, but the men would work with broken legs and bloody stumps to be gone from here."

"Then send word to the harbormaster."

Fish sprang to his feet. "Gustav! Muster the crew—everybody!"

Aiden got up clumsily, his knee stiff now after all the walking. "Where is Christopher?"

Fish's smile vanished. "In the cabin. He hasn't come out all day. He's in one of his moods."

"I'll see to him," Aiden said, but did not immediately get up. After months together on a small ship, everyone was used to Christopher's moods, but Fish's frown and tone told Aiden that it was more than ordinary melancholy.

Christopher lay on his bunk, curled on his side, facing the wall. Sweat had bloomed in the hollow of his back between the shoulder blades, then drifted down as he lay, making a stain the shape of India. The bottle of brandy and the bottle of laudanum sat on the little table beside his bed. Aiden had marked both with scratches in the glass, and both were at the same level they had been last night. It was both a good and a bad sign. Although he had taken it yesterday for his pains, Christopher generally scorned laudanum as a woman's medicine. And despite his fondness for the drink, he did not use it in his melancholy moods. In those times, he could sink without assistance.

"What are you doing?" Aiden poked him hard in his damp shoulder. "It's stinking hot down here."

"Go away."

"No."

Christopher did not move. Aiden sat down on his own bunk. He looked around the little cabin, trying to imagine what it must have been like in here when the wave hit. Something like being in a packing crate rolling down a hill. Besides the swollen nose and black eye, most of Christopher's bruises were deep purple lines, from slamming into edges.

"No one is in the mood for your moods," Aiden said. "Everyone has had a time of it. You're being a baby."

"You're a bastard—go away."

"No."

"I mean it."

"No. And I mean it too."

"Shut up." Christopher buried his face into the pillow. "I can't bear another day in this place."

"Then we will leave tomorrow," Aiden said without fanfare.

"Don't tease."

"Barring unforeseen complications—but we are on the docket."

"I will nail myself to the mast to make it so!" Christopher moaned. "Or do the keelhauling thing. Whatever is required. I will do anything to escape this place."

"Good of you to offer," Aiden said. "But you won't have to. If any ship can load tomorrow, it will be ours." Christopher sat up, and Aiden explained their good fortune.

"We could make it home by Christmas!" Christopher said.

"Not likely," Aiden interrupted. "The wind is against us going north. And we will be heavy. Fish says two months would be good. So late January, maybe February."

"Oh well, I suppose after this place every day will be Christmas."

26

Despite the choking clouds of dust, there was an almost festive mood aboard the *Raven* the next day as they loaded the guano. As wretched as the work was, once it was done, they would finally be leaving this place. Bag after bag slid down the chute onto the cargo nets, which were then hoisted up, swung over the deck and lowered through the hatches into the hold. Machinery made the job much easier, but down below the men still had to move the heavy bags around to trim the weight. Guano was a tricky cargo. It had to be kept dry. It could not even touch the sides of the hull, for it would pull moisture through the timbers like a sponge. Once wet, the guano would spoil. Worse, it could grow so heavy that it could sink the ship. It might even explode. No one was exactly sure what conditions led to exploding, but it was known to happen. Fumes from the ammonia could build up, and whole crews could be overcome. There were stories of men dying where they fell within minutes. The guano was even said to be a different kind of weight in a ship's hold. Fish wasn't sure how a hundred tons of guano could differ from the same weight of grain, but the captains all agreed it did. The *Raven* had special platforms in the hold to keep the guano well out of the bilgewater. Strong cargo nets would keep the sacks from shifting too much in heavy seas and allow crucial ventilation all around.

There was nothing for Aiden or Christopher to do but

stay out of the way. Christopher accomplished this easily by having himself invited to spend the day aboard another ship. But Aiden spent the day on the island. Jian had to have seen the *Raven* loading, or at least known about it. Even in so tightly controlled a place, information always had a way of traveling. Aiden was sure Jian was clever enough to find a way to get a letter to him. No coolie could walk right up and hand Aiden anything, of course, but he might surreptitiously leave it in a place where he knew Aiden would find it. So he walked a slow, regular loop from the wharf up to the top of the loading area, pausing each time to rest for a few minutes on some crates near one of the side tracks, where it would be easiest for a coolie to drop something for him. Whenever he saw the scar-faced guard, Aiden paused, giving the man opportunity to say something or hand him something, but all day long there was nothing.

Aiden still didn't know if he believed Jian. He had given Fish his word that he would not interfere with the coolies, but even without that promise he wasn't sure what he could, or would, do. While he pitied Jian, of course, he did not like him. In Jian's original world, he would be just another arrogant rich man, despising people like Aiden.

The day passed with excruciating slowness. The noise was constant and deafening. Tackle blocks squeaked, guano carts rumbled and, as always, the birds screeched constantly overhead. The canvas chute swayed and creaked in its braces as the bags of guano slid down. Sometimes the canvas sagged and the bags would pile up, so men had to climb up the scaffolding and poke the chute to unblock it. Around noon the braces actually collapsed, and the full chute tumbled precariously over the side of the wharf, like a clumsy python with an overweight pig in its belly. It took over an hour and required every available man to wrestle the chute back up into place, then another hour to shore up the scaffolding and get it all working again. It was an annoying delay that pushed the *Raven*'s departure awfully close to the turning tide. The storm had indeed dredged up sand close to shore. The harbormaster and Fish had both looked at the soundings and agreed that when fully loaded the *Raven* would probably still have clearance at low tide, but it would be close. It was not a chance anyone wanted to take.

There was still no message from Jian. Aiden felt mostly relieved—really, what more could he do? When he got back to San Francisco, he would go to the Chinese Merchants Association, tell them the story and let them sort it out. The cargo kept coming and the *Raven* sank lower and lower in the water. By late afternoon, the hold was full and the men were beyond exhausted. But finally it was done. The men closed and battened down the hatch covers. They hauled up buckets of water to rinse themselves and wash down the decks. A signal flag was hoisted up the mast to announce their departure, and aboard the German ship where he had sheltered for the day, Christopher folded his hand of whist, drank the rest of his sherry and made his farewells. The harbormaster and Fish signed and stamped some papers. The launch returned Christopher. He climbed up the boarding ladder and sprang nimbly over the side. The deck was still slick and he slipped, laughing like a child sliding on a frozen pond.

"Homeward, lads!" he cried out. "Let's heave away and haul about and all of that!" The men gave a cheer, despite their stinging eyes, cracked lips and sweaty fatigue. Who could feel bad, after all? This place was finally done. Nothing ahead but the open sea and homeward journey. Two months' sailing, less if they were lucky, and they would all be home. To wives and children and friends; to spend their good money on toys, dresses, false teeth for grandmothers and new boots. Gustav would get married and buy his bride a little house. Sven the Baby and three of his friends were planning to pool their money and buy their own lumber ship. Twenty new futures would blossom from the profit of this journey. And in China, hundreds of futures would vanish as more young men were tricked, sold or kidnapped into this hell.

The sailors cast off the mooring lines. The towboats approached and took their lines. Fish stood on the quarterdeck, supervising their departure. The tide was starting to go out, so everyone was eager to get under way. Guano dust had settled on the sails and puffed off in stinging clouds as the canvas was unfurled. The sailors swore with annoyance but stayed at their ropes.

"That's it, then, we've done it!" Christopher leaned against the rail beside Aiden. "All we have to do now is sail home and tally up our profits."

"Yes," Aiden said. But how should that tally be made? he wondered. If a five-pound sack of guano could keep a hundred people from starving, and two hundred coolies each dug five tons a day, but one coolie died for every thousand tons, what was the final price of a man's life? Aiden would never know how to work this math. And so he pushed it out of his head. He could not change the system any more than he could change the tides.

The *Raven* creaked away from the wharf, and Aiden felt a wash of relief. There had been no message from Jian, so no duty left to be done. But as he looked at the widening gap of water, the relief vanished. He felt uneasy. This did not make sense. Jian Zhang had spent every minute of his life on this island figuring out ways to escape. He had to have known the *Raven* was loading today, and if he had wanted to get a letter to Aiden, he would have found a way. That could mean only one thing: Jian had never intended to rely on any letter for his salvation.

"Excuse me," Aiden said to Christopher. "I must go tend to something."

"What's the matter?" Christopher looked at him and frowned. "You look like you've seen a ghost."

"No," Aiden said. He would welcome a ghost. "I just—I have to check something."

Aiden hurried to the companionway and slid down the ladder. The first deck, where everyone lived, was easy to search, and he swept it in a few minutes, every cupboard, cabin and locker. There was no place for anything bigger than a mouse to hide. Besides, how could Jian have slipped aboard unseen? The loading hatches to the cargo hold had all been sealed, but there was an access hatch in the stern from this deck. Aiden opened this and crept a few steps down the ladder.

"Jian Zhang?" Aiden peered through the haze of guano dust. The only light came from the deck level behind him, and it was so dim he could barely see ten feet into the hold. He pulled his kerchief over his mouth, but the caustic dust still made him choke. "Are you here? Come out. I know you are here." He heard nothing but the creak of timbers and a gentle squeak of the wooden pallet frames settling under the weight of the guano.

"You must come out. We will not sail with you aboard." Aiden tried to make his voice strong, but it sounded pinched. How could Jian have snuck aboard with so many people around? There were a hundred other reasons why he wouldn't have been able to get a message to Aiden. He couldn't be here. But somehow Aiden knew he was. What wouldn't I do myself for a chance to rescue my own sister? he thought.

"Please," Aiden said. "I can help you if you come out now!"

There was a small sound, a scuffling like a mouse creeping over the sacks.

"You will take me?" The voice came from beneath the guano very close by. It was choked and faint, but steady.

"I will get you back to the island before they find you are missing," Aiden said. In the next minute, there was a chance. "And I will get word to your sister. I swear. But you must hurry!"

There was a long silence, then he saw Jian's slight figure edge out from behind the sacks of guano.

"You can jump into the water," Aiden said, trying quickly to think up a plan. "We will say that you fell off the wharf. You will . . . hold on to a pylon . . . and . . . and I will see you there by chance as our ship pulls away! With so much noise from the loading, no one heard you calling for help!"

"Your men will see me jumping off."

"My men will say nothing," Aiden assured him. But what about the twenty men rowing the towboats? They would certainly notice a man jumping off the deck of the *Raven*.

Aiden groped for a new plan. "I will say you were helping us load and were overcome with the fumes. You fainted and fell into the hold, and I just found you now as you were climbing out."

"No coolie ever helps load a ship," Jian said. He did not sound like a man pleading for his life. He sounded like a patient nanny trying to explain things to a stupid child. "There is no story."

Aiden rushed ahead with a new idea. "I will say I asked you to bring me more pottery bits. I will tell Koster that I asked you to come aboard because I wanted more Inca pottery—for a museum."

"And where are these pieces that I brought you?" Jian said.

Aiden's heart sank. Alice had taken all the authentic shards with her to Lima, and the others had been lost in the wave. The ship turned and the afternoon sun beamed through the portholes on the upper deck. The light spilled through the open hatch and striped the dusty air with a cruel brightness. Jian's body was coated white with guano dust, but his sweat carved out the lines of his skeleton.

"I can't take you," Aiden said. "I'm sorry." Was there actually some place he could hide Jian where he would not be found? Back below the guano in the bilge? The *Raven* was at least twenty minutes from sailing freely—what if they were ordered to stop? Once the alarm bell was sounded, everyone in the anchorage would know that a coolie had escaped. What would the other ships do? The captains all depended on this trade for their livelihoods. Even if a few might be sympathetic, would they risk their own futures? They were already at the lowest levels of the shipping world. Where would they sail if they were banished from the guano trade? A couple of well-rowed launches could easily overtake the lumbering *Raven* under her harbor sails. Assisting in the capture of an escaped coolie would gain a ship favor in loading for the future, favor worth thousands of dollars a year.

"The guards will discover you are missing. They must already be counting. I cannot change the numbers."

"I have chosen my fate," Jian replied.

"Well, you can't choose mine!" Aiden felt angry, feeble, tricked, annoyed, desperate and resentful all at once. "If they find you aboard, they will take our cargo and our ship. We will lose everything."

"I am offering you my fortune."

"I have a fortune right now in this ship!"

"I saved your life," Jian said sharply. "In the mine, when the guano came down. And the night of the wave, when the others wanted to kill you."

"Or maybe you were the one getting everyone riled up against me in the first place!" Aiden said. "How do I know? Maybe it was you who caused the slide yourself and only warned me to make me beholden. You said how you were always planning."

Aiden heard the creak of sails being raised and felt the ship lurch as the first of them caught the wind. Perhaps Jian would not be missed in time. Perhaps Aiden would not have to decide. Delicate motes of guano dust whirled in the dim light.

"They will put me on the rock," Jian said softly.

"No." He remembered the sparkling little fishes darting about in the water, feasting on tattered bits of skin grated off the still-living man. "We can think of something."

"I made a rope," Jian said. "Out of scraps of cloth I found

on the beach after the wave. I hid the rope beneath the wharf. That is how I climbed down onto your ship. The rope is still there."

There was no possible explanation now.

"No one will find it," Aiden said. Of course someone would find it—and know immediately what it was for. "How did you climb aboard, even then?" Aiden asked. "The guards are always watching."

"Last night I made cuts in the frame that holds the guano chute," Jian said. "When it broke today and all the men were busy to fix it, I climbed down the rope, then through an open hatch."

It was a brilliant plan. It had worked perfectly. Almost.

"Aiden?" Christopher's voice came from the deck above. "Aiden, where are you? Are you there? Where have you gone? Fish is asking for you. He wants to be sure you're aboard before we sail."

"I'm here," Aiden called. Christopher's face appeared over the hatch, peering down and blinking his eyes against the dust.

"What are you doing down there?"

Aiden hesitated. Christopher would not see Jian unless he actually stuck his head down the hatch, which he was certainly not about to do.

"I'm just checking the cargo," Aiden said.

"Checking? For what?"

Jian could easily wiggle back down below the pallets of guano, down to the center of the ship, and hide. The ship was moving; no bell had sounded.

"Aiden, is something wrong?" Christopher pressed.

He could help this man escape. But why? Why him and not any of the other two hundred? Bread for the world and a fortune in his own purse. Aiden blinked against the stinging dust.

"Tell Fish"—Aiden looked up at Christopher—"tell the captain—" His voice caught in his throat and he coughed to clear it. "Tell the captain to come here. Tell him come quickly."

"Is something wrong?"

"Please just go—tell the captain."

"Yes. All right."

Aiden heard Christopher's boot soles scrape as he turned. Good leather had a unique sound. Everything about the rich was different. Even when you didn't know what it was exactly that was different, you knew it was something. The smell of a body that ate good food, the sound of their clothing as they moved. You could probably dig up bones from ancient times and know who was rich or not, Aiden thought.

"I'm sorry," he said to Jian. "I have no choice."

"Of course you have a choice!" Jian said bitterly. "You choose to kill me."

What other endings could there be now? Aiden thought. Angels might appear—or elves. Sweat ran down his face, stinging his eyes.

"If you will not help me, then you must kill me," Jian said. "Do not let them put me on the rock. You must have guns on a ship. But a knife will do—if you cut well and fast. Here"—Jian stretched out his neck and tapped the veins in his throat—"you must cut much deeper than you think."

"Shut up! Stop talking!" Aiden turned away.

"Kill me quickly," Jian said. "This much favor I have the right to ask."

"Aiden?"

Fish came to the hatch.

"I'm here," Aiden said.

"What are you doing in the hold? What's wrong?"

"A coolie—" Aiden hated himself already. "A coolie has hidden in the hold."

In the Bible, the end of the world went on for a whole book. But the real end of the world, Aiden knew, would never be more than a paragraph or two. The real end of the world would just be small things piled up.

Fish shouted out some commands in Swedish. Aiden heard two sets of boots leaping immediately down the companionway ladder and running toward them.

"Will he come out peacefully?" Fish asked.

Peacefully? Aiden blinked. What was Jian going to do? For one thing, he was trapped like a rat. For another, the sailors were twice his size, with hands strong enough to snap one of his arms if they wanted to. His nerves already stretched, Aiden had to strangle back laughter.

"He will come out," he said, his throat so constricted he could barely talk. "But can you—is there something you can do?"

"I will ask for mercy," Fish said. "Koster knows there is objection to the rock."

Objection, Aiden thought. What a polite word. "He speaks English. He says he was kidnapped. . . ."

"Stop," Fish said. "It doesn't matter what he says."

Gustav and Jonas appeared at the hatch. Jian climbed slowly up out of the hold. In the slanting sunlight, his skin sparkled as if coated with diamond dust. It was the guano, though, infinitely more valuable. Each sailor took hold of one of his arms, recoiling at first at the slipperiness of guano and sweat on his skin. They looked to Fish to tell them what to do. They already knew what had to be done and what would happen next, but a captain's command was an order and therefore absolution.

"Bring him." Fish barely looked at Jian. Gustav and Jonas followed him up onto the deck with Jian between them, each holding one of his wrists. Aiden came last. Most of the sailors were in the rigging and unaware of anything going on, but the few on deck all began to talk excitedly.

"Quiet," Fish commanded.

"Jesus Christ!" Christopher said. "What is a coolie doing on our ship?"

"Be quiet," Aiden whispered sharply. "Please say nothing."

"Is he a stowaway? Where was he?"

"Nothing. I beg you."

On the island, the alarm bell began to sound. Jian had been discovered missing. So they would have found him anyway. The choice would have been taken from him anyway. Did that make him less a Judas? The *Raven* was only about forty feet from the wharf. The men in the towboats stopped rowing, looking back and forth between ship and wharf, awaiting orders.

"Keep your pace!" Fish called to them. "No slack." The wind was against them and would push the *Raven* back toward the wharf if they stopped towing. Koster and two Negro guards came out to the end of the wharf.

"Halt the ship!" Koster shouted.

"I cannot, sir," Fish replied.

Jian stood silently with his head bowed. His body wavered slightly, like one of Daisy's dolls when she tried to make it stand alone.

"Hold him fast, Captain," Koster shouted to Fish. "Don't let him jump!"

Jump? Where would that get him? Aiden thought. It wasn't like he could swim anywhere. Then he realized what Koster meant. Jian might try to drown himself, and Koster did not want such an easy death for him. Gustav and Jonas were still holding Jian's arms.

"Halt your ship!" Koster shouted. "That is a command! You must return that coolie at once!"

"I cannot stop my ship here," Fish shouted. "It is dangerous. I will heave to in the harbor. You may send a boat for the coolie, Mr. Koster."

"Drop your anchor, then!" Koster demanded. "I insist you stop at once!"

Even from this distance, Aiden could see Koster's face was red with fury and his round little body was quivering with rage.

"Pull us on!" Fish called to the towboats. "Pull ahead!"

Even Aiden knew they couldn't drop an anchor this close to the wharf. There wasn't enough room to play out the chain. Besides, dropping an anchor and hauling it up again would take time. Fortunately, the towboats were manned by sailors from other ships who understood the situation. They kept up their rowing, and the *Raven* continued to inch out into the harbor. It was like two worlds were going on at once, Aiden thought. The big world of the ship, with men scampering along the ratlines and tending to the sails, and the little world here on the deck, where one man's life was counting down as surely as the tide.

"What a poor, wretched creature," Christopher said, stepping closer to examine Jian. He had not seen any of the coolies since the first day they had visited the island, which had been the only day for Christopher. Even then, he had never seen one this close. Jian lifted his head and looked directly at Christopher. Aiden thought he saw recognition, maybe calculation, in Jian's eyes. In another world, they would be equals, maybe friends.

"Please, sir," Jian said in his most carefully enunciated English, "may I have a drink of water? I am very thirsty. I would be most grateful."

Christopher and the sailors nearby were all startled to hear him speak English. "Um—yes. Of course," Christopher said, unnerved. "Someone get him water."

Sven the Baby was closest to the scuttlebutt. He pulled up the dipper, but then hesitated. He looked at his shipmates. No one spoke. The men looked down at the deck, folded their arms and shifted from foot to foot.

"Well, come on," Christopher said. "What's wrong?"

Aiden knew what was wrong. There were usually tin cups tied to the barrel, but they had been lost in the wave, so the men had all been drinking from the one dipper. They did not want the coolie to drink from it. It was the same way in the logging camp—the Negroes and Mexicans always had their own dippers. He ought to do something, Aiden thought, but could not think of what. He was tired of thinking. Fish was too busy handling the ship to notice the standoff.

"You're not afraid of him, are you?" Christopher went

on, oblivious to the men's real fear. "Here, give me that." He took the dipper from Sven and carried it back to Jian. "Give him a hand free to drink it." Christopher looked at Jonas. The sailor let go of Jian's arm.

"Thank you, sir." Jian took the dipper and raised the water to his cracked lips.

Aiden saw the tiniest twitch ripple through Jian's body and felt the back of his own neck prickle. He had learned to see this motion—sense it, really—in the lumber camp fights. It was a small tightening of neck muscles in his opponent, a subtle shift in posture that showed when he was about to attack even before the attacker knew it himself. It was this sense that gave Aiden an advantage against bigger and stronger fighters. But this time Aiden was not quick enough. Everything happened so fast. Jian swung the dipper at Gustav, smacking him hard in the forehead. The dipper was light but the blow was vicious and startling. It split the skin, and blood ran down into Gustav's eyes. Gustav let go of Jian's arm. Jian spun around and leaped onto the man's back, throwing both arms around him in a bear hug as if trying to wrestle him to the ground. What a stupid thing to do, Aiden thought. Jian was half Gustav's weight. Why not just jump overboard while he had the chance? But Jian Zhang was not intending to drown.

Gustav, like most sailors, wore a knife in a sheath on the middle of his back. Here, it was always handy to grab with either hand, but out of the way when climbing the rigging or hauling ropes. Jian grabbed this knife. He slashed upward, cutting Gustav from the small of his back to his shoulder. An arc of blood spattered on the freshly rinsed deck, and

Gustav staggered forward. Jian swung his other arm into Christopher's side and kicked at his knee. As Christopher crumpled to the deck, Jian grabbed hold of his hair with his left hand and thrust the knife up against his throat with his right.

Only seconds had passed. The fallen dipper was still rolling back and forth like an abandoned toy.

"Get back!" Jian shouted at Aiden. "I will kill him!"

"Jian, no!" Aiden raised his hands. "Don't do this."

"This ship will go now!" Jian shouted. "Now or I will kill!" Christopher's blue eyes were wide with surprise, but he was surprisingly steady. Jian pulled Christopher to his feet and, keeping him in front as a shield, backed up against the ship's rail.

"I will do what you want," Fish said calmly. "Do not hurt this man."

"Please," Aiden said to Jian. "Your anger is for me. Let him go. Take me in his place." It was not a brave or noble offer. Aiden simply knew that he had a much better chance than Christopher. A rich merchant's son like Jian probably had not been in many knife fights. Jian might cut him some, but Aiden would not likely die. Gustav was still standing, though blood was pooling on the deck around his feet. Sven the Baby took off his shirt and pressed it against his cousin's wound.

"I will sail the ship," Fish said. "But think. How long can you hold that knife? One hour? A few hours? Release him now and I will make Mr. Koster promise to spare your life."

"No!" Jian said. His hand was trembling. He had to know there was no chance, Aiden thought. But a man with no chance was especially dangerous. What reason was there not to slash Christopher's throat?

"Our captain's word is good," Aiden said.

"But Koster is false," Jian said, pressing the knife hard. One of the sails caught the wind and snapped with a crack like a gunshot. Everyone jumped. Tiny droplets of blood bloomed from Christopher's throat.

"Death must be my end today," Jian said calmly. "But I will choose how we meet." He stared hard at Aiden. "I choose you will kill me."

Time stopped. The low sun melted the sky. It was not a plea, Aiden realized, but a command. Aiden looked at Fish, not sure if he understood what Jian was saying.

"Please, Fish," Aiden said. "We can take him with us. Koster can't stop us! So what if we're banished? We want no future here anyway!"

There were shouts from the water, and the splash of oars close by. Aiden and Fish looked out and saw two skiffs rowing rapidly toward them. Each held two Negro guards armed with rifles. Another boat was just leaving the wharf with more armed men.

"They won't shoot us," Aiden said.

"I don't know what they will do!" Fish said. He looked up at the sails, which were only half raised, flapping in the feeble breeze. "They have authority to board us, and if we try to resist, they can shoot."

"They won't!" Aiden insisted.

"I will not risk our men."

"Captain." Jonas appeared at Fish's side. Aiden saw that he carried two rifles and a pistol from the *Raven*'s weapons

locker. They had never expected to need guns on this voyage. Piracy was not a problem for guano ships, and mutiny among a crew of family and friends was not likely. Would Koster's men really fire on a merchant vessel? Koster, a bit mad to begin with, had spent a long time on a maddening island.

Fish took the pistol.

"No!" Jian tensed and pressed the knife blade harder against Christopher's throat. "He must do it!" Jian glared at Aiden. "He will kill me."

"I am the captain of this ship," Fish said evenly. "It is my duty."

Jian slashed at Christopher's ear. Bright red blood gushed out. Two of the guards in the rowboats raised their rifles and pointed them at Jian's back.

"Stop!" Aiden yelled. "Don't shoot! You will kill them both!" A rifle bullet from so close could easily pass through Jian's body into Christopher's. "I will do it," he said to Jian. "Let him go and—and—I will do it."

He turned to Fish and held out his hand for the gun. Jian, still holding Christopher by the hair, pushing him in front, walked a few steps away from the railing. He did not intend to give the despised guards a chance to kill him. Christopher's face was white. The blood had soaked the front of his shirt.

"Crew muster on the foredeck," Fish commanded. The sailors on deck scrambled quickly to obey that order, collecting in the front of the ship, well away from any bullets. Aiden raised the pistol. Jian shoved Christopher forward so he fell to his knees. Aiden's hand shook. Maybe there was still another way to end this. But as if reading his mind, Jian raised

the knife again and pressed the point against Christopher's throat.

Aiden blinked and took a deep breath, then let it out steadily. He stepped forward. He raised the gun, aimed and squeezed the trigger.

27

There were no cheers or rockets as the *Raven* sailed out of the anchorage. Though no one on the other ships knew exactly what had happened, they had all heard the alarm bell and the gunshot, had seen the *Raven*'s delay and knew it could not be good. The sailors did not line the rail to wave farewell; they were busy hauling up buckets of water and scrubbing away the blood on the deck. The first sweet taste of clean sea air brought little relief. Fish allowed generous rations of pisco that night, but even that brought no lightness, only a grateful numbness. The slash across Gustav's back, though long, was shallow, requiring no stitches. Christopher's earlobe had been sliced nearly through, but Sven the Baby made neat work of it.

It was a gloomy ship for those first few days. Christopher mostly stayed drunk and Aiden mostly stayed still. It was like a job, being still: to eat nothing, to breathe as little as possible, to move only as needed. He did not read or pace the deck as he had so often on the journey down. He did not talk and he did not think. He put his mind into the sky and the wind and left it there, away from everything.

Though Fish had never set foot on the island itself, the evil touch of the place had affected him, even before that awful final day. But with a ship to run, he had no time for depression. There were no moral questions for sailing a ship—it was just ropes and muscle and judgment. No one questioned why the wind blew the way it did; they just had to work the sails to fit. So the days passed and the sea lengthened behind them. The men came back to life the way men do—and must. The horror of the place was too big to live with, and they had to live, so they wooed forgetfulness in the rhythm of the sea and the working of the ship.

After a few days, Aiden began to climb and reef and haul along with the sailors, for it was good to be doing something useful. Even Christopher began to stand watches, for it was something to do. Fish would not let either of them climb higher than the lowest yards or do any work on deck in rough weather, but he understood that hard work was the best repair for damaged souls. Miles passed and days passed. The sky was blue and the sea was a different blue. Christopher mostly stopped drinking, except for the day the Christmas pig was slaughtered. He saw it hanging over the lee rail, the cut throat gaping, the blood spattering the waves in arcs with the tossing of the ship. Aiden saw him turn pale and begin to shake. They had not talked about that day. What was there to say? Christopher stumbled to the cabin, and he drank and he cried so he choked and lost his breath, and Aiden held him like he would one of the ducklings until, spent, he fell into a deep, ragged sleep. They never spoke of that again either.

The ship slipped hemispheres, and the men pulled out sweaters and flannels against the winter chill. Though they had a fairly steady course and could often see land, Fish still took a sight with the sextant each day at noon. It was like a religious ritual for him. On New Year's Eve, they shot off rockets and toasted the year 1867. Four weeks later, the *Raven* slipped into San Francisco Bay, just another cargo ship in a busy port.

Everything in San Francisco felt strange to Aiden. Of course it would, after almost six months away. There was solid ground, for one thing, and all the colors, especially green. There were dogs. Fresh water flowed from taps—clear and unlimited. His bed alone was nearly as big as the whole cabin he had shared with Christopher aboard the *Raven*.

It felt especially strange to be standing here now in Mr. Worthington's office. He gazed down to the garden below, where Christopher and Elizabeth were sitting on a bench eating hothouse cherries. They spat the pits into the bushes, competing for distance. The heavy oak door opened and Mr. Worthington entered, walking soundlessly across the thick carpet. That was another strange thing—how quiet it was here. Of course it wasn't really, but city noise was different—it was not the relentless screech of a million seabirds or the constant noise of the wind and waves. And here in the sheltered world of the Worthington estate, it sometimes was actually silent. In the middle of the night anyway.

"Thank you for making time for me, Mr. Worthington," Aiden said, swimming out to meet him in the center of the vast room.

"I've been wishing for such time," Worthington said, taking Aiden's hand and looking at him closely. "You have been rather monkish since your return." There was a tenderness and concern in his gray eyes that Aiden had never seen before, except with the ducklings. Aiden looked away.

"I'm still adjusting," he said vaguely.

"Of course."

Aiden didn't know what Christopher had told his father in their private council, but he suspected the old man knew most of it. In front of the family, Aiden had said almost nothing about their journey, and Christopher had told only the lightest of stories, enthralling the ducklings with descriptions of jumping dolphins and sea lions and the odd giant accordion player who would never stop playing. He told about playing cricket on a field of bird poop. The little girls thought an island full of bird poop hysterically funny to begin with, so it was easy to go from there. All unpleasantness was left out, and they were young enough not to even know there were questions to be asked. The tidal wave was simply excitement and high drama. The scar on his ear? Stupidly trying to shave in rough seas, of course.

"Sit down." Mr. Worthington led him to the comfortable chairs by the window. "You want to talk about some business."

"About the *Raven*," Aiden said nervously. There was no overture with Mr. Worthington. One got straight to the point or was soon dismissed. "I would like to arrange to relinquish my ownership half to Christopher. The guano license as well."

Mr. Worthington frowned. "Have you spoken to Christopher about this?"

"Yes. He doesn't want me to do it. But I don't want payment. I know you will say that is foolish and bad business, but I have decided. I believe it would just be a matter of drawing up papers."

"Christopher made it clear from the beginning that he

wanted me to have no part of this endeavor," Mr. Worthington said somberly.

"Yes, but now the endeavor is over." Aiden did not believe for a minute that the man had not scrutinized every deed and writ that his son had entered into, but he was willing to play along. "I only ask you for the name of a lawyer who can do papers. I don't know any lawyers."

"Of course," Worthington said. "I will make an appointment for you."

"Thank you, sir."

"So, you will be rid of the devil's ship and the devil's business. What do you intend to do, then, with the devil's profits?"

"Excuse me?"

Mr. Worthington leaned back in his chair.

"I understand the guano business has turned out to be more than either of you expected," he said. "Now you wish to divest yourself from the poisonous trade. But you have already earned a healthy fortune from this trip. So what do you intend to do with your—blood money?"

The glimpse of fatherly concern had vanished. The question was meant to be biting.

"I—I don't know, sir," Aiden said quietly.

"Throw it into the sea?"

"No."

"So you will keep it? Invest it? Live richly? Give it all away to the poor?"

"I don't know."

Mr. Worthington went over to the little table and poured two glasses of cognac.

"The poor will always be with us—Jesus himself said

that. And do you know why he said that? Because Jesus was crap at business." He handed Aiden a glass and stood by the window, looking down at his son and daughter in the garden. "He could have charged a penny apiece for all those loaves and fishes, and people still would have been happy, still would have known it was a miracle. Then he could have taken all those pennies, picked a dozen men out of the crowd and handed them each enough money to start a business." Mr. Worthington swirled his glass around and held it up to the light to watch the golden liquid slide down the crystal. "But no—everyone went home with nothing but a free lunch and a blessing of their poverty."

The smell of the cognac made Aiden feel sick to his stomach.

"You've had two months since you left the island with nothing to do but think."

"Yes," Aiden said. "But I have found no answers."

"Of course you haven't. Because there are none. There never have been and there never will be." Aiden wondered if the man had already been drinking. As long as he had known him, Mr. Worthington had been an abstemious man, but now he seemed slightly unmoored.

"What about Christopher?" Worthington looked at Aiden with a sharp gaze. "Do you despise him now?"

"No, of course not."

"But he has no qualms about profiting from this evil. Doesn't that make him despicable?"

"I am loyal to Christopher and will remain so."

"Why?"

"He is my friend."

"Yet by your sentiment, if he continues in this trade, he is at least evil, if not a murderer."

"No. You're—you're twisting things up." It seemed all the air had gone out of the room. Aiden stood. He wanted to leave, but the carpet was endless as the prairie and he didn't think he could cross it. The colors all swirled together. How were rugs made? Were people slaved to the looms? *What do your nice boots really cost? Or the sugar in your coffee? Do you lie in your comfortable bed on your soft sheets night after night, fretting for the slaves picking cotton and the little children who work in the mills?*

"Oh, sit down," Mr. Worthington said. "You are in no shape to be deciding your future right now. Neither one of you. Christopher is like an old man. I never thought I would long for his mercurial tempers, but . . ." He could not finish the thought. His hand shook as he lifted his glass. "And you are a wraith," he went on, his voice returning to mild paternal scolding. "You hardly eat at meals, you wander the house and the garden all night. Christopher says you haven't slept a night since you left that place. I know you've had a harsh lesson—"

"And what lesson would that be, sir?" Aiden interrupted angrily.

Mr. Worthington sighed. "That industry is a machine that can't be stopped. That a machine cares for nothing except feeding itself—like a thresher in the wheat cares nothing for the field mouse it catches up and crushes."

"Men are not mice."

"But machines are still machines," Worthington said wearily.

"You're right," Aiden said, trying to keep his voice steady.

"I have learned much about business now. I've seen harsh labor. I've done it myself. I've seen slaves worked. But the guano mines are beyond any of that. They are beyond hell. The coolies are starved and worked to death, most in a year or two! Tell me, how does that make sense in any way? To transport them from the other side of the world—six months in a ship—then work them to death? What if the coolies had three cups of rice a day instead of two? And two quarts of water instead of one? What would that cost to business?"

"You tell me," Mr. Worthington said, setting his glass down on the little table. "You've just been there. You know the cost of rice and water. You know the cost of labor and shipping and ground transport, and the price of guano in the market. Do the sums. If three cups of rice will yield your investors a better profit—or at least ease their consciences for a small enough price—you may fatten the coolies as much as you want."

"I don't know the cost of a human life," Aiden said.

"The cost doesn't matter if no one will pay it," Mr. Worthington said.

"How much profit do the rich really need?" Aiden looked down at the luxurious carpet with its elegant swirls. "Would your investors really flee if this were a lesser rug?"

"Yes," Worthington said, with genuine sadness. "My investors would flee if there were a flaw in the seam of my suit. If my cigars were from Florida, not Cuba. If that decanter were Bohemian crystal instead of French." He looked out the window and sighed. "I could probably get along without the polar bears, however. So how would your life have turned out then, my rich young man?"

274

Aiden's face burned with anger, embarrassment and confusion. "I would have made do."

"I'm sure you would have." He said this earnestly, with no sarcasm.

"The rich would still be very comfortable."

"No one dreams of being comfortable." Mr. Worthington stood up and smoothed out his jacket. "The dream of being comfortable brought us better stoves and lamps. The dream of being rich is bringing a railroad across a continent." He tapped the toe of his impeccable shoe on a crimson rosette. "You did not walk across the country hoping for potatoes."

Actually he had, Aiden thought. When he and Maddy had started their journey, he might have killed for a potato.

"I don't want to live that way," Aiden said.

"Well, you don't have to," Worthington said. "That is your decision to make. And you know what a rare privilege that is. I will ask you one favor. Give yourself time before you decide anything. You've been home barely three days. Wait until you can sleep through the night. The worst demons always haunt the midnight garden. The guano is in the warehouse, the ship is safely in the harbor. Peter has missed you, I think—who can know? But the ducklings certainly have. Come back to life for a while. There is plenty of time to decide. It's winter, everything is bleak. And you're only seventeen."

28

Aiden left the house by the front door. He didn't want to have to talk to Christopher and Elizabeth in the garden or the servants in the kitchen. All he wanted was to walk and think—or not think. He had no idea what he was feeling, only that he hated this new life, with its constant traps and riddles and slippery ideas, where everything was really something else and then something else behind that, like the shifting scenery and illusion in the theater. But what life would he choose instead? What life was there to go back to? Bribing his way to a job on the docks? Slicing up dead horses in the knacker's yard? Back in Kansas, stuck for life behind the plow? The lumber camp seemed very attractive right now—that dark green world where the work was hard but the rules were simple: cut down trees, eat, sleep, fight. Was it really only a year since he had left? It felt like a lifetime. But he could not go back there without risking jail or worse.

It was early evening and the streets were busy. Carriages carried businessmen home. The day maids walked home in laughing groups, gathering up their friends from other grand houses as they went. The winter dark came early, and the lamplighter was already working his way along the street, leaving a string of little glows behind him as he passed. There was a good job, Aiden thought. How did one get to be a lamplighter?

What he really wanted right now was a good fight. Sometimes he just felt his insides build up like a storm and there was no other way to let it go. Even the pain from a fight was comforting in a weird way. Pain from a fight was clear. You hurt because someone punched you. It wasn't like this inside pain, this unending twist of doubt and confusion.

The Barbary Coast was not at all scary now—it seemed more like a silly charade of badness. The same touts and thugs still lurked in the shadows, but they were like actors on a stage. Aiden knew the tangled streets by now, even after months away, and felt at ease walking through them. He went into one of the basement saloons and drank a shot of bad whiskey. Almost immediately a woman came up beside him. Her eyes were cloudy, and the red powder on her cheeks was caked into the wrinkles of her skin. She had thin, raised scars across her forehead, nose and chin. She wasn't old, but plenty had gone wrong for her.

"Are you looking for company?" she said.

"No," Aiden said, sliding off the rough stool. "Thank you."

"Come on—I'm gifted."

"What would you do for a hundred dollars?" Aiden asked.

"I'm not a hundred-dollar whore," she said, scraping some blackened ooze from the corner of her eye. "But if you're daft enough to pay that much, I can do whatever you want."

"What if I told you a man had to die for that hundred dollars?"

She sighed and rolled her eyes. "All the more reason to spend it on me, as he won't be needing it."

"Ah, well, that's true." Aiden had to smile. He gave her a dollar and went back out into the muddy street. He wasn't likely to find any fight in that place. Or anywhere this early. Neither liquor nor passion would be high enough for hours. A thin fog had settled in, condensing on the wool of his coat in tiny droplets that the ducklings called ladybug tears. The mud sucked at his boots.

He saw Blind Sally in a dark corner across the street. She was dressed the same as when he had last seen her, in the military coat, but with a bright red-and-blue-striped scarf added to thwart the cold wind. She was leaning against a wall, one palm pressed on the stone as if feeling the vibration of the city. Somehow she looked both frail and mighty at the same time, like she was holding up the building but quivering under the exertion of it. The Moon, as always, sat attentively by her side. The dog stiffened as Aiden approached, and gave out a low woof of warning.

"It's a friend, Blind Sally," he said. "Aiden Madison—if you remember me."

"Of course I remember you," she said. "New lad jumped and robbed, turned a fancy lad with the rich boy, turned a sea captain and went to sea. Now you're back alive. So I'll take my fee!" She held out her small, crooked palm, steady as the equator.

"And what am I paying a fee for?" he asked, fishing for coins in his pocket.

"For the ship I sent you, for that's what! The black bird ship."

His heart skidded sideways. "The *Raven*?"

"Aye. That one." She curled her fingers. "Give on, then."

"What do you mean, you sent me the ship? I won it in a card game."

"Yes, you did—ha! So you did. And that happens every

day about the place, does it? 'I'll see your jacks and here's a ship'—easy as that."

Aiden pressed some coins into her tissuey palm.

"What story are you telling?" he asked.

Blind Sally felt the coins and deemed them adequate, then gave an exaggerated shrug and pulled her scarf tighter around her shoulders. "Too cold to be standing around outside telling stories. Especially as being thirsty."

"All right, then, come have a drink with me," Aiden offered, as he knew she expected.

"Not in your fancy place. They won't let The-Moon in, or me either."

"Anywhere you like."

"Come down the way, then. Where they like The Moon and pour a good level. Come down to Paradise."

Aiden followed her down the darkening street. Paradise was slightly better than a cellar with planks, but not much. It had tables and chairs, a few lamps and a stuffed bear's head with peeling strips of fur on the wall. It actually seemed like a cozy place, friendly even. The kind of place where murder was infrequent—though more from lack of initiative than virtue. The Moon led them to a table in the far corner and sat attentively. The waiter girl appeared almost immediately. The Moon looked at her adoringly. She was a very pretty girl, part Mexican maybe, not young, but with a young girl's eyes.

"Good evening, Miss Sally," she said. "And hello, dear The Moon." She held out a crust of bread. The big dog took it delicately from her fingers, then curled up on the floor in a surprisingly small bundle. Blind Sally ordered three whiskeys. Aiden, unsure how many of those were meant to be his, looked blankly at the waiter girl and shrugged. She beamed him a far better smile than ought to be found in a place like this and pivoted away with a flip of her skirt. She returned a minute later and set down three small glasses in front of Blind Sally and one in front of Aiden. He took a small sip and waited for Blind Sally to talk. She tipped back one of her whiskeys, then another.

"I will say, and you must believe, I did not mean for such bad to come for you in it," she said, looking away. "I do swear that on The Moon."

"Why would you think it turned out badly for me?"

The old woman curled her fingers around the third glass.

"I'm not so blind as all that. You're down the Coast now here of a bad night, but hardly two days home and all alone with yourself when you have a fancy house instead, and the fancy place to drink. What says that but trouble?" She took a smaller sip from the third glass and scrunched her veiny knuckles around the dog's ears. "Talk says it's a murder ship now."

"A murder ship?"

"Man was killed on it, yes?"

Aiden nodded. However did she know that? "Yes. A Chinaman." He wasn't sure how that tipped the scales.

"I might have seen it for the devil's dealing."

"Why—what do you mean?"

She fanned her crumpled fingers across the stained tablecloth. "The man comes to me on a night—asks can I find him men would burn a ship. I say will take a few days. He says no, must be done that night. So do the job yourself I say. Isn't hard to burn a ship. But then I say why burn the ship at all? A burn may not cure the haunting—may even make it worse for turning loose the spirits and having them adrift. Go lose it in a gamble I say, not advising it, but just I'm tired of him. He says yes, then he will do that, so I send him to you at that place."

"At the Elysium? You told him to lose the ship to me?"

"I told him your face and form. But there onward is off my hands." She finished her last whiskey and pushed the three little glasses into a triangle.

"Why me?"

He pushed his own glass toward her.

"I knew you were about."

"Lots of men were about. Why me?"

"Why not you? Things have to happen to someone."

29

Aiden walked off alone into the night streets. His anger was spent, his frustration had collapsed, leaving only tiredness to carry his body home. Blind Sally's queer tale was likely just the imagining of a nutty old woman. But what if there was some hand of destiny twisting the threads of his life? Would that absolve him now? What if there really had been no other choice for him to make?

He did not fall asleep until nearly dawn, and woke just after ten to rare sunshine streaming in through his window. Breakfast was long past, but the coffee was still warm on the back of the stove. The house was quiet. He found the ducklings in the conservatory. They lay in a row on the floor, each one in her own patch of sun, reading or drawing pictures. Peter's wheelchair was parked nearby. The boy slid his hands back and forth through the light, fascinated by the shadows crossing his fingers.

"Good morning." Aiden walked over and patted his shoulder. Peter looked up briefly, screeched a greeting and turned back to his light play. Aiden knew he could not distract the boy for lessons until the sun vanished.

"What are you drawing?" Aiden looked down at Annalise's paper, which was covered in colorful blobs like burst flowers.

"Molecules," Annalise said somberly. "Professor Tobler taught them yesterday in science class."

"They are the smallest parts of things," Annabelle said.

"They make up everything, like bricks make up a house—but you can't see them, even with our microscope. You just have to believe in them."

"Like God," Annalise offered.

"But molecules are real," Daisy said.

"Molecules are proven by science," Charlotte broke in, with the imperious tone of the oldest. Her molecules were lacy constructions of green and yellow swirls. Some had faces, arms and legs. Daisy's were simply circles, squares and triangles connected in long, wiggling chains—more geometry than chemistry.

"If you change only one molecule," Daisy said gravely, holding up one small finger, "just one molecule, that can change a thing completely!"

"So if I change a molecule of you, would you be different?" Aiden asked playfully.

"Would I be?" she asked seriously. "Would that make me a boy? Or an animal?" She frowned. All four ducklings looked at each other in consultation.

"Well, one molecule different will make water not be water," Annalise said tentatively. "That's what Professor Tobler said."

Daisy stroked her hands across her cheeks as if trying to smooth all her molecules into place.

"It probably isn't really easy to change molecules around," Aiden tried to reassure them. He didn't really know much more about molecules than they did. "Or else things would be changing all the time, wouldn't they? I mean, you can't just change bricks around once they're in a house, right? Let's not worry about it now."

But what if one molecule could really change everything?

he thought. One thing done differently, one decision. "We'll just ask Professor Tobler when he comes again." Aiden sat down on the floor with them, sharing Daisy's patch of sun. "In the meantime, let's draw—tigers."

"Have you stopped being sad?" Daisy asked, laying her small hand on his.

"No one can be sad with four beautiful girls around," he said lightly.

"Christopher said you were sad about the Chinamen," Daisy pressed. "Because they had to work so hard."

"Yes."

"Did you tell them you were sorry?"

"The Chinamen? No. I suppose not."

"You should. When you apologize, you feel better. And also make, um . . ." She hesitated.

"Amends," Charlotte said, in a tone that sounded like deeds requiring amends had recently occurred.

"Like if you borrow a ribbon and then lose it, you have to give one of your own ribbons," Daisy said. "You can't just say sorry. Even when it wasn't your fault. Even if it just fell out when you were running in the wind."

30

The *Atlas of the World* had eleven pages about China, four maps, two photographs and five illustrations. Though Aiden remembered every detail from his countless readings of that holy book during the endless prairie evenings, he knew almost nothing about the real Chinese living in San Francisco. They did not go to the same shops, saloons, theaters, music halls or dining houses as the whites. Like most white people, Aiden had never even talked with one.

The only Chinese who ventured outside Chinatown were the silent men washing dishes in the backs of restaurants, picking up trash, digging ditches or wheeling carts of laundry through the streets. The man who collected the laundry from the Worthington house twice a week did not even talk to the servants. The sacks of dirty laundry were left in a bin outside the kitchen door. When he returned four days later, he put the clean bundles, wrapped in brown paper and tied with twine, in the bin and jangled his bells for the maids to come collect it. They always peeked through the kitchen curtain to see that he was gone before they came out.

The only thing most people in San Francisco knew about the Chinese was that they were filthy, sneaky, idol-worshiping criminals. A few of them were smart—or at least cunning and clever enough to run a business—but most were simple brutes. They were all addicted to opium and kept prostitutes in every basement. Half the newspapers would go out of business without daily stories of Chinese villainy. Except for the opium dens, Aiden had heard and read pretty much the same things about Negroes, Mexicans, Indians and the Irish all his life.

He had visited Chinatown a few times with Christopher and his friends. It was popular as an exotic adventure in the same way that their visits to the Barbary Coast were, but they had stayed mostly on the main streets of Stockton and Kearny. On these border streets, where the two worlds came together, there were shops full of bright souvenirs for tourists: painted fans and carved ivory pagodas, silk purses and painted scrolls. There were restaurants and teahouses catering to the white patrons.

"Genuine Chinese dinner!" touts called, beckoning the tourists in. "Chop suey restaurant here. Very clean! Come see—very clean, very good chop suey. . . ."

But today he was wandering deeper into the heart of the place. The cries soon fell away, replaced by a constant low din, the background clatter of thousands of people living on top of each other. The buildings were constructed to crooked heights, like toy blocks stacked up perilously high, with facing balconies so close together that neighbors could almost hand things across the street from one balcony to another. Every inch of space was precious, and so every inch was used. Most of the shops were barely big enough for a single person to sit behind a counter the size of a child's school desk. The merchandise was stacked to the roof on three sides and spilled out onto the stoop in front. Out on the street, spindly ladders leaned against walls, with more merchandise hanging from every rung: cloth, kettles, slippers, shirts and hats; live chickens and ducks in cages; wooden tubs of live fish; pig heads hanging from hooks outside the butcher shop. At the base of each building, a stone stairway, narrow enough that even a small man would have to turn sideways to pass through, led to dark underground rooms. It was reported that half of Chinatown was actually underground, where the poorest and most unlucky lived in the tiny dank rooms.

The streets themselves were so narrow that little sunlight ever reached the ground, and it was perpetually damp. So many people trod the streets that the mud was packed to a firm surface. It was like walking on moss. The Chinese mostly ignored Aiden, though some cast suspicious glances. A few, probably deciding that he looked too young to be a policeman, beckoned to him, pointing to some dungeon entrance with a whispered offer of one sin or another.

How in the world was he ever going to find Jian's sister in this place? Except for some older women in the shops and restaurants, there were no Chinese women out at all. A common laboring man could not afford to bring a wife from China, or support her if he did. No Chinese woman came on her own, for there was no work for her here. Wives and daughters of the wealthy would be kept safely in their homes.

His idea had been to go to the Chinese Merchants Association and try to find out where Silamu Xie lived, but then what? He had no pretense for seeking the man out, and certainly couldn't simply go knock on his door and ask to speak to his wife. No matter how bad Lijia's life might be, Aiden knew, he could make it worse with the wrong questions. What did she know about her brother's fate? And what could she do if she did know? It was difficult enough for a white woman to leave her husband, even when he beat her, even if she had family to take her in. Where would a Chinese woman go to escape? He had messed enough things up by now, Aiden thought. He should think this through a little more. He turned and found his way back through the streets to the outside world.

The kitchen and dining room were bustling as the servants cooked and set the table. Aiden found Christopher in his room, dressing for dinner. They exchanged glances in the mirror. There was a distance between them now, a kind of wariness. Like little boys who had, for no reason, started throwing rocks at a stray cat one day and wound up killing it.

"Come in," Christopher said, winding his necktie around his stiff shirt collar. "I said you'd be here for supper. You weren't around to ask."

"That's fine," Aiden said. "I can dress quickly."

"And there's this for you," Christopher said, picking up a leather folder from his desk. "The papers from the lawyer. The cargo has sold—your bank statement is there too. Like it or not, you've made a good bit of money."

Aiden took the folder but didn't open it. He didn't want to see the number. He knew it was huge.

"Winning the ship wasn't an accident," Aiden said.

"What do you mean?"

"The captain set out to lose it."

Christopher frowned.

"Captain Newgate asked Blind Sally to find him someone who would burn his ship," Aiden went on. "She suggested he lose it in a card game and sent him to the Elysium."

"Well, there you have it. It was all fate and we have nothing to feel guilty about," Christopher said. He was trying for humor, but there was a bitter edge to it.

"Does your father do any business with the Chinese?"

"No. Of course not," Christopher said.

"Why 'of course not'?"

"They don't do our kind of business. The richest of them made their money by bringing in coolies for the railroad. But now, with the railroad nearly done, there are too many coolies, so that's dried up. They import some regular goods—tea, silk, ivory—but nothing that really matters, no commodities, no industry. Even their banking is private. What are you after?"

Aiden had not told Christopher about his promise to Jian. He had said nothing of the full story even to Fish. He had told them only that Jian had brought him the pottery shards, then had begged to be rescued. Aiden had refused, which was true. He knew Fish had some questions—he certainly remembered Aiden asking about buying a coolie's indenture—but he also trusted Aiden. Leaving out some of the details, Aiden thought, was not betraying that trust.

"It wouldn't take much to make things a little better for them," Aiden said. "At the very least, the Chinese merchants could make what is happening known back in China so other men aren't tricked into going."

Christopher dropped into a brocade chair. "You think they don't know?"

"How could the harshest businessman—thinking only of his profits—allow men to be tricked into that place?"

"Because he wouldn't believe it was true," Christopher said. He leaned forward, running his fingers through his hair. "Who could imagine that place was true?" His voice was quiet, resigned. "But if you really want to meet some Chinese, I suppose you could just go to their New Year's banquet."

"New Year's was a month ago," Aiden said.

"Ours was—not theirs. Theirs depends on the moon—but it's always late January or early February. I'm sure it hasn't happened yet this year—we'd have seen or heard something. It goes on for two weeks. They have parades and shoot off firecrackers every night. Were you not here for it last year?"

"No," Aiden said. "I had just arrived last January. I would have still been living at Fish's mother's boardinghouse. It's not so close to Chinatown."

"Wow," Christopher said. "Has it really been only a year?" He got up and pulled his dinner jacket on. "Well, the Chinese merchants host a New Year's banquet for us every year. Businessmen, politicians—you know, their top people and our top people. Father always gets invited, of course. Come on, then." He led Aiden into the small anteroom beside his father's office, where the secretary's desk and file cabinets were kept. He began to poke through the little wooden slots and trays of letters and invitations waiting to be copied or answered.

"Look for a red envelope," he directed. "It's always a red envelope—lucky color. Ah, there." He plucked the invitation out of a tray. The red paper was thick and smooth, and there was an intricate Chinese symbol stamped into the broken wax. Christopher lifted the flap and pulled out the card. "It's postmarked just two days ago, so it isn't likely a refusal has been sent yet, but you can ask Mr. Butter in the morning. New Year starts February fifth. Tomorrow; the banquet is on the tenth." The invitation was hand-painted with Chinese symbols and watercolor flowers on the outside.

"Pretty, isn't it?" Christopher said. "They get very serious with the decorations. I went once with Father. Wives are invited, but Mother never wanted to go."

Aiden examined the card. Five days from now. He thought of Jian chipping away at the guano. Five days seemed an eternity. "You don't think your father will mind if I go?"

"No. He'll probably be glad. He went a couple of times, but not for years now. There's no point, really. But even if the Chinese are not really competitors for anything, he always likes having spies out." Christopher put the invitation back on the desk. "So, now will you go hurry and dress? We must be prompt. Cook is making a soufflé." Christopher fastened his collar stud.

"What's a soufflé?"

"Something French. Apparently all the rage."

The next five days passed in a strange mix of social whirls and quotidian peace. It was the midwinter ball season, with dances that went on all night, followed by lavish breakfasts. In between, there were days to recover, when everyone was happy to shuffle around the big, comfortable house in loose clothing and undone hair. They read books, played cards and games, ate cheese toast and cold meat and ignored the rest of the world. Elizabeth helped the ducklings write a play, which they performed for the family and the servants. No one really understood the plot—there were lots of fairies and spells and a magical orb stolen first by an ogre (Christopher), then by a wolf (Aiden), and finally recaptured, only to turn out to be a magical egg that hatched a magical bird.

Aiden spent hours each day with Peter, still trying to find a way to communicate with him. The boy had changed little physically over the months, but he seemed to get frustrated more easily. Mr. Worthington had tried two other tutors in Aiden's absence, but neither had worked out. They were proper trained teachers, and they felt it was a waste of time. Aiden still did not believe the boy was feebleminded. He read to him every day and was convinced Peter was listening, but when Aiden pointed to words, he would not repeat them. He loved playing with a set of alphabet cards but would not put them in order. He would not try to write letters or even trace over them. In fact, he recoiled as soon as the tip of the pencil touched the paper.

Though he did not like to admit it, Aiden sometimes felt annoyed with the boy, even angry. Why couldn't he just point at the letters on the board or tap for *yes* or *no*—anything to communicate? Crippled as he was, Peter still had a hundred times more advantage than most people in the world. Aiden remembered his own mother drilling them hard on lessons in the tiny Kansas cabin in the middle of a brutal winter. Learning was precious. Knowledge was breath. Daily life was all plows and aches—but then came evening, and in the long summer light, or if there was kerosene for the lamp, there was escape in study and reading. They had to struggle to buy books, paper and pencils. All this boy had to do was point.

31

An enormous lion danced in the street, a great sparkling beast with golden scales and goblet eyes, a scarlet tongue and a fringy beard of blue and green. It twirled and bobbed and cocked its head like a dog. It charged toward the crowd, sending people squealing backward with delighted fear. Though even the children knew it was a puppet—the two men holding it up were clearly visible—it had such personality that it seemed completely real.

The lion danced to a raucous chorus of drums, bells, gongs and flutes, while a dozen men in red and yellow silk jackets marched alongside it holding swaying lanterns on poles. The whole block was a carnival. Bright banners fluttered from the windows, and red paper lanterns glowed from every fence post and entryway along the street. Strings of firecrackers snapped in fiery bursts, sending up acrid drifts of smoke that hung in the chill air. It was easy to find the restaurant where the banquet was being held, since it was the only place other white people were going to. Servants stood by the door with trays of champagne and glasses of punch. Aiden took a glass of champagne. He still did not like champagne but had learned to deal with the bubbles by barely wetting his lips at every sip. It gave him something to occupy his hands, and since it took him an hour to get through one glass of it, he did not worry about dulling his wits.

Aiden was nervous. Though he was practiced at parties by now, he knew that was largely because he had always had Christopher around to entertain, amuse and charm enough for the both of them. This was the first time he had ever been to any kind of social event on his own, let alone a foreign one. He recognized some of the other guests from parties at the Worthington house. He nodded and was greeted in return, though each time, once they realized that he was there alone, they quickly moved on to more important people. Aiden didn't care. He actually found it sort of amusing. Though he was rich by any normal standards now, he would need profit from another dozen shiploads of guano to really count for something in their eyes.

He found a place off to the side where he could hang back and observe the whole room. There were ten or twelve Chinese men who were clearly the most important—mandarins, as they were called. These mandarins were all older men, forty at the youngest. They wore exquisite robes of embroidered silk with heavy cuffs of gold brocade. Aiden didn't know enough about Chinese clothing to be able to tell their ranks or social positions. It had taken him months to learn the nuances of dress for Americans. When he first got to San Francisco, every shopgirl was wearing a ball gown. He would never forget the first time he went to the Worthington house and thought the butler was Mr. Worthington.

Seven of the mandarins had wives by their sides. Aiden assumed they were wives, for they wore equally opulent clothing: silk jackets with voluminous sleeves and skirts covered in elaborate embroidery. They had ornately styled hair adorned with ivory combs or strings of pearls. Most seemed to be much younger than their husbands. Any one of them could be Lijia, Aiden thought, his anxiety growing. What would he do when he met her anyway? He didn't even know if she spoke English. Would Jian's tutor have included her in his lessons?

But even if Lijia were here and spoke English, and he could somehow speak to her alone, what should he say to her—*I'm sorry, but I had to kill your brother?* The first challenge, however, was simply to find her. Each mandarin had an interpreter by his side. Most were younger men, several in Western-style suits, but three were women—perhaps daughters who had grown up here. There were also a dozen or more young men who were escorting the American guests around and introducing them to the mandarins. Aiden crossed the room and began to examine the display of Chinese crafts and paintings. Some were scenes of mountains, some of flowers or animals. Many were done simply with ink and brush. But not simple, really, Aiden thought. He didn't know much about art, but these seemed unique and beautiful.

When one of the introducers finished with his guests, Aiden boldly stepped up and handed him his calling card.

"I am Aiden Madison," he said. "Will you introduce me, please?"

The young Chinese man held the card reverently with both hands as he bowed.

"Mr. Madison," he said with polite deference. Then he glanced up and looked to either side of Aiden, and his expression briefly shifted. He looked puzzled, suspicious even, to see Aiden alone, clearly too young to be an important man.

"I am eager to meet our hosts," Aiden said with what he hoped was casual authority. The man was in no position to question or object.

"Of course. Please come with me, sir. I will make the introductions for you, sir."

He began to lead Aiden through the gantlet of mandarins. The introductions, fortunately, were brief, but the Chinese names were difficult to remember, and each man who was not Silamu Xie was a waste of time. Aiden forced himself through polite questions and offered the briefest mentions of his own business. "Shipping and transport," he would explain.

"Allow me to present . . ."

"Allow me to present . . ."

He had never really spoken through an interpreter before, and it was awkward at first. A few of the mandarins knew of Mr. Worthington, or at least politely pretended they did. But one couple, a stout, animated little man with a stouter but silent little wife, had actually toured the zoo. As near as Aiden could make out, he had donated some kind of Chinese bird to the menagerie, but whether it was a finch or a pheasant, Aiden could not tell. The little man talked so fast the interpreter was struggling to keep up. Other guests were beginning to bunch up behind them by the time the introducer finally succeeded in moving Aiden along.

"Allow me to present the Honorable Silamu Xie." The introducer made a deep bow. Aiden felt his heart thump in his chest.

"Good evening," Xie said. He did not look sinister or imposing in any way. From the story Jian had told, Aiden had pictured him as some monstrous villain, but he really had little presence at all. He was a small man with a round face, close-set watery eyes and a thin, scrimmy line of dry skin around the edge of his scalp like hoarfrost. The voluminous robes hid his body, but the way he stood with his shoulders low and his feet turned out betrayed a soft condition. His voice was wispy.

"I am pleased to meet you," Aiden said. "I am Aiden Madison, a business associate of Mr. Worthington's."

Silamu Xie's narrow eyes did not betray much, but the corners of his mouth tightened and there was an allover bristle of interest, like that of a cat that doesn't move a whisker but alerts to a mouse in the room.

"It is my pleasure," he said. This appeared to be the extent of his English, for he then spoke in Chinese. His translator was a woman, young, Aiden guessed by her voice, though she kept her face down and so he did not get a good look at her. Not his wife, Aiden assumed by her plainer clothing and subservient demeanor. She stood as still as a statue with her hands clasped in front of her.

"I know Mr. Worthington's endeavors with great interest," she translated.

Aiden felt a sudden stab of panic. What exactly did the man know? And how stupid not to have thought of this! The *Raven*'s voyage to Peru, the names of its owners and its cargo of guano had been reported in the shipping news. If Xie really had arranged Jian's imprisonment on the Chinchas, he must have a connection to someone there—perhaps even to Koster. So he might also have received word of Jian's death aboard the *Raven*! It was almost two weeks since they had arrived home, and much faster ships had sailed past them. A letter could easily have reached Silamu Xie. Aiden felt like the stupidest man alive. Here were a hundred snares he had never considered. *I know Mr. Worthington's endeavors with great interest*. The interpreter shifted ever so slightly, and Aiden realized he needed to say something. Maybe she hadn't translated it exactly. Maybe Xie was just making a polite remark.

"Mr. Worthington has interest in, ah, many different businesses," he said cautiously, pushing away his panic.

"Of course." The translator spoke in a stronger voice than he would have imagined from such a slight woman. "I have interest in mining machines such as his company has devised for the silver mines of the Comstock."

Aiden felt a cautious relief. He knew little about the actual machinery that had built the Worthingtons' fortune. But he had to think of some way to talk to the man longer. Xie appeared to have no wife—no Lijia—here by his side, so this was the only chance Aiden would have to find out anything about her.

"Perhaps you might tell me more about your interest in mining equipment over dinner," he suggested. "I could relay your questions to Mr. Worthington, as I am his close associate."

Silamu Xie fixed Aiden with a steady, inscrutable gaze, then nodded and lifted his hand slightly. Immediately one of the servants sprang to his side. Xie spoke to him briefly in Chinese and the man scurried away.

"You will be most welcome to join our table, Mr. Madison," the interpreter said. She looked up for the first time, and Aiden felt the air go heavy. She was beautiful. Her eyes were a rich, dark brown and framed by expressive brows. Her skin was creamy and clear, her features delicate. She wasn't older than twenty, he guessed, and could be as young as fifteen. Her glossy black hair was pulled back in a simple bun, not encumbered with the loops and dangling jewels of the fancier women. Her ears were little seashells, each studded

298

with a tiny pearl earring. She was sunrise on four continents. He felt hot and disconnected.

"Thank you," Aiden managed to say as ropes twisted tight around his chest. She gave a small nod and gestured for him to follow.

As soon as all the guests were seated, the servants rushed through the room, setting bowls of fragrant soup at each place. The interpreter sat beside Xie and was kept busy making introductions all around. Her English was very good. She was amazingly calm and never seemed to falter. Could she be Xie's daughter or niece? But wouldn't he have introduced her as such? Their eyes met. Aiden's insides jolted again. She smiled, but quickly looked away. Two spots of crimson bloomed on her cheeks. Her fingers nervously touched a button on her blouse. Aiden tried to focus. He couldn't tangle up his strategy now because he was smacked silly by a girl.

There were twelve people at Xie's table, including two other Chinese men, one some kind of builder, one an official of the Chinese police. The American guests were two couples and three other men. Aiden knew one of the couples slightly, Mr. and Mrs. Larson, parents of a school friend of Christopher's. He recognized one of the men as a city councilman.

Despite his anxiety, Aiden felt enormously hungry and began to eat the soup. The broth was rich and delicious, with a dark, sweet saltiness he had never tasted before. He was halfway through the bowl before he looked up to see the other American guests either sitting silently before their untouched bowls or simply pushing their spoons around. Aiden gulped. The Chinese men were eating their soup, so he knew it was the right time. He had not slurped or sloshed. He had no idea what he had done wrong, but the American guests were looking at him like he was insane. He put the spoon down. There was an awkward silence.

"I was admiring the Chinese paintings," Mrs. Larson said, rescuing the conversation. "I do like landscapes. Though ours usually have more"—she glanced back at the paintings, trying to decide exactly what was wrong—"scenery in them."

There were murmurs of agreement among the Americans as the comments were translated. Aiden knew what Mrs. Larson meant about more scenery. Landscape paintings in rich houses were full of mountains and clouds, usually with a waterfall and some grazing deer. They were thick with oil paint. The Chinese paintings looked like they had been painted by little birds with tinted water on their feathers.

"I am happy that you see the beauty in these paintings." Silamu Xie's translator spoke. "I regret we do not have finer examples to show to you here." The tone of her voice did not change as she said this, but she stiffened and her dark eyes flashed. Xie went on talking. "The artist of these paintings is a member of my household who has some simple talent and a little training," the translator continued. "I give her permission now to speak to you herself."

Then Silamu Xie stopped talking and nodded to the young translator, waving his hand, as if in a royal permission.

"I am the painter," the woman said, addressing the guests for the first time as her own person. "I will graciously be happy to answer your questions."

"You painted those pictures?" the councilman said with surprise.

"Yes, sir. I have studied painting in China since I was a small girl."

"Girls can be very good at watercolors," Mr. Larson said dismissively. "It's simple, you know. Not like real painting."

The other men nodded in agreement.

"Thank you for the kind compliment," the woman said. Her expression did not change, but her jaw tightened with anger at the insult. Aiden wished he could get up and punch the man.

"What is your name, dear?" asked Mrs. Larson, who, with her kindly nature, also recognized her husband's slight toward the girl.

"I am called Ming."

"Well, Ming, I think they're lovely just the way they are. Your flowers are especially pretty. They aren't realistic at all, not like botanical prints, yet somehow I think they're even more real. Do you know what I mean?" She looked around the table. "What do you think, Aiden?"

"Uh, yes," Aiden said. "It's like, well, when you left out all the details, you painted what most made it be a flower." That sounded extra-stupid. It wasn't like a flower would otherwise be a buffalo. But he didn't know how else to say it. Ming smiled at him. Aiden felt his face flush and wondered if there had been hot peppers in the soup that he hadn't tasted at first.

"Chinese art show philosophy of China is unity of heaven, earth and human," the police official broke in. His English was not nearly as good as Ming's and he didn't seem particularly artistic, but he spoke with authority regardless. "Order of all in picture is great way of Chinese picture."

The American guests looked confused.

"He points out that in our tradition, a painter seeks to

capture the essence, not the detail. To show the balance of man, nature and the spirit," Ming explained. "But of course I am not a great painter," she added quickly. "I am still on the journey of learning."

Silamu Xie raised his hand, and the servants swooped in to clear the soup bowls. Aiden tried to think of anything to say that might keep her talking. She was a member of the household, he thought excitedly. While some kind of servant, then, she must have standing. She spoke English and had studied painting. If Jian Zhang's family was indeed very wealthy, Lijia must have brought a maidservant with her from China. Assuming Lijia had some education, she would have wanted a girl who could be a companion to her as well.

"Did you paint the invitations too?" Aiden asked, trying to think of ways to learn more about her.

"It was my honor to be asked."

"And the calligraphy?"

Ming brightened. "Yes," she said. "You know Chinese calligraphy?"

"Oh no!" Aiden said quickly. "I mean, I've read about it."

Mrs. Larson looked vaguely scandalized. Oriental crafts were not generally in the curriculum for refined young men.

"Calligraphy most fine art supreme!" the police chief broke in. "Best Chinese great art!" He gestured back at the place card with a flick of his long, curved fingernail. "This okay. Better than child make."

Ming's expression did not change, but Aiden saw angry rays beam off her, like the sun at noon in the desert. He almost laughed out loud. She was like one of her paintings, communicating much more with what she left out. Then Silamu Xie began to talk, and Ming's voice once again became his tool as the conversation switched to manly topics: building and the railroad.

The Americans were served steak, boiled carrots and potatoes for their dinner, but there were also platters of Chinese food offered. Aiden watched the other guests devouring the beef and realized the reason they hadn't touched the soup was simply because they distrusted Chinese food. It was said that the Orientals ate all kinds of awful things, but this smelled delicious to Aiden. Heck, he had eaten bugs; how much worse could this be? It turned out to be not worse by any means—and in fact really delicious. Layers of flavor and texture rippled through his mouth like waves. Crunchy things and soft things and spicy, sweet, sour things.

"The dinner is delicious," Aiden said with sudden inspiration. "Does your wife prepare this kind of food in your own home?" he asked Silamu Xie.

"Some of these dishes are special for the New Year celebration," Ming translated his reply. "But my cook is very good."

Of course he would have a cook!

"And are you married, Mr. Xie?" Mrs. Larson asked, unintentionally helping Aiden out with a more direct approach.

"I regret that my wife was unable to attend tonight," he said.

"I am sorry to hear that," she said.

You can't begin to imagine how sorry, Aiden thought. Slammed up in a dead end—where to go now?

After dinner, there was a singer from the Chinese opera. Aiden wasn't sure what to make of it. She sang notes he hadn't known even existed—like notes between the regular notes. He kept his eyes on the singer, but all he could really see, at the edge of his vision, was Ming. She sat perfectly still and also watched the singer, but somehow Aiden knew she was looking at him too.

"Very nice!" Mrs. Larson said, clapping enthusiastically though looking bewildered.

Chairs scraped throughout the room as people stood to leave. The American guests were almost racing to the door. The duty was done—everyone could go home and have nothing to do with each other for another year. Aiden felt desperate. He had to find a way to talk to Ming in private—even for just five minutes. She was most certainly his path to Lijia. But she had not been farther than two steps from Silamu Xie all night. Aiden wrenched his brain for an idea.

"Mr. Xie," he said. "I hope it is not presumptuous to ask, but my associate Mr. Worthington has five daughters who are quite devoted students of the arts." He paused to let Ming translate. "I wonder, would you consider . . ." Aiden groped for the right word. He couldn't ask to hire her—that would be insulting. But neither could he make it sound like a social invitation, for that could also be interpreted as mocking, since there were no social dealings between the races. "Perhaps consider honoring our household by allowing Miss Ming to visit one afternoon to demonstrate this beautiful traditional Chinese style of painting and calligraphy. I am sure Mr. Worthington would be very appreciative."

Ming fixed her gaze on Aiden as she translated this, and that gaze was surprised, amused, shy, excited—all expressions shifting within a few seconds, like a summer storm passing on the prairie. Silamu Xie pulled a silk handkerchief from the sleeve of his robe and dabbed along the arc of his flaking forehead. He had not drunk much wine at dinner—Aiden had been watching—but his face was flushed.

"It would be my honor to share with you the modest talents of my servant in this way," Ming translated, dropping her gaze and bowing her head now. Aiden saw her small hands trembling slightly.

"Thank you," Aiden said. "If you will send a note to the house informing us when Miss Ming would be available, I will make the arrangements."

The streets of Chinatown were still crowded and noisy with New Year's revelers as Aiden left the banquet hall. Lingering smoke from the firecrackers tinged the foggy air, and bits of red paper fluttered everywhere. He felt relieved and lighter than he had in months. His mission was not yet achieved, but he could at least see a clear path to it. Ming would carry a letter to Lijia. His duty to Jian would be done. He could not have dreamed up a better messenger. Ming might even know how to help Lijia. She was clearly smart and, as a translator, probably more in touch with the outside world. And, he thought with a shiver, he would get to see Ming again. But he should not even think about that. This lightness he felt now, this fluttery distraction, was from relief, nothing more. Anything more was impossible. Even if she were just an ordinary Chinese girl, it was impossible, but she was a servant in the house of the villain. This feeling was relief, nothing more.

32

The ducklings were excited about their visitor. None of them had ever seen a Chinese lady before.

"Can she see?" Annalise asked.

"Of course she can see," Aiden replied, puzzled. "She's a painter! Why would you think she couldn't see?"

"Chinese don't have eyes," the girl replied.

Aiden realized the only Chinese she had seen were the cartoons in the newspapers, where caricatured drawings gave them only slits for eyes.

"Their eyes are just a different shape," he explained. "Miss Ming has very pretty eyes."

Mrs. Worthington was apprehensive, but Aiden assured her that Ming was a most respectable young woman. Elizabeth, who had no interest in painting at all but loved the idea of meeting an exotic Oriental, finally persuaded her mother to allow the lesson.

"But how will she come here?" Mrs. Worthington fretted. "Do they have a carriage?"

The Worthington estate wasn't even a half mile from Chinatown, but Aiden knew it was a problem. A Chinese servant might walk or catch a ride in a laundry cart, but Ming wasn't a servant. An American cab would not transport a Chinese person, and Aiden didn't know if the Chinese had cabs or carriages.

Silamu Xie solved the problem by promising to arrange

the transportation himself. So then there was debate about whether Ming should be brought to the front door, to the garden door or through the servants' entrance and whether she should be offered tea and, if so, which china to use. Racism, Aiden thought, was really an awful lot of work.

But eventually, after several days of notes sent back and forth, all the details were sorted out. Mrs. Worthington, unable to decide how to handle the social protocol for having a Chinese woman in her home, even if only to give an art demonstration, had decided to avoid the encounter altogether by scheduling a tea that afternoon with the cotillion committee to discuss plans for the spring ball season. On the appointed afternoon, the ducklings waited in a row by the window, eager for the first glimpse of her. Even Christopher, who tried to appear his usual nonchalant self, was hanging about the house. Finally a small buggy driven by a Chinese man pulled up in the gravel driveway. The horse and buggy were modest, but both had been cleaned and polished so they gleamed.

"Oh," Charlotte gasped when Ming stepped out of the carriage. "She looks just like a doll!"

"She's ethereal," Daisy sighed.

Ming wore a blue silk skirt and blouse embroidered with yellow and blue flowers—clothing much finer than what she had worn at the dinner, clothing chosen to impress. Elizabeth was clearly impressed. Aiden was not sure what he was—dizzy, mostly, like he'd been slammed to the ground in a lumberjack fight. Elizabeth, seeing him frozen dumb, stepped in to make introductions.

"I'm Elizabeth Worthington," she said. "These are my sisters, Charlotte, Annalise, Annabelle and Daisy. We are so pleased to meet you, Miss Ming."

"It is my pleasure." Ming bowed.

Aiden recovered his voice. "Yes. Thank you for coming."

Then a Chinese man walked around from the other side of the buggy. He was big as a cathedral and as scary-looking as one of its gargoyles. It was something Aiden had not anticipated, but should have. Of course no Chinese woman would travel outside Chinatown by herself, especially one who was a member of an important household. Still, it was a problem. The front door had been allowed for Ming, but a Chinese manservant could not come in the front door or be received into the family areas of the home. The servants would not welcome him in their kitchen, but he could not be left to wait outside like the laundryman.

"This is Gouzhi," Ming said. "He has kindly accompanied me today. I wonder if you would allow him to visit Mr. Worthington's most renowned zoo while I am visiting with the delightful girls."

"Yes, of course," Aiden said, relieved. She had rescued them all with grace.

Gouzhi was a big man, for either American or Chinese. He was only an inch or so taller than Aiden, but more broadly built, with heavy bones and ample muscle connecting them. He wore the typical Chinese quilted jacket and loose trousers, and his hair was braided into a traditional pigtail down his back. He was solid and expressionless as a wall, and Aiden suspected he was more bodyguard than servant.

"Aiden," Elizabeth said, subtly kicking his ankle. "Why don't you show Mr. Gouzhi around back to the zoo while I take Miss Ming inside to the nursery." She smiled at Ming. "We are looking forward to our painting lesson."

Aiden led the silent Gouzhi along the side of the house, past the conservatory and up to the gate of the zoo.

"You're welcome to stroll as you wish," Aiden said. He had no idea if the man spoke English. "The polar bears are our main attraction."

Gouzhi didn't seem quite as eager to see the animals as Ming had reported, however, and simply sat himself down on a stone bench where he could see the house and the buggy that had brought them.

"All right, then," Aiden said. "You're also welcome to sit there."

Aiden went back inside, stopping in the kitchen to cajole the cook to send tea outside for the man. She glowered at him but pulled out a battered old tray and a chipped old teacup.

"No toast," she muttered as she scooped a meager spoonful of tea into the pot. "Look at the great size of him already! I'm not fattening up any Chinaman on Mr. Worthington's good bread and butter."

"Thank you, Cook," Aiden said. He sprinted back up the stairs but forced himself to slow down as he neared the nursery. He nervously fingered the letter in his pocket. It had taken him two days to write it, facing a blank page each night with an equally blank mind. The letter had to be perfect. It had to tell her everything, but not really everything. Lijia did not need to know the details of the guano island. She did not have to know how horribly her brother had lived the many months of his imprisonment there, or about the rock. She certainly did not need to know all the details surrounding his death. It was unlikely Aiden would ever meet her in person. There might be a few more notes between them, but he would worry about that if it came to it.

It is with regret that I must tell you that your brother died in a tragic shooting . . . a tragic occurrence . . . a tragic accident . . .

He finished each night with many burned pages and no letter. Should Lijia know that her husband was responsible for Jian's kidnapping? Did she already know—or suspect? What could she do about it if she did know? The final letter was short.

I had occasion to meet your brother Jian Zhang on my recent trip to Peru. I was working with some scientists, and he brought us samples of ancient pottery. I am terribly sorry to have to inform you that unfortunate events led to his untimely death. He wished me to convey to you his enduring love and affection.

In the nursery, Elizabeth and the ducklings were already sitting around the table. Peter's chair was parked nearby. Ming had brought several of her paintings to show them, which she propped against the wall on top of their bookcase. She was even prettier than he had remembered. His skin felt prickly and his heart was still beating fast. He leaned in the doorway, feeling like an intruder on such a scene.

"This style of painting is called *shui-mo,*" Ming said. "It is ink and water. It is more than one thousand years old." She opened her bag and took out brushes, sheets of paper and a little wooden box that held an inkstone and a stick of ink.

"These are called the four treasures," Ming said. Her voice was different from the voice Aiden had heard as she translated for Silamu Xie at the banquet. It was softer but clear, with a tiny precision to the hard consonants, like a little silver bell. "The inkstone, the ink stick, the paper and the brush. With the four treasures, you may show all of the earth and the heavens! I have brought one that each of you may try."

She set out little boxes in front of each girl. The inkstones had smooth depressions in their centers. The ink sticks were the size of dominoes, with gold Chinese characters pressed into them. Ming dipped her brush into a cup of water and made a small puddle on the stone. Then she picked up the ink stick and began to rub it in circles against the stone. "You must not grind the ink," she said. "Let the ink come willing. As you make the ink, your mind will come away from the world and change."

The girls began rubbing their ink sticks. Not one of them made a sound or even shifted in her chair. When the ink puddles were glossy and the consistency of melted butter, Ming gave them each a sheet of paper and demonstrated how to hold the brush.

"One brush has in it one hundred different strokes," she said. She dipped a brush in the ink and drew a fine black line as thin as a cat's whisker. Next she turned the brush slightly and made a pale swoosh that looked like a curled ribbon. Then she pushed the brush tip down and spun it up again with the tiniest flick of her wrist, leaving dainty blossoms.

"Please try now!" She smiled at the ducklings. "Do not worry to be perfect. Only learn how to feel the brush."

Elizabeth, who had endured more years of restraint at the Clairidge School for Ladies, was tentative, carefully trying to copy Ming's examples. But the little girls began to swoop and twirl their brushes across their papers. They scrubbed the bristles against the inkstones and splattered droplets on their smocks. Ming never reprimanded them, except with demonstration of her own tranquillity. With a few strokes of her brush, she painted a rabbit. The ducklings clapped with delight.

"Why don't you paint with colors?" Annabelle asked. "We have colored paints."

"Sometimes I do," Ming said. "But plain ink . . ." She hesitated. "You must feel the shape and weight of a thing— what is the essence. With color, I may paint a pretty picture of a bird. With ink, I must make the bird alive." With a dozen quick strokes, Ming painted a swallow soaring across the page.

Daisy nodded very solemnly. "I understand."

Ming painted a few lines, and a tiger sprang. Aiden saw that Peter was watching quite intently. His body was still with concentration. Aiden walked over and squatted beside him.

"Do you want to see the pictures?" Aiden asked.

"Anndeee!" he said. "Anndeee!"

"He likes them," Daisy said to Ming. "He says they are very beautiful."

"Shall I paint a picture for Peter?" Ming said playfully.

"Yes! Please!" The ducklings all clapped. Aiden pushed Peter closer to the table, where he could watch.

"What would you like me to paint, Peter?" she asked softly.

Peter made only a soft grunt. The big orange cat roused himself from his nap by the stove, stretched and leaped onto the back of the couch.

"Shall I paint your pretty cat?" Ming asked. She dipped her brush, then swept it across the paper, and the cat appeared, sitting just as he was, licking one plump paw. The girls squealed with excitement.

"Look, Peter, it's the cat—the one you like," Charlotte said.

"Now the cat jumps!" Ming painted a second picture, capturing the muscular grace of a leaping cat in a few washes of gray and black. "And now he catches a little mouse." She made a second image on the same page. The little mouse took only six brushstrokes but was so lifelike the ducklings giggled with delight. Ming painted a Chinese character on the page.

"This is how we write *cat* in Chinese," she said. "Take up your brushes. I will show you how."

The girls clutched their brushes and began to copy the character.

"Very good, Miss Elizabeth!" Ming said. She picked up Elizabeth's page to show the others. Peter began to grow agitated. He jerked his head back and forth and slapped his hands against his table. Aiden snatched the cat picture out of his way, afraid he would tear it. This seemed to make the boy even more frantic.

"Peter, calm down. Come on, I'll take you out." He knew Peter's outbursts could be disturbing to someone not used to them, and did not want Ming to be upset. But as Aiden started to turn the chair away, Peter suddenly quieted down. He struggled to calm his body and turn his head back toward the table.

"He wants to stay," Charlotte said. "Look, he wants to see the painting."

"Do you like the paintings?" Annalise went over to her brother's side. "Do you want to see them some more?"

Peter stared at the big orange cat, then back at the paper.

"Att," he said, touching the picture. Then he patted the calligraphy and repeated, "Ka-at."

"He knows what it means!" Daisy picked up Ming's calligraphy and held it in front of Peter's face. "Do you see it, Peter?" She tapped her tiny finger on the Chinese character. "Do you know what this means?"

Peter smiled, and it was like light came pouring out of him. Slowly he straightened his arm, uncurled the clenched fingers and pointed at the big orange cat.

"Kh-aaat!" he repeated, the voice still strained, but the meaning clear. "Aaat!" His eyes looked at the Chinese character, then back to the cat.

"He knows," Elizabeth whispered in amazement.

Ming was looking lost and a bit frightened.

"He's never understood letters or words or even symbols before," explained Aiden, as surprised as anyone.

Charlotte ran to the toy shelf and took down a wooden horse. "Here," she said to Ming. "Draw this, and the symbol for it—the cali-gee . . ."

"Calligraphy," Annalise said. "Yes, please draw it!"

Ming painted a horse and the character for *horse*. Annabelle snatched the papers up and showed them to Peter.

"This means *horse*, Peter!" she said eagerly. "Do you understand?"

"Hold it still," Elizabeth said, steadying the girl's hand. "You're shaking it like laundry on the line."

"But he knows what it means!" Annabelle chimed in excitedly. "You do, don't you, Peter?" She touched the toy horse, then the picture, then the character. "This means this! It's a horse. Can you say *horse*?"

"Ooorse." Peter forced out the tangled word.

"Yes!" Charlotte exclaimed. "It is a horse!"

"Do a dog!" Annabelle said.

"Elephant!" Daisy shouted.

"Wait, wait," Elizabeth admonished the little girls. "Don't overwhelm him. And Peter's never seen an elephant." She looked at Aiden for help. "Do you think he really understands?"

"I don't know," Aiden said. "He's never responded like this before. Could you paint the symbols on separate papers?" he asked Ming. He took the pictures Ming had already painted and folded up the bottoms so the Chinese characters were not visible. Ming saw what he meant to do. She tore a sheet of paper into small pieces and painted characters on each one. Aiden laid these out on the table below the paintings, mixing them up.

"Which is the horse, Peter?" Aiden said. "Will you show us?"

They all watched silently as Peter struggled to aim his hand. He touched the drawing of the horse, then the character for *horse*, then the bird and the character for *bird*.

"He knows Chinese!" Annalise said.

"Is Peter Chinese?" Daisy asked.

"No," Aiden said. "It just—I don't know." He looked at Ming, who seemed a bit unnerved.

The ducklings scampered around the room, gathering up other toys and objects and thrusting them at Ming to paint as fast as she could. "Do a shoe or a cup. . . ." The poor girl grew flustered. "Not all Chinese characters mean exactly the thing itself," she explained. But gamely she painted pictures and calligraphy for *house* and *cup*, *tree* and *shoe*. Peter really did seem to be comprehending. He still struggled with the words, giving only "ooo" for *shoe* and "ha-ha" for *house*, but it was still more than he had ever done before. They were all surprised when the butler rapped on the nursery door. Two hours had flown by.

"The visitor's buggy is ready," Mr. Butter said. If he was puzzled by the gaiety of the little girls and the litter of Chinese characters all over the table, he very professionally did not show it.

"You must come again, Miss Ming," Elizabeth said. "Please!"

"Yes," Aiden agreed. "I don't know why, but he understands."

He suddenly remembered his real mission—the whole reason he had thought up this painting-lesson ruse in the first place. Aiden reached into his pocket and fingered the letter he had written to Lijia. He couldn't just hand the letter to Ming without some explanation. He had counted on having a few minutes alone with her to explain. Even if he did manage to slip it to her now, did she have a pocket in her skirt to put it in? She had already closed her painting box, so he couldn't sneak it in there. But most of all, he thought, if he didn't give her the letter now, he would have to find a way to see her again. And he desperately wanted to see her again.

33

"**A**re you telling me my son speaks Chinese?" Mr. Worthington frowned.

"No. Of course not, sir," Aiden replied nervously, looking to Elizabeth for support. "Only that, for whatever reason, the Chinese characters just made sense to him. Suddenly it registered in his mind that a symbol could mean the thing itself. And look"—Aiden pulled the calligraphy for *horse* out of the pile—"the symbol really does look like a horse. It has legs and a head. However abstract."

"You are the sixth tutor I've hired." Mr. Worthington glared at Aiden. "And, as you yourself have acknowledged, the least accomplished. Others have tried symbols and pictures." He looked down at the pile of Ming's paintings and calligraphy. "Why would Peter suddenly understand that these—these foreign squiggles—mean *cat* or *horse*?"

"I think *because* they are so foreign," Aiden said. He had a flash of Ming's small hand holding the brush—so delicately and powerfully at the same time. He shivered. "We've always thought Peter doesn't notice things, but I wonder now if he notices too much. What if sights and sounds are hitting his mind like a thunderstorm all the time? I think the ducklings have understood this, in a way, but didn't know how to explain it to the rest of us." *It's that bread has a thousand ways to taste. . . .*

"What if I sent you down to the china pantry right now,"

asked Elizabeth, perched on the edge of her father's desk, "and told you to fetch six Davenport Lattice cream soup bowls, four Coalport Adelaide consommé bowls, a dozen Spode London shape butter plates and two luncheon settings of Wedgwood—could you do that?"

Mr. Worthington looked blank.

"No, you could not," Elizabeth went on, not expecting an answer. "But you could probably tell a teacup from a soup tureen."

"Yes?"

"Well, maybe we've been confusing Peter with china patterns, and now Ming is simply showing him teacups from soup tureens." •

"Even so, we're not all going to learn Chinese just to communicate with him," Mr. Worthington said.

"Of course not," Aiden said. "But now he at least has the idea that symbols can mean actual things."

"So what do you propose we do now?"

"I would like to have Ming come back," Aiden said. "We'll have her paint words—in English—along with the calligraphy and the pictures."

"Why can't you do that?" Mr. Worthington frowned. "You don't have to do actual Chinese writing. After all, he isn't going to know the difference."

"Peter liked her," Aiden said. "She has a very gentle way about her." There was no explanation to offer. Perhaps the boy had also been smacked senseless—or sensible, as it were—just as Aiden had been.

"She does," Elizabeth added. "Please, Father, we all liked her."

They knew there was little Mr. Worthington would refuse his daughter.

"Very well, I have no objections. If your mother approves."

"Thank you, Father." Elizabeth leaned over and kissed him on the cheek.

Aiden sent a note to Silamu Xie that afternoon. The next morning, though it was a typical dreary, damp February day, Aiden was exhilarated and cheerful. He could not manage a bite of breakfast nor concentrate on his book as he waited for the morning post. He was not worried when there was no note from Silamu Xie. He hadn't really expected a reply so soon. But by two o'clock, the earliest the afternoon post ever came, he felt restless and vaguely sick. Twice he walked down the pebbled driveway to check the road—perhaps it was too muddy for the mail carriage. By three o'clock, when there was still no mail, he felt a blunt squeeze in his head. Elizabeth came home from school at three-thirty and wasn't the least bit concerned, which made Aiden, quite absurdly, want to strangle her.

"What in the world is wrong with you?" Christopher asked when he saw Aiden idly wandering through the library. "You've been fidgeting about all day."

"Nothing," Aiden said. "It's the weather, I suppose. I miss the sunshine." He was surprised his friend had noticed. Christopher had been holed away in his own room lately, working on some new business idea, he said.

At four Aiden decided that the pressure in his chest was caused by his ribs somehow turning themselves inside out and he was bound to die before supper. But then the post came and he was miraculously cured of everything. Ming would come tomorrow at eleven. He tucked the letter into his pocket. She had written it herself. She had blown the ink dry with her own breath, folded and creased the stationery with her delicate fingers. And tomorrow she would be here, breathing in this house. What in the world was he going to do?

The ducklings were disappointed that they were not to have Ming for themselves this time, but understood this lesson was for Peter. They did insist on bringing her first to the nursery to see the Chinese paintings they had done. Ming admired their flowers and praised their tigers. They had invented their own "Chinese" characters as well—though most of these consisted of stick figures and dots.

"I think they missed the part about the ancient traditions," Aiden apologized.

"Every language was once invented for the first time," Ming said.

Peter's nurse had set up a table and chairs in his room for Aiden and Ming. The door of the room was left open to her own adjacent bedroom, where she sat knitting, observant and suspicious. She was a sturdy, kind, illiterate woman who was good with the boy's physical care but distrustful of all efforts to educate him. She was proud to have raised her own five children with no schooling and thought it mean, if not actually cruel, to torture a feeble mind with the confusion of the alphabet.

Peter was clearly happy to see Ming. He did not recoil when she touched his hand, and even reached out to her, brushing his fingers lightly across her offered palm.

"Would you like to paint today?" Ming asked the boy. Peter nodded. Ming sat down, opened her paint box and set each item out on his table. Inkstone, ink stick, brush, paper—the four treasures. Aiden had only been to Catholic Mass a few times in his life, but her soft, sacred motions reminded him of the Consecration. Ming poured water on the inkstone and began to rub the ink stick around. She took Peter's hand and wrapped it over the stick. She guided his hand and together they mixed the ink until it was glossy and ripe. This was holier than any Communion.

Her blouse seemed fancier today than last time—more threads of color in the silk. And it was tied a little tighter beneath her breasts, so there was more outline of her shape. She picked up the brush, but hesitated.

"Can you hold the brush?" She spoke directly to Peter but glanced at Aiden for guidance. Before Aiden could say anything, Peter thrust his hand toward Aiden. Aiden laughed.

"I made him this." Aiden picked up the splint. "But he's never liked it before." Aiden tied the splint around Peter's hand, and Ming slipped the brush into it.

"Don't feel bad if he won't do it," Aiden said. But Peter eagerly dipped the brush himself, then brought it to the paper. He pressed the brush down, then lifted and pulled it across the page, exactly as Ming had done in her first lesson.

"It's amazing," Aiden said. "I've tried with everything—charcoal, chalk, pencil, even pen and ink—and he acts like I've given him a hot poker."

"Hmmm," Ming said. "I wonder . . ." She picked up the slate and handed Aiden a piece of chalk. "What do you feel when you draw with that?"

321

"Nothing," Aiden said.

"Close your eyes," Ming said. "How does the chalk feel?"

Aiden closed his eyes. The chalk felt like chalk.

"It is rough and it scratches. I don't like chalk either. Now feel the brush." Ming slipped the brush between his fingers. Aiden jumped at her touch and his eyes popped open.

"Go on."

Aiden painted an inky line across the rice paper.

"The brush is smooth like silk," Ming said. Aiden thought that was what she said—he couldn't really hear anything except the waterfall rushing through the middle of his brain.

"Painting," she went on, "is like . . . touching softly? I don't know the word—softly touching, like petting a cat?" She moved her hand in a sensuous wave.

"Stroking?" Aiden's voice caught in his throat. A cat would die instantly of happiness with her stroke.

"Peter feels the roughness—the scratchy feelings—more, I think."

She guided Peter's hand and he slowly copied Ming's bird. She painted the character and he copied that too. It took all of his concentration, but he did not grow frustrated. Finally she painted the letters *b-i-r-d*. Peter, growing more adept with the brush, quickly copied the letters. Instead of stopping, he dipped the brush in the ink again and—shockingly—began to write more letters: *c-a-n-d-e*. He looked at Aiden and smiled, as if happy that Aiden had finally figured it out.

"*Candy* is his word for anything good," Aiden explained, laughing.

"Then we will make some more candy pictures," Ming said brightly.

As the afternoon passed, it felt like they were in a separate little world. The nurse's rocking chair squeaked and her knitting needles clacked from the next room, but she did not interfere. Aiden and Ming began to talk more easily. It was only small, careful subjects, the sort of polite parlor talk that would offend no one and reveal nothing, for the squeaking rocker was a constant reminder of their chaperone. But sometimes their eyes met as they bent over the table, and Ming did not look away so quickly. Sometimes their hands brushed together over the sheets of paper. Ming had a light scent—spicy, sweet and something else, like Christmas cake and the pine forest. The sun peeked through the clouds once and streamed briefly through the window, making her silk blouse sparkle and her black hair glow with a blue sheen. Aiden felt sick and dizzy.

Ming told Peter a story about a fox and a fish and the moon falling into a pond. She illustrated each scene as she told it. "Now you will keep these pictures and you may write the words, yes? I think this is enough lesson for today." She dipped her brush in the water to clean it. Peter gave a weak squawk of protest, but Aiden could see he was clearly exhausted.

"How do you know to do this?" Aiden asked. "Have you seen a child like this before?"

"No, but"—Ming watched the ink swirl in the water—"I know what it feels like to have no voice."

The nurse came abruptly into the room. "It is time for Master Peter's supper."

Ming got up immediately and bowed. "I am grateful that you have allowed me to visit with Peter today."

"Hmm." The woman scowled. She looked at the paintings and her expression relaxed. "Well, those are real pretty." She commandeered Peter's wheelchair and pushed him out of the room.

"Thank you," Aiden said, feeling awkward again now. "This is amazing." *You are amazing,* he wanted to say. "Um— uh, does Silamu Xie have children?" he asked. He had to keep her a little longer. He was failing at his real task once again. He had to find out about Lijia. He had to stop being a stupid love-struck boy! He wanted to both smack himself in the head and sink into a field of daisies. None of this made any sense.

"No," Ming replied.

"So you, um, mostly just work as his translator?"

"When he is in need of my service, I am happy to assist."

"How did you learn to speak English so well?"

"In Shanghai, where I am from, there are many English people."

"And how did you come to be here? In San Francisco?"

"It was my destiny."

Clearly, she was growing uncomfortable with his questioning. How did Christopher always know what to say so smoothly?

"Would you—would you like to see the zoo before you leave?" Aiden asked.

"Yes." Ming's face brightened. "I would like that very much."

"Then, please, I would be honored to show you our zoo! But come down the back stairs, or the ducklings will capture us."

He led her down the servants' stairs and through the

conservatory. He hurried past the orchids and lemon trees and parrots, though he expected she would have liked to see them. He was eager to be outside with her, where no one would be hovering and spying. When he pushed the heavy leaded-glass door open and the damp, cool air hit them, they both laughed. Though the afternoon was foggy, the world felt bright.

Aiden had forgotten, however, about Gouzhi. As they rounded the corner of the house, they saw the stony bodyguard waiting on his stony bench. He stood immediately and without even a nod began to walk toward the side gate, where the buggy waited. Aiden's heart sank. But then Ming said something in Chinese. Gouzhi stopped and turned, a shocked expression on his broad face, as if a tree had just spoken. Ming said something else that sounded very sweet and calm to Aiden but that made the bodyguard scowl. Even in this most foreign of languages, Aiden recognized her tone as commanding. Gouzhi's face turned red, and he stared hard at Aiden, squaring his chest in a challenge. Aiden had fought bigger men—not successfully. But no fight was necessary. Gouzhi sat back down, folding his ham-sized arms across his bull-sized chest and staring straight ahead as if he had never intended to go anywhere.

"What did you say to him?" Aiden asked as he opened the iron gate to the zoo.

"Many pretty words," she said as she slipped past him, "to thank him for the work of protecting me. Then I told him that the fence around the zoo is like the Great Wall of China, and this is the only gate. If he is meant to protect me, he must protect the gate."

"What is he meant to protect you from?" Aiden asked.

Ming smiled. "You hear stories about Chinese villains," she said. "We hear stories about American villains."

"Fair enough."

Aiden closed the gate behind them, happy to feel the latch click firmly into place. Ming looked around and gave a small sigh of relief. Her whole posture changed, as if all the little shadow birds in her paintings were lifting her up.

"This is the first time since I have come to San Francisco that I may look and see no buildings," Ming said.

Even a rich man's house in the crowded warrens of Chinatown would offer little garden space or view of the sky, Aiden realized. The zoo was carefully landscaped with terraced rock walls, winding stone paths and green plants everywhere, even in February. The clouds were thin enough to let a soft wash of sunshine through. They walked in a gauzy quiet, casting no shadows. The air seemed distorted—it was like looking through water. How was it that in her presence he could feel completely calm and completely crazed at the same time?

"This is an aardvark," Aiden said. "It comes from Africa. In the wild it eats ants and termites, which it digs for furiously with its enormous claws. But here we raise crickets and mealworms to feed it." The aardvark was curled up and sleeping in its shelter. "This is a coatimundi," Aiden went on hurriedly. "It comes from South America, is thought to be in the raccoon family and eats fruits and grubs." The coatimundi was also sleeping. It was in fact a sleepy little zoo.

"These are a kind of antelope called dik-diks," Aiden said. He realized he was almost reciting Christopher's standard girl-at-the-zoo speech word for word. But what else could he possibly think of to talk about? As easy as it had been in Peter's room, now his brain was full of noise and sand. Ming shifted the air as she walked, made it denser and loaded. Aiden showed her the monkeys and an enormous waddling porcupine. Ming stopped in front of the bobcat's cage. She pulled her jacket tighter around her neck.

"What is this animal?"

"A bobcat," Aiden said. "Also called a lynx."

"It is beautiful."

The bobcat had a thick caramel coat spotted with brown, and tufts of black fur on its ears. The cat stared at them with a defiant gleam in its yellow eyes. It had worn a track around the perimeter of its enclosure with its pacing.

"It is very wild?"

"More shy, really. It won't attack a person."

"I mean, it doesn't like the cage."

Aiden didn't know what to say to that. What animal did?

"It gets plenty to eat here," he offered. "A rabbit every day, and lots of mice."

"That is good," Ming said sadly.

Aiden desperately did not want her to be sad. "Come see the polar bears—their cage is enormous and they have a pool. The cubs have grown up here—they're really very happy."

He led her along the winding stone path. She bent the light around her. The polar bear cage was carved out of the hillside, and a thick hedge along the walkway obscured any sight of it until you rounded a corner and arrived directly in front. The approach was designed to have a big impact, and it certainly did now. The two cubs, nearly full grown, charged the bars. Ming cried out and jumped back. Aiden touched her shoulder. It was like touching lightning. The bone fit perfectly in his palm, like it was carved to the exact shape of his hand. He could feel her slender body trembling, but she stood straighter, as if embarrassed to show fear.

"They can't get out," he said, not moving his hand. Her body leaned closer to his, naturally, like a reed in a current. Her hair smelled of ginger. A swarm of noisy angels started buzzing around inside Aiden's skull.

"They're just excited to see people," he said. "And I usually bring them hardtack."

"Hard tacks?" she said.

"It's a piece of toasted bread," he explained. "Crunchy." His lungs were melting. "For a treat."

He reached in his jacket pocket in hopes there might be a crust but instead felt the letter to Lijia. Leftover angels crashed. His skull was full of dust. There would be no better chance. The letter to Lijia was the whole reason he had pursued Ming, after all, wasn't it? To fulfill his duty, to secure the absolution he needed. But once he gave Ming the letter, everything would change. And right now, he wanted nothing to ever change. He wanted only to stand next to her until her breath filled up the sky.

"I—I have something to give you," he said. His fingers squeezed the letter and slowly began to draw it out. But what would it matter if Lijia didn't know for a little longer? Her brother would still be dead. Maybe it was mercy to let her hope a little longer. He let go of the letter, pulled his hand out empty, bent down and plucked a crocus from one of the planter boxes.

"Here."

"Thank you," Ming said. "It is very pretty."

"It's a crocus," he said. "The gardener forces the bulbs in the hothouse."

"Yes, we have crocuses in China." She tucked the flower into the button loop at the neck of her blouse. The fabric shifted, and he caught a glimpse of her collarbone. The ground shook, the clouds swirled, every animal roared and a thousand crocuses burst open across the globe. He could be happy with just the bones of her, he thought. The seagull arc of her collarbone, the gravel of her wrist.

"What is that?" Ming said, looking at his chest. Her glance cut through his ribs like an axe. Aiden clutched awkwardly at the leather pouch that he wore around his neck. It had swung free when he bent to pick the flower.

"It's, ah, it's an Indian pouch," he stammered. "To keep tokens."

"Tokens?"

"Little things that have meaning."

"Like a charm? An amulet for luck?"

"More like to remember things that have taught you something. Or to help you remember things that are important."

"Tokens are for guiding?"

"In a way, yes."

"Have they guided you well?"

"I don't know," he said honestly. "But I like where I am right now."

Ming blushed and dropped her gaze but did not move away. "Are there Indians in San Francisco?"

"No," Aiden said. "I came across the country in a wagon

train. I met Indians on the journey. I come from Kansas. Do you know where that is? I'm sorry," he added hurriedly. "I know very little about China. So I don't know what you know. . . ." Why did he sound so stupid around her? He had learned to talk to regular girls well enough.

"I do not know about Kansas. I know about New York. Is Kansas far from there?"

"Oh yes," Aiden said. "Kansas is far from everywhere."

The bears, as if frustrated by his most lame conversational skills, turned away from the bars and tumbled into their pool. They were big enough now that they nearly filled it.

"How did you come to be here?" Aiden asked. "In San Francisco."

"I suppose because I had no tokens to guide me." Ming's smile vanished, and it was like a cloud had darkened the earth.

"You are unhappy here," Aiden said.

Ming looked at him steadily. Aiden could see a galaxy of stars in the dark irises.

"I—I should go now," she said.

"Are you—are you ill treated?"

"No," she said quickly. "I am sorry. I did not mean to sound ungrateful with my destiny. But I must go now—Gouzhi is not a patient man."

"When can you come again?" Aiden said.

"I think there is nothing more I can teach Peter," Ming said hesitantly. "I think the secret is only the brush and the ink. And simple pictures. You will do very well as you are."

"But I—we— want to see you again. The little girls and—and Peter and I—I want to see you again." He yearned to touch more bones of her: the trellis of her ribs, the seashell of her ear, the bent-willow jaw. But he restrained his greedy hand, curled his fingers away and just brushed his rough knuckles across the crocus in her blouse. When he dropped his hand, it touched hers, and she didn't pull away. Her fingers melted into his palm. Her body leaned into his. Aiden kissed her on the lips. They both stiffened at the pure surprise of it, then realized the kiss completely—every soft, trembling moment of it.

A purposeful step and cough sounded from the path back beyond the hedges. Aiden and Ming sprang apart.

"Mr. Madison, sir?" Mr. Butter certainly knew enough about the zoo to keep a discreet distance.

"Coming," Aiden called, his heart pounding. "Right away." He looked at Ming. "I must see you again," he whispered, taking her hands. "Tell me how. Tell me where to go and I will go there."

"There is nowhere." Her voice cracked. She leaned into him and spoke into the dip of his shoulder, where motion joined breath. "This must be enough."

"It is not."

"It is impossible," Ming said. "It is not my destiny."

She pulled away, her body slow and reluctant. Aiden brought her hand to his lips and kissed her fingers. "Destiny changes all the time. You just take one step on a different path. One step different, and there's a new destiny. Say you'll meet me again."

Finally Ming gave a little nod. "Tomorrow night is the last night of our New Year—the Lantern Festival. Everyone will be out in the streets to celebrate. Women are allowed to walk freely on this night. Go to the steps of the restaurant where the dinner was held—just after dark. Can you find it?"

"Yes." He would find a single crocus in the desert, one petal floating on the ocean. "I will be there."

34

Aiden slept but a few restless hours that night and woke before dawn, just as the sky began to lighten. How could he wait for dark again? Dark was a year away. How could he pass all the minutes of this day? He splashed cold water on his face, dressed and walked to the harbor and back. The sun had risen by then. He read the newspaper and drank his coffee; he visited the polar bears and played with the ducklings and sat in the conservatory looking at the orchids that would never be beautiful again because now everything was compared to Ming. It was not yet ten. He worked with Peter and it was still only noon. The piano teacher came and the little girls plunked away another hour. Time seemed like a cruel mirage. His throat was closed to food. His blood was thin and fizzing like soda water. He played chess with Christopher and it was still only two o'clock.

"What is wrong with you?" Christopher pressed. "The sun is out today, and you're still as restless as the ducklings on Christmas Eve."

"Nothing," Aiden said.

"If I didn't know better, I'd say you were in love."

Aiden blushed and zipped his bishop recklessly across the board.

"Good thing you know better, then," he replied. Christopher looked at him suspiciously but was distracted with the opportunity to entrap the bishop.

Finally the afternoon passed and the dusk began to purple the sky. Aiden slipped out of the house through the kitchen while the cook was busy preparing supper. He had not told Christopher he was going out, for he knew that his friend, already suspicious, would see through any excuse Aiden offered. But he did tell the cook not to set a place for him, so the family would not be worried at his absence. He walked quickly down the drive, keeping to the grass along the edge so as not to scrunch on the gravel, then set off down the road, forcing himself not to run. As he neared the border of Chinatown, he saw other Americans also headed that way. Clearly, he was not the only one to know about the Lantern Festival. Any entertainment was welcome on a February evening. Aiden kept his head down. He knew enough people in the city by now that there was bound to be someone who would recognize him. At lunchtime Christopher hadn't had any plans for the evening, but it was quite possible one of his friends might have sent a note in the afternoon post, looking to get up a group to go. Aiden wore the jacket from Fish's mother's old dead cousin and his denim trousers. He knew he could never blend in among the Chinese—he was far too tall, for one thing—but at least he could be not terribly obvious.

As he neared Chinatown, he could see a glow, and when he turned the corner onto Kearny Street, he suddenly saw a river of red light, as if the streets were flowing with lava. Hundreds of people were gathered there, and everyone, from the oldest man to the smallest baby able to hold a stick, carried a lantern. Lanterns hung over every door of every building and from every signpost, sending curls of candle smoke up into the plummy dusk. Most were plain red globes, made of bamboo frames with paper skins, but some were elaborately painted with fish and dragons and birds or Chinese symbols. Vendors wiggled through the mob with bouquets of small lanterns on bamboo sticks held over their shoulders.

Aiden wormed his way through the crowd, looking for the restaurant. He quickly realized, with dread, that all the buildings looked alike. This time there was no stream of white guests and swarm of attendants. He could not, of course, decipher the Chinese signs. He climbed the stairs of several places and peeked in the windows, but that didn't help, as all the restaurants were also furnished and decorated pretty much the same. He felt cold prickles of sweat race down his back. A little over a year ago, when he was trying to find his way through mountains in a blizzard, he had not felt such a sense of panic. Finally Aiden decided to just pick one of the restaurants, wait there and hope she would see him. He scanned the crowd, certain that he could spot her despite the hundreds of people and the bobbing lanterns and the clouds of smoke from firecrackers.

But what if she wasn't coming? The way she looked at him, the way her body seemed drawn to his own—that could all be his imagination. And even if she did feel something, any relationship—even just as friends—was impossible. Aiden pressed his fingers hard against his eyes, trying to smash back his thoughts. Red lanterns bobbed through the street below. The full moon inched up into the sky.

Had Silamu Xie suspected something and locked Ming away? Like Lijia was locked away? Aiden felt a new wave of guilt. He would tell Ming tonight. He had to. Unless the universe shifted somehow, he would never see her again. But that was an impossible life to accept. The red lanterns spun luminous threads through the darkening street. Faces were distorted by the lights, carved into arcs of glowing chins and cheeks. Drumbeats tattered the night, and strings of fire-crackers snapped. Two little boys darted past in green silk jackets, a protective swarm of family lighting a ring around them. The full moon rose higher—and still she had not come.

A young boy appeared by Aiden's side. "Are you lost?"

"No," he said, startled. "Thank you, but I'm just watching the lights."

"They are very beautiful."

"Yes."

Only then did Aiden realize that the boy was Ming. She wore a man's blue cotton pants and quilted jacket. She had braided her hair into a pigtail and wore a little cloth cap.

"It's you!" he said.

"Yes." The candle in her lantern flickered and Aiden saw her smile. It was all he could do not to grab her and kiss her.

"Come," Ming said, stepping quickly back, also evading the urge. She led him down the steps, into the swirling river of light. Time stopped. Nothing mattered now but this moment, and they were together in the moment and that would be enough for all time. Aiden felt like his senses were mixed and overlapping. Solid objects melted while mist turned to stone. Colors were sharp against his skin. Sounds had weight inside his head. People and objects froze completely still or moved so fast they were a blur. Although they were among hundreds of people now, Aiden felt like he and Ming were alone and invisible, walking in a cloud of fireflies. They could not hold hands, or even touch. They could not really even talk, for a common Chinese boy speaking near-perfect English with an American man would be suspicious. When

Ming did speak, she feigned the simple words and broken speech that one of the Chinese tourist guides or restaurant touts might use.

"See lantern, yes!" She pointed at a particularly elaborate lantern covered with Chinese symbols. People were gathered around it, chattering and laughing. "Chinese word on lantern tell joke. Joke with answer? People guess?"

"A riddle?"

"Ah, yes—riddle!" Ming smiled and rolled her eyes, laughing with him.

"What is the riddle?" Aiden asked. It was too noisy to hear the whole thing, but he loved the chance to bend his ear close to her lips and feel her breath on his cheek for a few seconds. A vendor interrupted, carrying two baskets on a pole over his shoulder. In the baskets were little paper-wrapped bundles.

"Ah, good!" Ming pulled a coin out of her pocket, and the man handed her one of the bundles. She unwrapped the parcel, which held two little rice balls.

"*Yuanxiao,*" she said. "Tradition food of Lantern Festival." She took one out and fed it to him. Aiden could not tell if it was sweet or salty, only that her finger had touched his lips. They walked together through the crowd. Because they could not talk freely, they spoke with their eyes and postures, inventing a new language of brushed arms and secret smiles. Ming would point out something, as a guide would do, but her hand would linger in the air, seductively as an exotic dancer's, then brush the length of his arm as it fell. Aiden could touch her shoulder now and then, for the crowd was so dense he might rightfully fear getting lost. The thick jacket muffled her shape, leaving him only the knob at the top of her back and the plow blade of her shoulder. Sometimes she clutched his coat sleeve and he could feel the curl of her knuckles through the fabric.

Aiden had almost starved to death once. Love felt exactly the same, only completely opposite. Starvation had scraped out the center of his bones, numbed his hands and feet and shimmered his vision. It conjured weird, distant music in the back of his brain and made everything he touched feel oddly unreal. The same symptoms seized him now, only the ache in his gut was a lump of silver. The strings that fastened his heart in his chest had come undone, so the muscle skidded around with every beat. His lungs could never get enough air, for the air contained the breaths she had exhaled.

Firecrackers exploded nearby, and both of them startled and reached for the other—then quickly pushed away. It was insane not to take her hand. Insane to be kept apart not by mountains or rivers or deserts, but by stupid social rules.

"Come," she whispered, a bright, conspiratorial glint in her eyes. She led him away from the river of people and down a small street, deeper into the heart of Chinatown. She hesitated several times, looking around for some landmarks as the streets grew more narrow, twisting and dead-ending, but finally she led him into a square. There was an ornate building in the center, which Aiden guessed was a joss house, or temple. Lanterns hung across the entry, strung between two ornately carved wooden posts. Three elderly men sat on a bench outside. Ming mumbled something, bowed and backed up, pulling him along, back into the dark street.

"I am sorry," Ming whispered once they were out of sight. "I thought there would be no people there now because of the festival. I thought it might be a place for us to be alone."

Aiden said nothing. In this dark corner, for a moment at least, they were alone. He slid one hand behind her velvet neck, pulled her face to his and kissed her. That kiss could not have been long enough had it lasted a year, but it was only a few seconds before they both heard voices coming. They jumped apart. Aiden turned his face to the wall and hunched his shoulders to hide his height. Three Chinese women came around a corner, walking toward them. One carried a lantern that cast enough light to show them. The women muttered something but hurried on their way. Aiden and Ming both choked back nervous giggles and clutched each other again.

"Come outside," Aiden said. "We won't go far," he promised. But where could they go outside Chinatown? He couldn't take her to a café or a hotel lobby or a theater, and certainly not a saloon. No Chinese would be allowed in any white establishment except for the worst Barbary dives. He could not bring her to the Worthington house with no lessons as an excuse. The night was too cold to sit outside for long. But they could walk at least. They could have another hour.

"There is a hill nearby," Aiden said. "You can see the ocean from the top. Well, just the bay, actually, but it's lovely in the moonlight. I will bring you safely back. Before the festival ends. I promise."

She twisted her fingers harder into his sleeve. Her whole body was trembling.

"I will go with you."

He took her hand, his heart soaring. He had no idea which way to go. "Do you know how to get to Washington Street?"

"I don't know streets outside," Ming said. "I only know from the main street here to the temple and to Silamu Xie's house."

Of course. No woman was allowed to wander freely through these streets even in daylight. Aiden looked up at the sky. During the long sea voyage, the stars had become a familiar map, but here the city chopped the sky into tiny patches that could tell him little. In the forest, the moss on the trees would point him north. But right now there was nothing that offered guidance through the maze of China-town at night.

"Where I met you tonight—which way is that?" he asked. Ming pointed.

"Can you keep us headed opposite, then?" Even if she didn't know the streets, she would at least have more sense of this warren than he did. She could read the shop signs and know if they were going in circles.

"I will try."

Despite the full moon, it was dark in the narrow passages. There were no streetlamps, only occasional faint stripes of lamplight seeping through the slats of wooden shutters. But Ming managed to navigate with only a few dead ends and soon guided them to the edge of Chinatown. She hesitated at the boundary as if she were on the edge of a chasm. Aiden longed to just take her hand and run with her, but they still could not be seen walking together. A white man and a Chinese boy inside of Chinatown could be explained. The boy could be taking him to an opium den, a gambling house or one of the wretched basements where women were forced to work as prostitutes. But out here they would certainly be suspicious. So they walked apart, resisting the urge to even look at each other.

After two blocks, the streets became less crowded and the fog grew thicker, offering disguise. They eased closer to each other, close enough that the white puffs of their breaths mixed in the chill air. Ming slipped her hand into his. They were alone now. The rules were gone for now. They stopped by a mossy stone wall, neither one guiding the motion of their bodies, and tumbled into each other. Her braid lay across her chest and pressed between them like a rope as they kissed. Her forehead was fringed with wisps of foggy hair that brushed against Aiden's face. He could almost feel her body through the baggy clothes. Small as she was, she was not frail.

"I know a place we can go," Aiden said with sudden inspiration. "A place indoors." The Larsons' house had caught fire last spring and was being rebuilt. Aiden knew it was still unfinished. He had seen Mrs. Worthington and Mrs. Larson visiting in the conservatory two days ago, looking at furniture catalogs. "If you want to."

Ming nodded. Aiden took her hand. Nothing more would ever go wrong in the world. They ran together through the misty street, past iron gates and yellow windows, past Grace Church, then up a steep, short hill behind it. The house was completely dark, as he had hoped it would be.

"Who lives here?" Ming whispered as he led her around to the back.

"No one right now," he said softly. "There was a fire last spring," he explained. "It's being rebuilt. There is a loose window in the pantry that we used to sneak my friend in after curfew." Aiden paused, looking for a watchman, but there didn't appear to be anyone around. Anything worth stealing—barrels of nails, slabs of marble or planks of wood—would need to be hauled in a cart, and the streets at the bottom of the hill were guarded well enough to prevent that.

Aiden saw, to his great relief, that the small pantry window was still easy to jostle loose.

"No one will come here?" Ming asked in a shaky voice. "Are you sure?"

"Absolutely," Aiden said. "Give me your knee." He cupped his hands and boosted Ming over the high sill, then pulled himself up and wiggled in. The house smelled of damp plaster and sawdust. The dining room was newly papered with French wallpaper, an intricate pattern of flowers, fruits and vines. All the salvaged furniture had been stored here, stacks of chairs and iron bedsteads, sofas and tables covered with sheets. The room was even a little bit warm. There was an iron stove with a bed of carefully banked coals. Plaster and paint would never dry in the damp. Aiden opened the stove vents, stirred the embers and tossed in a few lumps of coal from the hod nearby. Then he shut the iron door, leaving only glowing stripes of light peeking around the edges to illuminate the room.

He did not turn around. He had no idea what to do or say now. But he did not have to think or move or speak. Ming came over silently and stood before him. She pulled her braid over her shoulder and untwisted the glossy strands. She slipped the loops from the cloth buttons and let the quilted jacket fall open. She took his hand and kissed his palm. Aiden picked her up and carried her to the couch. Little puffs of dust rose from the sheets as their bodies fell together.

35

Afterward, when their skin had cooled and their breathing eased and they lay together tucked into the curl of the sofa, the sheet scrunched into ridges beneath their bodies, Aiden still could not stop touching her. Her skin was like nothing that could exist in the world.

"Your skin is so smooth, it's like . . ." What was it Christopher had said? "It's like a teacup."

"A teacup?" She laughed.

"A—a fancy teacup," he fumbled. "A teacup made of"— for his very life and the fate of the world, he could not remember the word *porcelain*—"the finest kind of clay."

"Oh?" Her dark eyes danced with amusement. "Well, thank you."

"And your arms are like branches!"

"Branches?"

"From plum trees—with blossoms that are swaying in the wind. Oh God." He laughed and rolled over as much as the narrow couch would allow. "I'm trying to say how beautiful you are."

"So I am clay and branches," she said lightly. "Next you will say I am bread and water?"

"Oh yes." He kissed her neck, her shoulder, her heart. "You are most definitely bread and water."

"So common?"

"As common as air is to a drowning man."

She pushed him away, looking into his eyes, with just a velvet inch between their bodies. "Can I also be one thing—grand? Can I be—a bit of starlight?" She pointed to the faint sparks appearing through the window. "From that little one there?"

Aiden sank his fingers into the black river of her hair. "You can be no little thing." His breath collected in the dip of her throat, and he breathed it back saturated with her. "You are the North Star. Without you, I am dashed upon the rocks and lost."

"Do not say that." The playfulness vanished. Her voice was sad now. "I am not that." She sat up, one soft hand trailing down his arm. "I cannot be even bread and water to you. We must go back now. The festival will be over soon." The golden firelight showed chill bumps on her skin. She picked up the cotton shirt and slid her arms into the coarse sleeves. "My maid will be punished if she returns without me."

"When can I see you again?"

"You cannot. It is impossible."

"But that was before—this!" Aiden sat up and took her hand.

"I said impossible!" Ming pulled her hand away. She had the same tone of command that had forced Gouzhi back to his place on the bench. "That doesn't mean maybe, or if the stars are in order, or if—if—" She choked up. "It means impossible." She pushed her feet into the trousers, then jumped up, keeping her back to him. She pulled the baggy trousers up and tied the drawstring. She all but vanished in the dark clothes in the dim light.

"Wait," Aiden said. "Have I done something wrong? Have I offended you?"

"No, I am sorry. Not at all." Ming's eyes filled with tears. "It is just a fact."

"I know there are difficulties," Aiden said, groping for his own trousers. "But we can figure them out."

"There is nothing to figure out."

"Ming, I love you."

"I am to be married."

"Married?" Aiden froze. It was like a brick to the face. "You're engaged?"

"'Engaged' is your word. It is different for Chinese."

Aiden stood still, trying to understand the words she had said.

"Do you love him?" *Do you love me?* was what he really wanted to ask.

"It doesn't matter," Ming said.

"Of course it matters! Was tonight—was this all false?"

"No. Do not think that." Her hands reached out and her body moved toward embrace, but then she stopped herself. "There is nothing false in my heart for you. Never think that." The slow tears spilled over and rolled down her cheeks. "I don't know what love is. Only from stories and songs. But when I first saw you at the banquet, my heart became joyful. Every time after that we are together is beautiful, and all the time we are apart is a beautiful ache. So I think that is love. But it does not matter."

"Of course it matters! It is the only thing that matters!" Aiden grabbed her shoulders, small and cold and shaking. She pulled away.

"I am sorry, Aiden. I never thought yesterday that we would be this way tonight. I thought only that we would walk together in the festival for an evening. That it would be a small time with feeling love and to be free—and then I could remember the rest of my life one happy night."

"Are you sorry that we have been together this way?" Aiden asked.

"No." She touched his face, then his chest, her hand weighing on his heart. "I am sorry only that I am selfish. I wanted to know how it feels to be like the bride in the arms of the man who loves her. And who she loves." She brushed the tears off her cheeks. "For this I give you my apology."

"I don't want your apology! I want to be with you. No one can force you to marry! Come away with me now. I have money to keep us!" Aiden felt a thrill of excitement. He did have money and so, for once, he could fix something. "We can make a new life. There must be some place we can be together. New York, maybe!"

"I want with all my heart to be with you." Ming smiled sadly. "But the arrangement cannot change. I must marry Silamu Xie."

"What?" Aiden's insides turned to lead. "What do you mean? Silamu Xie is married already. He has a wife. I know he has a wife."

"Yes," Ming said. "But soon—two days or maybe three from now—she will die. She has been ill for a long time. After the mourning period, I will become his wife. It is arranged."

Aiden felt a wash of guilt, but also relief. It was sad, of course, but with Lijia dead, his duty would be released.

"I—I'm sorry that his wife is sick," he said, trying to choose his words carefully. "But it doesn't mean you have to take her place!"

She pulled the dense black waterfall of hair over her

shoulder and combed it with her fingers. "I was brought here from China only for this agreement—to marry Silamu Xie," she said in a toneless voice. "It was arranged long ago between our families."

"I don't understand. It was arranged while he was already married?"

Ming began to braid her hair, moving the heavy strands slowly, as if that might weigh down time. "It takes six months to sail to China," she said. "Silamu Xie sent his emissary more than one year ago. His wife had been ill for a long time and Xie believed that she would die before I arrived. So my family was told she was dead. There are many years of trouble between our families. This marriage was supposed to bring the families together—for greater business."

The fire had burned down and was only embers now, casting a low red glow on the emptiness of the room.

"My brother Jian came from China with me as my guardian," Ming went on. "When we arrived and learned this wife was still alive, Jian was angry at the deceit. He said it is trickery to make me number two wife. It is disgrace for me to be number two wife."

Aiden felt a buzz creep up the back of his skull. This could not be happening. Jian might be a common Chinese name. Arranged marriages were common enough. The trembling he felt might be an earthquake. Please, God, let it be an earthquake. But Ming did not seem to feel any earthquake. She was buttoning up the quilted cotton jacket, closing the fabric around her throat with grim resolution.

"Xie said we will wait for number one wife to die," she went on. "My brother said no, the insult is too great. The agreement is broken." Ming smoothed out the baggy jacket, tugged on the hem, then sat on a crate, folding her hands, shifting back into the guarded servant, the untouchable object. "My brother can be"—she drew herself up in an imperious pose—"very haughty and without grace. He cursed the house of Xie. He told me our trunks will not be unpacked and we will leave in the morning. That night he vanished. Silamu Xie's wife did not bear him children. He wants a son. He promises when we are married my brother will return."

Aiden felt like all the blood had drained from his body. There could still be an earthquake. There could be a tidal wave.

"You said your name was Ming."

She looked at him, puzzled. "Yes."

"What is your full name?" Aiden had to concentrate on how to make words come out.

"Lijia Ming Zhang. I use only Ming here." Her voice was floating away now, and it seemed she was sliding backward down a long tunnel away from him. "It may be silly, but I think it is a way I may keep something of myself. Aiden, what is wrong? You look—ghostly. Why do you shake? What have I said?"

There was no way to say it but plainly—no outcome but a landslide. "I know of your brother," he said. "I didn't know that you were Lijia. I thought you were her maid." His throat was drier than it had ever been from the guano.

"Her maid? What do you mean? How do you know my brother? Where is he?"

"I'm sorry. He's—there was an accident. He asked me to take a message to you. I searched for you. I'm so sorry," he said.

"I don't understand," Ming said. "You searched for me? But here I am! He is all right?"

"No," Aiden said. "No, he died."

"How could you meet my brother? How do you know it was really Jian? It wasn't Jian! I am sure! You don't know!"

"He told me a story," Aiden said softly. "About how your father tied a rope around him to teach him to swim. He held Jian from a bridge, and you ran up the bank and threw flowers in the water and you told him to reach for them, and so he learned to swim."

Ming began to tremble but she did not cry. Her expression was blank.

"Tell me everything," she said.

"I met your brother in Peru," Aiden said. "Silamu Xie sent him there to work in a mine. I was on my ship—Christopher Worthington and I owned a ship—and I met your brother. He told me he had been kidnapped and asked me to take a message to his sister Lijia. But Jian said Lijia was the wife of Silamu Xie. I went to the banquet hoping I would find her. Xie said his wife was unable to attend. So I thought you were her maid or companion. Then I thought that you might be able to take a letter to her to explain about her brother. Also, I was already in love with you."

"You never gave me a letter," Ming said.

"I meant to. The first time you came to the house. I had it in my pocket, but then everything happened with Peter. I had no chance to talk with you alone to explain." Even as Aiden was sick with this new truth, sick with having to tell her and sick with his own hand in the awful story, he was beginning to feel a flicker of hope as well. With Jian dead, she would not have to marry Silamu Xie. He could have her love, her magic,

349

all the bones of her. "I had it the second time too," he went on. "But I was afraid if I gave it to you, that would be the end. That I would never see you again."

"My brother was made a prisoner in this mine?"

"The workers are indentured," he explained. "They mine fertilizer for growing crops." How easily he embraced this lie now! "Jian was unable to convince the manager that he had been brought wrongly. So he wasn't allowed to leave."

He did not have to tell her all the details. Wasn't it kinder not to? He told her about all the plans her brother had thought up to escape, but nothing of the wretched conditions they lived under. He told about Jian quoting Shakespeare but left out his cruel remarks about the other coolies. He did not mention the rock at all. Ming shivered as she listened but would not move closer to the stove. So he sat across from her, leaving the dark shadows between them. He told her as carefully as he could, and the moon passed fully across one of the new windows before he finished.

"I wanted to help him," Aiden said. That wasn't really a lie. He had wanted to help Jian. Hadn't he offered to surrender the cargo? "But our ship had to leave quite suddenly. I didn't have a chance to speak with the manager." Would he really have done it—given up his fortune to save one man? "Then your brother tried to hide on our ship as we were leaving."

Jian's death, in this telling, was quick and undramatic. Koster discovered Jian was missing. Men rowed out to the ship and Jian was shot. That was what happened. Aiden felt the clutch of panic again at the memory, but in a strange way, he was beginning to believe this version himself. He had done everything he could. Ming sat silently all this time, rocking slightly. When Aiden finished and she finally spoke, her voice was steady.

"You are certain that my brother was killed?"

"I—I saw it all."

"What was done with his body?"

"There is no place to bury a man there," Aiden said. "He was given rights as a sailor."

"He was put into the sea?"

"Yes."

"You saw this?"

"Yes."

Ming took a deep breath and stood up. She had stopped shaking, though she moved stiffly, her body strained from the long tension.

"Did my brother have time to know he would be killed?"

"Yes."

"Was he . . . brave?"

"Yes." Aiden said this with no hesitation. That answer, to a loved one, was always yes.

"Does Silamu Xie know that Jian is dead?" she asked.

"I don't know. The news could have come on a faster ship."

Ming nodded but said nothing. Her eyes were dull with sorrow and fatigue.

"I will take care of you, Ming," Aiden said. "You don't have to worry. I will take you home to China if you want, to your family. I am—I have money." He wanted just to go back an hour in time, to lying with her in his arms, fumbling over tree branches and teacups.

"I cannot go back to China," she said softly. "My family will have shame."

"We don't have to decide anything right now," Aiden said. His emotions were churned worse than any storm. He felt exhilarated, for Ming was now free, and relieved, for duty no longer hung over his head. But he could also feel the cold pistol in his hand and see the look of hatred in Jian's eyes. It would change nothing for Ming to know this. It would be no mercy.

"You can't go back to Xie's house now," he said. "Come home with me. Everyone will be asleep—no one will even know you're there. Tomorrow we will think what to do. I am not as rich as Silamu Xie, but I have enough to keep us well forever."

Ming nodded. Her face, even in the dim light from the stove, was shivery white. When she stood, her knees gave way. Aiden caught her and held her. She was not goddess of the sun, not plum branches or the North Star, but a girl his own age thrashing out a path to her own life, and he loved her more for that. He eased her back to the sofa, and they sat, holding each other for a long time. The fire died down. The moon set.

"We must fix the house," she finally said.

"Yes."

They shook out the sheet together, billowing it up and letting it float gently down, erasing the creases of their love-making, shrouding it against their passion. Aiden banked the coals and closed the drafts on the stove, then silently they slipped out of the empty house.

The night felt terribly cold. Aiden wasn't sure if the temperature had actually fallen or if they were both just so wrung out. He guessed it was well after midnight, though time had long since vanished. The cold had hardened the muddy ruts in the road, so it was difficult to walk. They did not see anyone else on the streets, but Aiden did not begin to feel at ease until they neared the Worthington home. Hopefully it was late enough that there would be no servants sitting up in the kitchen. All he wanted to do right now was lie in his bed and sleep with Ming in his arms. Even with the stress and confusion, the memories of their lovemaking tumbled through his body like small avalanches.

When he turned the corner and saw the blurry glow of the gas streetlamp by the back gate, Aiden felt a wash of relief. The iron gate was locked, but there was a key hidden behind a loose stone in the wall just inside. Aiden reached his left arm through the bars and felt for it. Suddenly he heard Ming cry out. Aiden saw a shadow lurch out from behind the shrubs. Before he could pull his arm back through the bars, a hard fist slammed between his shoulder blades, knocking him into the gate. Then one large hand grabbed the back of his neck and smashed his face against the iron bars while the other landed hard blows to his side, sending jaggers of pain through his body.

Aiden heard Ming shouting in Chinese and felt the vibrations of a grunted reply. It was Gouzhi, Aiden realized as he struggled to break free. He had come looking for Ming. She was not at home, and this was the only place she would be outside Chinatown. It was over a year since he had last fought a man in the ring, but Aiden's instincts and training were still sharp. Gouzhi's hand wasn't big enough to wrap all the way around Aiden's neck to choke him from behind. So he guessed Gouzhi's next move would be to try to slam his head against the iron bars again. As soon as Aiden felt a twitch in the fingers that signaled Gouzhi pulling him back,

Aiden pushed himself off the bars and jerked his head back as hard as he could, smashing his own skull into the man's face.

As Gouzhi fell back, Aiden pulled his left arm free from the bars, jabbed that elbow into the man's belly, then spun around and followed with a strong right hook to the man's eye.

"Run, Ming!" Aiden shouted. "Get away!" Gouzhi staggered but did not fall. In the flickering lamplight, he looked like a stone statue. But he was far quicker than any statue. He lunged at Aiden, slamming a rock-hard fist to his head. Aiden ducked most of it and managed to catch the man's sleeve. He twisted and pulled as he let his own body fall and roll backward, pulling Gouzhi over with him. Aiden kicked him hard in the groin, then rolled out of the way. He scrambled to his feet, but his legs collapsed beneath him. He saw black birds in a black sky. Then he felt the wet swish of Ming's trouser hem against his face and felt her hands grabbing his coat. Her wet socks had slipped down and, insanely, this aroused him. He pressed his face into that wet bunch of sock like it was a perfumed silken pillow. If he could only touch this much of her, the elegant tendons of her bare ankle, he could die happy. He grabbed hold of her ankle and she pulled him to his knees. Strength flowed into his legs and he got to his feet.

"Run!" he gasped. Gouzhi would not be down for long. Aiden pulled her around the corner of the wall toward the front door of the house.

"Go to the house!"

"No!" Ming stopped.

"They will help us."

"No." She pulled her arm away. "It is danger to the family."

"One night won't matter."

"And danger to me! Xie will know I am there," Ming whispered. "He will demand me to go back. They will send me back. They must."

Aiden tried to focus. Silamu Xie would certainly not send a band of men to storm the house tonight, and Mr. Worthington could summon all the guards he needed by noon. But then what? Worthington had lived through the toughest mob years in this city and knew violence too well. He was fiercely protective of the family and would never tempt those fates. Eventually he would return Ming to Silamu Xie rather than risk the man's anger. Aiden heard a grunt and rough steps behind them: Gouzhi on his feet and searching for them.

"This way," Aiden whispered. He pulled Ming along and they ran to the hedges on the far side of the lawn. They pushed inside the branches and flattened themselves on the ground. The piney scent was luscious, the fat bud tips swollen with resin. If only they were children stealing away for hide-and-seek, it would be a perfect place. No lights came on in the house, but in the last of the moonlight, Aiden could see the shape of Gouzhi standing at the far edge of the lawn. Aiden was pretty sure he would not dare trespass this close to the house. They just had to wait him out, then go—where? Ming was shivering so hard Aiden could hear her teeth chattering. He opened his coat and pulled her body against his, wrapping his arms around her, wrapping them both against the cold and the world.

36

Paradise was nearly empty. And it was warm. Aiden paused in the doorway, keeping Ming behind him in the shadows. There were three men sitting at the bar, steam paddy diggers, Aiden guessed by the mud spatters on their trousers. The two tables nearest the stove were occupied, one by three young women who looked like pretty waiter girls, the other by an old man who seemed quietly glad just to be sitting near them. He had sunken eyes and wore a heavy gray wool coat. One empty sleeve was pinned up with a brooch, a carved gutta-percha oval holding a flower woven from strands of human hair. Keepsakes made of hair had been fashionable during the war, but they always made Aiden shudder.

In the back of the room, at the corner bench where they had sat last time, was Blind Sally, with The Moon curled up tight at her feet.

"Come on," he whispered to Ming. The atmosphere was quiet, the weary bar girls talking softly, the old soldier nodding off, everyone contentedly to themselves. The light was low, with only two lamps behind the bar and some candles and lanterns scattered around the tables. They should be all right if she kept her head down. He had given Ming his own coat and cap to wear over her Chinese clothes, and no one had noticed her so far as they had walked through the streets of the Barbary Coast. Aiden's first thought had been to take her to Mrs. Neils's boardinghouse, but there was no place in a bunk room full of sailors to hide her there for long. Mrs. Neils had the only private room in the house, and that was little more than a nook just off the kitchen. Besides, Ming couldn't walk that far. Though she hadn't complained, Aiden knew she was near exhaustion, and her feet would be freezing in her thin cloth shoes.

The pretty half-Mexican girl was behind the bar, wiping glasses. She smiled as they entered. Aiden couldn't tell if she recognized him, or if she just smiled for everyone. The Moon gave a woof of warning as they approached the table, and Blind Sally looked up, sniffing and squinting.

"Blind Sally," Aiden said softly. "It's Aiden Lyn— Madison." He was so tired he had almost used his real last name.

"And who else?" Blind Sally said suspiciously.

"A friend. We need your help."

"Ah! A friend!" Blind Sally said. "There's a mystery way to put it."

"May we sit?"

"Sit!" she demanded. They slid onto the other side of the corner bench, Aiden keeping Ming on the outside, farthest from Blind Sally.

"There's cold come off you like an ice block." The old woman sat up and waved her crumpled hand at the barmaid. "Girl!"

The barmaid came over to the table.

"Whiskey all around. And something hot with sugar in it. And plenty of sugar. Don't be stingy—they've gone a lost way."

"The kettle's warm on the stove, Miss Sally," the barmaid said. "I'll make some tea."

Ming, looking up for the first time, saw the snarling bear's head on the wall and gave a little shriek.

"A girl?" Blind Sally said in wonderment. "A girl is your friend here now?"

"Yes," Aiden said.

"Does she speak?"

"I do, ma'am," Ming said softly.

"A China girl!" Blind Sally whispered. "Hmmm. Ohh— what tangles now? All sorts here of a night."

The barmaid put two steaming cups of tea and three glasses of whiskey on the table, plus a small jar of sugar and a plate of buttered bread, sliced ham, cheese and apples. It was the loveliest meal ever. Aiden poured half a shot of whiskey and a spoonful of sugar into one of the mugs of tea and gave it to Ming, who wrapped her icy hands around it. She was like a sleepwalker now, silent and dazed, drained.

"We need some place to stay," Aiden said. "For tonight at least—maybe a few days."

"I want no Chinese trouble," Blind Sally said. "They gut you." She made a quick slashing motion across her belly. "Say with a sharp blade you feel nothing, but I say gutting is painful, sharp knife or not."

"No one knows we're here," Aiden reassured her. "Chinese or anyone. We just need a place to sleep tonight. Please. I have money—I can pay."

"I have a bag of diamonds big as your balls!" Blind Sally snapped. "And a gold platter you could sleep on! You shame to offer coin for love danger!"

Ming recoiled—only from the tone, Aiden supposed, for there was no way any of that would have made sense to her. He squeezed her leg under the table. The Moon unwound his shaggy head for a glance but did not think the tirade enough to rouse himself for.

"I meant no insult, Blind Sally," Aiden said. "You know that." He never knew what to think with Blind Sally. She had requested payment for the bullets she had used to drive off his robbers, yet now acted offended that he offered to pay for a bed.

"Girl!" Blind Sally called out again. The sweet barmaid never seemed at all put out by the old woman's snappishness. "Make them in the baron's room!"

The barmaid went back behind the bar and fetched a ring of keys from a hook. She brought the money box over to the table, where Blind Sally then pulled it onto her lap. She took out her enormous pistol to guard it. Aiden and Ming ate hungrily and gulped the sweet, milky tea, dosed with the whiskey. Everything felt a little better.

The barmaid returned with a lamp. "The room is ready."

"Go on, then," Blind Sally said.

The barmaid led them through a curtain at the back of Paradise, showed them the outhouse, waited for them to use it, then led them upstairs. The stairs were steep, hardly more than a ladder, and so narrow Aiden had to turn sideways. At the top were four doors that opened outward onto a landing not more than a yard square, so small that only one door could ever swing open at a time. The barmaid slid a key into one of the locks and squeaked the door open. There was a bed inside the room. Inside the entire room. Wall to wall, front to back, except for a foot-wide aisle by the door. A gigantic headboard nearly touched the ceiling. It was of some dark wood, carved completely with cherubs, clusters of grapes and apples, flowers, great leafy vines and birds. A shorter but equally elaborate footboard pressed against the other wall so tightly the spindles had gouged the wall. Aiden wondered if the room had been built around the crazy bed. The walls were thin, partitions more than walls, made only of unplastered boards. Covering those makeshift walls were at least twenty oil paintings, heavy dark portraits of stern ancient people in gilded frames.

"It's very nice," Aiden said, wondering if Gouzhi had actually hit him hard enough for hallucinations. "Thank you."

The room had one window, with a flour sack nailed to the frame for a curtain, and a narrow shelf with a jug of water, a tin cup and a small stack of newspapers. The barmaid set the lamp down on the shelf.

"There's a chamber pot beneath the bed if you need—but you empty it yourself, not me."

"Yes. Of course. Thank you. What is your name?"

"Avia."

"Thank you, Avia. May I ask, please, we would like it if no one knew we were here—especially the Chinese girl."

"No one asks anyone's business here," Avia said. "Though you'd do best to stay in the room, miss, and not be seen."

She left them then, and Aiden latched the door. Ming sat on the edge of the bed, still silent and numb.

"You're safe," Aiden said. He knelt and slipped off her wet shoes. He unrolled the damp socks and pulled off her trousers, the hems heavy with mud. There was nothing sexual about any of this now—only something like peacefulness. He pulled back the rough blankets and nudged her between the coarse sheets. He climbed in beside her and pulled the heavy blankets up over them, spooning up against her back with an arm around her. Ming took his hand in hers and pressed it against her chest. She was still shaking, not constantly, but in little spasms like an injured bird.

Aiden woke disoriented, but strangely calm. He opened his eyes and saw Ming, wide awake, her brown eyes gazing at him. A thin gray light washed through the narrow window, painting the room in watercolor softness and lighting up the flour sack's proclamations. *Finest Grade. Highest Purity. Guaranteed Best Quality.* Her face was luminous above the rough gray blanket.

"Hello," he said. What a strange glory this was—like waking up in mythology. He touched her hand and it still did not seem real. "You are so beautiful."

"I did not choose it."

"But you still are."

"You fight in your sleep," she said.

Aiden sat up in alarm. He saw there was a bruise on her cheekbone and slight swelling at the corner of her eye. "Did I hit you?"

"No, this was from Gouzhi. You fought against the little angels." She reached up and stroked one of the carved cherubs on the headboard. The dark portraits stared indifferently across the room at each other.

"Is this . . ." She hesitated. "A usual sort of house?"

"No," Aiden laughed. "Not at all."

"These are ancestors?" Ming said.

"I suppose," Aiden said. He stroked her hair. "Do you feel all right?"

"I don't know how I should feel. I am in mourning for my

brother. I am joyful to think I will not marry Silamu Xie. I am afraid of what will come." She smiled shyly. "And I am happy to be with you."

Her body moved toward his, as naturally as the morning. What began as comfort soon flamed into passion again. It was different this time—slower, intuitive, their bodies tuned to each other so that every touch and movement rippled back and forth between them. They could stay forever, Aiden thought as they lay curled together after, right here on this wall-to-wall bed. He would buy soft quilts and smooth sheets and fluffy down pillows, paints and brushes and paper for Ming to paint with, bags of cookies and bread and ham, piles of books, dresses with lace and jars of cream for her skin (though she didn't need it—her skin was perfect—but girls always wanted creams), and day after day could pass in perfect love.

"I must tell you something," Ming said. "I am feeling shame to my brother. The story he told you, of how he learned to swim? That is not the truth."

"What do you mean?" Aiden leaned up on one elbow.

"My father did tie a rope to Jian and hold him from the bridge. It was a very little bridge—only two feet above the water. Jian was a soft and lazy boy and did not want to swim. He screamed and cried that he was drowning, but no boy will drown with his father holding the rope. I did throw flowers into the river, but I was not giving him help, I was laughing at him. I was mean. I said, 'Here, my silly brother! Here are some beautiful blossoms to decorate your tomb. Come and get them before you sink to the bottom.' I was teasing him. Now I feel shame."

"I'm sure he didn't even remember that," Aiden said.

"Oh, I am sure that he did," Ming said. "After, he threw clods of dirt at me and put me in the cupboard with the spiders."

"Well, then, I think that was payback enough. He loved you just the same," Aiden assured her, though he had no idea if Jian really had or not. "I had a sister," he said, stroking her hair. "She died in a river. I would have walked across the world to get her back."

Ming took his face in her hands and they kissed again. Why didn't people just kiss all the time? Aiden wondered. But finally he had to force himself away.

"I have to go," he said. "There are some things I have to take care of. You'll have to stay here. Don't leave the room. I'll be back as soon as I can."

"Where do you go?"

"I have to send word to Christopher," Aiden said. "To let him know I'm all right. Then I'll go talk to my friend Fish. He was the captain on our ship, and he can help me think where we might go."

"Go?"

"You can't stay in San Francisco. At least for a while. Fish will help us know our choices."

Ming lay back and scanned the faces of the ancestors. "I have never had choices," she said softly. "How does one know what choice to take?"

"You pick the one that seems most likely to work out," Aiden said.

"How can you know that?"

"Sometimes you just have to trust what feels right." A watery sunlight illuminated the flour-sack curtain and cast blurred word shadows on her bare shoulder. *Highest Purity. Guaranteed Best Quality.* "Does this feel right?"

Ming nodded. "Yes."

"I won't be long." He bent and kissed her, then kissed her again. He should not feel so ebullient when her whole world had turned upside down, but he couldn't help it. "There's water in the pitcher there, and I'll ask Avia to bring you something to eat. What do you like?"

"I don't know," Ming said. "I've never had American food before. I liked what we ate last night. I liked cheese."

"Cheese?" Aiden laughed. "I can get you cheese. I promise you a lifetime of cheese!"

Aiden ducked his head and climbed sideways down the narrow staircase. The door to Paradise was locked, so he had to exit into the alley past the outhouse, thread his way through the narrow passages to the main street. The morning was foggy, gray, damp and cold, but Aiden felt exhilarated. He felt bad for Ming, of course. He had lost everyone in his own family and knew the pain too well. But while there was room in his head for pain, his soul felt only love—with its unexpected weight and hum. And he felt relief. He had done his duty to Jian. There was a needle of dread still lodged inside him, a stab of guilt, but really, what could he have done differently? And if he helped Ming—Lijia—as he had promised, didn't that balance it all out? On Market Street, he went into the Penny Post messenger office and wrote out a note to Christopher.

I am well, but it is urgent that we talk. I'm in a bit of a mess. Sorry I must be mysterious, but meet me at noon at the Elysium.

Aiden stopped, anxious sweat blooming on his forehead. Would Gouzhi still be watching the house? With so many private guards in the neighborhood, a Chinaman lurking about would be challenged immediately. But what if he was disguised as a laundryman or garbageman? A wealthy man like Silamu Xie probably had lots of men he could muster.

Please beware that a Chinaman may be watching the house and try to follow you, which would not be good. I am in need of $100 cash and some clean clothes—ordinary things. I hope this will not be impossible for you, but in case it is so, please send a message to me at the Elysium indicating such.

After Aiden sent the letter, he walked to the wharf. Captain Neils's lumber boat was moored in its usual place, and Aiden could see men working on the aft deck but couldn't make out if Fish was among them. He asked some men rowing out to another ship to take a message. The only thing left to do now was visit the shipping office and see what ships were scheduled to leave in the next couple of days. San Diego, Hawaii, Mexico—Mexico might be good, Aiden thought as he pulled his coat tight against the February cold. It wouldn't have to be forever, just long enough for Silamu Xie to get over being angry and import another replacement bride for himself.

Aiden pictured a little house on a white sand beach, Ming painting in the courtyard, their walls covered with her pictures, fresh pineapples and oranges to eat every day. They could come back to San Francisco after a while. Or they could go to New York. He didn't know if Americans and Chinese were allowed to marry there, but there were all kinds of races in New York anyway, and no one, it seemed, could hate the Chinese as much as Californians did.

"You are a mess," Christopher said as he plopped down in a chair beside Aiden at the Elysium. He dropped a small canvas satchel on the floor. "Here are your clothes—and the cash." Christopher pulled an envelope out of his jacket pocket and handed it to Aiden. "In case the Chinese come storming in while we're here and you need to flee out the back door or something. But I don't think they followed me. And no one would let a Chinaman in here anyway. But really," he went on, leaning closer with a conspiratorial whisper, "I had no idea this would cause such an uproar! I thought they should be happy!"

Christopher was clearly in one of his bright moods— agitated, excited, talking fast, his blue eyes shining.

"Who should be happy?" Aiden said.

"The Chinese!"

A waiter arrived at the table.

"Coffee and brandy," Christopher said, motioning to the both of them.

"No, just coffee for me, please," Aiden said.

"Brandy." Christopher waved the waiter off. "I had a terrible night—sleepless with worry for you," he went on in a rush. "Then when I got your note this morning about lurking Chinamen—well, I didn't know what to think. I feared for your life. But I must admit, I was a little bit flattered that I had stirred them up so! But why would they be mad? I should think they would be grateful."

"Grateful for what?" Aiden said.

"My story."

"What story? Christopher, what are you even talking about?"

"My story in the *Chronicle*. That's what this is all about, isn't it? You mean you haven't read it?"

"No."

"Seriously? It came out yesterday. The entire city has read it by now! All about the island. About the guano and the smell and the coolie slaves and the rock—all of it. Father is livid, but I think maybe, secretly, he is a little bit proud. I didn't use my own name, of course, but everyone in our set will know. I thought you would be thrilled. Honestly, you didn't read it?" Christopher looked shattered.

"No, I'm sorry," Aiden said. "I was—no."

Christopher pulled a copy of the paper out of his coat pocket and thrust it at Aiden. The *Daily Dramatic Chronicle* was distributed free every day in saloons and coffeehouses throughout the city. It was full of theater news and gossip, sensationalistic stories about the most shocking crimes and occasional slaps at city officials. But lately it had been publishing more straight news, and a feature story once a week. The headline on this feature was huge: *Modern Slavery!* took up the whole first line in enormous type. *Wretched coolies dying for your bread.* Slightly smaller type. *Conditions unfit even for the yellow man!* Below that: *Two young adventurers discover the hellish reality of life on the guano islands of Peru.*

Aiden was stunned. "You wrote this?"

"Yes!"

"How?"

"How? I sat at my desk, that's how! For a really long time."

"Why didn't you tell me?"

"It was meant to be a surprise."

The waiter returned with a coffee service and two glasses of brandy. Christopher fidgeted as the man began to arrange cups and saucers and pitchers of cream. Aiden read quickly through the story.

A cloud of yellow dust swathes the island like the sulfurous breath of the devil himself. . . .

"Thank you. Just leave the tray, please," Christopher said. The waiter bowed and vanished. "I know it won't change things entirely," he said, pouring himself some coffee. "But it might get people thinking. Do you like it?"

If one of the wretches should try to escape, he is punished in the cruelest manner, chained to a rock where the relentless waves pummel him. . . .

Aiden didn't know what to say. He was certainly surprised, but more than that, he felt something like ashamed. He had done little else but anguish over the coolies, while Christopher, whom he had judged unmoved by their plight, had done something quite real.

"I know Charles and Michael de Young, the publishers," Christopher went on. "I'm sure you've met them." He tossed back half his brandy. "They're our own age—Charles is a little older, twenty-one, I think—though they don't really run with our crowd. They have the paper to put out every night, for one thing. And they're Jews." He shrugged, as if this explained everything.

"Still, I see them around often enough. They're at theater openings and some of the after-parties. They're smart—came from nothing and started the *Chronicle* with only twenty dollars. Anyway, they've been wanting to bring the paper up beyond theater news and gossip, so I offered them the story. What do you think?"

Aiden was trying to listen to Christopher's flood of words while reading.

> *The guano is more precious than gold. It has restored fallow fields to the bounties of Eden. But at what price do we enjoy these bounties? Shall your children's bread be wrung from the blood of the yellow slave?*

"Remember on the *Raven* when I said how I wanted to be something different?" Christopher said. "Well, this is perfect! Writing for a paper—it's artistic, but still a real job. I could even start my own newspaper. With the telegraph everywhere now, news is practically falling from the sky—it has to have some place to go. And the best thing of all, my father has nothing to do with newspapers! This would be entirely my own!"

Aiden was only half listening as he read through the whole story.

A Tragedy Ensues

> *As we prepared to depart that final day with our precious cargo, we were unwilling participants in the most desperate act of villainy. One of the unfortunate coolies, so despairing of his wretched existence, attempted to stow away. He hid himself among the sacks of our foul cargo. When we discovered him, there was some debate about his future.*

Any ship assisting a coolie to escape is sent home empty, its cargo confiscated. The decision was taken from us, however, when those on the island, upon discovering the man missing, demanded us to stop. Knowing that unyielding law would have him chained to the rock for a horrible death, the coolie leaped upon one of our sailors. He snatched away the man's knife, slashed him with it, then, nimble as a cat, grabbed me and took me prisoner. With the cold blade pressed against my own throat, shaking in his trembling hand, I could feel the desperate pounding of his heart in his wasted chest.

"Charles said to punch it up a bit," Christopher interjected as Aiden continued reading.

"Shoot me!" the poor man cried out. "Do not doom me to the slow death on the rock. Shoot me or I will kill this man!" There was nothing else to do. My partner had no choice but to shoot the coolie dead.

Aiden picked up his own brandy and took a sip. He felt like his skin had disconnected and he was slipping around inside it.

"I never imagined it would get the Chinese so angry, though," Christopher said. "Why are they angry exactly? It's their own people I'm trying to help, after all."

"They're not angry about your story."

"Then why the lurking and following?"

Aiden folded the paper. "It doesn't have anything to do with your story."

"So what, then?"

Aiden pressed his hands against his eyes as if he could

squeeze his thoughts back into his brain. "You remember Ming, the Chinese girl who came to the house to paint with the ducklings?"

"Yes, of course—everything with Peter."

"Well, I was—I was with her last night."

"With her?" Christopher frowned with puzzlement. "For what? Oh! Oh my God!" He looked both shocked and proud as he realized what Aiden was saying. "You mean you were *with* her?" he whispered.

Aiden nodded.

"She's the one you've been all dizzy about!"

"She's the one I love," Aiden replied quietly.

"Well, that is a problem," Christopher said. "I mean, she is very pretty, but you can't be serious. It's impossible!"

"I love her."

"So what is the immediate problem?" Christopher went on, ignoring that. "Her father? A husband?"

"She is betrothed," Aiden said. "Though against her will. And—" He took a deep breath. "And also"—he handed the paper back to Christopher—"she is the sister of our stowaway."

Christopher paled, and his hand went reflexively to the scar on his throat.

"Our stowaway? You mean the coolie who tried to kill me?"

"I only found out last night," Aiden went on hurriedly.

"Is this some kind of joke?"

"No."

"This is absurd! How would you ever meet his sister here in San Francisco?"

"I looked for her," Aiden explained. "I mean, I didn't

know Ming was her. I was looking for Jian's sister named Lijia. I thought Ming was her maid. I owed him some debt. The night of the tidal wave, Jian helped me."

"A debt? My God, did you help him stow away?"

"No! I swear to you, I did not." Aiden pushed back the urge to vomit up the brandy. "Jian was always scheming how to escape. I only suspected at the last minute that he might try to hide aboard the *Raven*."

"You never told me any of this before."

"I haven't. I'm sorry."

"Why not?"

"I don't know," Aiden said. "At first I doubted his story myself, then there didn't seem to be anything I could do anyway. And I—I didn't want to risk—" The words closed his throat. "Everything."

"What does she want from you now?" Christopher said.

"Nothing!" Aiden said. "We're in love. Only that."

"Nonsense."

"It's the truth."

"Be serious." Christopher got up from his chair and paced over to the window and back. The room was still mostly empty, though men were starting to come in for the lunch buffet. "It isn't hard to sort these things out," he said quietly. "Most men keep a mistress. There are apartments for them. It will be harder with a Chinese girl, of course. But I will ask around discreetly."

"I don't want her as a mistress in some apartment," Aiden said. "I want to marry her."

"You can't," Christopher said. "Besides all the obvious social reasons, it isn't legal."

"Somewhere it must be."

"Perhaps, but you would still be shunned from any decent society. You'd have no opportunities at all."

"Your world isn't the only world."

"Don't throw your life away, Aiden," Christopher said seriously as he sat back down in the plush chair. It was spooky how much he suddenly resembled his father: in posture, in tone and in sentiment. "My father has embraced you like a son. I have embraced you like a brother. We have taken you into our family and our empire. You have a future now—you cannot just throw that away! You might even be allowed to marry Elizabeth someday."

"I like Elizabeth very much," Aiden said. "But it is not a marriage affection. And she knows this," he added urgently. "It is her understanding as much as mine. I have never been false in my affections to her!"

"Still," Christopher said. "Even if this Ming were a white girl, you hardly know her! Good, well-bred girls are villainous enough when they sniff fortune—how much more so for a Chinese girl? There are plenty of ways to arrange for her."

"I don't want to arrange for her." Aiden looked down at the newspaper on the table, and through the tornado now swirling in his brain, he realized an awful possibility. The *Chronicle* was everywhere. It was dropped in stacks at every cheap saloon, then urchin boys gathered them up and sold them off again in bundles for toilet paper. Aiden remembered the stack of papers on the narrow shelf in the room. He pictured Ming in the little room, no one to talk to, nothing to do, taking down that stack of papers to pass the time.

"Oh shit!" Aiden grabbed his coat and started for the door. "I have to go."

"Where?" Christopher said. "We haven't sorted this out yet. And your clothes—" Christopher grabbed the bag of clothes and followed Aiden outside. They nearly collided with Fish in the street.

"Hello," he said. "Where are you going? Your note said noon."

"Sorry!" Aiden said. "I can't explain now." He took off running as fast as he could.

"Explain what?" Fish said. "What's going on?"

"A mess," Christopher replied. "Come on before he ruins his life."

The lunch buffet at Paradise was meager, but with beer only ten cents and a clientele unwelcome in the nicer places, it attracted a big crowd. Aiden had to shove his way through to the back stairs. It could all be fine, he thought, trying to calm his racing heart. Even if Ming had read the story, she wouldn't necessarily have realized that her own brother was the coolie, or that Aiden was the one who had killed him. He had told her only the barest details. He knocked on the door, then pulled it open, his heart pounding. She was waiting for him, sitting in rigid dread, but with a soft tilt of hopefulness in her shoulders, waiting to be told it was all a mistake, wanting to believe a better truth. The paper was on the bed beside her. Her pants were dry and brushed free of mud clumps but were stained at the bottom. She had smoothed and braided her hair, though little snarls frizzed from the lack of a real comb. The ancestors looked grim and sleepy. The cherubs gazed indifferently in their frozen innocence.

"This is the story you told me last night." Her voice was

toneless and steady. She pressed her palm upon the news-paper. "This is my brother."

"Yes," Aiden said.

"You did not tell it like this."

"I didn't want to hurt you."

"You lied to me!"

"No!" Aiden said desperately. "I never did. I—I just thought . . . you didn't need to know it all . . . so harshly. It wouldn't change anything."

He stepped into the room, but his shoulder knocked against the shelf and he stumbled into the edge of the bed. Ming recoiled. He wanted to smash this room now, break out the walls and put them both alone in the middle of the prairie, with nothing but horizon. He was such a coward. He could fight men and shoot wolves, swim a raging river and walk two thousand miles, but in this most important test he had failed utterly.

"I am so sorry."

Ming smacked Aiden across his face. He wanted a thou-sand more smacks—the sting meant something.

"The money you say you have," she went on. "The money for our life together—it comes from this? From the guano?" She held the paper up with a shaking hand. "From 'condi-tions unfit even for the yellow man'?"

"I am out of the business now," Aiden said.

"From my own brother's blood?"

"I have nothing more to do with it."

There was a scuff of footsteps behind them on the stairs. Christopher appeared on the tiny landing, with Fish right behind him. Ming did not seem to notice or to care who they were.

"It is the truth," Christopher interrupted. "Sorry, um, excuse me for intruding—I could hear on the stairs. But it is the truth, what Aiden is telling you. I was there. I'm Christopher—I met you briefly at my house. . . ."

"Christopher, leave us—please!"

"I'm trying to help!" Christopher leaned around Aiden. "Forgive me for intruding," he said to Ming. "He did give up his half of the ship! And he did not want to shoot your brother. There was just nothing else to be done!"

"Stop!" Aiden whispered urgently.

But Christopher yanked the confused Fish forward into the doorway. "This is the captain of our ship. He will confirm that!"

The little room went deadly silent, the only sound the click of a latch and squeak of a door as someone, curious about the commotion, peeked out onto the tiny landing from one of the other rooms.

"You killed my brother?" Ming whispered, her voice tight. She stood up so she was only inches away from Aiden. "You yourself?"

The world stopped. Aiden said nothing, but Ming searched his eyes and saw the truth. She gave one angry sob, then pushed past them all and ran down the stairs.

"Ming, wait!" Aiden shouted. He ran after her, his feet hitting barely enough steps on the narrow stairway to not fall. She ran into Paradise and darted easily through the crowd, though she jostled one man enough to spill his beer. Aiden pushed his way after her, but the man who had been bumped was angry and swung at Aiden. The blow caught him across the chest.

"Sorry!" Aiden held up his hands and tried to pass, but the man swore and flailed at him. Aiden punched the man in the stomach. The crowd cheered. A brawl was even better than a free lunch. But Aiden did not want a fight—just escape. He simply jabbed and ducked, kicked and shoved, his way through the crowd. He was almost at the door when a man threw a chair at his legs and tripped him. Aiden tumbled forward, bounced off a table and slid into the wall. The floor was slippery and gritty from wet boots, but he managed to get to his feet and shove his way the last few yards to the door. He burst outside and searched the street for Ming. He saw nothing but the usual drab men in their dirty brown clothes. It took him a few seconds to realize that he was indeed looking for drab, dirty clothes, not her blue silk skirt. But finally he saw her, running fast, already a block away.

He ran after her, down the sloggy street, straining to keep sight of her. As he neared, he saw two Chinese men run toward Ming from a side street. One of the men caught her arm and yanked her. Aiden dashed the last few yards and tackled the man, slamming him to the ground, then punching him so hard he knocked him out cold. Ming was flung to the ground. The second man, only a few steps behind, pulled a short club from the loose sleeve of his tunic and swung. Aiden raised his arm just in time to break the blow. He heard a loud crack but couldn't tell if it was wood or his own bone. He rolled away and kicked the man's feet out from under him. But the attacker was nimble and sprang up immediately. Two more Chinamen were running to the scene. Gouzhi had sent a small army; they must have followed Christopher from his home. Aiden launched himself on both of the men with a fury, but they knew how to fight the same way Aiden did. The fight was fast and brutal. His right arm was still numb from the blow.

The air was full of dirt and shouting, then Aiden saw with relief that Fish and Christopher had come to his aid. Fish, a good foot taller than the Chinese men, got one of them around the neck and wrenched him away. Christopher managed to distract the other. A crowd of men had gathered as well, giving Aiden hope. On the Barbary Coast, a fight was always entertainment, but no one would let Chinese beat white men for long. Aiden felt a kick to his knee, then one of the men grabbed his injured arm and spun him to the ground. Through the dust and chaos, Aiden saw Gouzhi. He had hold of Ming, twisting her arm behind her back, a dagger pressed hard against her cheek. He was not about to lose Silamu Xie's prize again. He bellowed a command in Chinese, and all his men immediately stopped fighting and came to his side.

"Don't hurt her." Aiden raised his hands. Fish let his captive go, and he and Christopher stood beside Aiden, a determined but futile phalanx. The men in the crowd fell quiet—no one knew what was going on now, and no one wanted to get involved in Chinese business, especially when there were knives involved. Gouzhi barked something. Ming translated, her voice quavering with terror.

"He says that—that Silamu Xie will not care if his—his pet dog—has an ugly face."

Gouzhi would not kill Ming, Aiden realized, but he could scar her cruelly with just a few slashes. She would still be useful for producing sons.

"Tell him all right," Aiden said steadily to Ming. "Go with

him. Don't be afraid. Tell him not to hurt you. We won't fight."

He wanted to tell her more—that he would come for her somehow, that she should never stop believing that, that he loved her. He just held her gaze and hoped his eyes could say enough. Hoped to see forgiveness in return.

Then a shot cracked out. People immediately began to scatter, ducking into saloons or behind wagons. Gouzhi looked surprised. He dropped the knife. He looked down at his chest with puzzlement. A dark stain of blood was spreading across the front of his coat. Then his knees buckled and he fell forward into the street. Ming screamed and darted away. Another of the Chinese men grabbed her, but Aiden sprang immediately and wrestled the man away. They both tumbled to the ground, fighting savagely. Fish ran over and grabbed Gouzhi's knife. Aiden punched and kicked, but the man drove a knee into his stomach, then straddled him, wrapped thin, steely hands around his neck and began choking him. Another shot sounded—so close Aiden could smell the gunpowder. The Chinese man screamed and twisted away, clutching his side and falling in a cringing agony. Aiden squirmed out from under him. He saw all the other Chinese attackers running away up the street. He saw Fish standing a few yards away, next to Gouzhi's body, holding the man's knife. His other arm was wrapped around Ming's shoulders. She was safe.

"Aiden, are you all right?" Christopher knelt beside him. It was only then that Aiden felt a burning pain in his thigh and noticed the sticky flow of blood. The world went very quiet and slow.

"Good God!" Christopher flinched. "I think she shot you!"

Aiden saw Blind Sally standing a few yards away. Her giant pistol was still smoking. The sunlight glinted off the gold braid of her tattered military coat. The Moon stood by her side, his back in a ridge of aggression, watching the crowd, growling at anyone who moved.

"Did I hit you, boy?" Blind Sally said. "Sorry for that. That big one was the easy one." She nodded at Gouzhi. "This one—" She waved her pistol toward the man who had been choking Aiden. "Skinny little man and moving fast as he was—well, sorry. Guess the bullet went clean through." She tucked the pistol into her belt. "You learn that today, boy—always hold still when a blind woman shoots."

37

"I'm sorry, Aiden," Fish said. "She still doesn't want to see you."

"But she'll go with you?" Aiden asked weakly. He had lost a lot of blood, and everything was melting in and out of foggy noise. The doctor had bandaged his leg but was impatient to do surgery while they still had good daylight.

"Yes," Fish said. "She will stay with my mother tonight. We will sail in the morning. I will take care of her. I promise."

Aiden nodded. "Thank you."

Fish would take Ming to Jefferson J. Jackson's compound north of Seattle. The old man, retired now from leading wagon trains, had a large extended family of half-breed Indian and Mexican children and grandchildren. He would not object to sheltering a Chinese girl. And it would only be for a little while, Aiden thought. Ming would come to understand. She would forgive Aiden, and they would get married and find a place in the world where they could live together. Aiden pulled the envelope of cash from his jacket pocket. Surprisingly, it had not fallen out during all the fighting.

"She will need clothes. Practical things, but a dress too. A nice one. And good boots and—"

"We'll take care of it," Fish said, taking the money. "Don't worry."

"She needs painting things—an inkstone and brushes for

her painting. There is special paper too." Aiden winced with pain. "It's called the four treasures."

"Be quiet," Christopher said. "Will you just lie still?"

"Get some presents too—toys and sweets. Jackson has dozens of children there."

"I need to operate now," the surgeon said crossly. Christopher frowned. He had wanted to send for their own family doctor, but Aiden pointed out that high-society doctors didn't tend to have much experience with gunshots. Dr. Patrick was well regarded on the Barbary Coast, when he was sober, and his table looked clean. His assistant, a light-skinned Negro man with short gray hair, set a little bottle of chloroform and the mask on the tray and rolled up his sleeves.

"Tell Mr. Jackson I will write to him soon," Aiden said. "And please, Fish—you can explain it all to Ming—tell her I'm sorry."

"Help get him on the table," the surgeon said to Christopher and Fish. "Then stay or go as you like, just shut up and stay out of my way."

When Aiden woke up, he was lying on a canvas cot with a coarse blanket over him. He felt cold as a stone. The room was dark, except for the light of the moon, just one day past full, shining in through the bare window. It gleamed on the white enamel operating table nearby. His head ached and his leg throbbed. He couldn't move. His right arm was splinted snugly between thin boards. The room smelled of blood and carbolic soap. He turned his head and saw a single candle on a table across the little room. Christopher was sleeping in the chair beside it.

The next time he woke, it was morning. The sky outside was gray and foggy. He tried to sit up, but the world spun. For a minute, Aiden thought he was on the lumber boat, the morning after the shark, a lifetime ago at the beginning of it all. He lay back and lifted the blanket. His leg was swathed in bandages. Blood had soaked through, but there was no smell of rot, so Aiden felt relieved. But the fog worried him. Would it be too dense for Fish to sail? He almost hoped for that, for then he could go himself to see Ming. She had had a whole night to soften her heart. Christopher, roused by Aiden's activity, sat up in the chair.

"You're still alive," he said sleepily.

"Yes," Aiden said. "Is there water?"

Christopher got up and poured him a glass from a tin pitcher. Aiden drank the whole thing down.

"Does it hurt awfully bad?"

"No," Aiden lied.

"You can't get up. There's a jug there if you need to piss." He refilled the glass.

"Thank you for staying with me."

"Oh, well." Christopher shrugged. "I wasn't about to go walking home alone through the Barbary Coast after dark." He stretched and slapped his face, then walked over to the window and peered out. "She disappeared, you know," Christopher said. "Your crazy lady."

"Blind Sally?"

"Just vanished! Shoots two people in broad daylight— well, three people, in fact—and then walks off."

"I'm sure she'll turn up again," Aiden said.

"The bullet is enormous," Christopher said, retrieving a

jar from a shelf near the washstand. "And it wasn't smashed, which the doctor said was good." He shook the jar and Aiden heard the metallic clank. "Will you put it in your pouch?"

"I don't know," Aiden said. What sort of token would that be except a reminder of his own stupidity?

"The doctor said he would come by this morning to check on you. He couldn't really tell if your arm is broken— it's not bad enough for him to feel anything anyway, but he splinted it to be on the safe side. He says you must not be moved for a day or two, but I think if we use Mother's new buggy, it would be all right. It has marvelous springs and is very smooth. You can't stay in this wretched place. That cot doesn't even have a mattress."

"I can't stay at your house," Aiden said.

"No, I know." Christopher pulled the chair closer and sat down. "I was really careful, you know—about being followed. Honestly, I looked all around. I went down different streets. I am sorry about that."

"Of course," Aiden said. "I don't blame you at all. You and Fish saved my life. You've learned something about fighting."

"Only more reasons to avoid it," Christopher said, dismissing the praise. "Anyway, I'll arrange a hotel room for you. And someone to look after you. I probably shouldn't visit myself, since, obviously, I'm not very good at sneaking about. But you'll be up in no time."

"Please give your father my deepest apologies for the trouble I have caused," Aiden said. "I will write to him myself, perhaps this afternoon. And tell the ducklings—" Aiden found himself suddenly about to get weepy. "Tell them I will miss them. And tell Elizabeth—"

"Oh stop!" Christopher interrupted. "You're not about to fall off the edge of the earth. The Chinese trouble will fade away, my father will get over his anger—with the both of us—and you and I will start my newspaper. First here, then we expand to Chicago and New York."

"Yes," Aiden said. "All right."

"All right, then." Christopher stood up. "I do need to get home before they all go crazy with worry. Goodbye. For now."

They shook hands. Christopher left and Aiden lay back down on the cot. The fog thinned and the sky grew brighter, and Aiden drifted back into sleep, dreaming of Ming standing by a window, painting soft gray birds.

He could see her through the window as he walked up the path from the dock, still just a shadow from this distance, but he immediately recognized the shape of her, the essence of her. It had been nearly a month, and he had no idea what she thought or felt now. He had received no letter. When Fish returned from dropping her off, he could say only that she had arrived safely and that he had tried to plead Aiden's case as well as he could. Ming had not spoken at all on the voyage.

A warm March wind blew up from the sound. Bright green tips were already sprouting on the pine trees, and Aiden smelled newly turned soil from the gardens. He saw some of the Indian women carrying bundles of fresh willow branches for weaving baskets. Then the children began to notice him and dashed in a swarm down the hill to greet him, racing in circles around him, pulling his hands and chatting gaily. Only a few of them remembered him from the last time he had been here, but they were always excited to have any visitor. Their commotion alerted everyone in the compound. He would have no quiet arrival. The front door of the main house opened, and Jefferson J. Jackson came out. He looked the same as ever, though he wore gold-rimmed spectacles now, and his wiry gray hair was a bit thinner.

"Welcome back," he said simply. "You alone?" He looked down at the dock.

"I took a steamer to Seattle," Aiden said. "Fish was on a lumber run, and I couldn't wait that long once I was fit."

"Heal up all right?" Jackson scrutinized Aiden with his experienced glance.

"After a while." The wound had gone septic, as wounds often did, but he had avoided amputation. "Is Ming all right?"

"Yeah." He tipped his head toward the door. "She seen you com'n." Jackson waved off the excited children. "Go on—go make your ruckus elsewhere!"

Aiden climbed up the steps to the porch but then couldn't make himself go inside. Jackson clapped his rough hand on Aiden's shoulder.

"I think she don't hate you, boy." He pushed Aiden toward the door.

She was still standing by the window. She wore Western clothes, a calico dress and apron, and her hair was in two braids, like the Indian women wore, but everything else about her was so true. Aiden felt like his heart—but no, not just his heart, his lungs, his kidneys, every unglamorous organ inside of him—might now be restored. If only he could say the right thing. If there was ever a right thing. He could not speak at all. Then he did not have to.

Ming walked through the beam of sunlight and stood in front of him. Shyly, she took his hand.

"You have come a long way," she said with a smile. "Would you like some bread and water?"

Author's Note

May 29, 2013

I was working as a Divemaster on an expedition cruise ship in the South Pacific when I first learned about guano. Each day we visited small islands and atolls where we ferried the passengers off to explore with a staff of naturalists. As my job was to take the passengers snorkeling or scuba diving, I was mostly focused on the underwater world, but one can't be near any island and not be aware of birds. The sky was always full of them, screeching and diving. Any cliffside was dotted with resting birds and "painted" with long white splotches of bird droppings. And there were ground-nesting colonies, where the birds sat as close together as buns in a baker's pan.

Every evening, the expedition leader gave a brief talk about the history of the islands, and after a few days, we jokingly started referring to this as the "guano talk," for every single island had indeed been drastically influenced by the guano trade.

The word "guano" comes from an Andean Quechua Indian word, *wanu*, which most likely came from an Incan word, *huanu*, meaning "dung." This guano—bird poop—was once the most valuable commodity in the world. Men sailed across the globe to obtain it. They fought for it, grew rich from it and enslaved other men to dig it out for them. Half the world would have starved to death without it.

Picture your grocery store with half of the shelves empty. Picture all the food your family eats in a week cut in half.

That is what our world would be like today if not for manu-factured chemical fertilizers.

As early as the mid-1700s, the world was experiencing food shortages. After even a few years of intensive farming, with the best practices of the day, soil was quickly exhausted and crop yields began to dwindle. By the Industrial Revo-lution in the nineteenth century, as populations grew and more and more people moved to cities, farming was at a cri-sis point.

The Incas had known for a thousand years that guano made great fertilizer, but Europeans were slow to realize its value. Early adventurers were more interested in gold and silver. It wasn't until around 1840 that farmers in Europe and the U.S. really began to understand what guano could do for their depleted farmland. It was estimated to be thirty-five times more effective than any other type of fertilizer (mostly manure) that was commonly used at the time. It truly was a magic powder, and the scramble to get it quickly grew intense.

Seabird droppings were harvested from every island and scrap of rock in the South Pacific, but the richest deposits of all were found on the three rocky islands known as the Chinchas, off the southwest coast of Peru. All of the details about guano mining in *Son of Fortune,* including the brutal treatment of Chinese laborers, are true. I have drawn them from the books listed in the "further reading" section, as well as shipping records, newspaper stories and many sailors' personal accounts from the time, found in archives primarily in San Francisco and Baltimore.

Estimates vary widely about how many Chinese men were brought to work on the Chincha Islands during the height of the guano trade, from 1849 to 1875. More than 100,000 were brought to Peru to work on cotton and sugar plantations, railroads and guano mining. (Another 10,000 died on the four-to-five-month ocean voyage, where they were packed in holds like cargo.) Some of these men signed contracts thinking they were going to work in gold mines or railroads. Some were prisoners or debtors "sold" to agents. Some were kidnapped outright. The guano mines on the Chincha Islands needed between four hundred and six hundred men working all the time. Many died within two years of arrival; few ever left.

In addition to the horrific practice of Chinese slave labor on the Chinchas, many of the guano operations on those beautiful islands I was visiting also depended on kidnapped and enslaved people taken from Pacific islands. "Blackbirders" would invite local islanders aboard their ships to trade or feast, then imprison them and set sail. In 1862, Peruvian blackbirders kidnapped over 1,500 people, probably half the population of Rapa Nui (Easter Island). The government finally intervened and forced the slavers to release those still alive, but only fifteen were returned. They brought with them an epidemic of smallpox, which destroyed most of the remaining population.

The guano trade was in decline by the 1870s, but only because most of the islands had been stripped bare. Guano is still collected on the Chincha Islands. You can buy a bag of it in your local gardening store. But today those who labor there do so voluntarily.

In 1909, two scientists, Fritz Haber and Carl Bosch, finally invented a way to make chemical fertilizer, and the world changed once again.

Sources

I am grateful to all the librarians and archivists, primarily at the California Historical Society, the San Francisco Public Library, the San Francisco Maritime National Historical Park and the Maryland Historical Society, who helped me discover dozens of old newspaper and magazine articles, agricultural bulletins, shipping reports, letters and pamphlets.

For Further Reading

The Alchemy of Air by Thomas Hager; published 2008 by Harmony Books (Random House, Inc.)

The Great Guano Rush: Entrepreneurs and American Overseas Expansion by Jimmy M. Skagg; published 1994 by Palgrave Macmillan

More Precious than Gold: The Story of the Peruvian Guano Trade by David Hollett; published 2008 by Associated University Presses